Within Her Grasp

ALSO BY DANIELLE GRAINGER

THE DENTON HEIGHTS SERIES

Under Her Wing (Book One):
The Shasti and Madison Story

In Her Cage (Book Two):
The Jaleesa and Tina Story

Within Her Grasp (Book Three):
The Marta and Shanice Story

THE BERNADETTE SERIES

Wrecking Bernadette (Book One)

(S)mothering Bernadette (Book Two)

Becoming Bernadette (Book Three)

Desiring Bernadette (Book Four)

Loving Bernadette (Book Five)

WITHIN HER
Grasp
DENTON HEIGHTS BOOK 3
DANIELLE GRAINGER

BIBI
BOOKS

Paperback ISBN 978-1-953734-31-0

First Edition 2023

9 8 7 6 5 4 3 2 1

Cover design by Sarah (Forcoverservice)

Published by:

Bibi Books Publishing Company, LLC

Dedication

This book is dedicated to those dealing with physical challenges. You are strong and tough and determined. You are my heroes.

Acknowledgments

Writing is a solitary endeavor...until it's not. I must thank the community of gentle souls that help me convey my thoughts and those that read them.

Readers—Please keep sending those emails and giving this author your feedback. Writers often feel like we work in a void, so your gentle touches are most welcome. Most of all, I appreciate your loyalty and encouragement. You keep me going.

Advanced Readers and Reviewers – Thank you for your thoughtful reviews of my books. Your encouragement, whether intended or not, keeps my writer's flame ignited.

Beta Readers – Jiske, Olivia, Tanya. You are all awesome and wonderful in your own unique ways. And still so giving, as well. You find things I miss and always find things for me to ponder over and reflect on.

Table of Contents

Chapter 1

Marta

Marta Ingersoll closed the front door as quietly as she could, not because she didn't want to disturb her neighbors at 0615 hours on a Saturday morning, but, yes, it was exactly that. She had been in Mrs. Pulaski avoidance mode for almost two years and had no interest in changing that any time soon. Marta just wasn't into people, least of all the nosy neighbor who had been her mother's best friend. The less Marta thought about her mother, the better.

With catlike skill, Marta made it to her pickup truck silently. She was just about to declare victory when the unthinkable happened.

"Good morning, dear."

Marta's heart leaped into her throat. Mrs. Pulaski had called to her from her front porch. With her blood pounding, Marta said, "You scared me." *Why are you stalking me at zero'dark fifteen, lady? It's not even light out.* Funny how Mrs. Pulaski was fully dressed already. No robe. No nightgown. Had she gotten up early to catch Marta on her way out? Maybe. Probably.

"How are you doing?" Mrs. Pulaski asked. "Did Nora have her surgery yet? How is she doing? Is she at Cincinnati General?"

Seven thousand questions already, and I've barely had my first sip of coffee. Marta had no choice. She'd been ambushed and had to engage. "She's having the surgery this afternoon. Her husband—"

"Brian," Mrs. Pulaski said as if showing Marta how much she knew about Marta's sister.

"Yes," Marta said, slowly dragging out the *s*. "Brian and their son will be with her all day." At least Mrs. Pulaski wasn't walking across her lawn to get closer. Thank God. *Stay on your own porch, woman!*

"Oh, good," Mrs. Pulaski said. "Please be sure to let me know how she is, won't you?"

"Sure," Marta said, not sure if she'd make good on the promise. *I need to change my morning routine. Or wear camo.* "I have to go now." And without fanfare, Marta dove into the driver's seat of her pickup and slammed the door shut on Mrs. Pulaski's presence. She didn't wait to hear a response or even wave goodbye. Why should she? The woman was a pest.

Marta drove the ten minutes to the nursery in a cranky mood. All she wanted was to be left alone, and Mrs. Pulaski sure made that difficult. Good thing it was Saturday, and the crew would be busy with the public, so she would be left alone to pull orders. Hopefully, Meyers & Sons Landscaping would have a big order she could spend all day fetching. The sun had just peeked over the horizon as she drove through the back employee gate. It was a bit cool for June, but then again, it was still early.

Marta made her way to the back office, thinking how sexist Meyers Landscaping was. What if Mr. Meyers' daughter, if he had one, wanted to work for the company? Marta inhaled sharply. What if she already did work for the company? "That would really suck," she muttered out loud.

"Who would suck, Ingersoll?" Jeff, another order-puller, asked as he reached the office door before she did.

"Who said you could talk to me?" She had been ignoring him the entire time she'd been working there. Over three years at this point. She never bothered to complain about the razzing she sometimes took from him or the other guys because that kind of banter was accepted at Carter Nursery and Landscaping on the outskirts of beautiful Denton Heights, Ohio, a sleepy bedroom community of Cincinnati. Nope, she didn't complain and barely bantered back. These were her Army days relived. At least in the Army, she had belonged. Here at Carter's, she wasn't sure.

She snuck a peek at the board of cart keys. No way! The Pope mobile was still up for grabs. Too bad the asswipe was blocking the board. No worries, she had a plan. She marched right over toward him and watched as his eyes grew wide. She inserted herself right into his personal space, reached behind him, and snatched the key off the peg. She grinned as she jangled it in his face and then walked toward the door as he choked on any comment he was about to make.

He regained his composure finally and spat, "Fuck you, Ing. I got here early to get the Pope mobile."

Her only answer was one middle finger raised high over her head as she grabbed the Meyers & Sons order and then slammed out the door.

"Asshole," she mumbled and headed to the cart.

"And a beautiful morning to you, too, Marta," Roger Freeman, the supervisor of commercial orders, said. There was no mistaking the sarcasm in his voice.

"Uh-huh," she answered without looking at him or breaking stride. He was an asshole, too. It was best *not* to engage.

Once inside the cozy motorized cart, she put her coffee thermos and water bottle on the floor next to her lunch cooler, checked the gas gauge to make sure she wouldn't have to stop by the office again until quitting time, and then pulled forward to hit up the tree section. True to form, Meyers & Sons were pushing dogwoods on their customers. Ooh, they needed a Japanese maple, too. Nice. She'd load up the trees first since they were the heaviest and most awkward to fling on the flatbed. She was strong, but it was best to get the heavy shit out of the way first. Her four years as an enlisted grunt made sure of that, even though she'd gotten out over a decade ago. Most of her jobs involved physical labor, keeping her strong. Her sister called her stocky, but she preferred to think of herself as solid muscle. Seriously, there was no fat on her. Well, not much, anyway.

Marta checked the order form. The list was long. Good. That gave her all day to fill the flatbed she pulled behind her and not bother with a single solitary soul for the rest of the day. She'd hit up the perennials near lunchtime, so she'd be near the public restroom up front. That way, the office asswipes wouldn't have anything to say to her. Up front, she only had to smile and nod if anyone talked to her.

She reached into her jacket pocket and pulled out her air buds. Fully charged, thank God. It wouldn't have mattered anyway because the Pope mobile had a USB charging port. Once she was far enough away from the office, she hit up the *TuneMeOn* App on her phone and wavered momentarily. Actually, it was no contest. She needed some old-school *Metallica* and a lot of it that morning. *Rammstein*, for sure, but later that afternoon. Heavy metal could only be played loud, so up went the volume through her earpieces, shooting Marta into her happy place. In that place, there were no people, no neighbors, and no sister having surgery.

As expected, the Meyers & Sons order took all day, and Marta pulled into the commercial pickup lot at 1445 hours. The commercial attendant signed off on her order because it was perfect, of course, and Marta punched out at precisely 1500 hours—quittin' time.

She checked her phone on the way. No text from Brian. That was okay, though. It was too soon. Nora was due to have the surgery at 1500 hours anyway. She got in her pickup and pulled onto the main road. She rubbed her ears. A little too much metal today, perhaps? Nah, never.

"If you don't text me by 1630 hours, Brian," Marta said out loud, "then I'm calling you and giving you a piece of my mind." She'd wanted to go down to the hospital, but her sister told her to stay home and come by the next day, Sunday. Nora wanted Brian to stay home and spend Sunday morning and afternoon with their son, seeing as it was Father's Day and all. Sounded good to Marta. A day without people? Perfect. Except she did like her nephew, Elliot. He was thirteen and had just finished eighth grade. He was awesomely awkward, but they understood each other. And he liked his Aunt Marta, so the kid couldn't be that bad, right?

She pulled into the driveway of the house she'd grown up in—the one she and Nora had inherited when their mother passed away almost two full years ago. It was two years that felt like two minutes in Marta's mind. Monthly payments to buy out Nora's share ensured Marta a life of solitude and privacy. Just what she needed at age thirty-five, almost thirty-six.

"Hey, Mrs. Pulaski," Marta called. She rarely engaged the enemy by going on the offensive like this, but desperate times and all that. Mrs. Pulaski stood up and waved from her rocking chair on her front porch. "No word on Nora yet," Marta said. She turned toward the house, not bothering to hear the return words that wafted in the wind behind her. She was safe inside the house in less than a minute.

Marta took a breath in the mudroom and took off her dirty boots.

Soft yet insistent meowing came from the other side of the door to the house. Marta chuckled and said, "I'll be right in, Snowball. Silly girl." Marta tucked her work boots under the bench her father had built in the small anteroom of the house. She couldn't remember exactly how old she'd been then but remembered that she and Nora had been in elementary school. She rubbed the well-worn seat and said, "Love you, Dad. Miss you." Tightness in her chest told her that tears were right there at the ready. She refused to let them out. What was the point? Tears wouldn't bring her father back from the stroke that killed him at age thirty-five while on a business trip in Texas. The fact that Marta was also currently thirty-five did not go unnoticed in her soul.

She opened the front door and was blasted with the stale stuffiness of the house. Shoot, Jessica was coming over tomorrow. *Mm hmm.* Marta let herself get distracted momentarily as she thought of the litany of things she wanted to do to her weekly submissive partner. Jessica coming over was not a bad thing. It just meant Marta had to spend the evening cleaning and airing the place. New sheets on the bed, too.

Snowball chirped as she wove around Marta's legs on their journey to the kitchen. Marta dumped her lunch bag and beverage bottles on the countertop and couldn't help noticing her mother's expensive KitchenAid Mixer. Her mother had barely used it, but she'd bought it as a way of sticking her middle finger up at the multiple sclerosis that was slowly killing her. Marta brushed her fingers over the rim of the silver mixing bowl and coughed down a sob that had burst out of her without permission.

She held her breath, daring another sob to come out, and when all seemed clear, reached down to pet Snowball. "How's my little girl doing? Are you hungry?" The long-haired white cat chirped and rubbed her head on Marta's dirty jeans. "I'll take that as a 'yes.'" Marta grabbed the cold can of cat food from the fridge and turned on the tap to warm up the water. Once the cold food was warmed and soupy enough for the princess, Marta placed it on the cat's mat and then headed to her bedroom to get out of her dirty work clothes. Nora kept telling her to move into their mother's bedroom with its sizable ensuite bathroom, but Marta couldn't do it. That was her mother's room. Okay, the hospital bed and other medical shit were gone now. It had been donated at her sister's insistence, but still. She couldn't move her stuff in. It just seemed wrong somehow.

Naked as the day she was born, Marta stopped to look at the framed photo on her wall. She looked so young in the picture. She'd been, what, twenty-two, maybe? Despite just making Corporal, her dress greens made her look more important than she'd felt in that picture. She thought she might make a career out of the Army, but that wasn't meant to be. Her mother needed her. Nora was about to be a new mom and had her own life to start. Marta opted for an honorable discharge and came home from Germany, where she'd spent the last year of her term after her tour in Iraq. She tapped the wooden picture frame, happy that no tears of regret came up this time.

After a quick shower in the bathroom she had shared with her sister growing up, she threw on sweats and a T-shirt. No bra. Why bother? A sharp meow from the backyard got her attention.

"Snowball, your girlfriend's here." Marta laughed when Snowball seemed unaffected and continued her post-dinner bath on Marta's unmade bed. Marta headed to the kitchen to grab a can of PBR and the bag of dry cat food and headed out the back door off the living room. She'd finally weaned herself off Keystone Light from her enlisted days and had graduated to Pabst. Not that many of her Army buddies would think that was an improvement, but fuck 'em. She liked it. And unlike many of her buddies, she only had one each night after work. It was a ritual she'd started after…Yeah, after that. She looked into the yard, resplendent in the late afternoon sunshine.

Ahh, the black cat was hiding in Marta's mother's barely recognizable flower garden. The small cat had piercing amber eyes and watched Marta suspiciously. But then again, they'd been playing this game for about a month at this point. Marta's movements were slow, and her voice soft and soothing as she said, "Hey, little girl." She filled a sturdy metal bowl from the bag of economy cat crunchies. She couldn't exactly afford to feed the strays with the expensive designer food Princess Snowball demanded, now, could she? She refilled the water bowl from the hose and placed it next to the food on the far edge of the concrete patio. She sat in the old but sturdy lawn chair on the back patio and popped open her beer. This was going to take a minute, but Marta was patient. Soon enough, the small black cat cautiously approached the food bowl.

Marta took a quiet sip of beer and diverted her attention from the cat by checking the nonexistent texts from her brother-in-law. She exhaled a sigh through her nose. Once this beer was finished, she'd text him to find out how Nora was doing. She felt guilty at the relief she had that Brian was her sister's primary caregiver. She didn't know if she could re-enlist after caring for their mother for so many years.

And Mrs. Pulaski, a voice in her head said unbidden. "Yes," Marta conceded softly, acknowledging that her widowed neighbor had taken on an integral caregiving role with Marta's mother. But Marta's mother was gone, and Mrs. Pulaski's role was done, and Marta didn't need to be taken care of, so Mrs. Pulaski should stay on her side of the property line and not cross it.

"Fuck," Marta spat, spooking the black cat into the bushes. That knot of sadness was right fucking there, trying to find its way out. "Son of a bitch." She took another swig of beer and threw the entire can and its contents far into the yard.

Realizing she had scared the little black cat, she willed herself to calm down. "Sorry, little girl. I'll leave you to it."

Without another thought for the beer can sitting in the unkempt yard, she headed back into the house to text Brian. She shut and locked the back slider and intended to head toward the far end of the couch that had been her designated spot since…forever. She didn't make it. Her bare foot caught on the throw rug she'd long ago tossed over the stains in front of her mother's chair, and she stumbled. Luckily, she caught herself on the coffee table before careening into it.

"Great," Marta said out loud. "No one would have found my body for days." She stood up and wrinkled her nose. "This carpet stinks. My decaying corpse would have been lost in this smell." She looked back at the rug that had tripped her up and saw the myriad stains on the ancient green carpeting underneath. The chair was in no better shape. It was worn out, marred with food spills, and most notably…empty. The chair was empty. She had not dared sit in it since her mother last sat there.

The sadness she had tried to keep bottled up finally erupted. Sobs burst from her soul, and she clamped a hand over her mouth to keep the universe from hearing how weak she was. Her other hand splayed over her chest to keep the broken pieces together. Gasping for air, she swiped at her eyes, annoyed at her inability to keep her shit together.

Only the ding of an incoming text knocked her out of her self-indulgent weakness.

> BRIAN: Nora did great, so sayeth the doc. She's in the post-op recovery room. No complications. They'll have her in a regular room soon. She was in good spirits before going in. Not much more to report than that. I'll text again later.
>
> MARTA: (Thumbs-up emoji)

She took a breath and let it out slowly. She wanted to sit outside with the black cat and catch her breath but opted for her bed instead. She wasn't very good company that afternoon, not even for the cats.

"C'mon, Snowball," Marta said, heading for her room. Snowball wasn't much of a metal fan, preferring soft jazz, so Marta tucked the air buds in her ears. "I need some *Korn*." Falling asleep to heavy metal was a skill acquired during her Army days and had served her well since then for times just like this.

Snowball made biscuits on Marta's blanket and then snuggled up against Marta's side. Marta fell asleep stroking the cat that had once been her mother's.

Chapter 2

Shanice

Shanice didn't want to stop, she was on a roll with the code she was writing, but everyone was walking into the conference room. Had she missed an email or something? She glanced at the doors closing behind the last person. An old-fashioned-looking white woman, impeccably dressed as if going out for tea with the girls in the 1960s or something, turned and looked straight at Shanice. She wagged her finger and shook her head as if to say, "No, no, no. You're not invited." The woman smiled knowingly and then closed the door.

Shanice tried to push her chair back. It wouldn't budge. Her heart raced. What was happening? She tried again and again but was trapped. She was just about to attempt to slide out of the chair and under the desk to free herself when her boss, Mr. Johnson, cleared his throat politely. "Now, now. You know you can't go in there with them." Like the old-fashioned woman, Mr. Johnson smiled at her sympathetically and then rolled his eyes skyward as if to say how utterly ridiculous she was being.

She desperately wanted to tell him she was stuck. She tried to ask him for help, but no words would come out of her mouth. She tried and tried until, finally, she managed something akin to a grunt. That was progress. She continued to attempt to move the chair to no avail, but she got another grunt out. The grunts turned to short pleas, sounding more like whines. The whines got louder and longer.

Something touched her. Where? Her arm. Bicep. She turned to look, but her eyes were sealed shut. She couldn't see. What was happening? Panicking, she thrashed her arms and legs. Her head whipped back and forth.

"Stop, stop, stop, honey," a voice said. "Wake up now. You're having a bad dream."

Shanice focused on the voice. She stopped thrashing and listened. The weight was back on her arm.

"I'm just taking your blood pressure and need you to keep still."

Her eyes fluttered open. A white woman with a surgical mask loomed over her. Are we still in the pandemic? Shanice recoiled.

"Stay away," she whimpered. "What do you want? Where am I?"

The masked woman stepped back. "I can't take your blood pressure now. It'll be too high. I'll just—" She grunted her disgust and said, "I'll come back later."

Shanice's gaze was laser-locked on the woman's retreating form. Once the door was shut behind the woman and Shanice was alone…she remembered. Adrenaline rushed through her, tightening her chest. She tried to sit up but couldn't. She felt heavy. So heavy. She took stock for a moment. Her left arm and hand were in a cast. Oh, yeah. She remembered the cast. And she remembered the bed.

She was in a hospital. Yes. But why?

She lay back and took slow, calming breaths. Yoga. She'd learned this breathing technique doing chair Yoga with Miss Macie. Dread filled her all over again. Who was taking care of Miss Macie? Oh, God, she needed to get out of there.

"Get me out of here," she yelled. For a solid minute, maybe more, she cried for someone to come and help her. No one came. She yelled for someone to call Miss Macie and check up on her. Miss Macie couldn't handle things on her own.

She looked for her phone. She could call Miss Macie's son if she could just get her phone. He needed to drive over from Louisville. Ugh, her neck was sore. And she couldn't really move it. She reached up with her good hand. Ahh, her neck was in a brace.

She stopped fidgeting and took a few more Yoga breaths. A car accident. Yes, someone had told her that. Broken arm, obviously. Did she also have a broken neck? She moved her neck gingerly. No, she seemed okay there. She was amazed at how calm she became as she began a checklist of her body. Was she paralyzed somewhere? Adrenaline spiked her bloodstream again. Ahh, maybe not so calm then. She wiggled the fingers on her right hand. Phew. She could move her left fingers, but they hurt a little. Oh, right. The cast. She looked down at the hospital sheet covering her body. She tried to lift one leg and then the other. They were inordinately heavy. She had braces on both legs. Were both legs broken?

She contracted her muscles and tried to lift the heavy limbs, but they wouldn't budge. She tried to wiggle her toes. At first, she thought she had been successful, but then she wasn't sure. Something was wrong. She couldn't see because it was dark. It was night. What day was it? Where was she? Why was she here?

And where was the stupid nurse? She cried out for help again and looked for a button to press to call for a nurse or anyone. How could they just leave her there in a room all by herself? Alone. She needed answers. Now.

Dizziness overcame her as the germ of a memory came to mind. It was the last thing she remembered before passing out.

~~~

"Ahh, good. You're awake," a different masked nurse said as she peered in the slightly opened door. She came in, leaving the door ajar. Shanice must have slept for several hours because the sun was now streaming through the lone window.

"I have an itch," Shanice said. "On my foot." She got no response from the new nurse as she fussed with the machines. Fine. "Do you have my phone?" Shanice asked, not failing to notice how rough and slightly panicked her voice sounded. "I have to tell Miss Macie where I am. Where am I? What day is this? What happened to me?"

The nurse gave Shanice a smile. It was one of those sympathetic smiles that all the foster kids got around Christmas when some church group or ladies' group remembered about the poor little orphans in Cincinnati. It was the kind of smile that said, "Thank God I'm not you."

The nurse said, "I'll put in a request for Admin to see about your phone
~~~

as soon as I'm finished with my rounds." The nurse paused, and her expression changed. This time it was serious. "Margaret tells me you fussed so much that she couldn't get your blood pressure reading last night."

"Sorry." Yep, that was all Shanice had to offer. "Where am I? What happened to me?"

"I'll let them know that you're more awake now. And that you're coherent and less combative."

Who's 'them'? Shanice wanted to ask. Why can't you tell me where I am or what happened to me? Why won't you tell me? She couldn't get any of the words out.

"Will you cooperate, young lady?" The nurse held up a blood pressure cuff. Shanice recognized it from her days as a foster kid getting yearly physicals. The families didn't get their money if they didn't show proof that they were taking care of the kids. And they didn't always take care of the kids. But that was a sore spot for another day. Or maybe never. 'Leave the past in the past,' Miss Macie always said, except she always brought up hers.

Shanice tried to nod to tell the woman to go ahead and put the cuff on, but the brace around her neck prevented that. "Do I have to wear this thing?"

"The doctors will determine that," the nurse said. She held up the cuff and raised her eyebrows in question.

"Yes, yes. Go ahead," Shanice said, hearing the irritation in her voice. She was not usually like this. She had infinite patience for Miss Macie, that was for sure, but not now. And she was bordering on being rude. She kind of felt bad, but also kind of felt like no one was helping her either.

She watched as the woman wrapped the thing around her good arm. It hurt as it squeezed, but she knew the momentary discomfort was the least of her worries.

When the deed was done, the nurse messed around with some clear bags hanging up on the side of the bed. "What are those?" Shanice asked.

"Your IVs," the nurse said succinctly as she swapped out one of the bags.

Shanice had trouble seeing what the nurse was doing for two reasons. One—she couldn't turn her head much, and two—she didn't have her glasses. "Do you have my glasses?"

"I'll put in a request with Admin. If they have any of your belongings, they will be in the safe in their offices. Today's Saturday, so no one's here today." Shanice tried to ask another question, but the nurse cut her off by saying, "I'll make a note for them, okay?" The irritation in her voice was loud and clear.

Shanice closed her eyes to rest but forced them open again. "It's Saturday?" The last thing she remembered was saying goodbye to Miss Macie Wednesday morning. On a crazy whim, she had taken three whole days off to go to Chicago. She'd never been. She'd planned to drive there to see The Benjies in concert. She was going to stay in a motel off the highway—she'd made a reservation and everything—and then go sightseeing all day on Thursday and Friday morning. She'd planned to get back home late Friday evening.

Frustrated as all heck, Shanice blurted, "Can you at least tell me how long I've been here?"

The nurse sighed as if Shanice were the absolute bane of her existence and looked up at the whiteboard. "That says you've been here for over two weeks."

Shanice recoiled. "Two? Two weeks?"

The woman put up a hand and said, "I don't know much more than that. I'll let them know you're coherent now." She fussed with a few more things, wrote something on a whiteboard near the door, and left without another word.

"Where *am* I?" Shanice called after her but got no reply. She wished she could make out what was written on the whiteboard, but without her glasses or contacts, no dice. It was one big blur.

"Did I even make it to Chicago?" she asked out loud. Why won't anyone tell her what happened?

She ran a hand through her hair, surprised at how even that motion hurt. As she suspected, her hair desperately needed washing. With a sigh, she lowered her arm. God, she felt bruised and banged up. And swollen. She was in a hospital, but where? Realization dawned on her. Maybe she was in a hospital in Chicago. She closed her eyes against the panic threatening to overtake her.

"I don't know anyone in Chicago. There's no one here to..." She swallowed against the sudden lump in her throat. What she didn't dare voice out loud was that there was no one in Denton Heights either. Well, there was Miss Macie, but she was in her eighties, hard of hearing, and basically, someone Shanice rented a room from for a reduced rate in exchange for taking care of the older woman. You would think at age twenty-five, Shanice would have a stable of friends or at least acquaintances. Wait. She knew her coworkers. They weren't friends, though. Only once did someone think to invite her out for their Friday happy hour. And that hadn't gone well at all. They eyed her suspiciously when she told them she didn't drink and then politely refused to smoke marijuana with them in the bar's back patio, where the management looked the other way. Once again, she was an outcast.

"Welcome to my life," Shanice said with a sigh. No one heard her, of course. "Crap." She was supposed to finish that coding project that weekend. That was the deal she'd made with Mr. Johnson for getting the three days off. She needed to call him. "Where's my phone?" She frantically searched for the call button again. No luck. "Where's my car? My suitcase?" Sadness filled her chest when she remembered Bernard. She'd brought her little furry musk ox stuffie with her to Chicago. Where was he? Tears filled her eyes as a huge lump settled around her chest as she silently apologized to Bernard for putting him in danger. She remembered where she'd gotten him. A bunch of high school kids in Cincinnati had collected clothes and stuffies for the fosters. They were a Key Club, maybe. She couldn't remember, but she'd been around seven then. She'd long since learned to pick the toys or stuffies from the donations that none of the other kids would want because if she did, no doubt one of the bigger, meaner kids would take it from her just because they could. So, she bided her time. None of the other kids at the Holiday Fair even looked at the brown raggedy-looking furry musk ox. He reminded her of herself. He was brown, of course, just like her. And he was a bit raggedy and small, also like her. Later, the other fosters laughed at her choice, but she stuck by Bernard—oh, yes, he had a name before they'd even left the warehouse. Since then, he'd gone everywhere with her. Even that time…

No. She took a deep breath and blew it out. It wasn't the time nor the place. She bunched up the top sheet, pulled it to her chest, and fell asleep, pretending she clutched Bernard and had been able to save him after all.

Chapter 3

Marta

This window needs cleaning, Marta thought as she looked out onto the parking lot from her sister Nora's hospital room. Wasn't her job, thank God. Although Marta was weary from working that morning, she was buzzing with anxious energy. If she never went to another hospital again, it would be too soon. And on top of that, the jerk Jeff made sure she didn't get the Pope Mobile that morning. He hid all the keys except one. The only cart left was Old Sparky—the one with the loose battery cable you had to keep putting on after every bump. "What an idiot," she muttered.

"Who's an idiot?" Nora asked, waking up from her second nap since Marta had gotten there five hours before.

"Ugh," Marta said, turning around. "Just some asswipe at work." She approached the bed and took her sister's hand. "Good nap? You still look tired."

Her sister blew out a sigh and flicked several stray locks of hair out of her face with her free hand. "I think the anesthesia's taking its damn time to leave my system." Nora's dark roots were growing in. It would be a while before she could get her hair dyed again. Why women went through that bullshit to preserve their *beauty* was beyond Marta. "And the doc wants me here for two more nights."

"Two more?" Marta was on full alert. Had there been a complication?

"Oh, the usual," Nora said, sounding resigned. She patted her overlarge belly. "Because I'm so overweight, he wants me to have the maximum post-surgery time before heading to the Chrysalis Center. He wants to be sure there are no 'complications' from the surgery." She used air quotes.

"Hmm," Marta grunted her response. She hoped there were no

complications for Nora's sake. And hers, if she was being honest. She didn't know if she could take that stress.

"Pip, I know the Chrysalis Center has bad memories for us," Nora said gently.

Marta grunted. Nora had used her childhood nickname. This was turning into a big-sister moment.

"Dr. Murdock says Chrysalis has a great skilled nursing center," Nora continued. "They have top-notch rehabilitation specialists, and it's right there in Denton Heights. You'll visit me while I'm there, won't you?"

"Of course." Marta softened her expression. Just because that was where their mother had died after spending her last days in the hospice wing didn't mean Marta would wimp out. She could be strong. She was ex-Army. She was a corporal who was tough and could handle anything.

"Get me a hair tie, Pip," Nora said.

Marta laughed as she rifled through Nora's bag. "You haven't called me that in forever."

"Well, you always were a little pipsqueak."

"You're six years older than me," Marta protested as she handed over the elastic tie. "I was always littler than you."

Nora pulled her hair back into a sloppy ponytail and sighed. "Much better." She grunted and said, "Do you know that Brian fussed at me last night? I mean, I was barely awake after the surgery."

"Fussed at you about what?"

Nora raised an eyebrow. "He reminded me that forty-one was too young to have knee replacements and that I have a lot more weight to lose before the doc lets me get the other knee done. And then he let all that sit there."

"Talk about kicking you when you're down."

"Right?" Nora said, finding an ally. "Men."

Marta busted out laughing. "I wouldn't know."

"No, you wouldn't," Nora said and added. "So, when are you going to settle down? When are you going to find the right girl—"

"Woman," Marta interrupted. She hated when people referred to grown women as girls. It was part of the whole weaker-sex, glass-ceiling conspiracy.

"Right, right," Nora conceded. She pointed toward the over-bed table for her Styrofoam cup of water. Marta pushed the table closer. "Marta, you have to get back out in the world. You're a hermit. Work and home. Home and work. Did you at least take down Mom's wheelchair ramp out front?"

"I've been meaning to," Marta said weakly.

"It's been almost two years," Nora said softly. "You're putting the pro in procrastination, and that is not like my little sister at all."

"I know." They sat in silence for an overlong moment until Marta blurted, "I have a date tonight, anyway."

"You do?" Nora's eyebrows rocketed skyward. "Good for you. Anyone serious?"

Marta shrugged and then looked at her watch. "Maybe I should get going."

"Yes, yes. And I want all the details." Nora giggled but then rescinded. "Scratch that. Not *all* the details."

Marta laughed and hugged her sister. "Give 'em hell, Nora."

"I always do." She kissed Marta on the forehead. "I love you, Pip."

Marta turned away as tears filled her eyes. "Me, too," was all she could muster. She composed herself and said, "I'll come back tomorrow after work. Okay?"

"Perfect," Nora said. "Ooh, I hear the dinner cart coming. I asked for extra chocolate puddings. So good."

"Yum," Marta said sarcastically and rolled her eyes. She was not a fan of that processed crap they hawked as food. "Text me if you want me to bring you anything. Or if you get bored."

Nora nodded. "Have fun on your date."

Marta smiled and let herself out of Nora's room. She stood outside the door momentarily to take a cleansing breath. She'd learned to do that with every hospital and doctor's visit with her mom. She had to show that brave face. She grounded herself and nodded at one of the nurses at the central station. The nurse either didn't see her or chose to ignore her. Whatever. As long as Nora got good care, that's what mattered.

Marta headed toward the hall leading to the bank of elevators. She stopped short when a piercing screech came from the room she was passing.

"No!" the female voice screeched again.

Marta leaned forward to continue her trek toward the elevators. This wasn't her business. She had no right to intervene. Not her person. Not her concern. But her feet remained rooted.

"Get away from me," the voice warned, clearly panicked.

Marta's feet decided for her. She threw open the door and assessed the situation quickly. A male figure. In close proximity to a female patient.

"Back away," Marta barked. When the figure didn't move or turn around, Marta approached from behind, wrapped her arm around his neck under his chin, and pulled him back. Once he was away from the patient, she spun him around and released him, effectively putting herself between him and the bed. "I told you to back away."

"What the fuck, lady?" He rubbed at this throat. His uniform indicated that he was a nurse or an aide. His nametag said Tyler. "I wasn't hurting her. I was just trying to get her ready for a bath. It's my job. Jesus."

"I'm not Jesus," Marta said. "But you'll see Him right quick if you approach her like that again." She heard a stifled giggle behind her. "Consent is the key to everything. She was clearly *not* consenting to you touching her."

"Yes, Ma'am. Okay, okay," he said, backing away. "I'll send someone else."

"A woman."

"Yeah, okay." He turned and waved his hand in surrender.

Marta's heart was pounding as she watched the door close. *I've met some amazing members of the male species, so I know they're not all bad,* she thought. *But, wow,* "that one was an idiot." There was another stifled giggle behind her.

Marta slowly turned around. She had no idea what the woman in the bed looked like, although she sounded young. As soon as she turned, her breath caught in her throat. The young Black woman took her breath away. She was a little worse for wear, but Marta was mesmerized by the woman's eyes and the depths in them. She was beautiful. The woman definitely looked like she'd been on the losing end of a fight, but it was her beautiful smile and hopeful eyes that pulled Marta in.

"You okay?" Marta asked, not daring to move closer to the frightened woman. She didn't want to see fear in the woman's eyes and be the cause of it.

"Yes, thank you," the young woman said. "You're kind of badass."

Marta scoffed but then lifted her arms to show her biceps. What was she doing? Fuck. She was attracted to the woman within seconds of seeing her. She was young, though. Probably too young. "How old are you, kid?" *Really? That's your next question?*

"I'm not a kid," the young woman said defiantly. She must get that a lot. "I'm twenty-five."

"Ooh, an old lady, already," Marta quipped, hoping the light banter would calm the young woman down.

The young woman giggled and put a hand over her mouth.

"What're you in for, kid?" Marta asked but then amended. "I mean, woman. Lady. Person."

More giggling came from the bed.

Marta turned to the whiteboard by the door. "Shanice Ward? Is that you?"

The young woman nodded.

"There's a question mark next to your name. And above it, it says 'Jane Doe – June.'" Marta narrowed her eyes and rubbed her chin as if deep in thought. She playfully mused out loud, speaking into her watch. "The suspect has various aliases. On any given day, she's Jane or June or Shanice."

"I'm Shanice," the young woman burst out with more giggling.

A flood of something smacked Marta's heart and rushed through her body. She wanted to dart over and pull the young woman into her arms, rock her, and tell her everything would be okay. She clenched her core and said, "No, seriously, Shanice, why are you in the hospital?"

"I think I was in a car accident." The floodgates opened as a sob burst out, and then tears fell. "Where am I? Where's my phone? Where's my wallet? Where's my car? I need to call my boss. Johnson Tech Group. And I need to make sure Miss Macie is okay." The young woman's gaze fell back on Marta. "Who are you?"

"Whoa, whoa, whoa," Marta said, stumbling backward. "That was a lot." She feigned dizziness and searched for a chair. This poor woman was frightened and confused, and Marta decided she couldn't leave the poor thing in such a state. So even though she didn't like people and never got involved, she sat down anyway. "My name is Marta Ingersoll. I'm thirty-five, and I like long walks on the beach." She thought that would get a giggle from the kid, but quite the opposite happened.

"No long walks for me," Shanice said. "Ever again." She gestured toward the bottom of the bed, and that's when Marta noticed for the first time.

Her heart leaped to her throat, but she heroically stifled a gasp. "Dang, kid." Marta was shocked that her voice was calm and even-keeled. "Did that happen in the accident?"

"Yes."

Marta wanted to ask if she could look but didn't. It seemed rude. The poor young woman had been amputated below the knee on both legs. God, life for her was going to be so different. Fuck. The kid was only twenty-five. Marta coughed to hide her emotion and then blurted, "You're in Cincinnati General Hospital. I don't know where your stuff is, but I can check the drawers and cupboards." She stood up and turned her back to Shanice to wipe away the tears in her eyes. A quick search revealed nothing. Not a single personal item. Not even clothes. "Sorry, kid. I didn't find anything."

"That's okay. The lady said she would talk to someone on Monday. I've been here for over two weeks but don't know what happened. No one's telling me anything."

Marta looked at the whiteboard. "Yes, it does say the day you were admitted."

"What day?" Shanice's eyes grew wide.

"Wednesday, June first."

Seeing Shanice's panic-filled eyes triggered something in Marta. As calmly as she could, she said, "I'll get to the bottom of all this, Seeing as you're a bit indisposed. But first, I have to ask you something. It's something I've been wondering about all day long."

It was obvious that Shanice was fighting a freakout. Her frown had reached epic proportions. "What?"

"Why *did* that chicken cross the road?" Marta bugged out her eyes to let Shanice know she was teasing her.

"The chicken?" Shanice was clearly confused.

"You know. The one that always crosses the dang road, and no one knows why."

"To get to the other side," a booming voice said from behind Marta. An official-looking nurse bopped into the room. "You," she said with a finger jabbing toward Marta, "cannot be in here."

"She's my friend," Shanice said.

Marta turned back to Shanice and clucked her tongue. "Yes, of course, we're friends." She faced the nurse again. "I'm her aunt. By marriage, of course. I can't get her to call me Aunt Marta, though. Kids these days. Am I right?"

"You're the first to show up for her," the nurse said suspiciously.

"No one else has come by?" Marta asked, real anger seeping into her voice. The young woman had been there for over two weeks.

"No one. Can you verify who she is?"

"Yes, of course. Shanice Ward. Age twenty-five."

More questions were fired quickly, and the only stumbling block in the charade was when the nurse asked where Shanice lived. Marta didn't hesitate and said, "Denton Heights." The vigorous head nodding from Shanice behind the nurse floored Marta. Shanice really did live in Denton Heights. Lucky guess. This day was getting weirder and weirder.

The nurse seemed satisfied with the answers and stopped fussing at Marta long enough to ask Shanice if she was ready to be bathed since Tyler said Shanice had requested females only. Shanice nodded, and Marta took that as her cue to skedaddle.

Marta went over to the whiteboard, wrote her name and cell phone number, and said, "I have to get going." She turned toward Shanice in apology. "I have an appointment. Is it okay if I come for a visit tomorrow after work?"

Marta melted when Shanice's entire face and body lit up with joy. Shanice nodded as much as she could with the neck brace restriction. "Aunt

Marta?"

"Yeah?"

"It was the turkey's day off."

"Huh?" Then it dawned on her. The chicken. The road. She burst out laughing. "I'm glad I found you, Shanice. I'll see you tomorrow."

Shanice waved vigorously with her unbroken hand, and Marta slid out the door. She pressed a hand over her mouth and made it to a chair near the elevator before bursting into tears.

~~~

Although hungry, Marta dove into the shower when she got home. Well, after feeding Snowball and the backyard stray, of course. Seeing that young woman so scared and so...broken had almost broken Marta. A hot scalding shower was just what she needed to shake off that stupid hospital. She shaved again, not that she really needed to, but Jessica would be there in an hour.

Marta needed chow for strength. She tossed a plate of leftover baked chicken and some green beans into the microwave and pulled out her phone.

MARTA: Don't be late.

There was no immediate response, but that was okay. It gave her a minute to plunk her plate of food from the microwave onto the kitchen table. The day after her mother died, Marta changed her usual seat at the kitchen table so that her back faced the living room. It was her father's old seat, and no one had dared to sit there all those years after he'd passed, but Marta simply could not face the empty living room with her mother's electric recliner staring right at her. She needed to toss that stinky stained thing out. And she would. Just not today.

She opened her web browser and typed in Johnson Technology Group. How cool that the young woman worked there. She must be uber-smart. Marta took several screenshots of phone numbers and would make calls in
~~~

the morning. Or should she call now? No, no one would get the messages until tomorrow anyway, and Shanice seemed to be in good hands. Hopefully.

A ding of a text knocked her out of the rabbit hole she was about to go down. She would call Johnson Tech tomorrow, she firmly decided. She swiped over to her text app.

> JESSICA: Yes, Ma'am. Can I bring anything? Do you have any instructions for me?
>
> MARTA: Be wet for me. No panties.
>
> MARTA: Pull in and park at the far end of the driveway. Like that one time. You're going to be impaled in the passenger seat. Face down like before.
>
> JESSICA: Yes, Ma'am. I'm already wet, but you made me more so just now. Thank you, Ma'am.
>
> MARTA: Don't be late.

Jessica knew not to text again. Marta had made it clear that she didn't like idle chitchat and that she was to have the last word in all text exchanges. Did that make her an asshole Domme? Who knew? It didn't matter because she didn't care.

She finished her dinner, washed the dishes, and checked in on Snowball. She found the cat in her mother's chair. Snowball, and asshole Brian, had been the only ones to ever sit in her mother's chair since she passed. And since Snowball wasn't an asshole, she had Marta's permission to hang out there.

"Date tonight, furball," she said to the cat. "So, you'll need to stay out of Nora's room." She needed to stop thinking of it as Nora's room. It was her designated playroom. Of course, all play toys and accouterment were stashed in Marta's room just in case Nora came by and got nostalgic about her old room. Marta never invited women into her own bedroom. It still looked like a high school kid's room. Army posters hung on the wall because that had been her obsession back then. Her track and weightlifting trophies sat on the shelf next to her high school diploma and her dad's Rubik's cube that he'd never mastered. Marta hadn't mastered it either, although she'd tried many times. Her room was her sacred space. Well, Snowball was allowed in, of course. But that was it. Even Nora didn't snoop in Marta's room. Thinking about the Rubik's cube made her nostalgic for her childhood when everything was okay, and she had both parents and wasn't an orphan like she was now. Was it possible to consider yourself an orphan if you were thirty-five? She went into her room and pulled down her father's cube. She spun it around a few times and got a solid color on top, but that's all she had emotional energy for. She put it down to get ready for her date.

Ten minutes before Jessica's arrival, Marta donned the apparatus she favored. Should she make Jessica put the condom on her? Nah, that would take too long. Marta was raring to go. Thinking about her session with Jessica that evening had helped her forget the troubling morning at work, her sister's surgery, and the poor young woman in 408.

The sun had already set when the familiar Honda pulled into the driveway. Marta headed out the back door and stood to one side with her hands on her hips. Putting her hands on her hips helped her get into Domme mode. Jessica parked her car, turned off the engine, and reached up to douse the interior lights. She got out of the car and was about to say something when Marta put a finger to her lips.

"You know what to do," Marta said evenly. She had no smile for Jessica. Not yet. Later. Maybe.

Jessica nodded and walked around the front of her car. Ooh, yes. Her soft dark brown hair was pulled back into a tight bun. She had that whole sexy teacher thing down pat, especially with that tight blouse showing off her lovely pillowy breasts. And the short skirt. The woman knew how to please, that was for sure. Marta admired the woman's legs as she got closer. Jessica was a sexy plus-sized woman with curves in all the right places. Why she'd chosen Marta to play with every week was beyond Marta, but that didn't matter at the moment, now did it?

Jessica paused in front of Marta and lay a hand on Marta's chest in greeting. Marta had a no-kissing rule, so they'd compromised with that gesture. Marta nodded and motioned with her head toward the passenger door. Jessica moaned in anticipation and opened the door. No lights came on. Good. She sat down on the passenger seat, facing outward toward Marta. She was waiting for more instructions. She was a beautiful sub, and Marta wished she could give her more, but she liked her solitude too much. Their weekly trysts fed her Domme soul and seemed to be enough for Jessica as well.

Marta reached into her back pocket and pulled out a gag. Jessica leaned forward to receive it without question. Marta gestured, and Jessica obeyed by undoing her button-down shirt, exposing her bra-clad breasts. Marta leaned down, caressed the top spillage, and then stroked each breast over the lace cups in turn. Later she would give them their due, but for now, she was letting Jessica know that those breasts belonged to Marta. Marta reached inside one cup and found the already hardened nipple. She circled her middle finger over it, causing Jessica to lean forward. Clearly, she wanted more as a soft moan escaped her gagged mouth. Marta brought her thumb over and gently squeezed the nipple. She increased the pressure until she got the reaction she'd sought. Jessica's moan caused a surge of lust to run through Marta's core.

Marta lifted one breast as if picking up the woman's body. "Turn over."

Jessica complied and knelt on the passenger seat. She leaned forward, resting her elbows on the driver's seat. Marta smacked Jessica's inner thighs gently, and Jessica parted her legs allowing Marta to take in all of Jessica's panty-less glory.

It was Marta's turn to moan. She unzipped her jeans slowly, making sure Jessica heard. In the quiet summer evening, sounds traveled. Hopefully, Mrs. Pulaski wouldn't choose this exact moment to bring over another one of her lemon Bundt cakes.

Marta pulled the skirt out of the way and tucked the hem into the waistband. Her warm hands caressed the ass presented to her. Jessica squirmed in anticipation. One well-placed slap stilled the movements, and Marta reached into her jeans and pulled out the phallus. She ripped open the condom and slid it on. She moved closer and let the phallus touch the back of one of Jessica's thighs.

"Mmm," Jessica moaned and clenched her ass cheek on that side. Marta grabbed two handfuls of ass and squeezed. Hard. Jessica moaned at the sudden pain, but her head lolled back toward Marta, signaling that she liked it, that she was ready, that she wanted this. They had safe words and safe snaps already in place, and Marta would remind her of those again once they were inside, but for now, she had to rely on their familiarity with each other.

Marta gripped one of Jessica's hips and guided the phallus toward Jessica's very wet center. Marta didn't have to physically check; she could see the arousal glistening in the fading light. Marta thrust her hips, gently guiding the phallus over Jessica's nether lips, rubbing over her clit. She pressed up on the phallus, causing more pressure as she rubbed. Jessica growled, making Marta chuckle evilly.

Marta pulled away, causing Jessica to groan at its absence. The groan was replaced by a moan when Marta tucked the tip of the strap-on inside. She pulled out and then pushed in a bit more. Oh, she could have simply impaled Jessica to the hilt. She'd done it before but wanted to tease the woman a bit more. Outdoor sex, no matter how secluded the back part of the driveway was, was still dangerous. Marta gripped the top of the door frame with one hand and stood up tall. The other hand gripped Jessica's hip while the dildo was tucked inside her sub. She toyed with Jessica for a few more thrusts but then made good on her unspoken promise and increased her thrusts in both speed and depth.

"Ahh, fuck," Marta muttered. The strap-on was hitting her just where she needed it. She was going to cum before Jessica did. And that was okay. A few more thrusts was all it took for Marta to explode. She continued to rock her hips into Jessica through her aftershocks. She dipped her head down and fell forward on top of Jessica. She gripped both of Jessica's hips tightly and rested on Jessica's back.

Once she'd caught her breath, she stood back up and pulled out. She smacked each one of Jessica's ass cheeks in turn, untucked the skirt, and said, "Keep the gag on. Lock your car and come inside."

Marta turned, laughed at the hard phallus sticking out of the fly of her jeans, and headed back into the house with it bob, bob, bobbing along.

Chapter 4

Shanice

Monday morning arrived, and Shanice stretched her one good arm overhead and her legs outward. She could feel her feet and toes stretching, but how could she? It was weird. She hadn't really looked yet, though. Looking would make it real. The big clock on the wall read seven. Miss Macie had a similar clock in the kitchen with a big hand and a little hand, so Shanice was used to reading clocks like that. She just never understood why they called them 'hands.' It was weird.

A small smile crept up her face. That woman Marta had nice hands and such a pretty smile. And her eyes were bright and playful and, yeah, a gorgeous light brown. And, good grief, the way she came storming in there like a superhero. It was kind of scary, but Tyler had been even scarier. *Jerk woke me up, touching me.* Like Marta said—idiot. Shanice giggled. Marta was so funny. Maybe she'd come by today after her work. Shanice wondered what a superhero with strong hands that told Dad jokes did for work. Firefighter. Yes. It has to be. *Or a Special Ops operative with the CIA, and she won't be able to tell me because it's all top secret.*

"She might not come," the pessimistic side of Shanice said out loud. Yeah, probably not. It's okay. She'd scrapped and survived her childhood and put herself through college with little help. She didn't need anyone. People, places, and things just let you down anyway, so getting attached made no sense. And besides, it was Monday. Hopefully, the Admin people would bring her phone and wallet up, and she could make calls, and all would be well in her world. She looked toward her nonexistent feet. Well, not all would be well.

Shanice sighed as she closed her eyes, waiting for someone, anyone, to help her piece together what had happened and what was next. Were they making prosthetics for her? That was the right word, right? This whole thing was a bad dream, but she kept waking up in it. She felt herself drifting off and let it happen. What else was there to do?

A while later, she woke up when she heard someone fussing near the bed. She opened her eyes. A nurse. Okay. She closed her eyes again.

"Blood pressure time, sweetie," the kind woman said.

"Okay," Shanice said sleepily and lifted her good arm.

"You're so helpful," the nurse said. Shanice had never seen this one. Of course, she'd been out of it for over two weeks, so who knew anything? "I wish I had more patients as cooperative as you are." The nurse smiled, and it was a genuine smile. Shanice couldn't help but smile back. It was then she noticed her superhero.

"Hi, Aunt Marta," Shanice said and waved with her good arm, totally disrupting the nurse's attempts to get the cuff on. "Oh, sorry, Ma'am."

The nurse just chuckled and said, "That one has been here for over an hour, just watching you sleep."

"She has?"

"I have," Marta said and stood up. "You're kind of cute and innocent when you sleep. But, yeah, we all know better. Don't we?" She laughed as if she and Shanice were old buddies, or truly aunt and niece, and had known each other forever.

"Thanks for visiting me," Shanice said, lowering her eyes.

"Pfft. I was in the neighborhood," Marta said but didn't elaborate. "Want the news now or later?"

"News?" Shanice grimaced as the cuff tightened on her arm. She scrunched her eyes and held her breath, making Marta laugh. "One sec."

"Understood," Marta said.

Aha! Shanice thought. That sounded kind of military or something. She was totally Special Ops. Maybe she was a renegade helping lonely orphans in hospitals.

"Okay, phew," Shanice said with a quick exhale. "Go."

"Yes, Ma'am," Marta said and stood straight. *Yep, Special Ops.* "I called first thing this morning and left messages at Johnson Technology Group. No one answered, and I was going to follow up with a call at lunch, but then I decided this was too important and drove over there on my way here."

"You did?" Wow, that was unexpected. "Was anyone there?"

"Yes, I met the handsome Mr. Johnson himself and the well-put-together Mrs. Washington."

"I love her," Shanice said, totally fangirling the Human Resources Director. "You told them?"

"Yes. I told them as much as I knew, which isn't much, but they were relieved to finally hear something. Mrs. Washington told me they've been calling your phone ever since you didn't show up that Monday for work, and then they tried to reach Mrs. Macie Clark, but the voicemail is full. They sent someone to your address, but no one answered the door."

"Miss Macie is kind of hard of hearing. And she never answers the door anyway. Too much crime, she always says. That's why I take care of her."

"To combat all that crime in Denton Heights?"

Shanice laughed. "I get reduced rent there because I help her."

Marta nodded. Shanice loved her gentle smile. It was one of sympathy, not pity, and there was strength in it. She wore a man's style button-down shirt, which looked good on her. The light brown in the pattern totally brought out her soft brown eyes. And her hair – it was dark blonde and wavy. Short, too. You can't have hair getting in the way of saving orphans, right? What sign was she? Cancer? Virgo? Leo? No, not Leo. Cancer and Virgo were the most compatible with Scorpio in love and communication.

"Shanice?" Marta said. "You okay?"

"Hmm?"

"You kind of zoned out there for a second."

"Oh, uh—"

"Could be the medications," the nurse said. "She's on a lot of them. I heard her call you 'aunt.' If she gives permission, I can share what I can with you."

"Yes, that's fine," Shanice said and grinned conspiratorially at Marta when the nurse turned back toward Marta.

"The docs typically make their rounds in the morning," the nurse continued, "so if you stick around, you can ask more questions."

"Where's her car?" Marta asked.

The nurse made a noise of regret. "I don't know. I saw a request for Admin to visit today, so they may have information about that. They may have details pertaining to the accident."

"Got it," Marta said, totally taking control. She must have saved lots of orphans because she sure seemed in charge. "What does her chart say about the accident? My niece doesn't remember anything."

The nurse pulled out her phone and tapped it a few dozen times. "Ahh, here it is. She came in early afternoon on Wednesday, June 1, and went immediately to trauma triage. Oh," the nurse looked up with a startled expression and said, "She went up to surgery immediately."

"Probably because of those," Shanice said, pointing to her nonexistent feet.

"We'll ask the docs when they come," Marta said firmly. She was going to get to the bottom of things. "Anything else?" She directed that to the kind nurse.

"It doesn't look like they induced a coma, but she's been on some heavy meds. She turned toward Shanice. "Because of all the trauma to your body. And you have a concussion. The docs will tell you more." She lowered her voice. "I really shouldn't have shared that much, but the wheels of communication turn so gosh-darn slowly here that, well, you ought to know something."

"Thank you," Marta said. She pursed her lips and nodded as if to say she understood the nurse's predicament and appreciated her breaking the rules. "Would you be able to light a fire under Admin? Get them up here sooner rather than later. My niece needs to know what happened. She needs to know so she can get busy healing. Right, kid?"

Shanice nodded as much as the collar would allow. She wished Marta would stop calling her kid. Even though she kind of liked it, she wasn't a child. And she didn't want Marta to see her as one.

"How soon before she can get that thing off?" Marta asked.

"A question for the docs." The nurse headed toward the door. "I'll put in that reminder to Admin right now, and then I'll come back to check on you later, Shanice."

"It's Jane," Marta quipped. "Maybe June. She's not talking."

Shanice giggled and hid her face behind the sheet.

"You two are cute," the nurse said. "Okay, I have to go. We're busy today. You have your call button?"

Shanice lifted it to show her. This nurse had wrapped it once around the bed railing on the good-arm side.

"Use it if you need anything."

They both watched the nurse leave and then Shanice said, "Thank you for looking after me. You didn't—" She swallowed hard against the lump forming in her throat. "You didn't have to do any of those things."

"You're worth it, young lady," Marta said softly. "It was just a happy accident that I was walking by your room yesterday when I was."

Shanice looked away. Okay, *young lady* was a step up from kid. She'd take it. She'd had lots of people offer to help during her twenty-five years on the planet, yet most of them either didn't come through or expected something significant in return. Sometimes that price was way too high. She'd long ago made a rule not to rely on anyone, and she wasn't going to break that rule now, even if she was faced with a handsome Special Ops orphan-saving superhero firefighter.

"You must be tired," Marta said so softly that Shanice felt guilty for lusting after her. She needed to reboot that silliness.

"Mmm," Shanice said noncommittally.

"I'm going to step out and let you rest. I'll just bop over and visit my sister across the hall. She had knee replacement surgery."

"Okay," Shanice said and closed her eyes. Marta was nice, but Shanice knew better than to fall for nice. She'd been burned before.

~~~

Shanice woke when she heard the lunch tray settle on the movable over-bed table. She heard someone say, "Thanks," which woke her out of a deep sleep. She groaned. Her body hurt. Everywhere. Even her invisible feet. She blinked her eyes open. How long had she slept? Wait! Had the doctors
~~~

come? She remembered…something. Answering questions or something. It was so muddy. Shoot, why was she so out of it?

"Hi, sleepy head," Marta said, heading for the food tray. "Ready for chow?"

"Hmm?" Shanice struggled to open her eyelids fully. Oh, shoot. She still had her thumb in her mouth. And everyone had seen it. Big baby. She pulled it out and asked, "Time is it?"

"Noon," the chipper voice said.

"'Kay." It was all she could muster.

"I'm going to raise you up a bit. The docs said you could be raised to eat, but lying flattish is best for your broken ribs."

"I have broken ribs?" Shanice said, now fully awake.

"Five," Marta said and added, "Ready to raise up?"

Shanice nodded.

"Stop me if it hurts."

Shanice nodded again. The new position was a Godsend. Something different. Hallelujah. "What else did they say?"

Marta moved the table closer to Shanice and adjusted its height. "Ooh, you got chocolate milk."

Was Marta avoiding the question?

"And there's baked chicken. That's what I had last night. Mashed po's and green beans." She handed a fork to Shanice.

"Not hungry." Shanice wanted to hear what the doctors said instead.

"Doesn't matter," Marta said matter-of-factly. "Tell you what. For each bite you take and swallow, I'll tell you something the docs or Admin told me while you were in dreamland."

Shanice sighed. "Okay." Marta must have kids or something. Ugh, and she probably had a husband. Oh, well. *Too bad, so sad,* Shanice said to herself. *No superheroes in my future.* Ahh, whatever. She'd made it this far without one, anyway.

She took a bite of potatoes first. She'd need Marta's help cutting the chicken, but she wasn't quite ready to ask for help. Marta must have read her mind, though, because she started cutting the chicken into bite-sized portions. Who was this woman?

"Good job," Marta said after Shanice swallowed the potatoes. She gestured toward the chicken. "You were in a multi-vehicle accident on I-74 where it merges with 275 near Miamitown. The accident wasn't your fault, so please don't worry about that. The driver of the tractor-trailer heading southbound lost control, crossed over the median, and careened into oncoming traffic. A bunch of cars were involved."

"Whoa. I don't remember any of that. I was going to Chicago."

"What for?" Marta smiled as Shanice speared a piece of chicken.

"Concert. The Benjies."

"The who's?"

Shanice laughed. Yeah, Marta was older than she was by ten years or something.

"They're so good. They're a girl group. It's K-pop. They're Americans of Korean descent, but it's still called K-pop."

Marta shook her head as if she had no clue what Shanice was talking about. "You're speaking another language there, kid. But I'm sorry you didn't get to see your concert. Maybe when you're better able to move around."

"Hmm," Shanice grunted grumpily. She was never going to get around. Was she going to be in a wheelchair for the rest of her life? "Am I getting fake legs?"

Marta gestured for her to eat the speared chicken bite, which Shanice did.

"Okay, swallow that first." Once Shanice did, she laid the fork down on the tray. There was bad news coming, she could tell. "I'm just going to come out and say it all, okay?"

Shanice nodded.

"Words."

"Yes, Ma'am," Shanice said.

Marta took a deep breath. "Apparently, an SUV took a direct hit from the out-of-control truck and went airborne. It landed on your car, and your legs were crushed." Her voice broke on the last word, and she took a moment to regroup before continuing. "You were medivacked by helicopter here to Cincinnati General, where your injuries were assessed—broken bones in that one arm, broken ribs, severe concussion. You have extensive bruising all over your body, but there was no real damage to internal organs besides the jostling your whole body took. And that, young lady, is a really good thing." Marta's expression softened, and Shanice realized that Marta was trying hard not to get emotional again. Marta encouraged Shanice to take another bite of food, and she did, sensing there was more. "Your legs. The docs told me there was no way to save them, honey. They quickly consulted with surgeons from another hospital and concluded there was no way to reattach either of the limbs."

Marta's voice caught in her throat, and she started crying. "I'm so sorry, Shanice. I'm so sorry this happened to you." Marta took a ragged breath and wiped at her eyes. "You're so young. So beautiful. This should not have happened to someone as lovely as you." She pounded a fist against her leg as she struggled to get her emotions under control.

Shanice reached for Marta's hand and held it. She rubbed the back of the hand with her thumb. She also had no words but found it odd that she was comforting Marta instead of feeling sorry for herself. That time would come, she knew.

"Marta?" Shanice said meekly. "I have a question."

Marta blew out a sigh, took her hand back, and wiped her eyes. "Yes, honey?"

"I've been wondering something."

"Mmm?"

"What side of the chicken has the most feathers?"

"What?" Marta asked and then rolled her eyes as she started to chuckle. "I don't know, honey. What side?"

"The outside, of course," Shanice said, laughing.

Marta broke down, both laughing and crying at the same time. Shanice reached for the box of tissues near her lunch tray and handed the whole box to Marta, which made Marta laugh even more.

"You're something else, Shanice." Marta took a tissue and wiped at her eyes. She turned away and blew her nose. "Ready for a few more things?"

"I guess."

"Listen, if you don't want to eat any more, that's fine. I'd have lost my appetite by now, too."

Shanice grinned and then ate some more to show Marta she was okay.

Marta smiled, blew her nose again, and washed her hands at the sink. She said over her shoulder, "Someone from your work is coming to see you today." She dried her hands and then came back to stand by the side of the bed. "Mrs. Washington told me they would give Admin your health insurance information, and, bonus, we can call your car insurance company right now if your card is in here." Marta reached into her back pocket and pulled out Shanice's wallet.

"My wallet. Oh, my gosh." Shanice sighed her relief. She took the wallet and opened it. Yep. All her cash was still there. That was a miracle. "All my insurance cards are in here." She pulled them out to show Marta.

"Cool," Marta said, all business again. "That was the only item Admin had. I signed it out for you as Aunt Marta. I hope that was okay."

"Yes, of course."

"And I didn't want to rifle through your stuff—"

"That consent thing?"

Marta's startled expression was almost comical. "Uh, yeah, something like that. And even though someone from your job will give them your health insurance info, I'll double-team them and show your card to Admin downstairs when I leave. But I figure after you're done with chow, we can call your car insurance company together from my phone. How does that sound?"

"Good. Thank you." Shanice sighed. "I wish I had my phone. I need to find out about Miss Macie. I'm supposed to be the one taking care of her."

"I couldn't find any info on her, but if you give me your address, I can stop there on my way home. I live in Denton Heights, too, by the way."

"You do?" Shanice couldn't help her excited expression. "That's cool. I moved there two years ago. For my job."

Marta beamed. "What's Miss Macie's address?"

Shanice dictated the address, and then they sat quietly for a few moments while Shanice ate. After a bit, Marta gestured toward the lunch tray. "Wow, you had a good appetite after all."

Shanice managed to eat all of the chicken and green beans. The potatoes were kind of fake and weird, but she ate them anyway. Food hadn't always been guaranteed in her world, so she ate all of it. She also hadn't wanted to disappoint Marta.

"Marta?" Shanice asked.

"Yes?"

"Did you go to work today?"

"Nah. Took the day off to help my new friend."

Friend? *Does she think of me as her friend?* No. Shanice didn't have friends. *No one ever sticks around.* She thought about her new lack of feet. No one is going to stick around now, that's for sure.

After a somewhat lengthy call to the car insurance company, which Marta handled most of, Shanice drifted off to sleep.

She woke up hoping Marta was still there but was sorely disappointed when she wasn't. Ooh, there was a note on the over-bed table.

> Hey, Beautiful – You were sleeping so soundly that I couldn't bring myself to disturb you. I'm heading down to Admin before they do something silly, like close their offices. I'll stop by Miss Macie's house to check on her. And I'll stop by to see you tomorrow, but it will probably be in the afternoon. Someone has to work around here. Ha ha. Get sleep. Cooperate with the nurses and docs, okay? Get going on that healing thing. That's all I want you to worry about! – Marta.

Shanice ran her fingers over the hand-drawn smiley face near Marta's name. Funny how they'd dropped the aunt/niece ruse already. Shanice reread the note, pausing on the word 'Beautiful,' and then folded it up small enough to fit in her newly recovered wallet.

~~~

"There she is," the kind nurse from that morning said as Shanice woke. "My shift is just about done." She gestured to a young nurse with long
~~~

blonde hair pulled back into a tight ponytail. "Miss Julie is taking over, and I just told her all about you. She has an interesting suggestion which I want you to consider."

"Okay," Shanice said cautiously. She wished Marta was there to help her.

The kind nurse headed out, and Miss Julie smiled as she fussed with the IV bags and meds and all of that.

"Here at the hospital," Miss Julie said, "we have chaplains who make rounds talking to people for their spiritual needs. I can ask for one to visit you if you wish, but I thought you might be open to another kind of spiritual healing method."

"What's that?" Shanice had never been religious, even though some of the foster moms and dads made them go to Christian churches.

"It's energy work. It's called Reiki healing. A healer of this sort hovers her hands over you and channels energy into your body to promote healing. Something like that. When I blew out my knee playing soccer, I had a few sessions, and I think it helped."

"Sounds like the laying on of hands," Shanice said, her hackles raising. She absolutely didn't want some exorcist person touching her.

"They don't have to touch you at all," Miss Julie said. "The neo-natal unit employs several Reiki healers. My healer said that the body knows what to do with the energy and uses it to heal whatever needs healing."

"I have a lot to heal," Shanice said. The list of injuries Marta told her about came to mind. "Would you be here?"

"If I'm on duty, absolutely. I have other patients but can check in on you while she's here. Want me to see if we can get someone to come up?"

"I don't know."

Miss Julie nodded, and her expression said she understood Shanice's hesitation. "Sometimes we just have to trust. You know? We have to accept help, even if it seems scary."

"Okay," Shanice said. "We can try." She was still cautious, but she was open to trying it. She believed in astrology and all that stuff, so why not this, too? Seriously, she needed all the help she could get at this point.

Chapter 5

Marta

Coffee tasted so much better outside on the back patio, Marta thought. That alone was a good enough reason to take Sunday off, but Marta had more plans than simply lazing around drinking coffee. The kid liked coffee, too, she had discovered during her daily visits after work. It had already been a week and a day since she'd met Shanice. The kid was interesting. Of course, all Shanice had at the hospital was that weak lukewarm crap they dared to call coffee. Maybe she'd stop someplace and bring some decent coffee to Shanice. Marta sat up taller. *I should bring things to her, shouldn't I?* What does she want? What does she need? A phone, for sure, but they still had to hear from the insurance company about how to get Shanice's stuff from the car. But, on the other hand, maybe her stuff had been trashed in the accident. Maybe her phone was smashed or lying on the side of the highway. Or, Marta thought cynically, someone has it and has been using it. "Assholes," she said to the backyard and took her last sip.

She was just about to get up when she saw a pair of amber eyes staring at her from under a bush. "Hey, backyard kitty," Marta said, making her tone gentle. "Want some crunchies?" The cat's gaze didn't waver, so Marta took that as a 'yes.' "Be right back."

She went into the house and pulled a fresh bowl from the cupboard. Snowball wound herself around Marta's legs lovingly. "No, fluffball. You've had your breakfast. This is for your girlfriend outside." With a clawed hand, she reached down and scritched the cat down her back. You need a combing, girl." She'd do it later after she got back from visiting Nora at the Chrysalis Center in Denton Heights, where she'd been moved on Monday, and then visiting Shanice at Cincinnati General in the city. But first, she'd take another stab at Miss Macie's. No amount of knocking or calling in the windows produced any results. Maybe the woman was being taken care of by someone else temporarily. Hopefully, nothing bad had happened to her. Shanice would blame herself. Shanice seemed to have taken the responsibility of caring for this Miss Macie seriously. And no amount of searching for the son in Louisville was producing any results.

The last time Marta had been to the house, she'd left a note tucked in the front door. It had her phone number and a brief message about Shanice's whereabouts. She omitted the major details, only saying that Shanice had been in a car accident.

As she fixed up a mixture of canned and dry food for the outdoor kitty, she wondered what it was about Shanice that kept Marta's trail hot to the city to see her. The young woman needed help, Marta reasoned. That was it. Once they'd gotten a few more things figured out and dealt with, Marta could back away and let Shanice return to her own life. And, of course, Marta could return to her "hermit ways," as Nora put it.

The backyard kitty moved toward the food bowl before Marta was even out of the way. "Whoa, look at you." Marta headed back to the house to let the cat eat undisturbed. She'd put out more food that evening.

Marta took one last look in the mirror and was satisfied that she looked nice. She headed out the front door, down the wheelchair ramp, and unlocked the pickup's driver's side door. Aha! Mrs. Pulaski wasn't expecting her to leave the house so late. It was already 0700 hours. Feeling lucky, she chanced it and went to the mailbox at the street. Yikes. The thing was full of a week's worth of stuff. Marta tossed the stack on the front passenger seat and frowned. The top envelope was addressed to her mother. A stab of…something hit her chest, and she sighed in disgust. "Don't they fucking know? It's been two years. Holy—" She pounded the dashboard in frustration, picked up the entire stack, and unceremoniously dumped it in the backseat.

She fumed all the way to Miss Macie's house. And then she fumed some more when she saw the note she'd left on Monday, six whole days ago, still stuck in the door. She knocked and rang the bell, knowing it was futile. By the time she reached Nora's room at the skilled nursing facility, she had calmed down outwardly. Inwardly was another story.

"Hey, Pip," Nora said cheerfully, and Marta wanted to tell her to tone it down. Instead, she laughed at herself. "You okay?" Nora asked with a cock of her head.

Marta shrugged. "I should be asking you that."

"Rehab starts tomorrow." Nora pointed toward her scarred knee. "Look. The swelling's pretty much gone. They're starting me right here in the bed."

"Not weight-bearing yet?"

"Nope." Nora nodded her head toward the other woman she shared a room with. "She sleeps a lot. Hip replacement."

Marta nodded and grabbed the fold-up chair from the closet. She unfolded it and plopped down into it.

"Not working today?" Nora asked, one eyebrow raised.

"Nope," came the one-word answer.

"Spill it."

"What?" Marta said. Even she heard the frustration in her own voice.

The infamous Nora scowl came next.

Marta rolled her eyes. Their mother had used the same scowl on them, and Marta was kind of powerless against it. "Fine." She took a deep breath and let it out as a long sigh. She looked at Nora again as if to ask if she really had to 'spill it.' When Nora gave her the 'I'm waiting' expression, Marta knew she was sunk. "Fine," she said again. "There's this young woman. She's twenty-five."

"And she has your attention."

Marta smiled. That was true. She went on to relay how she'd stormed into Shanice's room that first day and how devastated she was to see all the injuries on someone so young and innocent. She told Nora about the double amputations.

"She doesn't seem to have anyone in her life," Marta continued. "Not anyone who can help her, anyway."

"And so, you're helping her. You?" Nora said in disbelief. "The greatest hermit north of the Ohio River?"

"Shut up," Marta said good-naturedly. "I'm trying to make things easier for her."

"Mm hmm," Nora said as if she knew something.

"What?"

"You like her."

"What? I do not." Marta scowled at her sister. "There's a big age gap. And I don't really know anything about her. She might not even play on my team, if you get what I mean." She glanced over at the sleeping woman and then got up to close the privacy curtain. Not that those things ever did any good. You could hear everything anyway.

"If you say so," Nora singsonged. "What does your boss think about you taking two Sundays off in a row?"

"He's not happy. I used you as my excuse. I hope that was okay." Marta hadn't planned on spilling those beans, but she was kind of powerless over Nora's big-sisterly mothering. Nora took on a lot after their father died. Marta had been in elementary school at the time. On top of that, their mother's multiple sclerosis was getting worse. Nora had been the one to drive Marta and their mother everywhere before Marta got her driver's license. She had never known how to thank her sister. Maybe moving in with their mom and being the full-time caregiver had been Marta's way of giving back.

Fuck. Why did those thoughts have to intrude? She wiped at her tears when Nora looked away for a moment.

"Is this Shanice still in the hospital?"

"Mm hmm," Marta said, blinking back more tears.

"Ahh," Nora said knowingly, "so I'm only part of the reason you're taking time off."

Marta shrugged and looked down at her calloused hands. She picked at a raggedy cuticle.

"Tell me more about her. Do you have a picture?"

"No. I should get one. I'll tell her you want to see what she looks like."

Nora's laugh made Marta cringe. "If that's what you have to tell yourself."

"Shut up."

"Take one of us, and then you can do the same with her. Okay? It'll be a good cover story."

Marta only saw love and trust in her sister's expression. She nodded and stood up for the selfie. They both held up the peace sign, as was their typical sister picture-taking routine. Marta showed it to Nora for her approval.

"You know," Nora said, "I was wondering why you were dressed extra cute today."

"Nora!" Marta groaned and then hid her face behind her hand, embarrassed as all git out when the woman in the other bed giggled softly. She glared at her sister, who only smirked.

"I'm just helping her," Marta whispered through her teeth.

Nora held up her hands in surrender. "How's Snowball?"

Good. A change in subject. Marta stayed for another hour, keeping her sister company and showing her how to navigate the television's menu options. When it was time to go, her sister hung onto their hug for an extra long beat. "I love you, Pip," she said softly into Marta's ear.

"I love you, too. Text me if you need anything. Okay?"

They said their goodbyes, and Marta headed out the door. She purposely kept her head down as she passed the Long-term/Hospice wing. The memories down that hallway were ones she desperately needed to block out.

In her pickup on the way to Cincinnati, she debated stopping to pick up coffee for Shanice. No, she'd do it next time. Would Shanice like Rikki's Coffee Shop? She said she lived in Denton Heights, so she'd probably been there. Marta had gone there a couple of times when Nora dragged her out shopping. It was a cozy place, and the coffee was excellent. Maybe she'd take Shanice sometime.

"Whoa," Marta said. Why am I thinking about stuff like that? Nora's gotten into my head. I'm just helping the kid. That's it. *Shanice lost her phone and uses mine.* "She'll go back to her life, and I'll go back to mine soon enough." Saying it out loud made firm her resolve.

~~~
~~~

Marta nodded at the aide Tyler as she approached Shanice's door.

"Ma'am," he said politely and hurried by.

Marta smiled. Yes, that young man had learned a lesson. Hopefully. She pushed the door gently, just in case Shanice was sleeping. The joyful smile that greeted her was quickly matched by her own.

"Hey, there," Marta said. "Whoa! The neck brace is gone. Hallelujah!" Marta tried not to melt. Without the neck brace, she could see a more natural Shanice. And, yes, she was beautiful with her smooth skin, cute mouth, and tired but bright eyes.

"Hi, Miss Marta," Shanice said with a grin.

Shanice had used a polite reference even though it made their age difference more pronounced. Of course, if Shanice were her submissive, then that might be expected. She swallowed hard against that thought. Where the hell did that come from? *Dang you, Nora!*

"How are you feeling today?" Marta walked closer to the bed as Shanice raised herself up. It was good to see that she was figuring things out.

"Fine," Shanice said shyly. "What are you holding behind your back?" The grin she'd sported when Marta walked in grew bigger.

"What do you mean?" Marta turned all the way around as if looking for something behind her and, in doing so, revealed the bouquet of flowers she'd bought on a whim in the gift shop downstairs.

Shanice squealed when she saw them. "Are those for me?"

"They are." Marta held the bouquet out toward Shanice but then said, "Unless you think I should give them to Tyler."

"Nooooo," she said and made grabby hands.

Marta chuckled and handed the flowers over. It was so cute how Shanice smelled each one and ran her fingers over the petals. She seemed to like the carnations the best. Marta made a mental note.

"At school, Miss Abraham gave us each a green carnation on St. Patrick's Day. I think that might be the only time I ever got a flower. No, no, they gave us white carnations when we graduated high school. The institute people, not the high school people."

Marta choked down her emotions. Shanice had shared some of her life as a foster kid, and it had practically broken Marta's heart. She was glad Shanice appreciated the flowers. Marta herself had never made a big deal about getting flowers; she could take them or leave them, but this seemed like a huge thing to Shanice. Marta beamed with pride. She'd gotten it right. Yay. She reached over for the plastic shaker bottle she'd brought Shanice earlier in the week and said, "I'll bring a better vase next time, but we can use this for now. Sound okay?" Marta reached for the flowers.

"Just a few minutes more, okay?" Shanice hugged her flowers to her chest. "I miss Bernard."

"Who's Bernard, honey?" This was the first Marta had heard of someone else in Shanice's life. "Boyfriend?" Marta asked with a teasing lilt to her voice.

Shanice chuckled. "No, I don't have a boyfriend. I don't like boys that way."

"Ahh," Marta said knowingly but wasn't sure what she knew. "So, who's Bernard?"

Shanice chewed on the inside of her lip as if shy to answer.

"Go on, honey. It's okay," Marta said softly. "It's just me here." And why was she calling this woman who was a veritable stranger, *honey*?

Shanice looked up shyly and said, "He's in my suitcase, which is, hopefully, still in the car. I've had him since I was, like, seven, I think."

Marta narrowed her eyes, trying to figure out what Shanice was talking about.

"He's my stuffie." Shanice wiped the tears in her eyes. "And, yes, I know. It's silly. I'm a grown woman. Forget I said anything." She held out the flowers toward Marta.

"Oh, no, no, no, little one," Marta said, taking the flowers. "You will not deny your feelings. You have to feel your feels." *And did I just call her 'little one?'*

"Okay," Shanice said. "I have to call the insurance people tomorrow to find out which tow company has my car. They need pictures or something, and then they can reimburse me. It's not worth much, I'm sure. It was old. But I need to get my suitcase, phone, and whatever else I had in the car."

"Good," Marta said. "Things are in motion. I guess patience is the name of the game now. Don't you think?"

"I guess." Shanice squirmed in the bed. "My laptop is at home. If I had that or a loaner, maybe I could work. Mrs. Washington from work came. Did I tell you that?"

"You did."

"She said I'm on a paid leave of absence right now, so I guess I'm not supposed to work anyway. Parvati took over the coding project I was working on. I feel bad because Parvati had her own projects; now, she has mine." Shanice was working herself up again.

"Nope," Marta said. "No sense worrying about all that."

"What do you mean?"

"Can you do anything about those work things?"

"No. Not really."

"So," Marta said with a sigh, "no sense getting worked up about them. Can't control what other people will do."

"Mmm," Shanice said as if musing on this extreme Marta wisdom. "Kind of like no one can blame the driver of that 18-wheeler truck because he'd had a heart attack, right?"

"Yes, like that." Marta had done more research on Shanice's accident, and they'd found out that the truck driver died from his heart attack. Three other people were also killed. That was incredibly sobering to both of them, and Marta was on the lookout for survivor's guilt. Shanice was twenty-five, yes, but she also seemed very sensitive. And vulnerable. Marta felt that maybe she was helping the young woman in her own small way.

"Hey," Marta said after putting the shaker bottle of flowers near the sink where Shanice could see them. "I brought cards." She pulled the newly purchased deck of cards out of her back pocket. She'd picked the ones with kittens on the back.

"Ooh, kitties," Shanice said. "You know what? I have this list of things I want to do in my life."

"Like a bucket list?" Marta undid the cellophane and pulled the cards from the box.

"Yeah, yeah." Shanice sat up taller. She winced as she did so, though. Her healing ribs must have protested the movement. "After I pay off my college loans, I hope to one day be able to afford my own apartment with a cat who would be waiting at the front door for me when I got home from work."

"That sounds nice," Marta said. She told Shanice about her mother's cat Snowball and about the black stray in the backyard. Shanice seemed fascinated that Marta had a cat, and they talked about cats while Marta shuffled the deck. Shanice was fascinated when Marta showed off by doing a riffle shuffle with a cascade finish.

"Show me that sometime?" Shanice said in total awe.

"Let's make that a goal once you get that cast off your arm."

"Deal," Shanice put out her good hand, and they shook on it.

Marta wanted to pull the hand up and kiss the back of it. She resisted. She was here as a friend and helper. That was it. *Darn you, Nora*!

They spent the next hour and a half playing almost every card game they collectively knew. Shanice taught her a game called "Bullshit," which involved copious amounts of fibbing about what cards you laid facedown, and if someone thought you weren't truthful, they yelled, "Bullshit," and you had to turn the cards over. Marta jumped every time Shanice yelled the words, and the whole game had them laughing hysterically. Shanice turned out to be really good at the game, probably because Marta had never been any good at lying. Shanice said she'd learned the game while living at the institution as a teenager. It was a way for them to rebel and curse without getting into too much trouble.

As they played the game, Marta got to know Shanice better. Apparently, smoked turkey with collard greens was one of her favorite meals. Marta made a ton of mental notes, but way too soon, it was time for her to leave. She told Shanice she had an "appointment." No way would she tell the kid that she had a sex date. That was too private.

Earlier in her visit, Marta noticed something that looked like a phone jack and insisted to the nurse and anyone who would listen that a phone be placed in Shanice's room. As usual, she was told that nothing happened on the weekend, so perhaps a phone could be installed on Monday—tomorrow. It took all of Marta's strength not to roll her eyes. Installing a phone simply meant plugging one in. Before Marta left, though, they quickly made a to-do list of calls for Shanice to make from her room if she ever got the phone since Marta couldn't get there until after regular business hours.

"Bye, uh…Shanice," Marta said. She had been about to say, *Baby girl.* What the heck was happening to her? *Honey, little one, baby girl.* Even *kid.* Those were all things that her own mother or even Nora would have called her, yet she was calling Shanice those things.

"Bye," Shanice said. "Will I see you tomorrow?"

"Of course," Marta said as she stood in the open doorway. "My boss would like me to put in a full day's work tomorrow, so I won't be here until 1600 or 1700 hours."

Shanice narrowed her eyes as if she were thinking hard. "That's like four or five o'clock?"

Marta nodded once.

"Are you in the Army or something?"

"I was," Marta said but didn't elaborate. "It was a long time ago," She didn't like to talk about her time in Iraq, so she changed the subject. "Oh, shit, I forgot. Nora wanted me to show you this. She says hello."

Marta let the door close and found the selfie she'd taken with Nora earlier that day.

"You two don't look alike."

"Nora looks like Mom, and I take after Dad. Nora wants me to take a selfie with you to show her who my new friend is."

"She does?" Shanice smoothed down her hospital gown. "Okay. I'm as ready as I'll ever be."

Marta leaned in close to Shanice, and when she did so, she felt Shanice's warmth. It made her feel…something, but she couldn't put a finger on it. She'd lost focus and momentarily forgot how to work her phone. "Okay, I got it now. I'll take a few, and then you can pick the best one. Okay?"

Shanice nodded.

"I really have to get going now," Marta said after the photo shoot. "Snowball and the backyard kitty need their dinners."

"You have to name that backyard kitty."

Marta scoffed. "We'll see." To name her would be to claim her, and that wasn't going to happen. Snowball was all she needed. The last final goodbye was made, and Marta made it all the way to her pickup before breaking down crying. She hated leaving the young woman all alone like that. *I am such a freakin' softy. Oh, my God.*

Going home, Marta forced herself to think about her date with Jessica that evening. That way, she wouldn't think about poor Shanice alone in that cold, sterile hospital room. Marta hoped Jessica would wear that short skirt again. That thought alone got Marta's blood moving. Jessica was into breath play, but that was one of Marta's hard limits. There was no way she was going to hold Jessica down, wrap her hands around her throat, and cut off her airway with her thumbs. She'd seen it done at Dominique's club downtown but knew she could never do it. Jessica liked impact, too, but Marta just couldn't bring herself to strike another woman, with the exception of a rather vanilla spanking. She'd tried caning a lover once but hated every moment of it. The woman loved it, but Marta—not so much.

Marta originally planned to do needle-play this evening, but Jessica's texts indicated she wanted something more titillating. Knife play and fire play, that's what it would be. Ice would play a part as well, of course. She wouldn't blindfold Jessica during the fire play, though, because that was cool to watch as the fire traveled over the mousse trail Marta would lay out.

"I'll need the massage table," Marta mused out loud as she got off the exit for Denton Heights. "I have to clean that up." Even though it had been a while since she'd done fire play, she knew exactly where the fire-retardant cloth was to drape over the table. She should have gotten that ready before visiting Nora. No, no, there was plenty of time. Where was the fire extinguisher?

A surge of arousal went through Marta's core. The anticipation of a session was sometimes just as fun as the actual session. And she'd need ice, too. Jessica would be blindfolded after the fire play, of course, and turned over onto her back. Marta needed Jessica's lovely, sensitive parts accessible. Should they move to the bed? Nah. Best to make Jessica feel like an object on the table to be toyed with at Marta's whim.

Ice play would be next. Wax? No. The knife. Right, right. She needed to show Jessica the large knife *before* the blindfold went on. That way, she could picture and anticipate the knife's blade against her skin. Marta would keep up a running commentary about how vulnerable Jessica was as she tied her wrists to the table. Marta would yank Jessica's legs apart with one quick move and then tie her ankles down. A spreader bar? Maybe. Marta would have it ready. Not everything could be scripted.

Marta would press the blade of the knife against the fleshy part of Jessica's breast and then slowly trail the tip to Jessica's nipple. Of course, Marta would tell her how easy it would be to carve her initials into Jessica's flesh. The knife would flick the nipple and then travel down to Jessica's beautifully shaved mons. The cold flat side of the blade would rest there while ice cubes caressed Jessica's nipples, one after the other. Another cube would trail down Jessica's body past the knife to reach Jessica's center.

Marta would then scrape the knife edge against the mons as a quick reminder and then split Jessica's folds with her fingers to find the clit she had come to know so well. A fresh cube of ice would run close to the nub at first, so it would begin melting with Jessica's body heat. She had learned the hard way to never ever put raw ice on the clit. That was a surefire way to hurt your sub.

Once the ice was mostly gone, Marta would tuck it in between Jessica's lower lips so it could finish melting. The knife would be picked up again, and the tip run around the same path as the ice. The flat of the blade would press against the clit and then rotate until the tip remained in contact. Jessica, of course, would never know that the real hunting knife lay unmoved on the side table and that Marta was using the edge of an expired credit card made cold in the bowl of ice. Yes, that was a Domme secret and one she'd never reveal.

Marta pulled into her driveway and groaned. Mrs. Pulaski was heading over. Dang. Her arousal was about to be demolished by the woman holding, yep, it looked like a cake.

There were some things in life that you just had to resign yourself to. A nosy neighbor who couldn't mind her own business was apparently one of them.

Chapter 6

Shanice

Shanice wrestled the old-fashioned phone back into its cradle on the over-bed table. She'd gotten a lot of information from the insurance company and had to write everything down on paper napkins since she had no paper. They'd finally come to install the phone at one o'clock, and that was only after Shanice badgered the poor nurse into checking a few times. "Maintenance has a lot to do," the nurse said that morning. "It may not happen today." Shanice took that to mean that Shanice's needs weren't that important and that she should stop wanting things she couldn't have.

"Humph," Shanice had said out loud. How many times had she been told that in her life? "You don't always get what you want," the social workers in charge of placing her in foster homes would say. She'd been almost grateful that she'd been sent to that last foster house at age fourteen. It forced her to finally take matters into her own hands.

That creepy foster dad had just about licked his lips when the case worker brought her to the house that afternoon. After the case worker left and the new foster mom turned her back, he looked her up and down like a tasty snack. She pretended not to see when he rubbed his hand over the crotch of his jeans. There was no way she would spend the night there. No way. And she didn't. She was shown her room in the back of the one-story house. Her own room? She wasn't buying it. She'd seen the locks on the outside of the bedroom door. They were going to lock her in at night or whenever. This was yet another prison. The stupid thing those new foster parents did was leave her alone in the room without locking it. She tucked everything she could into her backpack, including Bernard, and snuck out the back door. She didn't even care that she'd left a suitcase full of clothes and schoolbooks there. Didn't matter to her.

She climbed over their back fence, impaling her palm on the sharp spikes, but she didn't care. The scar she'd developed was a constant reminder to keep away from people and not put herself into the care of others. She found a few safe-ish places to sleep and dumpsters to raid for food. Taking makeshift sponge baths at the gas station was getting old, though, especially when she had her period. But she'd lasted almost two whole months on her own. See? She didn't need anyone.

She'd made friends with the stray cats behind the pizza place, the one that backed up onto a small stand of woods. She made sure to pull out dumpster food for them, too. One time a bunch of teenagers found her back there, and she ran, looping back hours later to get her well-hidden backpack. It was then she decided to show up on the doorstep of the institution where hard-to-place kids lived. She told them in no uncertain terms that she'd had enough of the slaps, yelling, and subtle and not-so-subtle sexual advances. She'd managed *not* to get raped during her years in the system and told them she planned to keep it that way. If they tried to place her with another family, she assured them she would run away again and again.

Shanice took a cleansing breath like the Reiki healer had taught her. She had to shake off the memory. She relaxed a little, knowing that the healer was due to come back again that afternoon. And maybe Marta, too? Marta didn't come every day but said she would come by after work today. Maybe not, though. People said they'd do something and make promises, but in Shanice's experience, they didn't follow through most of the time. People didn't stay.

A few days before, Shanice and Marta tracked down Miss Macie's landline phone number. Shanice had been embarrassed that she hadn't known it, but Marta said she understood. There really hadn't been a need with all the info in her phone. Shanice punched in Miss Macie's number again. After a few rings, it tried to go to voicemail, but it was apparently full. She was dismayed when Miss Macie didn't answer, but Miss Macie never answered the phone anyway. That was usually Shanice's job. Shanice took another cleansing breath to steal herself for the call to Alstead's Towing in Miamitown. The insurance company had the police report and gave her the towing company's name, address, and phone number. She found the number on one of the napkins. One of the aides, not Tyler, had gotten her a pen and went in search of paper but never came back. There was a lot of that going around at that hospital. But she had the napkins, so all was not lost.

She punched in the numbers.

"Alstead's Towing," the gruff-sounding man said.

She explained who she was and what she wanted to know.

"It's in collections, lady," the guy said.

"What does that mean?"

"The car's not drivable, and no one's come to claim it. You shoulda gotten a notice."

"I'm in the hospital," Shanice said. "I can't get there to claim the car. I'll definitely pay you. How much is it?"

"Name?"

Even though she had already given him her name, she gave it again. And then she repeated all the details. After several back-and-forths and much miscommunication, she finally understood that someone had to physically go to Miamitown and claim the car. Alstead employees weren't allowed to touch any personal stuff in the car, so, no, they couldn't clean it out for her and hold it. She had to send someone to get her stuff and identify the car so the insurance company could move forward and pay them. Shanice wanted to give up on the whole thing. She'd left clothes and stuff behind before. But…Bernard. He was in her suitcase which was in the car.

"Oh, fuck," the guy on the phone said. "I remember that car. Kia Soul. Cool color. Alien metallic."

"Yes." Shanice thought of it as green, though.

"You survived?"

"Yes, sir." She didn't elaborate.

"How? Holy shit. Wait'll Manny hears this. Damn."

She rolled her eyes as several more excited expletives assaulted her ears, and then he said, "I'll put an extension on the collections, but you have to send someone here." He explained what to put in the note she would have to give to someone else for it to be legal and legit. And they needed a copy of her driver's license, too. Maybe Marta would let her use her phone to scan a digital copy for them. *If* she came back, that is.

"Thank you, sir," she said as a wave of exhaustion flowed over her.

She hung up the phone. "Think positively," Shanice said out loud, mimicking something the Reiki healer had said. "Yeah, easier said than done, lady."

Hopefully, someone from the insurance company could go up there. Or someone from work. It wasn't too far. Was it? She couldn't remember how far Miamitown was from Cincinnati.

She succumbed to the exhaustion and let sleep overtake her.

She woke to find the Reiki healer Katherine working on her broken arm. "Hello," the woman said softly. She had such a soothing voice.

"Mmm," Shanice said, blinking the sleep out of her eyes. "Hi, Katherine."

"Hello, Shanice." The voice was so smooth and just…calm. So calm that Shanice wanted to go back to sleep. "Have you asked your friend to pick up some crystals for you?"

"No, I forgot," Shanice lied as she closed her eyes. The truth was, she had no friends, and she wasn't about to tell Katherine that. Marta was a nice person and all, but not her errand girl. She wasn't going to ask favors of anyone, especially when she had no way to return them.

She had no idea how she was going to be able to function once she got out of the hospital. Somebody along the way said she'd be sent to a skilled nursing facility. When? They didn't say. For how long? Again, no information. But maybe they had told her, and the pain meds had knocked it out of her brain. That was a distinct possibility. A group home. She'd end up in a stupid group home for disabled people. *Disabled.*

"Positive thoughts, Shanice," the healer said gently. "I can feel your energy changing."

Shanice sighed. "Sorry," was all she could muster. This healer didn't need to hear about her troubles. She could clearly and plainly see them. And the lack of feet. She could see that, right? The stumps? Yes. The new stumps that used to be her legs. *Hey, at least I'm not paralyzed. Right?*

Since her eyes were closed, Shanice felt rather than saw the healer move away from her. She kept her eyes closed but heard rustling near the door.

"I don't have any amethyst, but I do have this clear quartz crystal," the healer said.

Shanice opened her eyes and took the slender inch-long crystal the healer handed her.

"I want you to hold this and think those positive thoughts we discussed the other day."

Katherine's smile calmed Shanice somewhat. The woman really was trying to help her. And at no cost, either. Shanice had tried to set up a payment, but the healer said that her services fell under a spiritual heading and were provided to patients at no charge. Later, a nurse confirmed that, so Shanice stopped worrying—about that, anyway.

"Yes, Ma'am."

"Cleansing breath, please," the healer said, and Shanice complied. "I'm going to work on your lower extremities now. The energy there is confused. I'm attempting to promote healing. The crystal will aid us."

Shanice nodded and felt herself relax even more. Nothing was going to bring the lower half of her legs back, but maybe this energy stuff would help heal the rest of her body.

"The quartz you're holding," the healer said, "is considered to be a master healer. It helps align your chakras and amplifies energy."

It just felt like a smooth rock to Shanice, but, hey, whatever. She always felt so much better after the healer had done her thing.

"Now, amethyst will help relax the mind. And that's why I'd like you to get one if possible. It helps relieve stress and anxiety."

"Thank you for letting me hold the quartz," Shanice said, figuring she should say something.

"It's yours now," Katherine said and then did some weird motions with her hands as if scooping away bad energy, mojo, or whatever.

"Cool." Shanice heard the almost-happy lilt to her own voice.

"Jasper is another good one for times of stress. You can put the crystals under your pillow when you're not holding them."

"Okay," Shanice said. "Thank you for helping me."

The deep smile the healer shot Shanice almost made her cry. People had helped her in the past, but this woman was making her feel...something.

Alive, maybe? Worth the woman's time and energy? Even Miss Macie kind of took Shanice for granted. Mrs. Washington at work was nice and seemed to have Shanice's interests at heart, so maybe not everyone was out for something from her.

Katherine finished the session, pulled energy off herself, and flicked it away into the universe. This was a step of protection, so she didn't walk around with the energy of others clinging to her. The first time she did this, she told Shanice not to be offended, and she wasn't. Every healer did this final step, apparently.

Shanice sighed into her relaxed state. She still didn't quite understand the whole energy-healing thing, but she was a believer now. Katherine pulled a business card out of her bag. "If you remember, ask your friend to visit this shop. It's near Blackwell College. I'm not affiliated with the shop, so I don't get a commission or anything like that, but they're reputable and fair, and they have a nice selection of crystals." She put the card on the side table. "Of course…"

The healer hesitated so long that Shanice finally asked, "Of course, what?"

"You should be there to pick out your own crystals. The ones that resonate with you."

"Yeah, that may not happen for a while," Shanice said, looking down where her lower limbs should be.

The healer nodded sympathetically but said nothing. Was she emotional? Were things worse than Shanice had feared?

"I'll be back when I can," the healer said, briefly touching Shanice's shoulder.

Shanice recognized the pitying gesture. She'd seen it often enough as a foster kid. The people always had temporary sympathy for her situation, but no one ever came through in the long run. Shanice watched the healer pack up and go. She wouldn't be back. Shanice wasn't sure how she knew, but she knew. And then there was Marta. Pretty, strong, and attentive superhero Marta who made her feel things she had no right to feel. There was going to come that moment when Marta, too, decided she wasn't going to come back. She just knew it. It would be a hand on the shoulder or lack of eye contact, something that would convey Marta wasn't going to invest any more energy or time into Shanice. No one ever did, so there was no sense wishing for it.

Even Mama Lauren and Mama Deborah didn't come through. They had been ten-year-old Shanice's best shot at security and happiness. They were such a nice white lesbian couple. Shanice closed her eyes and let herself get drowsy. Sleep was healing, they all said. Great. She'd do it and not remember how Mama Lauren had cheated on Mama Deborah with a younger woman. Nor would Shanice remember how Mama Deborah demanded Mama Lauren move out. Oh, how Mama Deborah had cried when she told Shanice she couldn't keep her any longer. Shanice understood that the circumstances had changed, didn't she? Yes, of course, she did. She didn't cry. She'd not quite allowed herself to believe the love she'd felt with the two women was real, anyway That had been the very last time she ever looked back at a room that had been all hers, if only for a year.

See? She'd been right. Everyone comes into the world alone and leaves it the same way. But her accident hadn't taken her life. Why not? She'd have been better off. It was a question she'd just begun to ask in the past few days. Before the accident, she felt like she'd gotten her life in order. Good job, her own lockable room at Miss Macie's, not to mention access to the entire house, including free use of the washer and dryer. And a dishwasher, too, except that hadn't worked since she'd moved in two years ago. The whole renting an apartment with roommates thing had saved money but had been a nightmare on so many other fronts. More than once, she'd come home from work to find that someone had rifled through her stuff. She never dared to confront any of the other girls. She couldn't. She had nowhere else to go. But when her most recent roommate Jenna started bringing her boyfriend to the apartment for overnight stays—that was it. Shanice no longer felt safe. He had looked at her in the way males often look at women, and she was having none of it. That's when she looked for and found a different situation. The move to live with and care for Miss Macie had been perfect. Things had been looking up. It had taken six months of scrimping and saving, but she had finally saved enough money to buy the Kia. Freedom! Finally. No more buses.

But now all of that had changed. All that freedom had been lost.

She had no idea how long she'd slept, but when she woke, her comfort thumb was in her mouth. And she was leaning on her side facing the wall. Oh, yeah. She vaguely remembered the nurse propping her over with pillows. They were watching for bed sores, she'd said. She pulled her thumb out of her mouth and wiped it on her hospital gown. One day she hoped to break the thumb-sucking habit. She was twenty-five years old, for goodness sake, but she just couldn't. It was a comfort habit she needed right now, especially with Bernard trapped in the car so far away. She stretched her bad arm overhead, surprised that neither the arm nor the ribs protested as much as they used to. Hopefully, she was healing, but it was probably just the good drugs that dripped into her IV.

"Hey," a voice said from behind her. She tried to turn her neck, but it hurt a little. And the pillows prevented her from rolling over.

"Marta?"

"Yeah," Marta said, her voice sounding closer. "You're adorable when you sleep."

Shanice said nothing but felt her face grow hot. Marta had seen her sucking her thumb. Again.

"I found this on the floor." Marta appeared on the far side of the bed, holding the clear quartz crystal. "Starting your rock collection?"

Shanice took it and then remembered the healer's veiled forever goodbye. The tears started despite her best efforts to keep them inside.

"Oh, honey." Marta rushed back to the bedside. "What's wrong? What's happened?"

Shanice swiped at the tears in her eyes and looked away. It didn't matter. Marta would be gone soon anyway. The floodgates opened, and she let out a torrent of worries. "I have nowhere to go. I can't possibly take care of Miss Macie anymore. My bedroom is on the second floor there. How would I get up the stairs? How can I help her up off the couch or out of bed when she needs help? How can I drive to work? I have no car and no feet to drive it with anyway. I have no place to live. I have no…legs." She gestured angrily toward the nothingness. She recalled bits and pieces of what the doctors said to her. "And, and, and…" She took a breath as her recollections aligned. "And, they said my stump incisions aren't healing well, and they're guarding against infection, but I can't stay at the hospital the whole time. I can't get prosthetics or whatever they're called until the stumps are fully healed and formed. At least six months, probably longer." She remembered something else. "The left leg was a goner, they said. They tried to repair bones and nerves on the right one, but they couldn't, so chop chop. Off it came."

Shanice couldn't stop her sobs. They came from deep in her core. And she didn't care. "She said to think positive thoughts." Another sob. "But how? How?"

A hand rested on her shoulder. A soft kiss landed on her forehead. And then another. "I have you," Marta said. A second hand cupped her face. Warm essence of something she'd almost felt with Mama Deborah came over her in waves. The hand cupping her face moved to caress her forehead and then smoothed down her out-of-control 'fro in a loving gesture. The other hand stroked her good shoulder and arm. It was as if Marta wasn't sure where to touch her. "You're okay, baby girl. I have you." A different feeling blossomed in Shanice's chest, nudging aside the sobs. She didn't know what it was, but she liked it.

Shanice fought hard to get control and eventually did. "Sorry."

"No, no, no," Marta said. "Look at me, sweetheart."

Shanice saw only love and compassion in Marta's face. Her expression held no pity or embarrassment. Maybe that was one of Marta's superhero powers.

"You are absolutely allowed to feel your feels," Marta said and stood back up. The funny thing, though, was Marta had grabbed her hand at some point and was still holding it. "And I've got some things that will hopefully change your icky feels."

"Yeah?" Shanice had no clue what Marta had brought this time.

"You need to be sitting up for this, though." And even though Marta let go of Shanice's hand, she still felt the warmth of her touch. People touched her there at the hospital, but not like that. Not in the loving, soothing way the superhero had.

The pillows propping her up on her side were moved, and Shanice rolled onto her back. "Wow, you're way down on the bed," Marta said. "Let me pull you up." She grabbed the bed controller, lowered the bed, and laid Shanice flat. She moved behind the head of the bed, grabbed the bottom sheet underneath Shanice, and said, "Ready?"

"Okay," Shanice said.

Marta pulled the sheet, and Shanice slid up higher in the bed. She couldn't help her giggles. Superheroes that could take you from sobbing one minute to giggling the next were...amazing.

Marta came back around and waggled her eyebrows. "All better." She handed Shanice the bed controller and said, "Sit yourself up now."

Shanice moved up as much as her sore ribs would allow. All the while, her eyes bore a hole in Marta's back. Marta was rifling through a bag but must have sensed Shanice's gaze because her head darted around, and she smiled at Shanice. Shanice giggled. Marta turned back to her bag, but Shanice saw Marta's back bob up and down as if she were laughing, too. Marta kept her back to Shanice but, in a sudden move, whipped her head around and looked at Shanice with playful eyes. Shanice couldn't help laughing. Marta did it yet again but turned her head in the other direction. Oh, my God, they were playing peek-a-boo. Shanice didn't care. It was fun. She shrieked in laughter when Marta faked and then faked again.

Marta finally turned fully around and held a to-go cup of coffee from Rikki's Coffee Shop in Denton Heights. She also held up a plate of something wrapped in tin foil.

"I've never been to Rikki's Coffee Shop," Shanice said. "You got that for me?"

Marta nodded and handed Shanice the cup. She placed the plate on the over-bed table.

"I wasn't sure how you took it, so I have half-n-half in this cup and sugars in my pocket."

Shanice couldn't help it. She started crying. Why was the superhero being so nice? Why was her superhero still here?

"Aww, kid," Marta said.

"Why are you being so nice to me?"

Marta's face scrunched up, and she turned away, clearly emotional. She took a moment and wiped at her eyes again before turning around. She approached the bed and reached for Shanice's hand. "I don't know."

"Honest."

"Always," Marta said and took a deep breath. "There's something about you that makes me want to hang around. I guess I like helping you."

"I do need the help," Shanice said, shocked that those words had actually come out of her mouth. "But you shouldn't take days off. And shouldn't you be helping your sister?"

Marta smiled, squeezed Shanice's hand once, and then let go. "I do. But she's doing fine. She has her husband and son that visit her at Chrysalis."

"That's the nursing home on Kirkland?"

"Mm hmm."

There was something odd in Marta's succinct response, but Shanice didn't know how to interpret it. "Tell Miss Nora I said hi, okay?"

"I will," Marta said. "Would you like anything in your coffee?"

"I drink it black, actually. Cream and sugar are expensive, so I learned to drink it plain."

"Got it," Marta said. "Are you ready for your second surprise?"

Shanice nodded vigorously. When Marta turned away to pick up the foil-wrapped present, Shanice wiped at her eyes and took a calming breath. Marta was here for now, and she should make the most of it.

"No way," Shanice said as the foil was unwrapped. "You brought me a piece of cake?"

"My nosy—" Marta started, but then seemed to think better of what she had been about to say and amended, "My neighbor made a cake for me to bring to Nora, and I figured someone here might need a pick-me-up. It's a lemon Bundt cake."

"Thank you. I love cake. And coffee." Shanice felt her waterworks starting again but swallowed back the tears. "And please thank your neighbor. I should write a thank-you card to her."

Marta's perplexed expression made Shanice laugh. It was as if she'd never heard of writing a thank-you card before in her life.

"And I should write you one, too," Shanice said shyly, hiding behind her coffee cup as she sipped.

Marta's face turned the cutest shade of red. Who knew superheroes could be so adorable.

Marta cleared her throat and unwrapped a plastic fork. She jammed it into the cake and pushed the over-bed table closer so Shanice could reach it.

Shanice took a bite of the cake and moaned. "This is so good," she said with her mouth full. She took another quick bite. Marta's pleased smile made that warm chest feeling hit Shanice again.

Marta cleared her throat and asked what other things she could bring for Shanice.

"Bernard," came the quick answer. Shanice filled Marta in on her call to the towing place, and Marta quickly volunteered to go up and claim the car and get Shanice's things. "No," Shanice said and looked down. "You've done too much already."

"Look at me," Marta said. Her voice was stern but not like the foster moms and dads. It was stern but had a superhero lilt to it. Shanice looked up. "Miamitown isn't that far from Denton Heights. I can help you."

"The car insurance people are going up there," Shanice lied. "I have to send the towing place a letter." She explained what the towing company needed in the letter, and since that part of the story was true, her lie quickly got buried. And even though she was ready to forfeit the car and her luggage, she couldn't hold back her tears when she realized that Bernard was all alone and probably scared. Marta took the cup of coffee from her hands and hugged her.

"It's okay, Shanice. It'll be okay."

Shanice clung to Marta with her good arm and let herself be soothed and cooed to. She knew the superhero holding her would eventually go away, but she'd let herself enjoy it for now. "Thank you," she mumbled into Marta's shoulder.

"Mm hmm," came the emotional response from the woman whose arms held her. "Let's at least get that letter written, okay?"

Shanice nodded. Her voice was too choked with conflicting emotions to speak.

Chapter 7

Marta

Marta leaned against the wall. She hated morning briefings with her boss. Roger only held them to make himself feel important and useful. He was neither. Marta just wanted to get out and pick her orders. And she also just wanted to be left alone. The other workers, Jeff included, milled about drinking coffee and talked about their Saturday night plans. They knew enough to leave her alone, especially with the obvious mood she was in. Why had she told Shanice she couldn't visit for a while? Why? She'd given Shanice some lame excuse about overtime and making up for the days she'd taken off. Lies. All of it.

She'd panicked. Pure and simple. Marta had started to feel things. Shit, she'd been feeling things from the moment they'd met. And then they hugged that day. It was too much. Marta needed out.

They'd written the letter together, and Marta took a scan of it and Shanice's driver's license for safekeeping. That's when the panic had set in. Marta was a hermit, just like Nora always said, and she'd found herself drawn to Shanice and feeling feels. *Feel your feels,* Marta thought sarcastically. Yep, that's what she'd told Shanice to do. *Great advice that you can't even take yourself, idiot.*

Feeling feels wasn't in Marta's repertoire. The repercussions weren't worth it. You love people, take care of them, and they leave. So, what's the point? You get your heart broken over and over again.

Marta sighed as Roger called them to order and started his pep talk. She'd been there long enough to know these briefings had no substance. It was always the same: watch for customers in the back areas, only take sanctioned breaks, don't speed in the carts, and remember to punch out. She tuned him out.

When Marta told her Shanice couldn't come for a while, the look on her face broke Marta's heart. Shanice tried to hide it, but the look of disappointment cut right through Marta's soul. And then Shanice's expression changed. She looked resigned to it as if she'd been subjected to rejection her entire life. Marta had almost caved and took back her declaration but didn't. A big part of her still craved solitude and hermitude, if that was even a word.

"Ing, snap out of it," a voice said, breaking her out of her fog. It was Jeff.

"Shut up," she said to him. Oh, shit. The briefing was over, and everyone was funneling out the door. Great, she'd end up with Old Sparky again. Whatever. She probably deserved that karma hit for abandoning the broken defenseless young woman.

She walked over to the board of keys, but no keys were hanging there. Jeff held two sets in his hand. Great, he was going to get immense joy handing her the keys to the worst cart.

He grinned, thoroughly enjoying her predicament.

"C'mon," Marta said and held out her hand.

He placed the keys in her palm, still grinning.

She turned without saying a word and headed to the worn-out cart. When she got in, the key didn't fit in the slot. She looked at the tag. "Wait," she said out loud. The key was for cart twelve. No air conditioning, but it was one of the newer models.

"You're in my cart, Ingersoll," Jeff said.

"Huh?" She stumbled out of the cart, her brain trying to process what was happening.

"Have a good one," Jeff said, slowly pulling Old Sparky away.

She stood and watched him go. "What the—" It made no sense. She lumbered over to cart twelve and drove it toward the tree section. She didn't get the Meyers & Son order form but still had a decent selection of plants to pull. "Two Redbuds it is."

After loading the trees, she headed to the shrubs section. "Green Giant Arborvitae," she read out loud. "Nice neighbor-blocking choice. I need to plant some of those on Mrs. Pulaski's side." Naturally, the customer wanted the biggest size, but she didn't care. She liked working her muscles. She loaded the shrubs and made a mental note to check into her employee discount to see how much they would cost her. When she got home, she'd measure the property line and see how many she'd need to block out the nosiest of neighbors once and for all.

She was about to pull away from the shrub section when she stopped herself. A thought had been niggling in her brain. She pulled out her phone and searched for information about amputees. She found a lot of stories, and each one broke her heart. Especially the one about the sixteen-year-old boy who loved horseback riding and lost his leg when the horse threw him off into some farm equipment stored against the tack barn. This other guy, a middle-aged man, had an infection from diabetes complications and had a "new normal," as he put it. He said it was a real challenge not to fall out of bed because he'd wake up and forget that he'd had one foot amputated.

"And Shanice has *no* feet," Marta muttered under her breath. "She was in the wrong place at the wrong time. It wasn't her fault, poor kid." Marta remembered Shanice telling her the stumps weren't healing well. "Good nutrition might help that. And a regular course of vitamins and minerals. And better food than that hospital slop." Marta sat up taller. "And regular workouts to make her muscles stronger."

Dread squeezed her chest tight. "Oh, my God. I'm an idiot. She needs help." Marta pulled the cart forward and punched it. She whizzed by Jeff and vaguely heard him say, "Where's the fire, Ing?"

She returned to the office, ran in, and said to her boss, "I have an emergency. I'm sorry. I have to leave."

She tossed him the key to cart twelve and made note of his disapproving frown. Whatever. If he fired her, she'd get another job. Whatever. She always landed on her feet. Sadness hit her chest as she punched out. Shanice didn't have feet to land on. Marta needed to help until Shanice got settled somewhere and was self-sufficient.

"Get her settled first, and then you can hermit," Marta said as she burst out the door and ran toward her pickup in the employee lot.

Marta fought her emotions all the way to the Cincinnati hospital. She thought about stopping at Rikki's coffee shop to get Shanice a to-go cup or stopping at home to snag another slice of the lemon cake. She didn't. That would have taken too much time. What she did do, though, was stop at the gift shop and pick up another bouquet of flowers. She picked a bundle of red, white, and blue carnations, Shanice's favorite. She pounded the elevator wall when it moved too slowly and then threw herself out the doors before they were fully opened. She raced down the hallway to room 408 and stopped short. She took the briefest of moments to compose herself and then opened the door slowly. She didn't want to wake Shanice needlessly. If she was sleeping, that was okay. Marta would sit and wait. She'd done it before.

She was not prepared for what she saw when she entered the room. The bed was empty. No sheets. Nothing. There was no IV pole. No beeping machines. She turned to look at the whiteboard. It was blank. Shanice's name was gone. Marta's name and phone number had also been erased. No one occupied this room.

Marta raced out the door to the nurse's station. "Where's Shanice?" she demanded of the nurse or tech or whoever it was typing something into a computer.

"Who?" the middle-aged woman said, not looking up.

"Shanice Ward. Room 408. Did she change rooms?" Marta wanted to push the woman off the computer and search for herself.

The woman hit a few buttons. "Discharged," the woman said and finally looked up.

Marta blinked, not quite understanding what she'd heard. "Discharged? Where?" Panic hit her gut. The kid wouldn't be able to function without help. Her mind went blank, but then a small thought found its way in. *Maybe the people at her job helped her.* That thought alone kept Marta's blood pressure from skyrocketing, but she was still panicked.

"Doesn't say," the woman said.

"When?"

The woman sighed, obviously annoyed that she was being disrupted in this manner, but Marta didn't care. "It says Thursday. 17:20. That's 5:30 in the—"

"I know what it means," Marta barked irritably. Shit, that was two days ago. "It seriously doesn't say where she went?"

"No. There's a home address, but I can't give that to you."

Marta wasn't about to claim to be Shanice's aunt again. She had the home address, anyway, and that's exactly where she was headed right now. Without another word, she raced back down the corridor but took the four flights of stairs instead of waiting for the elevator and then raced to her pickup. She carefully placed the flowers on the front passenger seat as if the flowers represented Shanice herself.

Once back on I-75 North, she let her tears flow. She pounded her leg. "I'm sorry, Shanice," she wailed. "I'm an idiot. You needed me, and I let you down." Marta held onto a glimmer of hope that Mrs. Washington from Shanice's job had arranged something. The woman had seemed quite capable and concerned the day Marta barged into Johnson Tech. And someone from Johnson Tech had come to visit Shanice, right? Or had they just called? For the life of her, Marta couldn't remember.

Marta stroked the waxy paper around the bouquet as if she were soothing Shanice. She pulled up to Miss Macie's house, which looked even more unlived-in than the last time. Marta bounded up the overgrown walkway, noting that the lawn hadn't been mowed in forever. That was probably one of Shanice's many jobs at the house. She rang the bell and then pounded on the front door. The note she had left a while back was gone. Maybe that was a good sign. Marta looked around the door, thinking it might have blown away. She didn't see it. She pounded on the door again and announced who she was in a loud voice. She put her ear to the door and heard nothing.

After one more door pounding, she jumped into the overgrown bushes and peeked in the windows. The blinds were drawn, but there was a broken slat at the bottom. She leaned down and looked in. The place was dark. And lonely. If a house could look lonely, this one did. There were no signs of life. No used drinking glasses or magazines on the coffee table. No remote control. It was strange. Marta made her way around the outside of the house, peeking in any windows she could.

"Hey, what you doing there?" a voice called to her.

"Oh, hey," Marta said, rushing toward the older white man, an obvious neighbor. "Do you know where they are?" She pointed toward the house with her whole hand, a gesture she'd learned during her Army years.

"Naw," he said. "Miss Clark keeps to herself. Her granddaughter moved in to help out, but I ain't seen neither of them lately."

Granddaughter? Maybe Shanice wasn't as forthcoming about herself as Marta had thought.

"Can I give you my cell phone number? Can you call me if you see them come home?"

He looked at her with distrust but took out his phone.

"My name is Marta, and I'm a friend of Shanice's. The granddaughter," she added when he looked confused.

She gave him her cell phone number without taking his, thanked him, and then headed to the other neighbors' houses. The others didn't even know the names of the people who lived there, but they also had the same story. They stuck to themselves, so nothing seemed out of the ordinary other than the "cute little green car" hadn't been in the driveway for a while.

From there, Marta drove to Johnson Tech, but the guard said they weren't open on weekends. She left a message for Mrs. Washington, and after pulling around the guard gate to head out, she took out her phone, called the company's information number, and left another message. Shanice told her she was on leave, but her employer must know where she was. They, hopefully, had an address or something. Marta decided to drive over first thing Monday morning and stalk Mrs. Washington until she got answers.

Marta held her head in her hands. "I'm sorry, Shanice. I messed up. You don't deserve to be abandoned this way." Marta's tears came when she recalled some of Shanice's stories about being a foster kid. "Everyone abandons her. Oh, my God." She cried in her pickup, idling in the Johnson Tech drive, until the security guard pulled up behind her. "I'm going," she called out the window and drove off.

She found herself heading for the Chrysalis Center. She needed her big sis.

After visiting with Nora, Marta headed home and now sat in her pickup in her driveway. Her visit with Nora had been pleasant, but Nora's concern about Marta being there on a Saturday—one of the busiest work days at Carter Nursery and Landscaping—further added to Marta's angst. Marta waved off Nora's concerns and avoided questions about Shanice. Instead, Marta steered the subject to Nora's rehabilitation. She was doing great with the rehab, but her doctor extended her stay one week longer than most patients. When Marta asked why, Nora just rolled her eyes and smacked her overlarge stomach. Her sister's obesity wasn't serving her. And Nora knew it. Everyone knew it. But Nora was the one who had to do something about it. Marta would help, of course, but she didn't know how.

The flowers were well received, and Nora complained that her husband didn't even bring flowers. There was no way Marta was going to tell her that the flowers had been purchased for Shanice. Marta made a mental note to bring Nora flowers or something every day. She needed to get her head out of her butt.

"Oh, my God," Marta said as she opened the pickup door. "Am I that selfish?"

It wasn't until she saw Mrs. Pulaski's plate on the kitchen counter that she realized she had forgotten to bolt out of her pickup and run up the ramp into the house to avoid her. The cake itself was long gone. After her last visit to Shanice, five whole days ago, she'd sliced up the cake to bring to Nora each day. Not that Nora needed more sweets, the woman was addicted, but it made her sister happy.

Marta pulled off her work boots. She should have done that in the entryway, but her mind hadn't been working right lately. Maybe she should go back to work to finish out her day, but no, she just wasn't interested. And besides, she'd already taken her boots off.

She headed to her bedroom and was about to change out of her work clothes but knew she had to stay occupied. She'd work on her mother's flower gardens out back. Not the ones out front. Mrs. Pulaski might see her and come over to "chat." Ugh. Marta couldn't handle that at the moment. She changed into an old t-shirt and grabbed her work boots from the front foyer. She sat out back and put them on. The backyard kitty wasn't anywhere to be found, but the food bowl was empty. She'd fill it later. The kitty would show up then, for sure.

It was early July, and the weeds in the back flower garden had overgrown the entire three-foot-wide bed. Marta got down on her hands and knees and began pulling. Her mother had loved gardening, but the MS had taken that from her. Many times, Marta set her mother up in a comfy chair out of the sun while Marta tended the flower gardens—under her mother's supervision, of course. Marta heard her mother's voice in her head reminding her to get all the roots, otherwise, the weed would just grow back. She put the pulled weeds in a bucket and, when full, walked it to the far section of the yard and tossed it onto the compost pile. After several buckets, her knees begged for a break, and she decided she was finished for the day.

Marta showered, and when she stepped out of the shower, she realized it was a holiday weekend. Duh. That's why everything was red, white, and blue. "You are so out of it," Marta said out loud as she toweled off. "Fuck." Monday was the actual fourth of July. Johnson Tech wouldn't be open. She wouldn't be able to bug them for information until Tuesday. "Son of a bitch." Marta slammed her hand against the doorframe of her room. She threw on sweats and a clean T-shirt. She didn't bother with a bra. Why? She wasn't going out, and clearly, no one was coming in. Not tonight, anyway. Jessica was coming tomorrow.

Marta grabbed a beer from the fridge, made a bowl of wet food for Snowball, who had been ecstatic that Marta had come home early, and then made a bowl of food for the outside kitty. She grabbed the Rubik's cube to fiddle with and, once out back, put the food bowl down and admired her gardening work. Her mother loved butterfly gardens, so Marta would plant that. Before bolting from work, she'd seen a few nice Black-eyed Susans and purple Coneflowers. She'd snag them tomorrow.

She stretched her back and sat in one of the chairs her mother used to sit in. It had taken her over a year to allow herself to do that, but now it helped her feel closer to her mother. Playing with the Rubik's cube also helped her feel closer to her dad. Lonely moments sometimes overtook her like this. But this was the life she wanted. "Everybody can just leave me the fuck alone," she murmured as she spun a section of the cube. Except for Jessica. Jessica was the one person besides Nora she let into her life.

Jessica had loved the knife play last weekend, and came really hard. She'd made a special request for this weekend, though. She wanted to be bimbofied. Great. Marta loved mind games. She'd undress Jessica herself, saying Jessica wasn't smart enough to do it on her own. She'd make Jessica sit on the edge of the bed while Marta put the play collar on her. This collar was a little different than their usual play collars. This one was snug around her neck and not meant for a leash or restraints. It was simply so Jessica would feel the fabric around her neck at all times. "When *it* is in the collar," Marta would say, completely objectifying her sex partner, "it will have no thoughts other than the ones I give it. It will now play with itself to the point of cumming but stop short. I will be the one to make it cum."

Marta sipped her beer and pictured the scene as she lay Jessica on her back on the bed. Once Jessica had edged twice, Marta would slip into her with her largest strap-on. "It welcomes my girth but does not cum until I say." Marta would be sure to bring Jessica just to the brink and then turn her over. Another one of Jessica's requests had been anal sex. Marta wasn't always a fan of that, it was kind of a soft limit, but she would honor Jessica's request. She wanted to make sure the schoolteacher was well-satisfied. Their sessions were a welcome end-of-the-week relief for both of them. Of course, she'd tell Jessica, or the bimbo as she would be called tomorrow night, that she was going to use the largest dildo in her backdoor, but Marta would swap out the phallus for the smallest one. She in no way wanted to hurt Jessica. That's why she never liked impact play or really rough stuff. Wasn't in her wheelhouse.

Marta squirmed in her seat and took a couple of sips of her late afternoon beverage. Then she saw movement in the bushes. She pretended not to see as the black stray approached the full food bowl. This was new. The cat rarely came out when Marta was sitting outside. *She must be hungry.* Marta stayed as still as possible. Her thoughts wandered, though, and she raised her arm to take a sip causing the cat to back away, scared.

"Oh, shit," Marta said out loud. "Sorry, kitty. I forgot you were here.

You're okay. I'm just sitting here trying to figure out how to undo my stupidity." She made sure her tone was soft and soothing. "Whoa," Marta said as she looked at the cat. "You're getting fat there, aren't you? Maybe I'm feeding you a little too well." Marta chuckled but then shut up. She looked away from the cat, so she wouldn't seem threatening.

It was then that an idea hit her. As soon as the cat finished her food, Marta was going to get dressed and drive over to Miss Macie's house. She'd sit in her pickup and wait to see if there was any kind of movement in the house. Maybe a light would come on at night. Maybe Shanice was actually in there and needed help. Marta sat upright. Maybe Shanice had fallen like that man in the amputee stories. But, then again, maybe Shanice didn't want her help. Maybe she had been home, heard Marta knocking down the front door, but waited quietly for Marta to go away. And Marta knew full well she deserved that treatment. She had been an ass.

"Yes, yes," Marta said out loud. She'd park up the street a bit, so no one would know what she was up to.

Soon enough, the cat polished off the entire bowl of food and scampered off into the bushes. Marta picked up the now-empty bowl and went inside. She put a pot of coffee on, intending to take a thermos with her. After all, it was going to be a stakeout, and she intended to be there a long time. Long enough to get some answers.

Chapter 8

Shanice

Shanice let Paola pull her on top. She made sure Paola's thigh hit her right where she needed it. She rocked against the strong thigh while soft lips kissed her own. The lips moved to her neck and kissed the tender flesh sending shivers throughout Shanice's body. "Cum for me, Shanice," Paola whispered into Shanice's ear. "Time for PT," she said. Her voice sounded farther away. "Up, up, up," Paola insisted, and it was then that Shanice understood. She'd been dreaming about Paola again. She wasn't at the institution. It wasn't her last night when Paola finally made her move and climbed into bed with her. They'd only just kissed that night, but Shanice had used that memory as the start of many late-night fantasies. And apparently, her subconscious used it as fodder for steamy dreams.

Reluctantly, Shanice opened her eyes. "Hi," she said to the physical therapist.

"Did you do your homework last night?" Elizabeth asked. Shanice nodded. She had done her leg lifts which she hated because she saw her bandaged stumps where her legs should be. She'd done her stomach muscle squeezes, too, and the neck stuff and the arm raises. She wouldn't confess that she'd done them on the broken arm, too. And her new roommate wasn't going to tell, either. Carol only did two things—sleep and groan in her sleep. She probably ate, too, but Shanice had requested that the privacy curtain remain closed between them. Of course, that meant she didn't get to see out the window, but whatever.

"Good," the small but mighty white woman said. Even her blonde braid seemed invincible and strong. She unpacked some stretchy exercise bands from her PT bag. Shanice wanted to hate the bands but knew better than that. These things were going to make her stronger.

"Did you have a nice Fourth of July?" Shanice asked. Since she was bound to a bed, she had to feel part of the living any way she could.

"I did. My husband and I took the boys camping at the lake."

"Sounds nice," Shanice said. When Elizabeth didn't elaborate, Shanice shut up. Some people were all business. Elizabeth was kind of like that. She probably had a lot of patients to see and had no time for chit-chat with a bed-bound amputee with no future ahead of her. Marta was kind of awkward sometimes when they talked, but Shanice always got the idea that she was nervous. No! No thoughts about Marta. Marta was gone—gone for good.

Elizabeth slid the stretchy band around Shanice's thigh and told her to resist the pull. Shanice pushed as hard as she could, but obviously, this fit and toned PT instructor was going to win every time. She had a nice body, Shanice thought. Not as hard as Marta's, though. Elizabeth was way more feminine than Marta. Shanice swallowed hard. Why did she keep thinking about Marta? Marta was just one more person who had come into her life, got her hopes up, and then dropped her. She felt like a fish thrown back because she wasn't wanted, forever bearing the wounds of the capture.

The PT session wrapped up in a precise twenty-minutes, even though it felt like two hours, and Shanice was ready to nap again.

"See that chair?" Elizabeth pointed to an odd-looking wheelchair. "It's a high back. I requested this from the other wing because of your healing ribs. We can't have you doing solo transfers yet because you're not weight-bearing on that arm yet. You have one more week in that cast, so we'll start next week."

"Start what next week?" Shanice asked, surprised at herself for being so assertive. She usually just nodded and tried to figure things out on her own.

"You have to learn how to get from the bed into a wheelchair all on your own. You have to learn how to get from the wheelchair onto the toilet. We'll start as soon as Dr. Patel okays you to be load-bearing on that arm." She made a note in her phone. "But later this afternoon, probably around four or so, I'm coming back with John, and together we'll get you into that chair. John will give you a tour of the place, so you can leave this room and breathe some different air."

"Can I go outside?"

"Yes, I don't see why not. There's a nice patio out back for patients. Do you smoke?"

"Yuck. No." Shanice said.

"I'm happy to hear that," Elizabeth said. "Make sure you stay away from the smokers, then."

"I will."

Shanice said goodbye, and even though she thought she'd been ready for a nap, she was wide awake and excited. She was going to go outside and see the sky for real and not outside a small window that she couldn't even see because of the privacy screen. She kind of wanted to ask for a room with a bed by the window, but she didn't want to bother anybody. If she got the courage, maybe she'd ask Miss Wilma, the kind night nurse with the Jamaican accent. The morning people never opened the blinds, so her room was always gray and cheerless. Carol groaning in her sleep didn't help the ambiance much, either. Of course, she could actually *ask* for the blinds to be open, but whatever.

Thoughts of Marta came back unbidden. Marta would make that happen. Marta would have made sure she was in a bed by the window. Marta would sit with her, bring her things, and play games. Her elated feeling turned sour fast. Marta was gone. She was a nice person, but whatever. Shanice hoped thoughts of Marta would fade soon. Shanice had enough on her plate and didn't need the fresh festering wound of Marta on top of all that.

Shanice allowed herself one more agonizing memory. Marta, a nervous texture to her words, had said, "I won't be able to come by for a while." She'd then made some fake excuse about work or something. Shanice could see right through it because Marta was a lousy liar. While her heart broke, Shanice steeled her chin, rose up as much as she could, and said she understood. 'Life goes on,' she'd said—something like that. Inside, though, she was trying not to cry. She felt her old familiar walls creeping up around her heart as she watched Marta leave. The closing of the door that day closed her heart once and for all.

Shanice hit her call button. She needed help reaching the room phone. No matter what she said, they always put it out of reach or on her bad arm side. She needed to call the insurance company and see if someone could get her stuff from the car. If not, then she'd call Mrs. Washington if the car was still there, of course. She pictured those car-crushing machines she'd seen in movies. Her suitcase crushing under the weight and Bernard. Oh, God. Bernard.

"I'm so sorry, Bernard," Shanice sobbed. She cried into her pillow until she fell asleep.

"It's the chair for you, little lady," John said, waking Shanice.

"Hmm?" Damn. She had her thumb in her mouth again. It was so embarrassing to do that in front of people.

John was a big Black guy, about her age, with muscles for days. His grin was always cheery, and she liked when he came to help her. Elizabeth burst through the door like she always did and got the process going. She lowered the bed as far as it would go.

"Okay, let's sit up like we've been practicing," Elizabeth said. She put her hand behind Shanice's back and pulled slightly. Shanice had to do most of the work, but Elizabeth was there to hold her in case her muscles gave out and she fell back. It wasn't easy but Shanice did it. They let her catch her breath for a moment, and then John wheeled the chair over.

"Now, this next part will be mostly us," Elizabeth said. "Mainly because of your arm. Don't fight us or squirm. You don't want us to drop you."

Shanice's nervous giggle was all she said in answer.

"Good arm around my shoulder," John instructed. Shanice did that and marveled at how strong his shoulders were. Maybe he was a superhero, too. A momentary pang of loss hit her as she remembered her other strong superhero, Marta. Nope. Can't go there right now. Got more important things to do.

John put his arm around her waist on one side, and Elizabeth did the same on the other. They put their arms under her thighs and lifted her off the bed together and onto the chair. It was scary, but Shanice was ecstatic. She was out of bed. She was sitting up. She did a quick check at Elizabeth's request. Nope, nothing hurt. She didn't exactly feel strong, but she wasn't in any pain.

"Can we go outside, John?" She looked up at the bear of a man and grinned like a little kid. She swung her legs. They felt weird without that extra weight. Really weird. She tried not to let her excited feeling drain from her, but it was hard.

"Anything for you, beautiful," John said with a grin. Marta had called her beautiful in her note. But Marta was gone, and John was here. He leaned down and released the brake on the left side. "Get the other for me?"

When Shanice didn't move, Elizabeth gestured toward the hand brake on the right side. Shanice reached down and pulled the brake off. Elizabeth gave her a thumbs up and reminded her to let John know if she was in any pain. Shanice threw her a thumbs up back.

John wheeled her out of the room, and Shanice felt like she could breathe again. He wheeled her down a long hallway, and then they were in a foyer-type area with a rec room on the left. A loud television blared a daytime story like the kind Miss Macie watched in the afternoons while Shanice was at work. Four women sat around a table playing a card game. Shanice doubted they were playing Bullshit because the game was going on kind of silently. There was another long hallway straight ahead, a long-term hospice unit or something. She didn't have time to ask because John took a quick and unexpectedly sharp left turn which was exhilarating. She squealed her delight at the suddenness of it.

Sliding glass doors whisked open at their arrival as if under her command. John slowed their pace, and she found herself outside. She was under an overhang but urged him forward into the sunshine. He wheeled her over the cobblestones toward a patio underneath an open-air pagoda covered in climbing vines.

Shanice breathed in deeply. She closed her eyes and let the sunlight warm her face and arms. She hadn't felt the sun on her skin in over five weeks. She wished she had more to wear than just this stupid sick-person gown, but at the moment, all her clothes were locked up in her room at Miss Macie's. Despite several phone calls, she still hadn't been able to reach the older woman. She tucked thoughts of Miss Macie aside and basked in the sunshine. John, meanwhile, had moved over to joke around with an older man in a wheelchair sitting in the smokers' area.

Shanice let herself lean against the tall backrest and looked up. Soft puffy summer clouds were making their way lazily across the sky. She tried to make shapes out of them, but she didn't have the mental strength. She was getting tired. Maybe if she leaned back, but that would require bothering John.

Feel your feels, came a message in her head. Marta had said that. "I *am* feeling my feels," Shanice muttered irritably to no one. *And I'm tired.* Marta would have adjusted the chair for her or at least asked John to do it. Shanice took a moment, steeled herself, and said, "John?"

"What's up, pigeon-pie?"

Shanice giggled. He was so silly. "Does this lean back more? I'm getting tired sitting so upright." She gestured toward her still-healing ribs.

"Anything for you, darlin'," he said. "Say when." It felt incredible when the back hit a certain spot. "When." She sighed in relief. "Thank you."

She soaked in the sun's rays, felt the breeze on her skin, and then remembered that she hadn't called the car insurance company. It was almost five o'clock, she mused and closed her eyes. Business hours are over. She sighed sleepily. She didn't care. She felt too content to move.

"Time to head in," John announced, waking her from a doze.

She groaned. God, all she did was sleep. She hated it. Maybe the drugs made her sleepy. Could she ask about getting a lower dose? Marta would—*No! There is no Marta.*

She was disappointed when they went inside but needed to get back in bed. The four women were still playing their silent card game. Maybe she should teach them Bullshit. That would be fun. But the four older white women probably wouldn't want to play with a twenty-five-year-old Black girl with no feet.

Elizabeth appeared out of nowhere to help John get her back in bed. "I bet you're tired," Elizabeth said.

"How'd you guess," Shanice said with a sigh. "Bye, John," she called to the big man leaving her room. He turned with a smile, bowed, and then headed out the door.

"It was a lot," Elizabeth said. "Do your homework tonight after dinner, okay?"

"Yes, Ma'am," Shanice said. "Before you go, can you put my call button in reach? I have to go to the bathroom. And the phone? I need to make calls tomorrow first thing."

"Sure, sure," Elizabeth said. "Maybe John and I can put you on the toilet tomorrow." She gestured to the private bathroom that neither Shanice nor her roommate Carol had ever used.

"Really? Bedpans suck," Shanice said with a laugh.

"Yep, I know." Elizabeth didn't elaborate but said, "I'll ask someone to come in to help you right now but go ahead and push the call button anyway."

"Thank you," Shanice said. "I appreciate your help."

"Aww, you're welcome." Elizabeth headed toward the door. "See you tomorrow. Don't forget your homework."

She was out the door before Shanice could respond.

~~~

Marta put her arms around Shanice from behind. The warm bubble bath was so soothing. Comforting. Marta stroked Shanice's stomach gently, making Shanice moan in encouragement. Soft lips kissed the back of her neck and then moved to the sensitive side. Shanice shivered and pulled away slightly.

"Too much?" Marta asked, her voice soft near Shanice's ear. She didn't wait for an answer as she sucked an earlobe into her mouth and flicked it with her tongue. Shanice squirmed. Marta's caresses were turning her on.

"Mmm," Shanice moaned and leaned into the touches.

Marta's wandering hands reached up and caressed Shanice's breasts. They were small, but Marta didn't seem to mind. Her wet fingers made circles around Shanice's sensitive nipples, making Shanice arch in need. She moaned at the erotic touch.

"Let me love you, Shanice," Marta whispered in her ear.

Shanice reached for one of Marta's hands and guided it down her torso
~~~

to her center. She opened her legs wider and arched up. Marta took over and stroked her slickness.

"Someone's ready for me," Marta growled possessively. Marta's other hand stopped torturing Shanice's nipple and snaked down to pull one leg away, opening up Shanice to her explorations. Her lips found Shanice's neck again, this time with more insistent kisses. The kisses finally moved along her shoulder as Marta adjusted so she could reach her goal better.

"You need this, Beautiful," Marta said, her fingers working around Shanice's area of most need. One of Marta's fingers circled Shanice's clit.

"Yes, yes," Shanice said as the spark of orgasm started deep inside her core. "Yes," she repeated. She turned slightly so Marta could kiss her properly. Had they ever kissed before? Shanice couldn't remember. Had they ever made love like this before? Or made love in any way? It was confusing, but she willed her silly thoughts away and let herself be loved.

Too soon, the feelings were fading. The colors were dimming. The feel of Marta's bare skin against hers was replaced by something else. Eyes closed, Shanice fought to stay asleep and finish the dream. She couldn't recapture it. Damn it.

She quickly assessed her situation. Carol's TV was on. Loud. That's what woke her up, dang it. Why had the woman taken this moment to come alive? The room was dark, though. It must be the middle of the night. She couldn't quite make out the analog clock in the darkness but didn't care. She had clearance.

She snaked her hand underneath her hospital gown and found the wetness she knew would be there. She stroked herself repeatedly, half listening for sounds from the hallway. Having a night tech come in and find her in this compromised position would never do. She was under the sheet and all, but still. Thoughts of dream-Marta's touch came back, and she let them. Her breathing quickened. Her fingers flew fast and furious. Her hips arched. And then all was still before the orgasm crashed into her. She kept her fingers moving, pulling out every last pulse and spasm, staying completely silent. It was a skill she'd developed at the foster homes and the institute. She didn't need anyone knowing her business.

She let out a long, satisfied sigh and then went back to sleep. She'd

examine the whole Marta sex dream thing tomorrow. Maybe.

Chapter 9

Marta

Marta kicked her muddy boots on the outside mat of the Chrysalis Center. She should have gone home to change after work, but she was so restless she had to see Nora. Her boots were overdue for a good clean, that was for sure. She'd do that when she got home. Roger had her doing inventory in the back part of the lot, and he didn't seem to care that it was raining. She knew it was punishment for bolting out early on Saturday, but c'mon, that was harsh. The guys picking orders knew it was, too. No one, not even Jeff, razzed her about the assignment. Whatever. She'd done her penance and was, hopefully, out of the doghouse.

She scraped her boots a few more times and headed inside the center. She signed in and headed to Nora's room. The door was shut, so she opened it slowly just in case Nora was dozing. Memories of doing the exact same thing in Shanice's hospital room came flooding back, and her throat closed with grief. God, how she hated how quickly she got choked up. She was supposed to be a tough Army corporal, dang it. Her face scrunched up in misery just as Nora said hello to her.

"Oh, Pip," Nora said, concerned. "Come here." She patted her bed.

Marta tried to get herself together but just couldn't. Visions of Shanice all alone with no one to help her came unbidden. Shanice beating her at cards. Shanice lighting up at the flowers Marta had brought.

"What's happening, Pip?" Nora said. "Get the chair. Sit. Are you okay?"

Marta nodded and wiped her eyes. Then she shook her head as fresh tears burst out. Marta sat in the fold-up chair that was now a permanent fixture on Nora's side of the room since Nora's roommate never had visitors. Marta pulled the chair close and laid her head on the bed near

Nora's hip. Nora petted her wet head.

"You've been out in the rain, haven't you, silly girl."

"I'm thirty-five, Nora," Marta said with a chuckle.

"Thirty-six on Saturday. You have three more days to be thirty-five."

"Don't remind me," Marta said glumly. Seriously, she didn't care about her age. She just said it because Nora expected her to.

"Tell me what's up."

Marta sat up and wiped at her eyes. "I lost Shanice."

"The cute Black girl?"

"Yeah."

"Go on," Nora encouraged.

Marta searched Nora's face and only found loving encouragement there. "I messed up. I told her I couldn't come by for a while, which wasn't really true. And she knew it."

"You panicked. My younger sister, the hermit, was catching feels and panicked."

"Shut up," Marta said and looked away. Was that true? "There's a stray cat in the backyard, and I've been feeding her."

"Random."

"No, it's maybe like that."

Nora scoffed. "The way you've talked about Shanice is different, Pip. She's not just a stray. I think she might be more than that to you."

"She's like ten years younger than me."

"I thought age didn't matter to you," Nora said and scrunched up her nose. She reached for Marta's hand and held it. "Age gap relationships can work, silly. Each person brings a different perspective, that's all. She won't know any of the bands you love to destroy your ears with, and you won't know the bands she likes."

That was kind of true. She'd meant to look up Shanice's favorite band, The Benjies, but kept forgetting. "She likes K-pop."

"Not sure what that is, but you get my point." Nora squeezed Marta's hand and let go. "Move me up in the bed, would you?" She lowered the backrest and let Marta pull her up by the sheet. "Much better," Nora said with a sigh. "My feet were jamming up against that stupid footboard." She raised her backrest again and said, "So tell me how you 'lost' Shanice."

Marta relayed her trip to the hospital and got a frown from Nora for leaving work early. The frown turned to astonishment when Marta told her about staking out Miss Macie's house every night for the past four nights and her plans to go back tonight.

"But there has been no discernible movement or lights turned on?" Nora said quoting Marta.

Marta shook her head. "No. I even hopped the fence and walked around the backyard once it got dark.

"Honey, she's obviously not there." Nora licked her lips and said, "Can you grab my water?"

Marta picked up the Styrofoam cup with lid and straw. "It's empty."

"I'll ring for someone." Nora hit the call button. "Hey, prop open the door there. If you see John or someone, call out for water."

Marta peeked out but didn't see the burly nurses' aide and propped the door open. She sat back down. With the door open, they could hear the noises of the rehabilitation center. A late afternoon talk show blared in the rec room as people tried to talk over it. Workers conversed in the hallways.

"I hate this place," Marta said, pushing back the memories of their mother's last days there.

"I know, honey. It's hard for me to be here, too."

They were quiet for a moment until Marta said, "She's all alone, Nora." She didn't want to be overheard by anyone in the hallway or one bed over, so she lowered her voice. "She doesn't have family. Mrs. Washington, at her job, said that since Shanice was on leave, they hadn't been in contact with her. Even *they* don't know where she is. Maybe Miss Macie showed up or something, but I have to know. I have to know. I'm hitting dead ends everywhere."

An alternate idea was forming in Marta's brain when Nora said, "Okay, okay. Let's not get all stalkery. I've never seen you like this. This is worrying me."

Marta tucked the plan aside. It would require taking another day off, but so what? She needed to know. She sighed in frustration. "I know. I'm sorry. I'm not thinking right. I even canceled my date with Jessica last

Sunday."

"Now I know there's something wrong with you," Nora quipped with a chuckle and put her palm on Marta's forehead. "Are you serious about her?"

"Who? Jessica?" Marta didn't wait for an answer. "No. No. We just…uh…"

"Sex buddy, hmm?"

A giggle from the woman in the other bed who supposedly slept all day made Marta bug her eyes out at her sister. But Marta nodded while taking a resigned sigh and said, "You look good. Recent shower?"

Nora nodded. "It made me feel so good." She ran a hand over her loose light brown hair. It wasn't pulled back in her usual ponytail and somehow made her sister look relaxed.

"How's the rehab going?" Before Nora could respond, Marta said, "Hey, now I can tell everyone my sister was in rehab." She followed it with an evil laugh.

"Don't you dare, you little brat."

"Have you ever played Bullshit?"

"Okay, that was random. Do you mean the card game?"

Marta nodded.

"Yes, my wonderful son brought that game into our home during fourth grade. I'm surprised he didn't rope you into playing it with you."

"Shanice—" Marta stopped her thought. She'd heard something—something out in the hallway. No. In the rec room. She put a finger to her lips when Nora started to ask what was wrong. She turned her ear toward the hallway and heard it again.

"Ten days?" the familiar female voice said. The speaker was in obvious distress. "I'm not going to be better in ten days."

"It's her," Marta said wide-eyed. "Oh, my God."

Without a backward glance at Nora, she bolted out of her chair, into the hallway, and toward the rec room. She stopped short when she saw her. Shanice was in a wheelchair and obviously distressed.

A young white woman wearing business attire stood over Shanice with a clipboard. Marta had seen this scenario before. It was Admin, there to discuss payment or insurance or something. That's all they cared about.

Marta pushed flashbacks of her mother's illness away and rushed to Shanice's side.

"What's going on?" Marta asked the businesswoman. She knew she had no right to, but she put a possessive hand on Shanice's shoulder. She felt rather than saw Shanice look up at her. Marta didn't look down because she didn't want to see whatever expression was on Shanice's face. It could be one of disgust, distrust, or any number of get-out-of-my-life expressions. Relief that she'd found Shanice flooded Marta's body and brain. She wanted to cry and take Shanice up in her arms but had to remain stoic in front of the worker.

"This is my Aunt Marta," Shanice said to the businesswoman who had started to protest sharing Shanice's personal information. "I give you permission to explain it to her.

The woman nodded and spoke directly to Marta. "Her health insurance will only cover ten more days. She'll have to leave next week."

*And go where? M*arta thought but didn't say it out loud. "Would she be able to stay and pay the full cost?"

The woman sighed and said, "I'll have to go back and work up the numbers, but it is prohibitively expensive for self-pay patients."

"That's just cruel." Marta squeezed Shanice's shoulder in solidarity.

The woman, looking about as uncomfortable as a person could, excused herself promising to work up some numbers for them.

Marta watched her walk away, took her hand off Shanice's shoulder, and backed up a step. She noticed John, the bulky nurses' aide, looking in their direction as if ready to swoop in and save Shanice from big bad Marta. Good. Shanice had someone else in her corner.

"I found you," Marta said.

"Here I am," Shanice said without much emotion.

Yeah, Marta had blown it. The tears hit her eyes before she could stop them. "I'm so sorry I left you. I panicked, Shanice. You thought I abandoned you. I didn't. I needed a minute to pull my head together."

"Mm hmm," Shanice murmured noncommittally and looked away. She looked over her shoulder and said, "Hey, John? I need to lie down now."

"You got it, Beautiful."

"Can I visit you?" Marta asked, not wanting to lose Shanice again.

Shanice shrugged. "I'm tired now."

Marta was panicking. She was losing Shanice again. She blurted, "Did you find Bernard?"

Shanice's head and shoulders dropped. After a moment, she shook her head.

Shit, Marta thought. I just made her more miserable.

John wheeled Shanice down the hallway, passed Nora's room, and entered the last room on the right. Marta made a mental note of where she was. She'd found Shanice again and vowed to make sure she helped the young woman get situated somewhere and settled. It was the least she could do to compensate for her karma-destroying abandonment.

A weird detail struck Marta as odd. The kid was wearing a hospital gown. Even Nora wore real pajamas in the bed. And the other people in the rec area also had on real clothes.

As she walked back to Nora's room, pieces were coming together. Yes, the plan she'd been scheming and tucked aside moments ago was going to become a reality. Shanice had no clothes and no Bernard. That could only mean one thing. No one had gone up to claim the car or gotten her stuff. Shanice's job seemed to have washed their hands of her for now. And Miss Macie was nowhere to be found. The car insurance people must not have helped either.

Realization hit Marta. Shanice had lied to her about the car insurance company going up to get her things and ID the car. She'd lied. Marta stopped just outside Nora's room. "And then I abandoned her." Tears did not come this time. This time Marta would not wallow in her past mistakes. No, Marta would fix everything this time, even if Shanice fought her on it. If there was one thing the Army taught her was that you never leave a fallen comrade behind.

~~~

Marta pulled into Alstead's Towing in Miamitown at precisely 0800 hours when the website said the office was open. She parked her pickup and
~~~

double-checked to make sure she had her phone in her pocket. She had no idea if Shanice's car was still there or had been junked already. Marta didn't talk directly to her boss about taking another day off but left a message on the office answering machine. More inventory was in her future, she was certain. But she didn't care. This was important.

She headed to the building that looked like an office and walked in.

"Can I help you?" a stout middle-aged Hispanic man asked her. His coveralls were stained, but he looked clean otherwise.

She introduced herself and explained why she was there.

"We still have it here," the man named Manny said, referring to Shanice's car.

Marta sighed in relief and let Manny take the lead. She showed him the picture of Shanice's letter, allowing the bearer to speak for her concerning the car. After a bit of fumbling with the technology, they managed to print out the letter, the picture of Shanice's driver's license, and the picture of her holding both items. The cast on her broken arm was prominent in the picture.

"Got gloves?" Manny asked.

"Yes, sir. In my truck," Marta said.

"Go get 'em. There's a lot of glass everywhere. We're not allowed to touch anything."

"I'll be right back." Marta was relieved that she could help Shanice like this but knew that seeing the crushed car was going to be rough.

Work gloves retrieved, Marta walked with Manny toward a side section of the large towing yard. There were at least fifty cars parked in the well-fenced lot.

"Someone came and took pictures," Manny said as they walked the long path.

"Who?"

"I'm fairly certain it was her auto insurance company. They totaled it. It would cost more to repair than it's worth. And, as you'll see in a moment, it's not repairable." He stopped walking and turned to face Marta. "I'm glad she lived."

Marta felt the telltale signs of dread coming over her. The last thing she wanted to do was cry in front of this guy. She'd planned to do that in the pickup on the way back to Denton Heights. Marta swallowed and thought about her first few days of Basic. The sergeants had toughened her up pretty quickly. She needed to harness that toughness right now.

"She'll need a lot of help," Marta said. "She broke some bones. But we're thankful she had no major internal injuries and seems to be doing well mentally and emotionally." She said the word 'we' as if Shanice had an entire army of people in her camp.

"So glad to hear that," Manny said, turning to walk on. "Fatalities are the tough part of this job."

Marta nodded, and when they turned the corner, she stopped in her tracks when she saw the mangled Kia Soul. Marta's heart leaped to her throat, and she couldn't help the tears. She clamped her hand over her mouth and cried. "Oh, honey," she said to Shanice, who was miles away.

"See why that young lady was lucky?" Manny asked quietly.

Marta nodded.

"I'll leave you to it. Meet me back in the office when you're done to make sure we've got everything signed and documented properly. Okay?"

"Yes, sir," Marta said automatically.

He chuckled. "Army?"

Marta scoffed. "Yes. How'd you know?"

"You walk with purpose. Back straight. Even cadence. When we stopped for a moment, you went right into 'at-ease,'" Manny said.

"You must have served if you noticed all that."

"Yes, Ma'am," he said with a wink. "I'm going to let you get to it then." And with that, he stood upright and saluted her.

She returned his salute, and then he headed back up the path to the office.

Marta was convinced he'd done that on purpose to distract her. He must have seen how upset she was and brought her back down to earth. She silently thanked him and got out her phone.

She steeled herself and took a couple dozen pictures of the outside. The driver's side was crushed in. A normal-sized person would have been completely broken. But Shanice was small. Marta took pictures through the broken driver's side door and tried not to blanch when she saw the dark, dried blood. *Her legs*, the quick thought came, but Marta pushed it aside as she noticed the Disney Stitch keychain dangling from the ignition switch now near the floor.

Marta cleared the remaining glass from the shattered window and reached for the keys, but they were too far away. She tried but knew there was no way the mangled driver's door was going to open, so she went around to the passenger side. With a struggle and a few heaves, the door opened, and Marta took pictures before clearing off the glass on the seat. She kneeled and snaked the keyring off the ignition key. No one would be driving this car again anyway.

Marta found a still-full coffee thermos and a full water bottle. She pulled everything out of both storage compartments, checked both visors, and looked under the floor mats. There wasn't much she could do on the driver's side because of the crunched seat and door. As she was doing a thorough check of the back seat, she accidentally knelt on a shard of glass that penetrated right through her jeans.

"Damn it," Marta cursed. She pulled the glass shard out, hoping a piece wasn't still in her skin. She'd check once she got back in the office.

Her heart lightened when she saw the suitcase in the small cargo section in the back. Satisfied that she'd scoured the backseat for personal items, she got out and yanked open the hatchback. She pulled the suitcase out and put it on the cleanest patch of dirt she could find.

"Phone," Marta said out loud. "She would have used it for navigation. With that single focus, Marta went back over the car meticulously but couldn't find it. "Damn it," she cursed. She closed her eyes, took a cleansing breath, and said to God, the Universe, or whatever was out there, "Please let this phone be here. Please let me find it. Please let this young woman find peace." Tears welled up again, naturally, but she pushed them down. She was on a mission.

She turned on the flashlight feature on her phone and slowly went over every inch of the front seats. She remembered a story about some rich guy who made his staff lay out a grid so they could meticulously search each square inch for shards of broken glass. She did the same using an imaginary grid, trying not to allow a single stray thought to deter her from her task.

"Look where you're looking," she scolded herself more than once when her mind strayed to some other part of the car where the phone might have flown to. With zen-like precision, she searched. She shined the flashlight in different directions hoping to find something. Anything.

She brushed away the glass and got on her knees to look underneath the broken driver's seat. Wait, what was that? Something glinted in the light. She moved the light again. Yes, something was there. She couldn't feel with her gloved hands, and despite the glass, reached up under the driver's seat and felt it. It had to be the phone. After much tugging and glass eating up her hand, she pulled it out.

"Victory," Marta said. She hopped out of the car, took a moment to regroup, and then with hyper focus, did one last look over every space of the vehicle.

When she reached the front office, blood was dripping down her right hand and arm. Manny rushed her into the restroom and helped her remove the glass shards.

"Worth it?"

Marta nodded. And it had been worth it. Shanice would have more freedom with her phone. And with the suitcase, she'd have clothes if they were still wearable. When Manny left her alone to check her leg wound, she wondered if she should take the suitcase home and wash the clothes. "No, no," she said. That would be a serious violation of privacy. Marta knew that doing what she was doing now was also a violation of privacy, but she'd take the consequences.

Manny took pictures of the items Marta had taken out of the car and took a picture of Marta as well. "For the file," he said.

Whatever.

"You did good, soldier," Manny said as they loaded the suitcase and the rest of Shanice's stuff into the passenger seat of her pickup.

"Thank you, sir," Marta said. This time she saluted him, and he returned it.

"Tell her we're all rooting for her."

Marta was surprised to see tears in his eyes. He blinked them away.

"I will," she said to him. "And thanks for holding on to the car for so long."

He simply nodded and headed back to the office.

~~~

By the time Marta pulled onto Market Street in Denton Heights, her frayed nerves had quieted somewhat. The bandages Manny had given her for her hand and forearm were soaked through with blood. She'd take care of it inside the coffee shop before ordering.

She headed inside, wondering why she hadn't spent more time there in the past. The overhead party lights gave the place a cool vibe. And the plants in the front window gave it a homey feel. Before she even made it to the restroom, a young woman stopped her.

"Whoa, whoa, whoa," the young blonde said. "What happened to you?"

"I lost a fight with some glass."

"I think Miss Rikki has bandages and shit in the back. I'll be right back with something."

Marta was about to say she didn't need any help but instead heard herself say, "Okay."

She washed up and did her square-inch method to see if any shards of glass were still embedded. She used her flashlight trick and didn't see any glints of light, so all must be good. A soft knock came on the single-serving door.

Marta unlocked the door, and the young blonde came in, followed by a tall, voluptuous redhead. The white woman was stunning in her long-sleeved poplin button-down shirt. Her long, gorgeous hair was pulled behind her head and held together by a beautiful, antique-looking clasp.

"What happened?" the tall redhead asked.

"Looks like I lost a fight," Marta said. "I was retrieving a phone from a friend's car that had been in an accident. There was lots of glass, but I wasn't leaving until I found the dang phone. She reached into her back pocket and pulled out the mangled thing.

"That's dedication," the woman said. She turned to the younger woman
~~~

and said, "Brittany, get the peroxide and bandages from the back storeroom. The gauze, too. Bring everything."

"Too bad Miss Shasti's not here this morning," the young woman named Brittany called over her shoulder.

"Yes, that would have been convenient," the tall woman said. "I'm Rikki, by the way."

Oh, shit. She was the owner of the shop. Marta tried not to be starstruck and squeaked out, "Marta." They shook with their left hands since Marta's right was currently bleeding in the woman's sink. Was that bad luck? Shaking with left hands?

Rikki took Marta's right hand gently and rewashed the obvious cut areas. "Anything hurt?"

"Negative. I think I got all the glass out."

"I hope your friend is okay," Rikki said, holding a paper towel over the largest cuts. "The one in the car accident."

"I hope so, too," Marta said. *Friend.* Yes, she'd like to be friends with Shanice. Hermitting might be compromised if Marta made a friend, though. She tabled the thought because she had vowed to help Shanice get settled and situated. She wasn't going to think beyond that. "Shanice is still at the nursing facility. She'll have some challenges ahead of her, but I think all her mental faculties are there."

"That's half the battle, I suppose."

"I stopped here to get real coffee to bring her. That and the phone." Marta didn't mention the suitcase or Bernard. She'd already shared way too much of Shanice's story already.

Brittany returned with a box of first aid supplies, and Rikki gently tended Marta's wounds. It was kind of embarrassing to be fussed over like that because Marta was used to taking care of herself. And then later, when Brittany gave her all three coffees for free, Marta insisted on paying.

"Your money's no good here," Rikki said, coming out of a side office or storage room. "Tell your friend to heal quickly so she can come in and see us in person. Tell her the coffee will be on me."

Marta refused to tear up, making her eyes go wide. Like Manny, she blinked them away. "Thank you, Rikki. You're an incredible human being."

“Go on,” Rikki said with a laugh. “We’ll see you back here soon, yes?”

“Sure,” Marta said, wondering why she’d said it. Well, Rikki’s Coffee Shop did have the best coffee in town, and now she understood why. Incredible people worked there—incredible people who put their hearts, souls, and love into what they did.

Marta hurried out with her carrying tray and headed toward Kirkland and the Chrysalis Center.

Chapter 10

Shanice

Physical therapy with Elizabeth had gone pretty well that morning. John wheeled her to the PT room just inside that long-term care hallway. She hadn't even known it was there. Elizabeth had her do lots of exercises in the wheelchair, and it was fun when the other people cheered her on when she had a difficult task to accomplish. And she found herself cheering them on, too. It was kind of like a PT solidarity. It was neat.

Shanice felt her muscles responding with more strength than ever. Okay, she was still a little sore and needed to lay down flat after their session, but whatever. She had nothing better to do anyway. Her breakfast tray was still in her room, so she lifted her backrest to see if any coffee was left. She already knew the answer but checked anyway. Nope. It was gone. Should she ask for more?

Before she could decide, the door to her room opened slowly. The Chrysalis staff never opened the door slowly. They just barged in and went about their business. Shanice's heart sped up. Only one person opened the door like that.

"Oh, good. You're awake," Marta said as she entered. She glanced at Shanice's sleeping roommate and said quietly, "I thought you might like some creature comforts." She handed Shanice a to-go coffee from Rikki's.

"Thank you," Shanice said, surprised that her voice was so calm on the outside. Inside, a storm was raging. She remembered the old saying—*Fool me once, shame on you. Fool me twice, shame on me*. She didn't intend to get sucked into Marta's orbit again, even if Marta was a superhero and all.

Shanice took a sip. It wasn't piping hot, but something about it tasted good. "Mmm," she moaned. "Thank you," she said again.

"I'm glad you like it." Marta was standing stiffly by the side of Shanice's bed. Not too close, which was good.

"I brought one for Nora, too. She said I was her favorite sister now."

"Aren't you her *only* sister?" Shanice asked with an amused tone.

"Exactly what I said to her," Marta said with a laugh. "I have a few more things for you. What do you want first, the big thing or the small?"

Gifts? Marta was trying to buy her off with gifts. No. There was no way she was going to accept Marta's guilt gifts. She wasn't going to keep them, anyway. When she left this place in ten days, she would leave whatever it was behind. She wanted no reminders of someone she had started to have feelings for who obviously saw her as a liability or someone to be pitied. She shrugged noncommittally.

Marta seemed nervous as she said, "Oh, okay," as if her bubble had burst. Yep, see how that feels? Shanice wasn't beyond retaliation, but she kind of didn't have real energy or strength for that sort of thing. And besides, Marta's obvious disappointment with Shanice's lack of enthusiasm was kind of heartbreaking. Kind of.

Marta reached into her back pocket, and it was then that Shanice noticed Marta's bandages. "Oh, my God. What happened to your arm?"

"It's nothing. I got cut digging this out from under your driver's seat." Marta held out Shanice's phone.

Shanice's eyes grew wide. "Is that…"

"Yes, your phone," Marta said, still holding it out. "I drove up to Miamitown this morning."

"Why?"

Marta sighed forcefully. "Because you needed help. And I'm able and capable of helping you, so I did." She tossed the phone on the bed and said, "I'll get the other thing." She turned and left the room, coming back in with Shanice's suitcase. "Where do you want this?"

"You did this?" Shanice asked. "For me?"

"Yes."

"Why?"

"You're as stubborn as I am." Marta looked frustrated. "You need help, Shanice." Marta pointed to Shanice's broken arm and lack of feet and twirled her fingers to indicate the whole room. "So, I'm sticking around and helping you. I need to see you settled and situated somewhere. And, yes, we're going to talk about your options at some point soon since they're kicking you out in ten days, right?"

Shanice nodded.

"But first, I think there may be someone in here," Marta tapped the suitcase, "who desperately wants to see you."

"Yes," Shanice said breathlessly. "Yes, please. Open it." Shanice shimmied over to one side of the bed so Marta would have room to heave the small suitcase onto the vacated space. Shanice indicated that Marta should go ahead and unzip it. "Where is he?"

Marta reached inside and found the brown seen-better-days musk ox.

"Bernard!" Shanice screeched and grabbed him from Marta's hands. She hugged him tight and cried so hard that her chest hurt. "I thought I'd lost you. I'm sorry I put you in danger like that." Marta must think she was such a baby, but she didn't care. She wiped at her tears and reached for Marta's hand. She was surprised to see that Marta was also crying.

"Thank you," Shanice said.

Marta simply nodded. She was obviously too choked up to speak.

Shanice held him up toward Marta. "Here, he wants a hug from you, too. Our superhero."

Marta laughed. "Superhero? Doubt that." She took Bernard carefully and hugged him. "Shanice and I have been so worried about you, Bernard," Marta said to the stuffie. "But we both know you were just hibernating until we could get to you, right?"

"Right," Shanice said. "Long naptime for Bernard." She took her furry friend back from Marta and kissed his worn-out furry head. "He's been with me since I was seven. For, like, eighteen years."

Marta's expression softened as she smiled. She had a really nice genuine smile.

Shanice took a breath and then said, "Can you find my contacts in there? It would be amazing to be able to see."

"Sure." Marta rooted around in the suitcase and found the contacts case and bottle of solution. She washed Shanice's hands for her using a washcloth she'd found in a cupboard and then watched while Shanice carefully put the contacts in.

"Oh," Shanice said with a sigh, blinking a few times. "Feels so good to be able to see."

"I bet," Marta said and stowed the contacts and solution in the drawer of Shanice's bedside table. "Hey," Marta said abruptly, "I have an idea."

"What?"

"I want you to meet Nora."

"Your sister?"

"Yeah," Marta said. "C'mon."

"Okay," Shanice heard herself saying. Wait. What was she doing? Moments ago, she had vowed not to, absolutely *not,* get sucked into Marta's vortex again, and here she was doing just that. Well, maybe she'd allow this one thing. Marta had brought Bernard back to her after all. "Wait. How are my clothes? Do they smell bad?"

Marta leaned down and sniffed the clothes. "Smell fine. Want to get dressed?"

"Oh, God, yes," Shanice said. "But maybe we'll skip the bra."

"Wise decision," Marta said, pulling out Shanice's clothes. As they picked out what Shanice could wear comfortably and still manage a bedpan, Marta told her about driving by Miss Macie's house a few times and how it had seemed dark and unlived in. None of the neighbors knew anything about where Miss Macie was.

"I need to call her son," Shanice said, picking up her phone. "I've been away from home for over five weeks. I mean, I hope she's okay and not..." Shanice looked away. She would never forgive herself if Miss Macie were hurt and lying in pain in the house. At this point, though, she wouldn't be in any pain. She would be...

"Quick question," Marta said, breaking into Shanice's morbid thoughts. "One of your neighbors implied that you were Miss Macie's granddaughter."

There was no actual question asked, but Shanice understood the implied one. She shook her head. "He or she must have assumed. I have no family that I know of." Except for the name on her birth certificate, but that was just a useless piece of paper and didn't mean a thing.

"Yeah, I figured he'd gotten it wrong," Marta said. "And, by the way, your phone is toast. Even if we could get a charger on it, that screen is so broken you can see the guts inside."

"I need a new one," Shanice said with a sigh. "I hope they can get my info off this phone, though. Ah, whatever. Hey, can you get John? I want to use the bathroom, and then he can put me in the wheelchair."

"No need for John," Marta said, raising her arms and flexing her biceps.

"Superhero arms," Shanice muttered and was mortified that she'd actually said it out loud. Thank goodness Marta laughed.

"Here's how I like to transfer," Marta said, outlining how she would pick up Shanice and place her in the wheelchair.

Shanice nodded her understanding.

"Words, please."

"Yes, I get it. Are you sure you won't throw out your back or something?"

"Nope." Marta picked her up as if she was as light as a feather. She brought her into the bathroom and set her down on the toilet. She lifted the back of the sleeping shirt so Shanice wouldn't be sitting on it.

"This is so sudden," Shanice quipped. "You're not going to buy me dinner first?"

Marta burst out laughing. "Shut up and do your thing." She made sure Shanice was balanced and said, "I'll be out here."

After she had 'done her business,' Marta came back in. Shanice was lifted into the oversized wheelchair, and the cardboard to-go tray with their coffees was placed in her lap.

"Keep that steady with the bad hand," Marta instructed. "And hold onto the wheelchair with your good one."

"Yes, Ma'am," Shanice said.

They headed toward the door until Marta stopped abruptly and said, "Wait." She ran over to the bed and grabbed Bernard. "You two have a lot of catching up to do."

Shanice caught Marta's gaze and held on. She took the stuffie without looking and squeezed him to her chest. She couldn't look away because it felt like Marta was looking into her very soul. Shanice wanted to somehow express her thanks to her hero but didn't know how. Without Marta, Bernard would have been thrown away. She knew how that felt. Too soon, Marta cleared her throat and looked away.

"Onto room 107," Marta said cheerfully and wheeled her out of the room. When they approached Room 107, Marta flung the wheelchair ninety degrees, making Shanice laugh as she desperately held onto the coffee tray. Marta laughed evilly, which made Shanice start to giggle.

"You seem to know your way around wheelchairs, Marta," Shanice observed out loud. She only got a grunt in response. Sore subject, maybe.

"Nora?" Marta said as she backed into the room, pulling Shanice with her. Once Shanice was all the way in, Marta let the door close and then wheeled Shanice around. "Look who I found in room 115 down the hall."

Nora's face lit up as she smiled. "You must be Shanice. It's so nice to finally meet you in person."

Marta wheeled Shanice closer to the bed and then unfolded a chair to sit beside her.

"Hi," Shanice said, suddenly shy. She expected Marta's sister to ask her how she was doing, but she didn't, thank goodness, because she wasn't sure how she would have answered that question. It was kind of obvious how she was doing, wasn't it?

Nora's eyes got big when she took in Marta's bandaged arm. One of the cuts was bleeding through, creating a red stain. Nora motioned silently toward the arm, but Marta simply shook her head as if it wasn't a big deal and she didn't want to discuss it at the moment.

Nora nodded to her sister and turned back to Shanice. "Oh, what a darling creature." She pointed toward Bernard. "May I see him? Her?"

"Him," Shanice said and handed Bernard over to Nora.

Nora took him gently and murmured such sweet words to Bernard that Shanice let herself be taken up by the love. "You are so handsome, sir," Nora said, giving Bernard a light hug. "Now, let me look at you." Shanice was a little embarrassed. Bernard had lost an eye a long time ago, and she had sewn a button in its place. It looked weird, but Bernard didn't seem to mind. And somehow, the stuffing in his butt had matted down inside, and he was kind of deflated on that end. There were clear worn spots, and yeah, he was a tired-looking creature.

"So," Marta said, taking her coffee from the tray in Shanice's lap, "Nora is a whiz at sewing and stuff." Marta looked at Nora with raised eyebrows.

"Absolutely," Nora said.

Shanice looked from one sister to the other and then to Bernard. What were they scheming? She pulled her coffee out of the holder and took a sip.

"Once we've both broken outta this joint," Nora said, waggling her eyebrows, "it would be my honor to give Bernard a spruce up."

"She's an expert at it," Marta reiterated.

Nora smiled. "I can give him a bit more stuffing in his behind."

Shanice giggled and hid her smile behind her coffee cup. Nora had said, 'behind.'

Nora's smile grew wider. "His derriere, if you will, and I may even have a working eye that would match his other one. Unless he prefers the button?"

"No, no," Shanice said. "He would love to be whole."

Marta made a weird kind of strangled noise beside her, but Shanice didn't know how to interpret it.

"Excellent," Nora said. "And I can redo this stitching where a very competent surgeon has obviously done some prior surgery."

"Me," Shanice said proudly.

Years ago, some stupid kid tried to take him from Shanice, and she yanked Bernard away, tearing one of his legs a little. She had cried, but thankfully the foster mom had a needle and thread that Shanice snuck out later that night to fix him.

Marta stood up and examined Bernard's sewn-up leg. "Wow, that's better than I would have done." Marta sounded impressed. Something weird was spreading through Shanice's heart. These sisters weren't teasing her. They weren't condescending. They were genuinely giving her loving attention. It was kind of like Mama Deborah had done, but she didn't let the sadness of Mama Deborah overtake her and stayed in the present.

"Okay, then. It's settled." Nora handed Bernard back to Shanice. "Sometime soon, we'll have a spa day for Bernard. Sound good?"

"Yes, Ma'am," Shanice said, getting shy again. That would be so awesome, but since it probably wouldn't happen, she wasn't going to get her hopes up.

"All right," Nora said cheerfully, "so let me tell you about the time Marta's stuffie Seymour the green frog got left in a hotel room in Illinois."

"Aww," Shanice said, looking up at Marta. She laughed when she saw Marta scowling at her sister.

"Oh, we got him back," Nora continued, "but I've never seen Marta cry so much in my life. We were about an hour into that day's trip when she realized he was missing. Daddy pulled over, and we searched the whole car and everyone's suitcases. Seymour was nowhere."

"What trip was that again?" Marta asked.

"You were four. You wouldn't remember, I guess. We were visiting Granny, Dad's mom, in Minnesota."

"Oh, right." Marta nodded her head.

"Marta was always a daddy's girl, so once our dad realized Seymour was lost, he turned the car around, and we headed back to that hotel."

"They said they couldn't find him at first, right?" Marta asked.

"Right, but Daddy persisted, and you crying your eyes out got them all moving. They finally found him bundled up in the dirty sheets from our room."

"I remember feeling so relieved," Marta said. She winked at Shanice. "So, you see? I completely understand about Bernard."

"Do you still have him?"

"Seymour? Yeah. Top shelf of my bookcase. He probably needs to be dusted, though."

The sisters chatted more about their childhood stuff, and although Shanice was envious that they'd had such a nice family together, it didn't make her feel bad about not having that for herself. She kind of felt like they were sharing their stories to make her feel included.

A sudden aching pain got Shanice's attention, and she winced.

"What's up, sweetie?" Marta said.

Shanice pointed to her stumps. "Can you raise them so they're sticking straight out horizontally?"

"Sure," Marta said cheerfully, then carefully lifted the leg rests. She adjusted each one so they hit Shanice's legs in a much more favorable spot just above her stumps. She hadn't known those things could be adjusted.

"Mmm," Shanice sighed. "Much better."

"How are you healing?" Marta asked gently as if afraid of the answer.

"Much better," Shanice said. She smiled up at Nora, who had a concerned but not a pitying expression on her face. These sisters were different than most people. "They took the staples out, and the wounds are closed up tight. I have to wear these lovely compression shrinker thingies to mold the stumps and keep swelling to a minimum. Elizabeth—"

"The drill sergeant PT lady?" Nora said with a stricken expression.

Shanice laughed. "Yes, she'd be the one." She laughed again and said, "Elizabeth rubs this oil stuff into the wounds, so they won't scar too much and give me trouble."

"Pip," Nora said, "find out what that oil is, so you can—" She gestured toward Shanice and nodded her head.

"I will."

Shanice was fascinated that they understood each other so well with just gestures and facial expressions. It was kind of cool. Shanice leaned over and whispered to Marta, "She called you 'Pip.'" Shanice snorted through her nose as if that was the funniest thing she'd ever heard.

Nora burst out laughing from her bed.

"Oh, no," Marta said. "No, no, no." She pointed first to Shanice and then to Nora. "I don't like this ganging up on Marta thing one bit."

The mirth in Marta's eyes told a different story, though. It was kind of weird the way Marta pointed. Most people used one finger. Marta used her whole hand. Maybe she'd ask her about that one day.

Once the laughter subsided, Nora shared that she was breaking out of the joint on Sunday and starting at-home physical therapy the very next day.

Shanice said, "Elizabeth told me my insurance would allow me about five in-home PT visits, and then I'd graduate to outpatient." She hugged Bernard close. She had no clue where "home" would be, but she would have Bernard, and it would be okay. She refused to choke up and covered it by saying, "You know, that's where you drive to a place and do the workouts there." Of course, she had no idea how she would *drive* anywhere, let alone to an outpatient facility. She'd have to find an Uber driver who could stash a wheelchair in the back or something. Taking the bus could work, too. She'd seen a few people in scooters and wheelchairs taking busses back when she had been using public transportation. That made her think about her car.

"What did my car look like?" she blurted to Marta.

"Umm," Marta said with hesitation.

"That bad?" Nora asked softly.

Marta nodded and blinked back some tears. She patted Shanice's good arm and then cleared her throat. "I took lots of pictures."

"Are you ready to see them, honey?" Nora asked. There was caution in her tone.

Shanice looked from Nora to Marta, seeing the love in their eyes, but knew it wasn't time. "Not yet," she said. "One day, maybe."

"Still too fresh," Nora offered.

"Yeah," Shanice said, hearing the worry in her own voice.

"Listen," Nora said to Shanice. "You have this ex-Army soldier in your corner, so you'll be okay."

"We're both lucky to have her in our corners," Shanice said shyly. She couldn't help smiling as she watched red creep up Marta's cheeks.

"Yes, we are lucky," Nora said. "It took forever for her to squelch that potty mouth of hers when she came home from Iraq."

Shanice's eyes grew wide. "Iraq? Really?"

Marta nodded, confirming Nora's statement.

They spent the next half hour finishing their coffees and mainly talking about Marta's and Nora's childhoods. Marta had changed the subject away from her Army days quickly. Must be a sore subject, Shanice thought. None of her business anyway.

Fatigue overcame her, and she asked Marta to wheel her back to her room. Once she was back in bed, she was dozing almost instantly. She felt Marta kiss her on her forehead and vaguely heard the words, "I'll come back tomorrow after work, kid. That is a promise."

Funny how Shanice felt like Marta would keep her promise this time.

Chapter 11

Marta

True to her word, this time, Marta visited Shanice every day after work. Marta hated that she had to work Saturdays and on her birthday to boot, but she went in, did the assigned jobs, and went home to shower. And even though Roger punished her by making her do composted cow manure duty all day in the hot July sun, she didn't care. In fact, she was cheery to everyone, even when they wrinkled their noses at her lovely smell.

As she was showering, she thought one thing was odd. Jeff told her to have a good birthday. He didn't razz her about the assignment like the other guys did. It was weird, especially because she hadn't told anyone it was her birthday. She thought she had quietly slid into thirty-six unnoticed.

After her shower, she dressed in casual summer clothes and did something she rarely did. She put on sandals. She was a work boots and sneakers kind of gal but thought sandals would make her look less ex-military. She didn't think about it too much because she knew she might change her mind and wear sneakers instead.

She tossed her clothes in the washer, set it on a double wash with triple rinse, and headed outside to feed the backyard kitty. She was nowhere to be found, but Marta left the food and a fresh water bowl anyway. She fed Snowball, gave her a quick scritch down her back, and then headed to the Chrysalis Center. Nora was getting out sometime tomorrow, probably while Marta was at work, so today would be Marta's last chance to see her there.

Marta stopped at the local supermarket and picked up two bouquets of flowers. One for Nora, of course, and one for Shanice. For her two best…girls. Marta blanched as the thought came unbidden. Shanice was *not* her girl. And she wasn't a girl. She was a grown woman in her mid-twenties.

And she was a friend, sure. Besides, Marta had her regular Sunday night date with Jessica tomorrow. Marta had agreed on a quasi-impact scene. It was rather vanilla, but Marta was going to "discipline" Jessica with a spanking. Then, Jessica would probably end up hogtied to the bedframe and made easily accessible for Marta to do anything she wished. And that was going to be needle play. That part Jessica had finally agreed to. Yay. Wait. Jessica would need to be relaxed for needle play. Okay, so somewhere before the needles came out, Marta would let Jessica orgasm. Why not? That's what they were both there for, right? Truth be told, Marta wasn't that interested in having that sort of release. She wasn't sure why. Probably her hormone cycle was at a low or something.

She pushed thoughts of her date aside and pulled into the center. She grabbed the bouquets and the other special surprise for Shanice, which had taken a few days to pull off, but she'd done it. As soon as the doors whooshed open, her senses were on alert. Something was different. She signed in, but the receptionist wasn't there to check her in. She used all of her senses like the Army taught her to find the discrepancies in the usual comings and goings of the place. She stepped forward cautiously, ready to ditch the flowers if she needed to fight.

It was quiet. That was the problem. Too quiet. Should she back away, go to her pickup, and call Nora? She had taken one step back when Nora wheeled herself down the hallway and into the front foyer. "Ooh, flowers for me?"

"Sure," Marta said, handing Nora one of the bouquets. Even Nora was acting weird. "What's going on?" She looked around wary.

"What do you mean?" Nora asked.

Marta grabbed the handles of the wheelchair and started heading back to Nora's room.

"Let's go to the Rec Room," Nora said. "Shanice has been teaching everyone Bullshit. It's hilarious."

Normally, Marta would have laughed at the thought, but something was really off. She trusted Nora, but still. As soon as they turned the corner, Marta barely had time to take in the dozen people as numerous explosions went off. She flung Nora's wheelchair behind her and dove to the floor, looking for her rifle.

The cheer of "surprise" died out, and Marta realized what had happened. "Fuck," she muttered. The pops she'd heard were from party favors. The kind that fling out streamers. She took the slightest of moments to sit up and said, "If that had been real gunfire, you all would have been toast."

Nervous laughter filled the room while Marta caught her breath.

"Pip," Nora said, "I'm so sorry. I didn't think. You haven't…in such a long time."

"I know."

"Thanks for saving me, though," Nora said with pride.

Marta's heart was still pounding as she rolled her eyes for Nora's sake. Marta put on a smile as Shanice was wheeled up to her by an attendant Marta didn't know.

"Happy birthday?" Shanice said cautiously and put her arms out in a sorry gesture.

Marta took another calming breath. "Thank you," she said to Shanice. Louder, she said, "Thanks, everybody. That, uh, really was a surprise, wasn't it?"

Everyone laughed, more genuinely this time, and someone played quiet party music for background noise.

Marta handed the now-crumpled bouquet of flowers to Shanice and then allowed Nora to fuss over her healing arm and hand. After a moment, Nora said, "C'mon, wheel us over to the cake."

"Cake? You did all this?"

Nora shook her head, and pointed to Shanice, who was grinning like a Cheshire cat.

"How'd you know?" Marta asked Shanice.

"Really?" Nora asked. "Are you that naïve? You didn't think us gals would get together and talk about our favorite Corporal?"

Marta shook her head and groaned good-naturedly. "Figures."

Everyone sang the happy birthday song, and then Marta was required to cut the first piece of cake for good luck or something. Someone took over the cake cutting after that, much to Marta's relief. Shanice insisted that

Marta take at least one bite of cake for luck, even though she protested that she didn't like sweets. Marta and Nora were polar opposites in that regard, and Marta sighed as she watched Nora wheel herself over for seconds on the cake.

"I have a surprise for you," Marta said to Shanice. They had managed to commandeer a semi-quiet table in the back of the room, far away from the merriment.

"Oh?"

Marta pulled out a brand new phone, the same color and cover as Shanice's mangled one. "The dude said he got all your information off the old phone and onto this one."

Shanice's eyes grew wide. "No way. And first of all, I can't believe you did this. How much did it cost?"

Marta waved her hand in dismissal.

"You can't pay for my stuff, Marta," Shanice said quietly. "I can pay my way. I've always paid my way."

"That's fine, whatever. Pay me back later." What Marta didn't tell her was that she had put Shanice on her own plan, seeing as they used the same mobile phone service and had the exact same phone. It was cheaper for both of them that way. She'd tell her at some point, but not right now.

"Can you wheel me to my room?" Shanice asked.

"Tired?"

"No." Shanice scoffed. "Well, yes. Perpetually. But I have a present for you in my room."

"Ooh, nice," Marta said, bolting out of her chair. She whizzed Shanice out of the rec room and sped down the hallway, probably breaking land speed records as they went. "Hold on," she called and made sure Shanice was holding on as she stopped abruptly.

The giggles coming out of Shanice made Marta smile. Yes, yes, yes. That was the birthday present she wanted. To see Shanice happy and having fun.

Once inside the room, Marta helped her onto the toilet and then back in bed. "You're getting stronger," Marta said. "I can tell by the way we transfer."

“Thank you. Elizabeth is working me hard. She told me I’m probably getting my cast off on Wednesday. And if it’s in the morning, we’ll do PT on it that afternoon. No real weight bearing yet, but she said sometimes bone breaks heal stronger than the original bone.”

“Yeah, I’ve heard that, too.” Marta lowered the bed a little so she could sit on the edge.

“She said we won’t be able to work on self-transfers, but she will put that in the home PT and on-site PT orders.”

“So you’ll be able to get yourself in and out of a wheelchair?”

“Yeah,” Shanice said succinctly. “Wheelchair. I guess I’m in a wheelchair now. Like, forever.”

Marta had no clue what to say to ease Shanice’s obvious pain, put simply put a soothing hand on Shanice’s forearm.

Shanice cleared her throat, obviously emotional, and said, “Elizabeth wants me to be more independent.”

“And that’s a good thing, right?”

Shanice nodded and then leaned to the side to open the drawer on her bedside table. She pulled out a folded piece of what looked like white printer paper.

“Sorry, I couldn’t get a real card.” Shanice handed the homemade card to Marta.

The drawing on the cover made Marta cry instantly. Shanice had used colored pencils to draw Marta in a superhero costume holding a brown blob that sort of looked like Bernard, the fabulous musk ox. Shanice had drawn a red cape and everything. It even looked like Marta. Over the top, it said, “Happy Birthday to my friend Marta.”

“This is so sweet. Thank you.” Marta smiled at Shanice, completely unashamed of the tears in her eyes.

“Open it up.”

Marta opened the card and inside was a drawing of Shanice holding a heart in her outstretched hands. Beside her was another drawing of the famous Bernard. “You are such a good artist.”

“Pfft,” Shanice said wide-eyed. “I like coloring and drawing. It’s soothing.”

"I get that," Marta said. "Oh, what's this?" She pulled out a loose rectangular piece of paper and turned it over. She read out loud, "The bearer of this coupon gets free coffee at Rikki's Coffee Shop anytime she wants." Shanice had signed it underneath and had drawn several cups of steaming coffee on the coupon. "I will always treasure this," Marta said. "And we'll definitely go get coffee as soon as you 'break outta this joint,' as Nora says."

Shanice chuckled, but underneath, Marta heard the fear. She wanted to console her young friend but decided it could wait. Instead, she challenged Shanice to a Bullshit rematch.

~~~

The next day Marta felt rushed when she left Shanice. She didn't want to leave. They'd been having such a good time playing cards and touring the Chrysalis Center together. They even played a couple of online games together now that Shanice had a phone.

It was funny, Shanice had scrolled past the war-type games and didn't even ask Marta if she wanted to play them. Maybe she didn't like those kinds of games, or maybe she sensed that Marta would have an aversion to them, which she did. They still hadn't talked about the incident in the rec room the day before, but Marta felt that maybe they should at some point.

"Another date?" Shanice asked innocently.

Marta nodded. There was no sense lying to her, especially because the Bullshit game had already proven that she was a lousy liar. She didn't elaborate on the date and promised to come by every day after work. She even promised to take the day off from work when Shanice was released.

Back home, Marta got Nora's room ready for playtime and fed the cats, although the outside kitty wasn't around again. The food kept disappearing, so maybe she was still hanging out. Hopefully, she was okay.

~~~

Marta figured Jessica had stood in the corner long enough. "Have you thought about what you've done, bad girl?" Of course, neither of them had discussed the supposed transgression. It was enough to say that Jessica had been a bad girl and needed to be punished.

A slow nod came from the nude woman standing in the corner. Well, nude except for the black high heels she'd put on to entice Marta. And, yes, it was working.

"Hmm," Marta grunted. "I doubt that. Come here." When Jessica hesitated, presumably because she didn't want to be punished, Marta barked, "Now!"

Jessica moved quickly and stood in front of Marta, who was sitting in an armless chair. Jessica's pinky was in her mouth as if she were the epitome of innocence. Something about the coquettish pose skyrocketed Marta's arousal. "Over my lap," she said simply. Once Jessica was positioned face down and balanced on Marta's lap, Marta rubbed the fleshy, smooth ass cheeks presented to her. "So lovely," she said. Being the mean disciplinarian was just an act, and every now and then, she let Jessica talk her into a spanking, but that's where she drew the line. Marta was not into impact. The first time she'd given a spanking was in Iraq at a lover's request. It had released a lot of tension for both of them, but it wasn't something Marta wanted to continue.

Marta lifted her hand and hesitated. She didn't like striking another human being but knew Jessica wanted this. Without warning, Marta brought her hand down on the fleshiest part of Jessica's ass. Jessica yelped as she jumped at the impact.

"Nice," Marta said and rubbed lightly with her hand. "I left a nice handprint on this side. Let me match it." She smacked Jessica on the other side. A similar yelp emerged, but Marta simply chuckled knowingly.

"I love the number five," Marta said, smacking one cheek five times and then the other five more. "Don't you just love the number five?" Marta asked as she rubbed the reddening skin.

"Mm hmm," Jessica said.

"Color?"

"Green, Ma'am," Jessica said.

"Ten just became my favorite number." Marta gave the promised number of smacks and then increased the tally until her arm was about to give way. Jessica's ass was fiery red, so Marta reached for the silk cloth on the bookshelf and ran it gently over Jessica's throbbing skin.

"Mmm." Jessica moaned again. Oh, yes, the schoolteacher was aroused.

Marta wrapped her arms around Jessica's back and pulled her up as she stood. "Face down on the bed," she instructed but helped Jessica lay down. Marta's voice sounded harsh, but she was truly a caring Domme and never wanted her subs to be hurt—physically or emotionally.

Marta stuck her face close to Jessica's. "Bad girls sometimes get a moment to regroup."

Jessica's eyes fluttered open. Marta smiled. Oh, yes, her sub was heading into that dreamy subspace they all craved. Good. It was the perfect time for the tie.

"Turn over," Marta ordered, and Jessica did so. The moment she put weight on her pulsing buttocks, she inhaled sharply. "Does that hurt?"

Jessica shook her head.

"You know what happens to bad girls who also lie?" Marta didn't wait for an answer. "They get tied up." She showed Jessica the coil of red silk rope. Marta had purposely gotten red because Jessica said that was her favorite color. And Marta had purposely gotten silk because it was sexy, and she didn't want her subs to have rope burns.

Marta slid off Jessica's shoes and placed them gently on the floor out of the way. She had Jessica raise one leg so her knee was in the air and the heel of her foot was near her sore butt cheek. Jessica was really flexible for a big girl, which was a good thing.

Marta doubled over the rope and tied a single-column tie on Jessica's ankle, making sure she left space so the rope didn't bind. Unbidden, Marta thought of Shanice. She would never be able to do something like this with Shanice. She must have groaned or something because Jessica stirred and said, "You okay, Ma'am?"

"Yeah," was all Marta could say. She wrapped the rope around Jessica's thigh and shin several times, ran a series of knots down the wraps, and then snaked the end of the rope through to the other side. She repeated the pattern of knots up the other side until spiraling the ends around the wraps making everything snug. She quickly checked the tightness, redid her final spiral, and then tied it off. It wasn't pretty, but it was a decent tie. A Shibari expert, she was not.

"Color?"

"Mmm," Jessica said.

"Color?" Marta asked again with a laugh. She loved subs in sub-space.

"Green."

A soft clearing of Marta's throat got the desired result.

"Ma'am," Jessica amended. "Green, Ma'am."

"Better."

Marta tied the other leg in the same manner, checked Jessica's color, and then pushed her creations apart, revealing Jessica's very wet center. Marta trailed a light finger from Jessica's knee up her thigh. She did the same on the other side. "Anything I want," Marta murmured.

"Yes, please, Ma'am," Jessica pleaded. "Anything."

"Be careful what you wish for." Marta lightly smacked Jessica's wide-open sex, making her yelp and whimper. Marta smacked her again and then split the furrow with the fingers on one hand before penetrating Jessica with two fingers from her other. Marta pistoned in and out slowly. Jessica arched her hips in time to Marta's rhythm. Soft moans told Marta that Jessica was close. She could tease and deny, but she decided not to. Sometimes you didn't have to be a complete sadist.

Much to Jessica's dismay, Marta stopped pumping, but that was okay. Her reward for being such a good "bad girl" was coming right up. Marta leaned down and kissed Jessica's mons, but she didn't dally there. Her tongue swirled around the swollen pearl, budding for Marta's caresses. Marta obliged and pumped her fingers again. She added a third finger and then pulled her tongue back so her lips could find the clit. She sucked rhythmically in time with her pumping. It was hard to stay latched on because Jessica's hips were undulating.

"I'm cumming," Jessica shrieked and bucked so hard she threw Marta off her clit, but Marta was ex-military and had a task to accomplish. She dove back in and continued sucking until Jessica's hand on her head moved her away.

Jessica's hips stopped moving, and the longest, most satisfied sigh

Marta had ever heard permeated the room. Marta kissed Jessica's mons again and then moved lower to check the tightness of the ropes. Still snug but loose enough.

She let Jessica doze for a few moments and took a swig of water. She'd make sure Jessica had some too. While she sat in the chair watching her lover doze, she tried to imagine this tie on Shanice. Could she do the initial tie near the stump? No, no, that would probably be too sensitive there. She made a mental note to ask Shanice if her stumps were sensitive. Maybe they were numb. Did they hurt?

A long sigh from the woman on the bed broke off Marta's thoughts. She made Jessica sit up and have a sip or two of water. Marta made sure she didn't need a break or need to use the restroom and then asked the question that had been burning in her brain since Jessica had green-lighted their next activity.

Marta picked up the colorful needles made explicitly for erotic play and asked, "Arms? Thighs? Butt? Belly? Or my personal favorite, breasts?"

Jessica's eyes went wide. She'd never done needle play before. "I want to watch, but I'm scared. Maybe butt, and you can take a picture?"

"Good choice," Marta said enthusiastically. She unwrapped the rope from Jessica's legs and asked her to stretch out and flex. Her color was still green, and Marta told her to flip over on her belly. "I'll take pics with your phone, so you can see what I've done."

Marta was going to do a simple design. One that didn't take too many needles. Jessica was a newb to it all anyway.

"Ma'am?" Jessica said, almost shyly.

"Yes?"

"Can I service you? Sometime tonight? Maybe after this?"

"We'll see," Marta said. "I'm not sure bad girls get what they want, though."

"No, Ma'am," Jessica said, sounding dejected. Marta would have played Jessica's tone off as role-playing, but there seemed to be something else underneath it. She'd ask later. Maybe. Marta wasn't big into sharing feelings.

"Ready?"

"Yes, Ma'am," Jessica said and blew out a sigh.

Marta excused herself to wash her hands and face. Not because she didn't enjoy Jessica's essence but because she didn't want to introduce any chance of bacteria into the needle sites.

When she returned, she said, "Relax for me," and swabbed Jessica's right butt cheek with alcohol. She preferred using the pre-injection swabs, which were 70% IPA alcohol. She took out the first needle, loosened it from the cap, and then pinched a small piece of skin. She used the smallest diameter needles she could find in each color to ensure Jessica's comfort. She almost laughed out loud. Comfort during needle play—that was a good one. She positioned the needle upward and punched all the way through the pinched skin.

"Eek," Jessica yelped but followed it with, "Green, Ma'am."

"Good," Marta said and took a picture with Jessica's camera. "No longer a needle virgin."

Jessica chuckled when Marta showed her the picture. It was a nice sound. She liked sharing this with someone. She'd taken one needle on a dare in the Army but decided she'd much rather give than receive.

Five needles were all she felt Jessica could handle, but maybe next time, they could do a more intricate design than the simple spiral she'd done using the colors of the rainbow. Marta took a few pics using Jessica's phone and then took one with her own phone, making sure Jessica gave the green light for her to do so.

"Feels weird, Ma'am," Jessica said drowsily.

"Looks awesome, though," Marta said. "Now it's time to take them out. I have to pinch each spot again, so get ready for that. And then I'll clean up the area."

As Marta worked on removing the needles, she couldn't help wondering if Shanice would like needle play. She grunted again. Why was she thinking about Shanice this way? Shanice was a good girl, probably not into kink at all. And maybe she wasn't even into women. No, wait. Marta remembered her saying something about not liking boys "like that." They'd held each other's gaze that day—the day Marta had rescued Bernard. Did it mean anything?

She shook off the thoughts and slapped Jessica on the other ass cheek. "You can clean this again when you get home," Marta said.

"Yes, Ma'am." Jessica rolled over on the bed. Her eyes went wide, and she rolled onto her side.

"Sore?"

"No." Jessica grinned and amended, "Yes, Ma'am. More from the spanking, I think."

Before Marta could respond, Jessica abruptly got up from the bed and put on the robe Marta always had ready for her. "Ma'am?"

"Yes?" Marta sat on the edge of the bed while Jessica stood before her. She gestured for Jessica to kneel, which she did, but then leaned to the side so her knees would get a break. That was an allowable modification since Jessica couldn't kneel directly on her knees. Marta handed Jessica the phone to check out the pictures.

The look of astonishment on Jessica's face was reward enough. "They look so good, Ma'am." She looked up at Marta with adoration. "Thank you for talking me into this." Jessica's soft expression changed. "Ma'am?"

"What's on your mind?"

"Can I please you somehow?"

Marta hesitated. "You already have."

Jessica nodded and looked down. "I, uh." It seemed like she'd wanted to say something more and then said, "Well, first of all, happy belated birthday."

"Thank you."

"And this is shitty of me to do this so close to your birthday, but…." Jessica looked up at Marta. "I kind of met someone."

"Oh," Marta said. She hadn't been expecting a break-up speech.

Jessica cringed, and silent tears started. "I'm so sorry. I love you. I love what we do, but…"

"I understand," Marta said. "I've loved our time together, too. We've had some good times, haven't we?"

Jessica chuckled through her tears and said, "Yes, Ma'am. I don't want you to hate me."

"Pfft," Marta scoffed. "I could never hate you, Jessica." She reached down and lifted Jessica's chin so she could make direct eye contact. "I can't give you everything you need. We both know that. I hope your new person can."

"I don't know that yet, but I didn't want to cheat on you with her. Or on her with you. Oh, gosh, does that make any sense?"

"You are an amazing woman, Jessica." Marta reached down to stroke her cheek, brushing away some tears. "Come up here." She scooched over to make room for Jessica to sit beside her on the bed. She pulled her into her arms, something she rarely did, and said, "It has been my honor to share these intimate times with you. You deserve someone who can give you all you need."

"Thank you, Ma'am," Jessica said, still clearly tearful.

"And if this new person hurts you in any way, I will hunt her down and do whatever you want me to do with her."

Jessica laughed and said, "Thank you, Ma'am."

Marta released her hold on her now-former sub and stood up. "I'll be in the kitchen. You go ahead and get cleaned up. Come say goodbye one last time, okay?"

Jessica nodded, took an emotional breath, and said, "I'm so sorry, Ma'am. And, yes, I'll say goodbye before I head out."

~~~

Marta had been stoic the night Jessica ended their relationship, but as the week wore on, a subtle sadness took over her heart. She hadn't loved Jessica but had gotten used to their closeness. They'd wished each other well but made no declarations of staying in touch. And that was just the way Marta wanted things.

It was Sunday, an entire week had passed since the breakup, and Marta was on her way to visit Shanice at Chrysalis. She was freshly showered and ready to make Shanice's last day at the center a good one. Shanice had gotten the cast off her arm on Wednesday, but the arm was still frail, and they didn't want her wheeling herself in the wheelchair just yet. Maybe Marta would push Shanice down the hallways really fast, making her giggle
~~~

with glee, only to be reprimanded by one of the staff, which may or may not have happened once before.

She pulled onto Kirkland Boulevard and knew that one thing was certain. She was going to make sure the rehabilitation center had set up Shanice's at-home physical therapy. Marta had helped Shanice in the evenings with the "homework" PT she was supposed to do but hoped that Shanice would be okay once she got settled back at Miss Macie's. And even though Shanice said they'd arranged transport for her for tomorrow, Marta was going to follow behind to get her settled inside. Having a bedroom on the second floor was simply not going to work, and Marta needed to make sure her friend had all she needed.

Because, like Jessica, Marta was getting ready to bow out. Marta was going to take Jessica's departure from her life as a sign that it was time to get back to hibernating and being the hermit she wanted to be. But she had to make sure Shanice was okay first.

When she pulled up to the center, dread hit her chest. Was that Shanice? Outside? Sitting in a wheelchair with her suitcase and a bag by her side? What was going on?

She pulled into the first open spot and leaped out of the pickup.

"Hey, hey," Marta said. "What's happening?"

Shanice shrugged. "We counted wrong. They kicked me out today. And the transport people never came."

Marta's head was whirling. "C'mon, let's go back inside and get some answers."

The answers they were given through the receptionist's window confirmed what Shanice had said. This was her last day. She had to move out. Transport canceled, they were told, saying they weren't authorized to bring a patient to a residential household or some such bullshit about liability. Marta wanted to blow a gasket but knew that would be counter productive. Instead, she calmly verified that the Center had Shanice's correct address and phone number. She verified the physical therapy sessions and demanded a phone number to verify with the actual PT company. The receptionist was getting agitated by Marta's insistence, but Marta didn't care one bit. She'd been there and done that while caring for her mother, and someone else's irritation didn't phase her when it came to protecting someone in her care.

Once satisfied, Marta said, "Ready to go, kid?"

"How?"

"I'm your transport." Marta tried to sound cheerful.

"She can't take that wheelchair," the receptionist said.

"How is she going to—" Marta stopped her question mid-ask. She looked down at Shanice and grinned. "No worries. This one's a piece of shit, anyway. We'll get you a better one. Okies?"

Shanice looked down. "Okay."

Marta's heart squeezed. Good lord, could this kid not catch a break? Apparently not. She over-politely thanked the receptionist and said she'd leave the wheelchair under the overhang after she loaded her friend in the pickup. She'd said the word *friend* deliberately so Shanice would understand that Marta was not going to abandon her in her time of need.

Once Marta had Shanice buckled up in the pickup and her stuff was in the truck bed, she said, "Couple questions before we head out. Do you have Bernard?"

"Yes, of course."

"Do you have your wallet? Keys to the house? Phone?"

"Yes, to all three."

"Good, because I never want to return to this place again." Marta laughed, trying to keep the mood light. "Look at us breaking you outta this joint." Marta's heart sang when she heard Shanice giggle softly in the passenger seat.

Chapter 12

Shanice

Marta pulled her pickup into a strip mall parking lot. "Dang it," she said and looked at Shanice. "I was hoping that medical supply place would still be open."

"There's a thrift store near my house. They have medical supplies, and I think they stay open late on Sundays."

Marta nodded and then gave Shanice a look that said so many things. It said she was determined to get Shanice what she needed and that she wasn't going to give up at the first setback. Shanice hoped that was true.

They pulled up to the standalone thrift store, and Shanice was embarrassed. Although she shopped there all the time, she pictured it through Marta's eyes and realized what a dump it was. The building looked like it should have been torn down years ago, but they had good stuff inside, and if you looked hard enough, you could find real bargains.

"Hmm," Marta said once she parked the pickup. She didn't turn off the engine, though. "I don't see any of those electric scooter things like the grocery store has, so maybe I should just carry you in, and we'll pick one out together."

Shanice was mortified. "No," she said quickly. "Can you go in? I can't…"

"Copy that," Marta said softly. "I understand." She left the pickup running and hopped out. It was not lost on Shanice that she would never be able to *hop out* of anything ever again. Marta was halfway to the store entrance when she turned around and called, "Keep the doors locked. And don't let anybody steal you."

Shanice laughed and threw her a thumbs up. There wasn't much activity in the lonely parking lot late on a Sunday afternoon anyway. No danger of a double amputee getting stolen. She watched with interest as Marta spoke with one of the workers who pointed toward the medical supply section in the back. Marta wasn't gone long and, in no time, was wheeling a newish-looking wheelchair to the pickup.

"Hey," Marta said, a little out of breath, "I know you're anxious to get home, but they have the cutest stuff in there." She opened the wheelchair and raised her eyebrows expectantly.

Shanice really did want to get home. She was anxious about so many things. Was Miss Macie okay? Why couldn't she reach Miss Macie's son on the phone? She couldn't even leave a voicemail for some reason. It was all very frustrating. Before she went too much further down that rabbit hole, she caught the waggle of Marta's eyebrows. Superheroes were hard to resist, weren't they?

Shanice had barely gotten the word "Okay," out of her mouth when Marta did a happy dance in the parking lot. She raced around and jumped into the pickup to turn off the engine. She jumped out again and flung open Shanice's door. Positioning the newly purchased wheelchair just so and double-checking to make sure the brakes were on, Marta put her arms out. "Ready?"

Shanice nodded and put an arm around Marta's shoulder. The movement had become familiar over the past two weeks since Marta had taken over most of the wheelchair transferring job from John at the Center.

Once in the chair, Shanice noticed that it was a lot sturdier than the ones at the Center.

"Good one, right?" Marta said. "I sat in all of them." She wheeled Shanice around the potholes and random debris and then used her back-in technique to re-enter the store since they didn't have automatic opening doors.

"We're closing in fifteen," one of the workers said.

"We'll be fast," Marta said and spun the wheelchair back around.

Shanice giggled. She loved when Marta did that. Her mirth was gone instantly when an unmistakable look of horror crossed the white middle-aged shopkeeper's face. The woman seemed transfixed on Shanice's stumps.

Marta didn't seem to notice and wheeled her toward a display of bags. "I thought you could use something like this for your wallet and stuff."

"So cute," Shanice said. It was kind of weird looking in the bin at eye level instead of standing height. Not that she was tall. On a good day, she could have claimed five-foot-one. Sitting made things different. She picked up a bag with Anna and Elsa from Frozen on it. Bernard would fit perfectly inside.

"I'm getting it for you," Marta said excitedly.

"I have my own money."

"It's no good here," Marta said with a laugh. She wheeled her to another section. This one had shirts hanging on racks. "I'm sorry, but I saw this shirt from across the store and thought you would look adorable in it. Is it your size?"

The t-shirt was a bit too girly and ruffly for Shanice's taste and kind of juvenile. But then again, an Anna and Elsa bag was kind of juvenile, too, wasn't it. "It's my size, but how about this one?" Shanice pointed to a Cincinnati Reds fan shirt. It was red and looked just like a uniform jersey.

"Yessss," came the enthusiastic reply. "Small okay?"

Shanice nodded.

"I love the Reds," Marta said. "Let's go to a game sometime, okay?" Marta threw the shirt at Shanice, who caught it deftly and placed it on her lap with the bag.

Shanice wasn't sure where Marta's enthusiasm was coming from, but it was fun.

"Okay," Shanice said as she perused the other t-shirts.

"Ooh," Marta said, "look. Shorts to match."

Shanice nodded. She was catching Marta's fervor. "Can we?" She pointed toward the haircare products. It had been forever since she'd been able to properly take care of herself.

Marta wheeled her over at lightning speed. The clock was ticking, after all.

Shanice couldn't remember what products she already had at home, so she bought a nice variety to restock.

Once they checked out and were back in the pickup, Shanice said, "You didn't have to pay for all of that. If I'd known—"

"I wanted to do that for you," Marta interrupted.

"At least let me pay you back for the wheelchair," Shanice said, hoping Marta heard how serious she was about that.

"Okay. Later, though." Marta was about to pull out of the space but then turned to look at Shanice. "That woman was rude. I want you to know that. Some people will be like that, but it won't be everyone. Just remember that she doesn't know you. The real you. The *you* that I've been getting to know. The happy, fun, extremely bright young woman who I accidentally met in a hospital."

Shanice looked down. It was a lot to take in. "You saw her looking at me, didn't you?"

"Yes."

"Maybe I'm some kind of monster now."

Marta undid her seatbelt and turned to face Shanice. She reached for one of Shanice's hands and held it with both of her own. "Negative." She took a breath as if gathering her thoughts and said, "You are not a monster. But the way I look at it, you are allowed to be sad about your new situation. Who wouldn't be? But you also have to think about it like a new challenge. I know it's not something anyone would have ever signed up for, but it's your reality now. So, when people are rude like that, remember it says more about them than you."

"That makes sense," Shanice said. She'd have to think more about it. "You're a wise superhero."

Marta laughed. She squeezed Shanice's hand and let go. "Okay, my lady, it's time for me to get you home."

Shanice gave her directions even though Marta already knew the way. And even though Marta tried to keep the mood upbeat by pointing out landmarks, stores, and restaurants, the ride over was quiet on Shanice's end. Several times in the past, Marta had said she wanted to see Shanice settled. What was the other word? Secure, maybe? Shanice couldn't remember, but what that meant to Shanice was that Marta was going to leave once Shanice got home. Maybe that's what the shopping spree was all about—parting gifts. *See you later, alligator. I bought you a cool T-shirt, and now I'm not obligated to ever see you again.* At least, that's what Shanice imagined Marta was saying in her head.

"You okay?" Marta asked as they neared the house.

"Sure," Shanice said, knowing her tone betrayed her true feelings.

"Oh, shit," Marta said, and Shanice looked up.

"What?" Shanice leaned forward. There was a For Sale sign plunked into the front lawn.

"No panicking," Marta said and put a hand out. She pulled into the driveway. "There's a lock box on the front door, but your key should work." Shanice took off her seatbelt, but Marta said, "Hang on. Give me the key, and let me make sure it still works, okay?"

"It should," Shanice said, confused. What was going on?

Marta went up to the front door and tried the lock with Shanice's key. She called back, "Are you sure this is the front door key? It won't even go in."

"I'm sure," Shanice said. "Try the others if you want." Maybe Marta had tried the wrong one. The only other keys she had on the ring were the key to her room upstairs and the one to her desk at Johnson Tech.

Marta came back wearing the bad news on her face. "Does this key unlock a back door?"

"I don't think so."

"Mind if I try?"

"Have at it," Shanice said, unsure how Marta was going to get into the small backyard. When Marta leaped up, grabbed the top of the shadowbox fence, and then flipped over, Shanice's mouth dropped open. Marta was a superhero, all right. Shanice would never have been able to do that, even with feet.

In no time, Marta was back. She shook her head. "Negative," she said and got back in the pickup. "Let's call that realtor." Marta had her phone out and was tapping in the numbers before Shanice could say a word. Marta left a message asking someone to please call her back as soon as possible about the house and that it didn't matter what time.

Shanice started crying. Why was she being punished like this? All she had wanted to do was go to a concert in Chicago. She'd only expected to be away for a few days. But days had turned into weeks, and in that time, she'd lost her feet, her home, and her stuff. Clothes could be replaced, and she had done just that many times in her life. But her new laptop and printers were in there. Those had cost her a lot of money. She'd already lost her car. And then there was that other thing. Receiving her birth certificate on her eighteenth birthday had nearly knocked her out. She hadn't known that she had one. And losing the certificate now seemed like the final blow. It felt like the last devastating straw in her stupid life because that certificate was the only link to the woman who gave birth to her. Her biological mother's name was on it. Shanice had searched countless times for the woman named Sophia Ward, but she'd never found her. She truly was an orphan.

She stopped crying and closed her eyes. When would the days of losing everything be over? Had Miss Macie or her son even tried to find her? Had Mrs. Washington or anyone at Johnson Tech tried to find her when she didn't show up at work?

"Well," came the soft voice from the driver's seat, "I guess you'll be staying with me tonight."

"No, just drop me at a motel or shelter." Shanice fake-smiled at Marta. Marta hadn't signed up for any of this.

"No fucking way," Marta said as if insulted. "Are you kidding me? You'll have your own room and everything. It even has a lock on it."

"I. Can't," Shanice said adamantly as Marta started the pickup.

"Why not?"

"You have ended up doing way more than you ever bargained for. I'm not going to be the stone around your neck, the charity case you can't get rid of."

"Hey," Marta said so sternly that Shanice jumped. "You don't get to tell me what I'm thinking or doing. Only I can. You are *not* a bother to me, Shanice."

"You just want me settled and secured away so that you can go back to your own life," Shanice said as calmly as she could. Marta's silence spoke volumes. "It's okay. I wouldn't want to be saddled with me in my predicament either." She pulled out her phone and hit up her Uber app.

"What are you doing?" Marta asked, trying to look at Shanice's screen.

"If you must know, I'm calling an Uber to drive me to a motel."

"Cancel it."

"No."

"Cancel. It." Marta said and glowered at her.

"Why? Tell me why I should impose upon you even longer than I already have." Shanice felt her face get hot.

Marta's face was also red. She was mad. That was okay. Shanice had seen a lot of angry people in her life. Marta was just one more. They stared each other down until a slight grin began to creep up Marta's face. "You're infuriating," Marta said with a chuckle.

"I know."

"Stubborn. Headstrong."

"Mm hmm," Shanice said. "Go on if you must."

"I betrayed your trust once. Honestly, I was scared of how close I was getting to you. Nora calls me a hermit, which I kind of am."

"And I'm going to let you get back to your solitude," Shanice said. It made sense. Easy peasy.

"I cannot, in good conscience, let you go off to a motel alone, Shanice." This Marta said softly. "Look, I've already taken tomorrow off. Mainly because I thought you were leaving Chrysalis tomorrow. So how about you stay at my house tonight, and tomorrow we'll get to the bottom of whatever's going on with this house thing. We'll get up at 0600 hours and call the realtor's office. If they don't answer, we'll go down there. Maybe we can stop at Rikki's to grab a couple of coffees on the way, but we'll get to the bottom of it."

Shanice didn't want to delay Marta's departure from her life any more than she already had, but all of that made sense.

"What do you say, kid?" Marta asked. "Snowball will love you."

Shanice's face lit up. She had forgotten that Marta had a kitty cat. "Okay."

Marta scoffed good-naturedly. "Oh, so you'll come to the house for Snowball but not for me." She pulled the pickup out of the driveway. "I see how it is." Marta was teasing, that was clear, but Shanice still felt guilty that she had to inconvenience the woman who had helped her for so long.

"Maybe I should call the realtor tomorrow and pretend to be interested in buying the house," Shanice offered. She'd said it as a means of letting Marta know that she accepted the plans, but it was also a kind of olive branch, too. She liked Marta and hated ticking her off like that.

"That's kind of devious," Marta said. "See? I knew you were a fart smeller. I mean, a smart feller."

Shanice burst out laughing at Marta's bad Dad joke. "That was kind of funny."

"Stick with me, kid," Marta said. "I got a million of 'em."

Marta's house was nice, and she was shocked to see a ramp from the driveway into the house. Marta didn't explain it, but it was evident by the wear and tear that the ramp had been there for a long time. The house looked nice, but it also looked kind of neglected, like it needed some TLC. Miss Macie's house had the same look. Shanice had always done her best to keep the front and back lawns mowed and some flowers planted out front, but those days were done, apparently.

"You have a nice house," Shanice said as Marta seamlessly backed her in the front door. Things were starting to come into focus. Marta must have taken care of someone in a wheelchair. A partner? A parent? A landlady like Miss Macie? Nora maybe?

The moment they were in the house, Shanice noticed the lifeless and tired furniture. They looked how she felt. She wasn't judging. Who in the world was she to judge when this amazing woman had offered up her home to the homeless.

"Do you have to go to the restroom?"

"Not yet," Shanice said.

"Okay, let me show you your room. It was Nora's old room. The sheets are clean, and it's always ready for company."

Company. Something dawned on Shanice. "It's Sunday. Tonight's your date night. Oh, no. Marta."

"Not anymore. She broke it off with me last weekend."

"I'm so sorry," Shanice said and touched her chest. "You didn't say. You didn't even let on."

"Thanks for being so concerned about my love life, kid, but I wasn't, you know, in love with her. She met someone new, so whatever. Life goes on."

They turned the corner, and Marta wheeled her through an open door. "We had all the doors widened so my mom could get into every room with her chair."

"Oh," was all Shanice could think of saying. She didn't want to pry and ask why Marta's mom had been in a wheelchair, but it now explained why Marta seemed at ease with them.

"Snowball," Marta said, pointing to the cat on the bed. "Sorry, she always liked Nora's room."

"May I pet her?"

Marta wheeled her close to the cat and instructed her to put a hand out. Snowball, curious as ever, came over and sniffed Shanice's outstretched hand. Shanice didn't dare move so as not to scare the fluffy white cat.

"She's beautiful," Shanice said but didn't look away.

"Yeah, she's a fluffball. Probably needs brushing."

Snowball sniffed higher up Shanice's arm and leaned over the bed to sniff the arm of the wheelchair. One paw went onto Shanice's thigh, and Shanice held her breath. "Marta?" She wasn't sure what was happening.

"She's used to people in wheelchairs, so she's okay with it."

Shanice must have passed the Snowball test because before she knew it, the cat was circling in her lap. "What in the world is she doing?" Shanice asked. She'd interacted with the dumpster cats all those years ago, but that was about it. This was new and weird.

"She likes you," Marta said with a chuckle. "She's trying to find a comfortable place to nap."

It must have been the word nap that caused Shanice to yawn. "Oh, my goodness. I think I'm tired, but I need to…Sorry."

"No worries," Marta said, picking the cat off Shanice's lap. "She'll probably nap with you if that's okay."

"I'd love that," Shanice said. That was the best thing she'd heard in a long time. Having a cat was still on her list of things to accomplish. Maybe this one night with Snowball would be a good trial run.

"You have evening PT to do tonight, right?" Marta asked as she pushed Shanice to the bathroom.

"Yes, but Elizabeth said I shouldn't put much weight on this arm yet." She pointed to her discolored arm that recently had the cast removed.

"Got it," Marta said. "So, every time you have to go, I'll be there."

"Sorry," Shanice said as Marta lifted her onto the bowl.

"I'm going to lift you a bit so you can pull down the shorts and drawers."

Shanice laughed at Marta's use of the word 'drawers.' "You and Nora say funny things," Shanice said.

"We're birds of a feather, I guess."

Once Shanice was situated on the bowl, Marta excused herself to give Shanice privacy. Shanice did her business and wished she could reach the sink from where she sat so she could wash her face and hands. She called for Marta, who came back in, helped her get the shorts and 'drawers' back up, and then plunked her in the chair. She wheeled Shanice to the sink, where Shanice was surprised to find she could reach the faucets. Yay for small victories. "My toothbrush is in my suitcase."

"Oh, here," Marta said and opened a linen closet. "Just borrow one of these." She pulled out five unopened toothbrushes, all different colors. "Pick."

"Red," Shanice announced. "For the Reds."

"I'm glad you like baseball. Maybe there's a game on tonight."

Marta handed her the red toothbrush and then returned for a washcloth, hand towel, and bath towel for Shanice to use. "Feel free to root around in here for anything you need."

"No, no, I won't need anything."

"Well, in case you do." Marta headed toward the door. "When you're done, try wheeling yourself out. I'll be in your room. If it hurts at all, either arm, call for me. Okay?"

"Okay," Shanice said. Wheel herself? Was that wise? Elizabeth said she shouldn't. But grabbing the wheel and pushing it along wasn't exactly weight-bearing, was it? Maybe a little bit?

Shanice washed her hands and face using the gentle soap on Marta's sink. So much better than hospital soap. She brushed her teeth and put the toothbrush in the holder next to the blue one that was already there. Was that Marta's? Something weird pinged her heart as she looked at them side by side. She shook her head and sighed. Nope. This was just for one night. That's it. Superheroes weren't girlfriends; it was best to get that notion out of her head before it took hold. After her nap, she'd look up homeless shelters and group homes for the disabled because she seemed to be both of those now.

With shaking hands, she reached down the sides of the chair and found the wheels. She tightened her grip and, when nothing hurt, pushed forward. Still good. She had to make precise adjustments as she maneuvered through the open doorway, but she did it. One doorway down. One more to go. She took the turn too sharply and had to readjust. Marta sat on an armless chair, grinning. "You're not going to help me?"

Marta shook her head and seemed amused.

"Fine." Shanice would show her. She backed away from the doorway, readjusted her approach, and confidently smacked into the doorframe.

Marta burst out laughing. "I need to get more house insurance. Try again."

Shanice sighed in frustration but did as challenged. This time she made it through without damaging anything. She didn't even scrape her knuckles this time.

"How do your arms feel? Any pain?"

"No pain. They feel good."

"Excellent."

It was then that Shanice noticed Bernard. He was on the bed waiting for her. Marta had gone out to the pickup and brought all her stuff inside. The suitcase and all of her things were in the room. "Thank you. And thank you for rescuing him." *And me*, she added in her mind, not daring to say it out loud.

Marta simply nodded and stood up to help her get onto the bed. And then, lickety split, Shanice was pulled out of her shorts and T-shirt and into her sleeping shirt.

Snowball was at her side instantly, circling to find a spot near Shanice's side. "Honestly," Marta said, "I've never seen her take to someone that fast."

"Must be my fabulous charm," Shanice said sarcastically, making Marta chuckle.

"Let me get you some water."

"Thank you." Shanice snuggled down in the bed. "This bed is so comfy."

"Glad you like it," Marta said, heading out the door.

Shanice tentatively put her hand on the cat's white fur. When the cat started purring, it startled Shanice, but she knew it was a sign of contentment. She'd watched enough cat videos on her phone to know that.

Marta came back in with a cup of water. The cup had a lid with a built-in straw. "Just in case you knock it over," Marta said, gesturing to the lid.

"Good idea." Shanice yawned and stretched her whole body. It felt good. For some reason, she felt safe here with Marta. And Snowball.

"I'm going to sit out back for a while and have a beer. This outdoor kitty sometimes comes around, but I haven't seen her in a while."

"Okay."

"Yell if you need anything. I'll hear through the screen door."

Shanice's eyes were closed already. "Mm hmm," was all she could manage.

When Shanice woke a while later, it was already dark. What time was it? She reached over to the nightstand and found her phone—nine at night. "Oh, my God," she said out loud.

"Oh, are you awake?" came Marta's far away voice.

"Morning," Shanice said with a laugh. It was far from morning.

Marta was at the door. "We have a situation."

Oh, no. Shanice closed her eyes. This was a Mama Deborah moment, wasn't it? Shanice fully expected to hear the words, "Circumstances have changed. You do understand, don't you?" And then, she would be packed up and dropped off…somewhere.

"The cat in the backyard," Marta said with the weirdest expression.

"What happened?"

"She…she had kittens." Marta bopped up and down, clearly nervous.

"She wasn't fat, she was pregnant. What do we do?"

Shanice sat up, surprised that she had the strength to do so and that nothing hurt. "Where are the kittens? Where's the mama cat?" She pictured the poor kittens dirty and crying out in a ditch somewhere. She flung the covers off and spun around so her legs dangled off the side of the bed. She was just about to stand up when Marta rushed over.

"Whoa, whoa, whoa, kid," Marta said, knocking Shanice's forward motion back. "That would have been a problem."

For just a moment, in the wake of the kitten news, Shanice had forgotten. She had forgotten that she had no feet, that she couldn't just stand up and walk. She had forgotten that she was now beholden to other people for help. And right now, she was beholden to Marta. She fell back, embarrassed.

"I'm sorry," Shanice said.

"For what?" Marta asked. "It was a natural thing to do. We'll figure something out later, so you don't careen off the bed and hurt yourself. Hey, do you have to use the bathroom?"

Shanice shook her head.

"Copy that." Marta positioned the wheelchair, and then Shanice allowed herself to be transferred into it. "We have to figure out what to do with the mama cat and her kittens."

Marta took off for the door, and Shanice couldn't help thanking her lucky stars that Marta hadn't thrown her out.

Chapter 13

Marta

Mama Cat, which Shanice officially named her, was amazingly compliant and allowed Marta to scoop her and the three kittens into the laundry basket to be brought inside. All of them, except Snowball, were now in Marta's mother's bedroom, making a cozy nest for Mama Cat to care for her babies. Shanice had suggested the bottom dresser drawer, which Marta heartily agreed with, except that she'd had to move her mother's clothes out.

Shanice had given Marta a soulful look when she realized that the clothes weren't Marta's but belonged to Marta's mother, who had died two years before, even though it felt like yesterday. Marta willed herself not to get emotional about her mother's things. Mama Cat needed the drawer.

"Hey, Mama Cat," Shanice said softly to the all-black cat who was licking one of her kittens. "You seem happy here."

"I can't believe I thought she was fat." Marta shook her head. "Let me get food and water for her. And I guess I'll set up a litter box."

"Yeah, that seems important," Shanice said with a laugh.

Once the essentials were laid out for the new mother and her babies, Marta suggested they go into the kitchen and get something to eat. Marta fixed a couple of turkey sandwiches and offered soup which Shanice accepted gratefully.

"Thank you for taking me and Mama Cat in today," Shanice said with an embarrassed grin.

Marta laughed. "At least you weren't about to have kittens, too."

The grin on Shanice's face was different this time. She seemed a bit more relaxed than when they first got to the house. Maybe the distraction of the cats was doing it. Marta didn't care. It was nice.

Shanice pulled out her phone and did some research. "Okay, this reputable-looking website suggests we keep the door closed between Mama Cat and Snowball. They can sniff under the door and get to know each other that way for a while." Shanice looked up and narrowed her eyes. "I assume you'll be keeping Mama Cat?"

Marta's jaw dropped open. Her eyes darted from left to right. When Shanice giggled, Marta moved her eyes even more comically. "I hadn't thought that far ahead."

Shanice raised an eyebrow.

"I guess I am." Marta wasn't about to deny that eyebrow anything.

"This site says to get the new cat checked out for diseases and stuff before introducing them. You don't want to compromise Snowball's health accidentally."

"Good point," Marta said. She wouldn't have thought to do that.

"And, just so you know, I've had all my shots." Shanice's grin was priceless, making Marta burst out laughing.

"Well, that's good to know," Marta quipped back.

As they ate, Marta noticed something odd about Shanice's eating habits. Shanice always leaned forward and wrapped her left arm around her plate and bowl as if guarding the food. She also ate very quickly. While in the Chrysalis Center, Shanice had confided in Marta that she'd been a foster child in and out of homes and institutions. Marta knew there was a lot more Shanice wasn't telling, but Marta wasn't going to pry. She wondered if the eating behaviors were coping techniques Shanice had developed growing up as a foster. Had Shanice been food insecure? Marta made a mental note to tell Shanice to help herself to any and everything she had in the fridge, pantry, and cupboards.

"Hey, I'm a bit wired," Marta said, "and you just got up. What do you say I teach you Gin Rummy?"

"No, thanks. I don't drink."

It took Marta a few seconds, but then she got the joke. "Har-dee har har," Marta said, enunciating every syllable like her father used to do. "You game?"

Shanice nodded and then looked at her phone. “No messages from Reggie.”

“Miss Macie’s son?”

“Yeah.” Shanice’s relaxed mood was changing.

Marta leaped up and got the cards. “It’s time.”

“For gin?”

“Yep, but not yet. No cast means you can use that hand to learn the riffle shuffle.”

Marta took the cards out of the box and did the two-handed mix.

“My turn. My turn,” Shanice said gleefully, and Marta could have sworn Shanice was bouncing in her seat.

“Two equal-ish piles,” Marta instructed. “Yep. Fingers on the far side. Thumbs on the inside. Perfect. Top knuckle of your index finger on the—you got it.”

“I watched you.”

“You’re a smart little cookie, aren’t you?”

Shanice scoffed.

“Okay,” Marta continued. “Now bend them. Yep, that’s it. Bend them. And then—”

“Oof.” Shanice put down the cards. “Maybe another time, okay?” She rubbed her hand.

Marta made an ice pack for the hand, which Shanice took without protest. “I guess I’m still weak.”

“And fatigued. Gripping the wheel of the chair contributed, I think.”

Marta made a mental note not to push Shanice too much. Marta needed Shanice to be strong and independent as quickly as possible because life was going to be hard for her now.

“Where’d you go, Marta?”

“Mmm,” Marta murmured, gathering her thoughts. “Just thinking about all we need to do tomorrow.” She shuffled the cards and dealt them out while listing all their stops. Maybe one stop could be at Rikki’s coffee shop. Yes, yes. That might break up the touchy parts of the day. Should they go to Shanice’s job? It might be a good idea while Marta was there to drive and help.

"What exactly did you break?" Marta gestured to the arm that had been in a cast.

"Forearm and this upper bone. They had scientific names for both, but I forgot."

"So. nothing in your hand was broken?"

"Nope," Shanice said, wiggling her fingers. "It's just weak from disuse."

"Good to know."

After losing the fifth game in a row to Shanice, Marta threw her cards down in exasperation. "Are you sure you're not cheating?"

"Nope," Shanice said with a smirk. "Just had a good teacher. And you have so many tells that holding back the cards you needed was easy."

"Like I said before, you're a smart kid." *Savvy, too. Streetwise, maybe?* Marta stood up and gathered the now-empty sandwich plates. "We should check on Mama Cat."

"Can I?" Shanice said and gestured for the plates. "I want to help." She put them in her lap and then wheeled herself toward the sink. "This is such a nice kitchen. So homey."

Marta hadn't ever thought about it that way but was glad Shanice liked it.

Shanice pulled up next to the sink, and Marta was happy that Shanice could reach the faucet. She rinsed the plates and pointed toward the dishwasher. Marta nodded and beamed with pride for some reason when Shanice successfully put the plates in and closed the door.

Shanice turned in her chair and gushed, "You hung my card on the fridge?"

Marta felt her face get hot. She was probably turning a thousand different shades of red and purple. She had forgotten she'd done that. Not knowing what to say, she simply nodded.

"Aww, thank you. Mama Deborah used to do that with my cards and drawings." Shanice sighed.

Marta wondered who this 'Mama Deborah' was. When Shanice didn't elaborate, Marta grabbed the handles on the wheelchair and headed back through the living room toward Mama Cat's room.

"Ooh," Shanice said and pointed toward a side table next to the couch in the living room.

"The Rubik's cube?"

"Can I? Can I?"

"Shit, yeah." Marta retrieved the colorful puzzle. "Go for it."

Unbelievably, by the time they traversed the hall to Mama Cat's room, Shanice held up the finished cube.

"What the hell?" Marta said. "Show off."

"In Coding Club, we all had cubes and raced each other. I wasn't really that fast, but I wasn't the worst."

"Coding Club?"

"In high school. My ninth-grade math teacher, Mrs. Alvarez, was also the Coding Club adviser and suggested I join. I loved it. We learned computer programming, wrote applications, and built websites. I even wrote a game based on Rock, Paper, Scissors which some of the kids said was fun."

"Ahh, and so now you work for Johnson Tech doing computer stuff."

"Yep." Shanice took the finished Rubik's cube and, with lightning speed, messed it up.

Marta groaned as she opened Mama Cat's door. "I'll never get that thing back together."

"I'll teach you."

"Deal."

Marta was ecstatic to see that some of the food had been eaten and the litter box used. Mama Cat was back in the dresser drawer nursing her very vocal kittens. Marta felt a pang of something go through her as she watched Shanice's pleased smile and her gentle manner of speaking to the cats. That feeling she felt was something protective. A feeling she hadn't felt for a long time.

~~~

Unanswered calls to the realtor's office the next morning were a huge source of frustration for both of them. It was still early, Marta reasoned. They'd wait and call again in a little while. But as soon as the thought hit her
~~~

brainwaves, she rejected it. No. Something had to give. An idea was forming. Since Mama Cat and her kittens seemed to be doing well, and Snowball was curious but not overwrought at the new additions, Marta made a declaration. "We're heading to Cincinnati. Downtown."

"Why?" Shanice finished her last bite of cereal and dabbed at her mouth with a napkin. For some reason, that subtle movement mesmerized Marta.

She snapped out of it to say, "We're going to show up at that real estate office and demand answers." Marta got up and put their breakfast bowls in the sink. She'd take care of them later. "If we leave now, we'll arrive at 0830 hours when they open. According to the website, that is."

"Let's do it."

Thankfully there was no sign of Mrs. Pulaski when they got in the pickup. She didn't know how she was going to explain Shanice. Marta was cautious driving on the highway, not wanting to trigger anything for Shanice. Although Shanice said she had no memory of the accident or even leaving on her trip, Marta still wanted to be careful. The littlest thing could trigger a memory.

One car was in the parking lot when they pulled up, and Marta took that as a good sign. She pulled into a spot wishing she had a disabled parking permit to make it easier for Shanice, but it was what it was.

Once inside, they waited for the lone person they heard on the phone in a back office to hear their "hellos."

"Oh, hey," the impeccably dressed thirty-something-year-old white woman said. "I didn't expect anyone this morning. Do we have an appointment?"

"No, Ma'am, but we have questions," Marta said, taking the lead. Shanice didn't seem to object.

The woman stretched out her hand first to Marta and then to Shanice. "I'm Penni Pepper. Yep. That's my real name. Are you looking for a property?"

Marta explained their predicament as succinctly as she could without violating too much of Shanice's privacy.

Penni invited them to follow her to a small office in the back. "Let me check into this for you." Were all realtors this cheery? "Oh, can I get you something? Coffee? Water?"

"No, thank you," Marta said, answering for both of them. She was anxious to get this thing moving and get answers.

"The property is owned by, yep, Macie and Reginald Clark, as you said. I'm not the listing agent, but I can go ahead and call the Clarks and see what's up, okay?" Penni winked at them.

"They're mother and son," Shanice offered.

"Oh, thanks for the heads up. That would have been awkward." Penni punched some numbers on the office phone. "It's ringing," Penni said to them, looking hopeful. "Hi, is this Mr. Reginald Clark?"

Marta barely heard the realtor's following words because Shanice's hand had reached over and latched onto one of hers. Marta squeezed and sent Shanice a reassuring smile.

"Excellent," Penni said. "Here she is." Penni handed the corded phone over to Shanice.

"Hi. This is Shanice."

Marta desperately wanted to ask Penni to put the conversation on speakerphone but knew she couldn't. This was Shanice's life.

Marta listened intently to the one-sided conversation, ready to grab the phone and get answers, but then Shanice's expression softened as she said, "Louisville? Oh, good. Tell Miss Macie I said hello then. I tried to call so many times." There was a pause, and then she said, "So, it's okay if I get my boxes out today?"

'Boxes?' That made it sound like Shanice was about to be homeless.

Shanice nodded a few times. "Yes, sir. Thank you, sir. And I'm sorry that—" She nodded a few more times. "No, I'm fine." She nodded. "Yes, sir. Of course, if I'm ever in Louisville—Yes, I'll be sure to stop by and say hello. I'm just glad she's okay." Shanice returned the phone to the realtor, who spoke with Reginald for a few more moments. Marta didn't hear a thing because she was searching Shanice's face for clues.

Marta whispered, "Everything okay?"

Shanice nodded. "Miss Macie called him right away when I didn't come home the day I was supposed to. She's going to live with him at his house now in Louisville. All this time, I thought she was—" Shanice cried quietly behind her hands.

"But she's not," Marta said gently. "She's okay."

Penni cleared her throat and said, "I have a couple of showings this morning, but I can meet you up there this afternoon to let you in and get your things out. I'll just need ID to verify that you are who you say you are."

"Thank you," Shanice said, pulling out her driver's license.

Penni gave each of them a business card and took down Marta's and Shanice's cell phone numbers. "I've sold quite a few properties in Denton Heights recently. Funny how I keep getting pulled up there."

They said their goodbyes, and Penni assured them she'd put their appointment in her phone calendar for one o'clock so she wouldn't forget. And if anything changed, she would call.

Once back in the pickup, Marta turned to Shanice. "Looks like we're going to be roommates for a bit longer then."

"I'm sorry."

"Are you kidding? Who's going to help me with Mama Cat and those kittens? Who's going to teach me the Rubik's cube? Who's going to beat my ass in Gin Rummy?"

Shanice giggled, but Marta watched as conflicting emotions raced all over Shanice's face.

Marta didn't plan on making their situation permanent, but she could do the roommate thing for a while.

"Hey," Shanice said, "since we're all the way down here, can we go to this crystal shop?" She pulled a business card out of her wallet.

"'Celestial Light,'" Marta read off the card. "Why not? You're the navigator. Punch in the coordinates and tell me where to go."

"Tell you where to go?" Shanice's tone was playful.

Marta laughed. "Wait, that didn't come out right."

Despite the setback to Shanice's housing situation, Marta kept the conversation light on the way to the crystal shop. Lifting Shanice in and out of the wheelchair brought back memories of caring for her mother, but she was surprised that she was somehow okay with the memories.

Metaphysical new-age healing stuff wasn't exactly in Marta's wheelhouse, but Shanice was eating it up. The shop owners seemed to be particularly helpful, especially when Shanice was drawn to the crystals. She bought several, including an Agate for Mama Cat, which supposedly helped animals adapt to changes. Marta didn't understand any of it, but that was okay. She supposed Mama Cat would feel the love that had gone into the purchase. Shanice also pulled a few business cards off the wall of cards just before they left, with Marta's help, of course, and most were for Reiki healers. The Reiki healer in the hospital seemed to have helped Shanice, so why not? Whatever worked.

They got back in the pickup, buckled up, and were ready to head back to Denton Heights when Shanice said, "Wait. Before we go, I bought something for you. Kind of as a thank you for taking me in for a while. Thank you for getting my wheelchair. Thank you for feeding me and helping me get dressed this morning." She pulled out a pretty purple hexagonal crystal made into a necklace. "This is an Amethyst crystal. I bought one for myself, too. It helps promote healing because it radiates peace and calm. I thought it might help your PTSD."

Marta lost it. She had tried so hard to hide her struggles, but the stupid birthday surprise outed her big time. Shanice noticed and was trying to help. Marta had gone to therapy for a while but tapered off when she didn't jump at every noise or sudden movement anymore. A hand reached over and rubbed her thigh.

"You're okay, Marta," Shanice said quietly. "I'm sorry I upset you."

"No, no, no, kid," Marta said, finally catching her breath. "That was very thoughtful. You took the time to notice something I'm going through. Even in the middle of all *your*...stuff."

"I think a Reiki session or two would help both of us."

"Maybe," Marta said, making absolutely no promises on that front. She took the offered necklace and put it around her neck. "Looks good?" Her voice faded on the second word. She was struggling to get her emotions under control.

Shanice nodded. And then she did something that Marta allowed for some reason. The young woman reached right into Marta's personal space and tucked the crystal inside Marta's shirt. "Keep this close to your heart."

She patted the crystal over Marta's shirt, effectively patting Marta's heart.

Shanice pulled out a similar necklace and put it on herself, tucking it underneath her shirt. "I will be so happy to get my clothes today. And my stuff."

"I bet," Marta said, grateful for the subject change. She pulled out of the parking lot and headed for the highway back to Denton Heights.

"I should rent a storage place for my stuff until I find a new place to live," Shanice mused out loud.

Marta wouldn't hear of it and told her there was plenty of room at her house. Shanice had full use of Nora's old room, and they could make room in the garage if necessary.

Reluctantly, Shanice agreed to the plan saying, "But only until I can find a place to go."

"I had a thought," Marta said, changing the subject. "Do you want to stop at Johnson Tech today?"

"Yes, but not today," came the quick answer.

"Cool." Marta didn't dig deeper, figuring it was Shanice's business. "Lunch then?"

"Yes, for some reason, I'm kind of hungry."

Marta pulled onto the highway and melded into traffic. She was glad Shanice didn't seem bothered by the high speeds or the traffic around them.

"Do you think we can get takeout from somewhere and then eat at that cool coffee shop on Market?"

"Rikki's?"

"Yeah."

"Fuck, yeah."

Shanice gasped. "Potty mouth. Nora was right."

"Sorry. It slips out now and then."

Once situated inside the coffee shop with tacos from Marta's favorite food truck, they settled in for a well-deserved break. Marta purposely picked a table near the large picture window in the front near the green plants. She even picked off dead leaves, much to Shanice's amusement.

"Since I'm on leave from work," Shanice said, "I want to figure out where I'm living before I tackle where I'm working. I can't drive anymore, and public transportation is so hit and miss, and with this—" She smacked both armrests with her hands. "This thing will make it even more dicey."

"I get that," Marta said.

"Yeah, once I'm settled and moved in somewhere, then I'm thinking about asking them if I can work from home. Wherever that is, it has to have good WIFI, though. I mean, I could go into the office now and then, I suppose."

"Maybe somebody from work could pick you up on those days," Marta offered. *Or I could drive you*, she thought in her head.

"Maybe." Shanice scowled.

"What's wrong?" Marta put down her half-eaten taco. "Are you in pain?"

"No, I just realized that I have to figure out where to send my mail. I don't think it'll get forwarded to Louisville because my last name isn't Clark, but maybe I can pick it up from the people that buy the house."

"Forward it to my house for now," Marta said quickly.

"No, I couldn't—"

"Sure, you can," Marta interrupted. "Until you have another option. I'll safeguard it and make sure you get it. No fuss. No muss."

Shanice was silent for a moment and then said, "You truly are my superhero, aren't you?"

Marta didn't have a chance to answer because a certain tall redheaded proprietor sidled up to their table.

"You're back," Rikki said to Marta. "Marta, right?"

Marta nodded.

"How's the injury?"

Marta held up her formerly injured hand. "Good as new." That was kind of a lie because there were tiny scars from the glass, but who cared.

"And this must be the woman you risked life and limb for."

Shanice giggled and hid her smile behind her hand.

"I'm Rikki."

Shanice shook the offered hand and said, "I'm Shanice, and I've never been here before. I mean, I've walked by the outside. But I love it in here. So welcoming."

"Thanks," Rikki said with a smile that lit up her entire face. "Coffee's on me. Don't forget."

"Thank you," Marta said. "That's very generous of you. We'll be sure to get to-go cups on the way out."

They made a bit more small talk, and as soon as Rikki left and was out of earshot, Shanice burst out laughing. "Marta, you have that whole pile of dead leaves on your napkin. She saw them. She knew you were picking her plants."

Marta bugged out her eyes. "Oh, shit. Well, she didn't ban us, and she's giving us free coffees, so I think we're off the hook."

A wave of pain crossed Shanice's face.

"Now you're in pain," Marta said matter-of-factly. "Tell me."

"I'm okay," Shanice said, clearly lying.

"Listen, I'm not good at that Bullshit game, but even I can tell you're bullshitting me right now."

"Such a potty mouth," Shanice murmured playfully.

"What do you need? Your meds are back at the house."

"Yeah, I'm due. But we have that appointment with Penni in a little while. My..." She used all her fingers on both hands and gestured downward. "My, you know. They're hurting. Elizabeth said I should keep them elevated."

"Ahh." Marta stood up. She maneuvered Shanice's chair in such a way that Shanice could lift her stumps and rest them on Marta's legs. "Better?"

"Yes," Shanice said with a long sigh. "So good. Thank you. They were throbbing."

Marta didn't even ask; she simply laid her hands on one stump and began an ever-so-gentle massage. She searched Shanice's face for signs of pain or irritation but saw nothing. "Color?" she asked but then almost choked. Wrong place. Wrong time. Wrong person.

"Hmm?" Shanice asked, clearly confused. "Black," she said with a laugh. "Thought you'd noticed that by now."

Marta grabbed the stump she was massaging and just laughed. She caught Shanice's eye, which got them both laughing even more. Once they caught their respective breaths, Marta said, "Green means go. Red means stop. And yellow basically means pause for a moment to regroup."

"Oh, why didn't you say? Green means go," Shanice said, gesturing for Marta to continue the personal stump massage.

Marta switched to the other stump. "Did Elizabeth give you any of that special oil to rub into the scars?"

"No, but she said vitamin E oil would do the trick."

"We'll pick some up on the way home. Don't let me forget."

It wasn't until Shanice said, "Okay," that Marta realized she had called it 'home.'

Chapter 14

Shanice

They got back to Marta's house late Monday afternoon after clearing out Shanice's stuff from Miss Macie's. Superhero Marta had carried Shanice up the stairs to her former second-floor bedroom, leaving the wheelchair at the foot of the stairs. Someone had boxed up all her stuff quite thoroughly, and Marta single-handedly brought all eleven boxes down the stairs while Penni, the realtor, sat in her car making phone calls. Marta then loaded the boxes and Shanice in her truck, and after thanking Penni profusely, they headed home, where Marta, once again, heaved the boxes out of her truck and brought them into Nora's room. The only things missing were a couple of coffee cups that had been in the kitchen. Oh, well. Those must live in Louisville now. But everything else had been there, including her laptop, her tablet, and her printers. And the other thing was there, too. She didn't show Marta the birth certificate. That was private.

Shanice had missed her electronics. And her gaming apps, she had to admit. But those would wait. She had clothes to put in the dresser. Yesterday had been exhausting, and Shanice barely remembered sleeping last night. But it was now Tuesday morning, and she was anxious to go through her stuff. She was currently in Nora's old room, surrounded by boxes containing all of her earthly possessions. She sat in the wheelchair and slowly picked out some clothes to put in the dresser that Marta had graciously cleaned out for her. This dresser didn't have any of Nora's clothes or anything like that in there. It had towels and sheets and other stuff like that.

After many reassurances to Marta that Shanice would be okay alone in the house, Marta finally went off to work. There was no way Shanice was going to let Marta take yet another day off just to help her. They compromised, though, and Marta was going to zip home at lunchtime to see if Shanice needed anything. A bathroom trip, for sure. Shanice hoped she could hold any toilet needs until then. Fingers crossed. She couldn't wait until she was strong enough to transfer to a toilet on her own.

She planned on staying at Marta's only as long as it took to get housing. Marta had set her up with some pens and a pad of legal-sized paper for taking notes because Shanice planned to make a ton of calls to disabled housing places or assisted living or whatever it was called. She also had to call her auto and health insurance companies. She had to put in a change of address on the post office website, too. There was a lot to do.

She folded a shirt and put it in the highest drawer. Oh, shoot, she also had to call the Chrysalis Center to give them Marta's address. The physical therapy people had to be called. "Ugh," Shanice groaned out loud. All she wanted to do was play games and hang with Mama Cat and the kitties. She forced herself to work for a while longer, sorting clothes and picking through her boxes. She made sure the rest of her stuff stayed neatly packed in each box, ready to be moved at a moment's notice. She even had a small stash of granola bars she'd pilfered from Marta's pantry. She didn't want to betray Marta's trust that way, but when the time came that Marta decided that Shanice had overstayed her welcome, Shanice wanted at least a few days' worth of food to sustain her.

Shanice stretched her arms and legs. She absolutely, one hundred percent, needed a better wheelchair. An electric one would be amazing, but those were freakin' expensive. Yes, she'd already looked up the cost online. For now, she'd like a chair with a high back that leaned so she could get relief. And it had to have something that would raise her legs in the air. Pointing down to the ground like this was so tiring.

Sick of looking through her stuff, Shanice wheeled herself to Mama Cat's room. Unfortunately, because she was so awkward with the chair through the open door, a certain white cat snuck into the room.

"Snowball," Shanice said in alarm. "You can't be in here. Dang it." She calmed herself, not wanting to freak out the cats or the kittens, and wheeled to the dresser drawer turned kitten nursery. Snowball looked over the edge at the mewling kittens but didn't seem aggressive, just curious. Mama Cat looked up at the white cat and was clearly wary and on guard, but thankfully there was no growling from either side—just a lot of nose sniffing.

Snowball continued to sniff and sniff, so Shanice slowly reached into the drawer and pulled out the first kitten she could reach. She held the gray fluffball out to Snowball. "See what Mama Cat brought us?" Shanice used her softest tone. Snowball sniffed the kitten for what seemed like days, and then Shanice pulled it away so she could hug the little creature. The kitten in her arms mewled its dissatisfaction about being away from its warm and comforting mother, so Shanice put it back in the drawer. Shanice laughed as Mama Cat licked the little one's head as if to quickly rid her baby of that vile human smell.

Shanice said a few gentle words and cooed to Mama Cat for a few more minutes, but it was time. Time to make those calls. Marta told her she wanted a status report when she called at ten, and the last thing Shanice wanted to do was disappoint her, especially because she'd seen the necklace she'd given Marta still around her neck. Good. Hopefully, there was something to this whole energy-healing thing. Ahh, another thing to put on the list. Make appointments with a Reiki healer—one for her and one for Marta.

Shanice headed out Mama Cat's door and, once outside, called for Snowball, who, by some miracle, followed her out. She gave Snowball a treat from the treat jar Marta had shown her. Best to reward good behavior, right? Mama Deborah used to say that.

Seven hundred million phone calls later, Shanice had updated her address everywhere and had made an appointment with not only the at-home physical therapist for late Friday afternoon but also with Reiki healers for both of them late Saturday. She made late appointments, so Marta wouldn't need to take a single minute off from work.

Her phone rang. An excited spike of joy shot through her.

"Hi, Marta," Shanice said and immediately chattered on about all the things she'd accomplished, Snowball pushing her way into the kitten room, the appointments, and everything.

"Yikes," Marta finally said. "Take a breath, kid."

Shanice giggled.

"I am so honking proud of you," Marta said. "You're really taking care of things, aren't you? And kitten-sitting on top of all that."

Pride bloomed in Shanice's core. She knew it was silly, but having Marta say she was proud of her was like a balm to her soul. "Thanks, Marta." Oh, gosh. Her voice sounded so juvenile.

"You're welcome," Marta said gently. There was a lot of noise in the background wherever Marta was at work, but she didn't seem rushed or anything. "How are you holding up bathroom-wise? Can you hold it another two hours?"

Shanice lied straight through her teeth and lips. "Doing good." The truth was, as soon as Marta asked, her bladder raised its fist in protest.

"Excellent," Marta said. "Put your legs up on the couch or the bed. Whatever's more comfortable for you, okay? I don't want them down all day."

"Okay," Shanice said and then heard an angry voice in Marta's background.

"I gotta go. I'll be home at lunchtime. See you soon. Bye." Marta hung up without waiting for a reply.

Shanice wanted to rest and put her feet up, but nature was calling. She had to try. Her arm and hand had to be strong enough by now, right? Of course, she hadn't quite worked out the mechanics of hopping from the wheelchair to the porcelain chair, but she'd figure that out when she got in the bathroom.

Just thinking about going to the bathroom made her need to pee even greater. God, why did she have that second cup of coffee and drink all that water while making calls?

She had no clue how to do it. She should have researched this on her phone, but there was no time. She was about to pee her shorts. She positioned her chair diagonally in front of the toilet and flicked up the closed toilet lid. She shimmied forward in her chair, grabbed the toilet seat with the nearest hand, and braced herself. Without really thinking, she flung herself off the wheelchair and twisted in mid-air. Her stumps pushed off the locked wheelchair, and to her freakin' amazement, she had done it. She'd landed on the toilet seat. Unfortunately, she'd landed hard, and everything from her arms to her butt to her stumps kind of throbbed painfully from the impact, but who cared. She'd done it!

Except she had forgotten one thing. She had forgotten to pull her shorts down first. Cursing her stupidity, she leaned to one side and held onto the convenient grab bar. She pulled the shorts down as far as they would go and then leaned back the other way. Three more of these moves and she was free to pee.

"Wherever ye may be," she singsonged, "let your stream flow free." She sat there for quite a while, making sure her bladder was indeed uber-empty. She thought maybe she might have another agenda stirring, but it didn't manifest. When the back of her legs started to get numb, she decided it was time to attempt the dismount.

Honestly, the at-home physical therapist couldn't get there soon enough to teach her how to navigate stuff like this. But he or she wasn't coming until Friday afternoon. And today was Tuesday, so she had a couple more days to figure stuff out. She'd come up with an idea about how to transfer from the wheelchair to the bed or the couch on her own, but she wanted Marta there to spot her just in case things went terribly wrong.

"Sounds like gymnastics," Shanice said out loud. "Okay, I've stalled long enough. I need to go pet some kittens."

She pulled her underpants and shorts up with her fabulous new side-leaning technique and then scooted forward on the toilet seat. She figured she'd just do the reverse move that got her there and didn't really think about it. She flung herself toward the wheelchair, but it slid away. She crashed to the tile floor. She did a quick inventory of her body and then a slower one. She'd hit the wheelchair with her hip and face. The fact that she was bleeding from a cut on her cheek didn't panic her too much because everything else seemed okay. Even the stumps weren't protesting much, which was weird because they were always first in the picket lines.

She needed a moment to regroup, so she pushed the wheelchair out of the way and lay on the cold tile floor. She lay there thinking how mad Marta was going to be when she came home and saw the cut on her face. It would be easier to just be honest about what happened than to tell her a lie. Lying usually came easy to Shanice, but lying to Marta seemed like a betrayal of everything Marta had done for her—a betrayal of their new friendship.

Shanice sighed and remembered the dream she'd had of Marta while in the Chrysalis Center. It was the dream she'd had to finish with her own fingers when she woke up in the middle of it. She knew that Marta wasn't ever going to look at broken Shanice as girlfriend material, so there was no sense even thinking about it. Marta never would have looked in her direction before she'd become disabled and a burden, anyway. And now? Forget it. And she was probably too young for Marta. Ten years difference was a lot, wasn't it? Shanice groaned. She clamped down those thoughts and decided it would be the last time she'd even come close to thinking them ever again.

Lying on the bathroom floor, she decided to gather her strength before attempting to pull herself up into the wheelchair. Of course, she had no idea *how* to do that, but maybe something would come to her. She pulled her phone out of her pocket and typed in "Housing for Disabled Adults." Several suggested websites popped up, most of them for senior citizens. She found one with the label "Special Needs Housing" and clicked on it. She frowned. It was a site begging for donations so they could build facilities around Ohio. Too bad they hadn't been built already.

She clicked out and tried a few more sites, each looking bleaker than the one before. A dull headache started in her temples, but she forced herself to fill in an application on the nicest-looking group home and then selected an appointment time to check out the place. She was excited to get an appointment right after their Reiki sessions on Saturday. She would be relaxed and thinking clearly after the session. Hopefully. Exhausted, she closed the phone. She'd do more research and set up more appointments from her laptop later. Okay, just a little rest, and then onto the problem of wheelchair climbing.

She woke up confused. She was shivering. Realization came flooding back.

"Where are you?" a voice called from outside the bathroom.

"In here," Shanice called.

"You okay?" Marta asked, her voice closer. She appeared at the open doorway. "Oh, fuck." She flung the wheelchair out of the way and instantly knelt beside Shanice. "Oh, my God. Are you all right?" She touched Shanice's swollen cheek. Her hand came back bloody. "Where else are you hurt?"

"I'm sorry," Shanice said. "I had to go, so I tried—"

"Shh, shh, shh," Marta calmed her. "I understand. It's okay. Tell me where you're hurt."

"I'm fine. I think." Shanice relayed her glorious escapades in the bathroom and that only her hip hurt a little.

Marta pulled up Shanice's shirt. "Yeah, your hip is bruising up. Can you sit up?"

With Marta's help, Shanice sat up. "I have a headache."

"Makes sense," Marta said. "You hit your head. C'mon, let's get you back in the chair so I can tend this wound."

With superhero strength, probably combined with adrenaline, Marta scooped Shanice up and popped her back into the wheelchair. She wheeled her to the kitchen table and went for first aid supplies.

Upon returning, she said, "Okay, the cut's not too deep and should heal on its own."

When Shanice reached up to touch the new Band-Aid, Marta grabbed her hand and gently put it back down. "No touchy. We don't want to risk infection. Especially not on this pretty face."

"Yes, Ma'am," Shanice said. Although she was incredibly embarrassed about her stupid accident in the bathroom, warm gooey feels swept through her body. She liked when Marta fussed over her like this. She liked when Marta took care of her. She was about to apologize again but heard herself say, "Thank you." Her hand, all on its own, reached up and touched Marta's face.

Marta held her gaze. "You sure you're okay?" She broke eye contact after a moment.

"I am now."

Marta nodded her head as if deciding something. She pulled out her phone, called her job, and said she had to stay home.

"Hungry?"

"Yes," Shanice said. Yes, she really did like being taken care of.

"Hello-o-o," came a cheery call from the open front door. "Anybody home?"

"Fuck," Marta muttered under her breath. "Nosy neighbor," she said to Shanice and headed toward the door.

"Marta," said the cheery older woman. "I came to collect my plate. I'm making a cake for the church coffee hour this Sunday."

"Oh, sure," Marta said. "Let me go get it."

Shanice heard Marta groan at the unmistakable sound of the neighbor letting herself into the house. Shanice sat as still as she could, not wanting to add any more *ugh* to Marta's irritation.

"Oh, hello," the older gray-haired white woman said to Shanice.

"Hi," Shanice said and introduced herself. "Are you the one that made the incredible lemon Bundt cake?"

"Yes. I'm so glad you liked it."

"It was so good," Shanice said, totally fangirling the baker of the cake. "Marta brought me a couple of slices. Thank you so much for your thoughtfulness."

"You're so welcome," the woman said again. "Where are my manners? I'm Mrs. Pulaski. Call me Paula. I live next door." She pointed toward the driveway side of the house.

"Nice to meet you," Shanice said again.

Marta stood next to Shanice, holding the plate and watching the exchange. Shanice could tell she wanted her neighbor out of the house ASAP, but Shanice didn't know how to facilitate that.

"Do you like red velvet cake?" Mrs. Pulaski asked Shanice. "With cream cheese frosting?"

Shanice exaggerated the dropping of her jaw. "Uh, yeah. It would be un-American to say no, wouldn't it?"

"Why don't I come over sometime, and we can make it together?"

Marta almost choked and said, "We're really busy, Mrs. Pulaski. Here's your plate. Thanks again. Nora loved it, too. She's doing fine. She's home now. Okay, we have to get busy here, so thanks for coming by." Marta headed for the front door with the plate.

Mrs. Pulaski hesitated, leaned down, and said, "It was nice to meet you, Shanice." She picked up the pen Shanice had been using earlier that morning and wrote a phone number on the top of the pad of paper. "This is my cell phone. Call if you need anything. Anything at all. I'm usually home, especially now that Henry's passed on."

"Thank you, Ma'am," Shanice said, wondering why Marta felt so uncomfortable with her neighbor.

The voices were muffled out on the front landing, but Shanice heard Mrs. Pulaski say, "I can help." And Marta's barely discernable mumble, "We're fine. Have a good day."

Shanice searched Marta's face when she came in but decided not to try and penetrate her scowl. Marta's movements were quick and precise as she threw together tuna fish sandwiches, no onions, thank you.

"Can we eat out back?" Shanice asked.

"Yes," came the succinct answer.

She was dying to see the backyard. A backyard had been on her ultimate bucket list, but she knew now that she had to scratch that one off. "Marta, I'm sorry."

"Huh? What are you sorry for?"

"You're obviously mad at me for…" *existing.*

"You? No, no, no, honey." Marta's expression softened. "I'm not angry with you. Mrs. Pulaski is a buttinsky. That's all."

"She's lonely," Shanice said. That had been obvious to the extreme.

"Not my problem," Marta said coldly. She loaded Shanice's lap with the sandwiches and sliced red peppers. "I'll wheel you out there and then come back in for drinks."

"Okay," Shanice said simply. This was Marta's house, Marta's space. Shanice needed to remember that and be more grateful.

Marta's mood seemed to soften after they'd eaten, and Shanice asked if she could see the flower gardens that Marta had been working on. One short bump off the concrete patio and onto the grass, and Shanice was able to take in the colorful flowers that Marta had planted to attract butterflies. She explained how employees could purchase unsellable ones at a considerable discount.

"I've always loved Black-eyed Susans," Shanice gushed. "What are those ones called?"

"Irises. They were my mom's—" Marta didn't finish her sentence. She simply turned away and uncoiled the water hose. She was clearly trying not to get emotional about her mom's passing. Shanice didn't know the details and didn't want to upset Marta even more by asking.

"Hey, can I water them?" Shanice asked.

"Hmm?" Marta said and turned with the hose sprayer pointed right at Shanice.

Shanice put her hands and knees up to block the onslaught of water. "Quit," Shanice screeched. "I'll rust."

Marta threw down the hose and raced over to Shanice. She put her face inches from Shanice's. "This?" She pounded the armrests. "Is. Not. You. You are a beautiful human being who is not defined by this tool." She pushed off the wheelchair and stood up tall. "Sure, there will be people in your life that will look at you and stare."

"Like that lady at the thrift store."

"Yes, but then there will be people like Penni, the realtor who never once coddled or ignored you. She spoke to you like the grown-up adult that you are. She didn't see you as merely a wheelchair that would rust." Marta's tone softened as she said, "And neither do I."

"You don't?"

"No, silly." Marta handed Shanice the hose and told her to go ahead and water the flowers.

Shanice looked from the hose sprayer in her hand to Marta and sported an evil grin.

"Oh, no, you don't," Marta said, clearly trying to figure out where to hide.

Too late. Shanice pressed the handle and hit Marta once with the spray. She didn't want to get in too much trouble, so she whistled an innocent tune and moved the spray over to the irises and other colorful plants.

"Turnabout is fair play, I guess," Marta said, wiping water off her face.

After a few minutes, Marta turned off the water and spread a blanket on the lawn. "Nora and I used to lay on a blanket out here and watch the clouds. She was going for a gorgeous tan—"

"You white people try to get as dark as possible in the summer." Shanice made sure her tone was playful. Some white people got tense when race was mentioned or even hinted at.

"Not all," Marta amended. "I just wanted to hang out with my big sister. And the only reason I even have this tan is because I work outside. It's not deliberate."

"Whatever you have to tell yourself," Shanice teased. And she really was teasing. It was fun to banter with Marta.

"C'mon," Marta said, holding her arms out. Shanice wrapped her arms around Marta's neck, let herself be picked up, and then set down on the black-and-white checked blanket. "Lay back so you can see the sky." Marta lay on the blanket but facing the other way. She shimmied over until her head was close to Shanice's. "This is how Nora and I used to lay out here."

"Cozy," Shanice said.

After identifying shapes in the summer clouds for a while, they both got quiet.

"Marta?" Shanice said, knowing she had to get this out. "I can't stay here much longer."

"Sure, you can," Marta said matter-of-factly.

"Today's…I'm going to call it a mishap. Today's *mishap* is proof enough that I need some kind of assisted living situation."

"No, you don't." Marta sat up and then spun around so Shanice could see her.

Before Marta could go on, Shanice said, "I have an appointment to check out a group home on Saturday."

"Oh," came the quiet reply.

The silence that followed echoed loudly in Shanice's ears.

Chapter 15

Marta

Wednesday morning, Marta turned the volume up and put the pedal to the metal. Tree section, next stop. There was no sense in changing one's routine. Hearing that Shanice didn't want or need her help as they lay on the lawn yesterday afternoon sent Marta screeching back inside herself. She acquiesced to Shanice's shy suggestion that Mrs. Pulaski come by during the day to help Shanice out. One quick phone call, and it was set up. Marta didn't have to worry that the kid was alone now. Good. Fine. Whatever.

Nine Inch Nails was doing the trick this morning. No outside world could intrude. And that's the way she'd wanted it since forever. And then the twenty-five-year-old young woman with an amazing spirit had come into her life, and Marta had abandoned the plan momentarily.

"Stop," she said aloud, forcing herself to focus on the physical work. She loved when landscapers ordered Japanese Maples. Ooh, and a Sugar Maple. Awesome. Some days she wished she'd stayed in the actual landscaping part of the business, but that meant dealing with people and customers, and she'd bowed out because of that. Picking orders was the best way to stay in the game.

Next stop, shrubs. She tapped out the bass rhythm pounding in her air buds and headed to the east side of the property. Oh, shit. Another customer had gotten in the back. She was either lost or sneaking around to find the best plants. Marta didn't have time for that shit and made a sharp left between rows of Rhododendron. Let someone else tell the woman where to go.

"Tell her where to go," Marta said out loud, thinking about the silliness she'd shared with Shanice the day they met the realtor. That was the day Shanice moved all her stuff in. It was the day Marta thought she had someone to take care of. Not that she'd been looking for someone to take care of, but it felt similar to caring for her mother. But it was different, too. This time, her ward didn't have a degenerative disease. This time the person was strong but didn't know it yet. Marta knew that her psychologist, the one she abandoned all those years ago, would have a field day with her right now. She could just hear him. "You're invested in this one because you think you can save her, Marta." *Unlike the last one,* Marta finished for herself. She told the imaginary Dr. Fieldston in her head to shut the hell up. He did, but she knew he'd be back.

She stopped short at the azaleas and hopped out to grab the required amount of each color. She jumped when the lost customer popped out from behind the flatbed.

"You fucking scared me," Marta said and yanked her air buds out.

"Sorry," the young Black woman said. "Are you Marta Ingersoll?"

Why does she know my name? Shanice! "Is everything okay?"

"Uh, yeah," the woman said. She reminded Marta of Shanice a little. Black, petite, cute smile. "They told me to come find you."

"Who did? Why?"

"No one told you?"

"Told me what? Get to the point." Marta didn't have time for this nonsense. She just wanted to finish her day and go home. Not that Shanice needed her or anything. She had Mrs. Pulaski now, didn't she? And then the kid was going to move out and live on her own.

"I'm shadowing you for the rest of the summer," the woman said. "Well, through Halloween, I mean."

Marta just stood there and blinked. *No,* she wanted to say but held back. She had more manners than that. "Why?"

"It's part of my Landscape Design Internship here. Mr. Carter taught one of the modules in my certificate program, and he offered me this position.

Mr. Carter could be a shrewd businessman. Marta understood that when she accepted the low hourly wage two years ago. "Do they pay you?"

"Yes, a little bit," the young woman said with a shrug. Marta wondered if Shanice had ever straightened her hair like this woman had, although Shanice's 'fro was uber cute and soft.

"What's your name?"

"Oh, sorry. I'm Dana Moore."

"How old?"

"Twenty-six," Dana said. She held up a shiny new pair of work gloves. "I brought my own gloves."

Marta was impressed. They were a good brand.

"What do you want to get out of interning here?"

"Oh, gosh." Dana exuded pure eagerness. That was good. Marta wouldn't have to motivate her. "Thank you in advance, Ma'am. My Domme, uh, I mean, my girlfriend would have my hide if I didn't thank you."

'Domme'? Did she just say 'Domme'? "Don't thank me yet," Marta said, turning away to get the all-important clipboard. Was this kid in the life? Holy shit. What a slip of the tongue. Her Domme should teach her to be more careful around the vanillas. Not that Marta was a vanilla.

Dana had been chattering about her goals for the internship, so Marta tuned back in.

"…so that I can design landscapes for people and companies but be knowledgeable about the plants. Like I don't want to plant a Japanese Maple in a spot where the winter will kill it." She pointed to the tree on the flatbed. "South side is best for them, near shelter if possible."

"Excellent," Marta said. She tucked her air buds and phone deep into her pocket. There would be no more music today. Marta showed Dana the clipboard and was surprised at how nervous Dana seemed with it in her hands. Marta wasn't sure what the issue was but went over to stand by her side, and they read the list together.

Marta gave Dana the literal lay of the land, pointing out the various sections of the property and that they were now in the shrubbery section. "Azaleas are next."

"Oh," Dana said with understanding. "Duh. That says 'azaleas.' Obviously." She waved her hand around the shrubs that surrounded them.

Could Dana not read? Was English not her primary language? Did she not know the names of plants? Marta wasn't sure what it was, but she would not make fun, be impatient, or anything like that. She would be patient and kind. That's how her parents had raised her. Marta's mother always said, "You never know what's going on in another person's life or their struggles."

It had been a productive morning, and by productive, Marta meant that she hadn't lost any time working with Dana. She had to explain many things to Dana, but having an extra person lifting plants onto the flatbed evened out the time. She deposited Dana back at the office to have her lunch with the guys and zipped home only to find Shanice and Mrs. Pulaski happy and content in their baking project. All was well with both Shanice and the kittens, so Marta ate her sandwich quickly and headed back to work.

At the end of the workday, it was obvious that Dana was weary. She was a chatterer, though, and talked kind of incessantly. That was okay. Marta didn't have to contribute much that way. The job was both physically and mentally demanding, but Dana had done well. Marta made a copy of the order list and suggested that Dana practice recognizing the names of the plants, so it would be easier as they went along.

After Marta punched out, she turned to Dana and whispered, "Say hello to your *Domme* for me." She emphasized the word, *Domme.*

Dana inhaled sharply. "Okay," she said in a high tight voice. "Ma'am," she added.

Marta laughed as she turned away to head to her pickup. *That one is well-trained, all right.*

Thursday and Friday workdays went well at the nursery. Dana took more initiative each day. She had clearly been doing her homework and knew how to recognize the names of the various plants, although Marta helped her pronounce any new ones that came along.

Since Dana's was a Monday through Friday internship, on Friday afternoon, Marta said, "Okay, minion, I'll see you on Monday."

"Ma'am?" Dana said, following her out the office door. She looked around and asked, "Would you like to come to my housewarming party? My Domme said she would like to meet you. She said it was obvious that you were a caring person."

Instant emotion hit Marta's core. "Just doing my job," she said, willing the warm feelings in her chest to disappear.

Dana looked a little lost for a moment. "Tina said I could invite some people if I wanted. I invited Kadesha, obvi."

"Obvi," Marta mimicked, teasing the younger woman. Dana had talked about her BFF Kadesha a lot over the past week, and apparently, Dana didn't get to see her much since moving to Denton Heights.

Dana patted Marta on the upper arm as she said, "Stop teasing."

"Who's Tina?"

"Tina's my Domme's girlfriend."

Marta heard the words, but they didn't compute. She replayed them in her head. Nope, not better. Clarification was needed. "Girlfriend?"

"Yes. My Domme said it's okay to tell people about our household. If they're in the *life*, that is. If they'd understand, and I think you will."

"Try me," Marta said. This should be good.

"Jaleesa, my Domme, has a girlfriend who is like her life partner. They sleep in the same room and all. I have my own bedroom upstairs, and I'm Jaleesa's submissive. She and I…"

The pause was overlong, so Marta said, "I get it. And this Tina is okay with that?"

"Oh, yeah," Dana said. "She encourages it."

"Really. Not conventional, but as long as everyone gives consent."

"Oh, yeah," Dana said. "It's working out really well. And then Harriet lives on the first floor near the kitchen."

"Another sub?"

"Yes," Dana said, "but Harriet's a service sub, not a sexual sub." She whispered the last part.

"Got it." Marta was intrigued. Not that she'd ever want a situation like that, but she had to admire the Domme's ability to have three submissives, all living peacefully in the same household. Yes, this she had to witness for herself.

"When's the party?"

"Sunday. One o'clock."

"I get off at three," Marta said. "But maybe I can get out early."

"Give me your phone," Dana demanded.

"Excuse me"? Marta chided, going into full Domme mode. "Did you forget yourself?"

"Ma'am. I'm sorry, Ma'am." Dana looked like she was about to drop to her knees but checked herself. She hung her head. "Oh, gosh. I'm sorry. I'll ask Jaleesa to punish me tonight for that."

"No, no, no," Marta said. "Just remember next time." She'd wanted to say, 'Just remember your place,' but Dana wasn't Marta's sub. There was a natural hierarchy to Dommes and subs, though, and Marta was certain that Dana's Domme would want Dana to remember that hierarchy and respect it.

"I will, Ma'am."

"Now, what did you want with my phone?" Marta pulled it out of her pocket.

"I was just going to put my contact info in there."

"Have at it," Marta said and handed her the phone. "You're just like Shanice, always updating my phone or adding apps."

"Shanice, Ma'am?"

Shit, Marta had slipped. She hadn't intended to mention Shanice, seeing as she could be gone as soon as tomorrow evening if the group home had space. A sudden sadness overcame Marta at the thought. "She's living with me temporarily."

"Oh," Dana said, clearly not wanting to intrude. "She's more than welcome to come, too, Ma'am." She handed the phone back. "I put my name and the address in your contacts. Miss Jaleesa wanted me to let you know that it will be a vanilla party for the most part. My parents are coming, and hers, and Tina's. Not Harriet's, though. And we're inviting some neighbors and stuff."

"I can be vanilla," Marta said with a laugh, gesturing to their environment. She checked the time on her phone. "I have to get going. Maybe I'll see you Sunday."

"Hope so," Dana said, and Marta almost cringed at the hopeful tone in Dana's voice. "Oh, and Ma'am?" Dana said.

"Yes?"

"It's a dry party. We're all in twelve-step programs of one sort or another."

"Ahh," Marta said. "There's more than one kind?" She shouldn't have asked, but the words had rushed out of her mouth before she could stop them.

"Oh, yes, Ma'am. There's one for alcoholics, of course." Dana waved, outing herself as a member of that group. "There's so many more. Narcotics Anonymous, Gamblers, Sex Addicts, Overeaters; I mean, the list goes on."

"Overeaters?"

"Mm hmm," Dana said. "My great aunt does that program, and she's so healthy now."

"Cool," Marta said. And it was. "It's great that people can get help for stuff like that. Okay, I really have to go now."

"Bye, Marta," Dana said. A few of the guys had just come out of the office, so Dana reverted back to vanilla. Not always an easy thing to do.

Marta wasn't a party person, so she'd decide on Sunday if she felt like going. But for now, she needed to rush home for Shanice's first physical therapy session.

As she drove home, she was determined to make sure the therapist did right by Shanice. Even though Shanice would be on her own soon, Marta wanted to make sure the young woman had every advantage.

Thankfully, Shanice was alone when Marta got home. Mrs. Pulaski had still been there on the previous two days, and it had been painfully reminiscent of the last few months of her mother's illness when Mrs. Pulaski would sit with her mother during the day. Before the move to the Chrysalis Center, that is.

"How was your day?" Shanice asked. There was a cautious tone to her voice. Things had been kind of strained and awkward between them since Shanice's Tuesday afternoon announcement about wanting to move out.

"Good," Marta said. "Dana did much better today."

"Oh, that's good." Shanice tapped her pen on the pad of paper. "So, uh, I called like you suggested, and some guy named Allan, spelled with two A's, is coming over in an hour. He made sure I got his name spelled right." Shanice laughed, but there was no mirth to it. "When I asked if I was going to learn to transfer today, he said that transfers were the occupational therapist's job."

"Occupational therapy? Do you have an appointment for that?"

"Monday."

"Here?"

"Yeah, I wasn't sure where I would be living. Was that okay?" Shanice didn't make eye contact.

"Sure, whatever," Marta said. "I have to shower. Are the kittens okay? Mama Cat? Snowball?"

"Everyone's okay. Including me."

There was something in her tone that hit Marta in the heart. Shit, Marta hadn't asked Shanice how *she* was doing. She hadn't asked if Shanice needed anything like she usually did. Damn it. Nora would say Marta was being a brat. She was. She knew it, but she couldn't let her heart get wrapped up in the young woman any more than it already had. Too painful. That was one of the many reasons she avoided interacting with people. Too hard.

Marta turned around and said, "Do you need anything? Bathroom trip before I get in there?"

"No," came the succinct and cold answer.

Yep, she deserved that.

After her shower, they waited in relative and extremely uncomfortable silence until Allan, with two A's, showed up. The session was mainly an evaluative one with some but not enough strength training for Marta's taste. The following four appointments were set up over the next two weeks, all in the afternoon. If Shanice hadn't moved on by these days, Marta insisted on being there. She didn't want a stranger in her house or alone with Shanice. Not on her watch.

"That wasn't enough," Marta said as soon as she locked the front door after Allan's departure. "C'mon, I'm going to take you through them again."

"Yes, Ma'am," Shanice said, unenthused.

"You want to be strong, right?" Marta didn't let Shanice answer. "For when you live on your own? You have to be able to do things for yourself without help."

Shanice's face scrunched up as she began to cry. "You're still mad at me." She reached up to touch the fresh bandage on her face that Mrs. Pulaski had put on that morning.

"I'm not mad," Marta said in an angry tone. *I'm an idiot*, she scolded herself and softened her tone. "I'm not mad, Shanice. I'm worried for you. That's all."

"You sure?"

"Sure," Marta said and then worked Shanice through the same exercises the physical therapist had done and tacked on a few more. "You can do most of these on your own. Just remember to use proper form."

"Yes, Marta." Shanice rubbed her arm, the one that had been broken. "I want to show you something I've been working on."

"Hmm?"

"Mrs. Pulaski said I was ready to show you but that you have to spot me."

"Sounds like you're about to do a tumbling routine."

"No," Shanice said with a giggle. "That's what I'm trying to avoid a repeat of." She gestured to the bandaged cut on her face. "Can I show you?"

"Go for it."

Shanice pulled the wheelchair up to the couch head on. She lifted her legs, put her stumps on the cushions, and then pulled her wheelchair forward until it made contact with the couch. "Brakes locked," Shanice murmured. "Ready," she said and gestured for Marta to come closer.

"Copy that."

To Marta's amazement, Shanice was able to move onto the couch by using her arms to pull and her butt and leg muscles to 'walk' herself fully onto the couch.

"Yessss," Marta screeched with joy. "Holy shit, kid, you're a rock star."

Shanice beamed her pleasure at the praise. She lay down and said, "See? Now I can rest these babies while I lay out flat."

Marta's heart filled with pride. "That is so awesome and is exactly what I want for you. This type of strength and independence."

"When Allan told me on the phone that we wouldn't be doing transfers today, Mrs. Pulaski and I looked up stuff on the internet together. Like how to transfer from a couch or bed to the chair, so I can probably get in and out of bed by myself now."

Marta nodded. "This is a monumental day." And she meant it. Like she had said before, she only wanted what was best for Shanice. "You'll definitely need to invest in an adjustable bed, though."

Shanice nodded. "Now, chair to toilet transfers? I think I'm going to need a different kind of chair. One where the arms fold down, and I can slide off the side." Shanice sat up on the couch without struggling.

"You're getting stronger. You couldn't sit up like that a week ago."

"I know. Thank you for helping me, Marta. And I'm sorry if I did something that upset you. I did all the dishes. I made my bed. I scooped the cat box, and Mrs. Pulaski put the bag in the outside garbage bin for me." Something must have changed in Marta's expression because Shanice said, "She's harmless. She's just lonely and wants to help."

Marta nodded. She wasn't sure about the truth to those statements, but since Mrs. Pulaski was helping out without getting paid, she wasn't going to look that gift horse in the mouth.

Marta's heart softened as she said, "If you're not too tired, how about we have dinner out? You can pick, but it's my treat." This might be Shanice's last night at Marta's house, so she wanted to give her a special sendoff.

"Really? Lobster and steak it is."

Marta knew that Shanice was teasing but said, "I know the perfect place."

"Really?"

"Yeah. Get a move on. We leave in half an hour. Do you need help changing?"

"Nope. Well, except maybe you can spot me getting on the bed. I think the chair is lower than the bed."

"You got it." Marta's smile was genuine. She decided to stay out of her funk and help Shanice for as long as she had her. "Oh, hey. Do you want to go to a party on Sunday? Dana and her housemates are having a housewarming party." *Oh, shit.* Why did she ask that? Shanice might have moved on and out of Marta's life by then.

"Yes," Shanice said enthusiastically. "Yes," she said again.

"Cool," Marta said, conflicted. "Head on to your room, and I'll text Dana." Too late to take it back now. But that's okay, Marta convinced herself. It might do the young woman some good to have a festive outing.

As soon as Shanice maneuvered back into the wheelchair, all on her own, and headed toward her room, Marta sent the text.

> MARTA: Hey, Dana. Thank you for the invitation. May I bring a plus one?

The reply came back almost instantaneously.

> DANA: Of course, Ma'am!

> MARTA: Great.

She debated for a moment but decided that planning ahead would be a good idea. She didn't want Shanice to be embarrassed.

> MARTA: My friend Shanice is in a wheelchair and doesn't transfer readily. Will that be a problem?

> DANA: Hey, Jaleesa here. (I grabbed Dana's phone). Yes, of course, we can accommodate Shanice's needs. We'll save a parking spot in the driveway for you. Dana will see to that personally. You can come through the side gate by the basketball hoop. I'm looking forward to meeting you. Dana speaks quite highly of you.

> DANA: It's me. I'm back. See you on Sunday. If you want, you can text me your ETA so I can make sure the drivway's cleer.

> MARTA: Thank you both. We're looking forward to the party.

Seeing the misspellings in Dana's text alerted Marta to an issue with Dana's reading or spelling ability. One thing was for sure, Dana's issues, whatever they were, had absolutely no bearing on her intelligence. That young woman was smart smart smart, just like Shanice.

Marta waited another moment to see if Dana or Dana's Domme responded again. She had a good feeling brewing inside. She wasn't sure why. She rarely felt like this. Oh, well. The days of miracles and wonders weren't over, apparently. She chuckled at the thought, tucked the phone in her back pocket, and then practically skipped to Shanice's room.

Chapter 16

Shanice

"Bye, Mrs. Pulaski," Shanice said as the neighbor let herself out the front door.

"Bye, dear." The kind woman looked back and waved. "Remember to lock the front door behind me, okay?"

"I will," Shanice said, waiting for the door to shut. When it did, she wheeled over and twisted the bolt closed.

She checked on the casserole in the oven, hoping Marta would like it. It was Mrs. Pulaski's recipe, and she assured Shanice that it was one of Marta's favorites. She knew that because she'd made it often when she helped out with Marta's mother during her illness.

Satisfied that the chicken and cheese dish was fine, she checked the rice and broccoli on the stove. Hopefully, Marta would be true to form and get home at the usual time. Making the dinner, with Mrs. Pulaski's help, of course, was Shanice's way of thanking Marta for the lobster and steak dinner she'd treated Shanice to the night before. She admitted that she'd never had lobster before, which surprised Marta. When Shanice announced that she was now an official lobster lover, Marta said they would have to go back to that restaurant again sometime. That made Shanice's heart sing. Maybe they could remain friends after Shanice moved out.

It was a big weekend. It was the first time Shanice had cooked for Marta. They had their Reiki sessions in a couple of hours, and then there was the group home to tour. She'd texted Mrs. Dupont, the group home mom or whatever her title was, and re-confirmed the appointment for later. And then there was the party tomorrow. She would ask Marta to help her figure out what to wear, but that wasn't what worried her the most. Not everyone, but a lot of people at the restaurant the night before stared at her. Didn't they know she could feel their eyes staring at her, even if she wasn't looking directly at them? It had made her so self-conscious. Marta even stared down one particularly rude lady at the next table. The wait staff was great, though. They moved the regular chair making room for her wheelchair to slip in. And she wasn't in the way, either. It was like Marta had said. Wise Marta. Some people would be rude, others merely curious, and others would be cool about her new situation.

Shanice went in to check on the increasingly noisy and rambunctious kittens and heard Marta come home even though the bedroom door was closed. A spike of joy went through her. Especially now that Marta wasn't moping around brooding over something. Shanice still hadn't figured out what Marta's lousy mood had been all about, but it had only lasted a few days, thank goodness.

"I'm in here," Shanice called so Marta wouldn't panic.

The door opened, and there she was—her superhero. "Hey, the house smells so good. I assume that's dinner before we head out?"

"Yes, Ma'am," Shanice said. "Come see these guys. They're getting so big already. I think they're one-week old today."

"Hey, Mama Cat," Marta said, petting the new mom. She picked up one of the black kittens and hugged it to her chest. "Two black and one gray."

"All these blacks outnumber you now, Mama," Shanice said, realizing her mistake. "I mean, Marta."

Marta's eyes comically darted from side to side, and then she waggled her eyebrows at Shanice. "I love it." She put the kitten back, gave the others equal time, and asked, "Do you need help in the kitchen, or can I shower first?"

Shanice pinched her nose shut and said, "Shower first."

"Oh, you're a real comedian. And, uh, it may be time to move on from those sponge baths of yours, too, you know."

Shanice was too embarrassed to comment.

"We have the tub. I won't look, I promise."

Shanice felt her face get hot. "Okay," was all she managed to squeak out.

"If we eat fast, we should have just enough time for a quick bath for you," Marta said as she stood up. She put a hand on Shanice's shoulder. "I mean, it's a good idea to be clean for the Reiki healer, right?"

Shanice inhaled sharply. She hadn't thought of that. "Yes, of course." She pulled away from the drawer full of fur and said, "I'll get dinner on the table. And, yes, I'll wait for you if I can't handle something."

"Good girl," Marta said, squeezing Shanice's shoulder and then letting go. "You're learning."

Once Marta was out of the room, Shanice groaned. "Oh, my God. I called her Mama. What the hell?" She didn't have time to examine it but remembered that it was what she used to call Mama Deborah. Was she feeling the same way about Marta? No time to think about it. She had dinner to put on the table.

~~~

After the Reiki sessions, Shanice pushed Marta's hand away, knowing she might get in trouble for it, and handed her credit card over to the receptionist at Astral Light Healing. "Mmm," Shanice said to Marta. "I feel so good right now."

"I hate to admit it, but I do, too," Marta stretched. "There just might be something to this whole energy work thing."

"Marta," Shanice whispered and turned away from the receptionist. "Am I supposed to leave a tip for the healers?"

Marta nodded twice.

"Copy that," Shanice said, mimicking Marta, who laughed. Shanice turned back to add a tip for each one.

The receptionist handed them business cards, and they headed out the door to the pickup.

"Plenty of time to get to the group house," Marta said as she stopped the wheelchair by the passenger door.

A hand came to rest on Shanice's shoulder from behind. Before Shanice knew what she was doing, she reached up and put her hand over the strong one on her shoulder. "Thank you for everything, Marta."
~~~

"You're easy to help, Shanice. Believe me when I say that it's my pleasure. And before you go on. You are not a burden. Not in the slightest. I already had the wheelchair ramps built and waiting for you at the house."

"And the handrails down the hallways, in the bathrooms, and everywhere."

Marta lifted Shanice and tossed her in, making her bounce on the passenger seat. Shanice giggled. She loved it when Marta did that. She turned to watch Marta fold up the chair and then heave it into the bed of the pickup truck like it was nothing. Marta must have sensed Shanice watching because her head darted comically from side to side, and then she ducked below the tailgate out of Shanice's sight line. Shanice giggled and then giggled even louder when Marta popped up momentarily and then hid again. She screeched when Marta popped up at the passenger window. So much fun. Marta put her hand on the glass and spread out her fingers. Shanice matched her smaller hand on the other side. They stayed like that for a moment, and too soon, Marta pulled her hand away and patted her own heart. Aww, Shanice melted at the gesture and did the same. She wasn't exactly sure what had just transpired between them, but whatever it was, it felt good. Was Marta missing her already?

Marta got in the driver's seat. "Onward and upward. Got the coordinates for the group house?"

"I do. Does that mean I can tell you where to go again?" Shanice teased.

"Always." Marta's tone was serious, and Shanice wasn't sure what had changed. Marta was a mystery in so many ways.

They made their way from one side of Denton Heights to the other and then beyond. "Are you sure it's out this far?" Marta asked.

"Yes, it's another two miles on the right side."

"Busy road," Marta commented.

"There it is, on the right," Shanice said when the two miles had gone by. It was an old house sorely needing a paint job and didn't look anything like the picture on the website. It reminded her of some group homes she'd lived in as a foster. She pushed down those memories as Marta pulled up the dirt driveway. At least there were big front and side yards.

"Isolated," Marta said.

"Mmm." Shanice had noticed the same thing.

Once in the wheelchair, Marta had trouble pushing her up the uneven dirt driveway cluttered with stones and clumps of grass.

A middle-aged woman came to the front door and waved. "You must be Shanice," she said cheerfully.

Shanice's heart sped up. Oh, no. This felt too similar to…before.

A calming hand rested on her shoulder.

"Yes, Ma'am," Shanice said. "Are you Mrs. Dupont?" The woman nodded, and Shanice added, "This is my good friend, Marta."

"Nice to meet you," Mrs. Dupont said from the entryway.

"Likewise," Marta said succinctly, then muttered, "Hmm."

"Come on inside," Mrs. Dupont said and beckoned them.

The fact that there were three steps leading up to the front porch didn't seem to register with the woman.

"Is there a side door or back entrance?" Marta called out.

"Oh, right." Mrs. Dupont came back out. She bopped down the steps and then lit a cigarette as she walked them toward the garage. "Through here." She opened the walk door to the garage and held it open for them. There was a door jamb that Marta had to bump the chair over, but it wasn't too bad. Shanice figured she could probably do that herself.

Mrs. Dupont tossed her still-lit cigarette in the driveway and then got in front of them. It was dark in the garage, so she said, "We can leave a light on for you." She opened the door to the house, and one more bump later, Shanice was inside a dark room with a TV and two stained couches. The rank smell was the first thing that assaulted her, and then the noise. It sounded like a fight was breaking out in the main part of the house.

"Kitchen?" Marta asked.

The woman pointed up the stairs toward the noise.

"She said a new girl was coming, and we have to hush up," a teenage girl's clearly irritated voice said.

"Okay," came the voice of a grown-up man. "Cockroach," he screeched and then laughed.

"You're a fucking idiot," the teenager accused, and then the voices bickered back and forth, getting louder and louder.

"Your room is in here." The woman opened a sliding glass door to what clearly had been a back porch. Shanice felt the heat of the non-insulated porch and knew instantly that it wasn't a legal space. "If you want it cooler, you just leave this door open a bit."

"Nope," Marta murmured near Shanice's ear, and the hand was back on her shoulder.

"Thank you for showing us," Shanice said graciously. "I have your number. And we have quite a few more to look at this evening. So, I'll give you a call."

"Utilities would be split between us," the woman offered, taking out another cigarette. She just held it and didn't light it, thank goodness.

Marta didn't need any hint from Shanice, and they were through both doors and back in the pickup in record time. Marta pulled onto the road heading toward Denton Heights. She pulled onto the shoulder once they were out of sight of the house.

"No," Marta said, gesturing out the windshield. "Just no. Negative. You will not live in a place like that. I forbid it. If we can make it work, I want you to stay with me. If we get on each other's nerves or you find the perfect living situation elsewhere or whatever, then fine, you can move out, but not to a place like that. Never ever. Not while I'm living and breathing on this planet." She finally turned to look at Shanice, her face bright red.

Shanice waited to make sure Marta wasn't going to blow an actual gasket and said, "I'd like that."

"Listen," Marta started up again, "there are people who'll try to take advantage of you. Like that woman. What a cluster fuck. Wait." Marta shook her head. "Did you say you'd stay? We can be housemates?"

Shanice nodded.

Marta started moving her shoulders up and down and then did some kind of white girl happy dance in the driver's seat. Shanice fell under the spell and joined in, with a little more soul, of course, and it wasn't long before they started laughing. Marta pulled Shanice into a hug that lasted a long time. Marta's warmth felt so good, and her warm exhales on her neck sent a wave of shivers through Shanice's core. The hand rubbing her back was soothing, too, but the "Thank you" whispered in Shanice's ear sent tingles from her non-existent feet to the crown of her head.

"You're welcome," Shanice said. "Wait, what? I should be thanking *you*. You're like an angel or something. My superhero guardian angel."

Marta released Shanice from the hug and ran the back of her knuckles down Shanice's face. "I wouldn't be able to stand it, knowing you were in a place like that. Or worse, not knowing *where* you were." Marta turned her attention toward the front of the pickup and said, "I think I needs me some ice cream. How about you?"

"You? You don't even like sweets," Shanice said. "But I'll take it."

"I have an idea. Do you trust me?"

Shanice nodded. Of course, she trusted Marta. After that 'cluster-fudge' of a group home experience, Shanice understood how much she implicitly trusted Marta.

The surprise turned out to be a local ball field where they watched a woman's softball game under the lights while eating ice cream from the concession stand. Marta sat on the bottom bleacher while Shanice sat in her chair. And, even though they'd had a lobster and steak dinner at a fancy restaurant the night before, and Shanice had made a surprise dinner for Marta earlier that day, this outing felt like home. Just the two of them, together, doing something fun. Yes, please. "Sign me up."

"How's that?" Marta asked. "You want me to sign you up for softball? C'mon, let's go talk to the coach." She faked standing up.

Shanice laughed. "Uh, I think there's kind of a big obstacle, though." She gestured as if to say, 'Duh, you've missed the obvious.'

"What?" Marta said. "I'll sign you up and tell you to go out there and land on your own two feet." Marta bugged her eyes out. Oh, yes, this was a challenge. Shanice couldn't help the grin creeping up her own face.

"Oh, is that so? You'd probably tell me to put my best foot forward next, huh?"

Marta snorted and needed a napkin to wipe up the vanilla ice cream that leaked out of her mouth from her old-lady creamsicle, which she had been properly teased about, of course.

"Oh, it's on," Marta said. "Keep your eyes on the stars, Shanice, and—"

"My feet firmly planted on the ground. Right?" Shanice shrieked with laughter, causing some of the fans in the bleachers to look their way.

"Sorry," Marta said to the scowling people and stood up. She unlocked Shanice's wheels, and they giggled all the way back to the pickup.

Once back at the house, they checked on the cats, all five of them, and sat out back for a while. Shanice was kind of quiet, though, while Marta did most of the talking. She was making all these plans to sturdy up the outside ramp and to build another smaller one out back, so Shanice could get to the driveway on her own where the outdoor garbage and recycling bins were. And a bed. Marta wanted Shanice to have an adjustable bed to make life easier. And two new wheelchairs—one that was electric and one that would be lighter and easier to transport. Although Marta mused that if she installed a chair lift thingy on the back of her pickup, they could take the electric wheelchair everywhere they went.

When Shanice tried to bring up paying rent, Marta wouldn't listen. It was really frustrating. Didn't she understand that for Shanice to feel all this independence Marta kept talking about, she needed to pay her own way and not accept charity?

Shanice now lay in bed, handsome and patient Bernard tucked in her arms, wondering where her life was going to go from there. She had no one. Not really. Marta, for now. That would change, but Shanice had given in and decided to accept the help until Marta's generosity waned. Which it would because resentment on Marta's part would eventually set in, and Shanice would move out and end up in a place like Mrs. Dupont's.

The tears started quietly, but Shanice couldn't get thoughts about all the obstacles in her future out of her heart. They ramped up, and she couldn't get a hold of them. She tried to muffle her sobs in Bernard's fur, but apparently, she hadn't been successful.

"Honey," Marta said, rushing to her bedside. "What's wrong? Do you hurt anywhere?"

Shanice shook her head.

Marta's tears started as she searched Shanice's face for the cause of the meltdown. "Does it hurt in here?" Marta pointed to her own chest.

Shanice nodded, letting loose a fresh batch of tears.

"Oh, my goodness," Marta said. "So many feels happening all at once."

Shanice nodded again and wiped at her wet face.

"Want me to hold you?" Marta asked softly.

That would be amazing. Shanice shimmied over, making room for Marta, who got in under the covers and lay on her back.

"C'mere," Marta said softly and patted her shoulder closest to Shanice. "Put your head here."

When Shanice lifted her upper body to move, Marta wrapped one arm around her back and pulled her close. Shanice's head now lay in the well of Marta's shoulder. Marta kissed the top of Shanice's head and said, "You're okay, honey. I'm not going to let anything or anyone get you."

"No?"

"You are so safe with me, little girl."

The words 'little girl' did something to Shanice's heart, and she softened into Marta's embrace. It was then that she realized that her chin had nestled into the top of Marta's soft breast. Did Marta realize that?

"Good girl," Marta cooed. "Relax now. Even though you might not have physical pain, that emotional stuff always gets us. You know?"

Shanice nodded and automatically moved her hand toward her face. No. She would not suck her thumb. Not now. Never again. She had to break that baby habit.

"You can," Marta said gently. "I don't see anything wrong with you sucking your thumb, kid. It's a comfort thing, I know. I understand. I do pushups when I need comfort, and you suck your thumb."

Shanice's waterworks started again, but she put her thumb in her mouth anyway.

"Shh, shh, shh," Marta said, rocking her gently.

A calmness overtook Shanice slowly. She found herself falling asleep when Marta started humming a soothing song. A lullaby, maybe? She was asleep before she could ask.

Hours later, she woke up, and Marta was still there holding her. Hmm, maybe Marta would stay. That was her last thought as she fell back asleep.

Chapter 17

Marta

Marta worked seven days a week at Carter Nursery and Landscaping. She worked so much to make ends meet. She'd fallen behind trying to pay her mother's medical bills, but those had finally been fully paid off from her mother's estate. Marta was, however, behind paying Nora for her share of the inherited house. Nora was okay with it; Brian, not so much, but he could fuck off for all she cared. And now her priorities were changing. She wanted to back off her busy schedule to spend more time with Shanice, making sure she got what she needed. How Marta would be able to do that *and* make enough money to pay the bills was a mystery at the moment. At least she got paid time and a half when working overtime. But then there was that other stuff. Roger had put her on manure duty again simply because she asked for Sunday afternoon off. Not only did he *not* give her those few hours off, but he sent her up front to shovel shit. Something needed to give. And soon.

While she took an extra-long time in the shower washing off the stink of Happy Cow Composted Cow Manure from her body, nails, hair, and aura, Shanice was doing an extra physical therapy session in the living room on her own. When Marta suggested the extra session, Shanice didn't moan or groan. She just said, "Yes, Ma'am," and got started. Shanice needed to be strong, and she understood that. They both did. Holding Shanice for a few hours while she slept last night was also a balm for Marta's heart. Shanice was definitely more relaxed this morning, that was for sure. At some point, she hoped Shanice would share what had upset her the night before, but Marta wasn't going to push. Shanice had every right to feel her feels. And Marta did, too. It had felt natural to hold Shanice in her arms and soothe her. And Bernard. Bernard needed soothing, too, apparently.

Marta chuckled as she stepped out of the shower. Going along with the whole Bernard thing had surprised Marta. She hadn't known she'd be so okay with that and Shanice's thumb sucking. Both were soothers for the young woman currently lifting three-pound weights in the living room. It was as if Marta's soul was responding to this person that had been placed in her life for some reason.

Marta dressed and headed back to the living room in time to see Shanice flex a bicep muscle.

"Nice," Marta said appreciatively, which caused Shanice to jump and hide her face.

"I'm trying to get big guns like yours," Shanice said, peeking over her hand.

"You've had this, like, burst of healing or something," Marta said, putting her keys and wallet in her pockets. "You have so much more energy than a week ago. You and the kittens are getting stronger simultaneously."

Shanice bopped joyfully in her chair.

"Time to go," Marta said. They were almost three hours late for the party, but that couldn't be helped. Once in the pickup, Marta texted Dana with their ETA. She put her phone away, and they headed out.

The ride was kind of quiet, and Marta sensed Shanice's nervousness.

"We don't have to stay the whole time," Marta said as Shanice pointed down a side street, giving her the navigation directions.

"Okay," came the short answer.

"Listen. Dana is a sweetheart. I think you'll like her, so there will be at least one nice person at this party."

"Okay." Again. One word.

Marta pulled over to the side of the road. "Tell me." She turned to look at Shanice.

"What if they look at me like that lady in the restaurant did the other night?"

"Then they look at you that way." Marta put what she hoped was a calming hand on Shanice's forearm. "Seriously. If they do, then it says more about them than it does you. Tell you what. We both know people will be curious, so how about we tell Dana how you got this way and ask her to spread it around casually."

"Okay."

"And I'll be with you, too. Don't forget that. Best foot…"

"Forward?" Shanice said and grinned.

"There's that smile I love." Marta squeezed the forearm she was still holding as calm spread through her chest. Shanice did this to her. Taking care of Shanice did this. Marta cleared her throat. "Onward and upward?"

"Yes, Ma'am," Shanice said. "The house is right up there. The last one on the right."

Marta whistled at the amazing landscaping in the front yard. "Wow. Dana wasn't kidding. She designed the yard for a class she was taking. Got an A-plus on it."

"I'll say," Shanice said. "It's so nice."

Marta pulled into the driveway and waved at Dana, who had obviously been waiting for them. "That's Dana."

"She's so petite. And pretty."

"Like you," Marta said and winked. "There's lots of room on your side, so we should be good to go."

"Hi, Miss Marta," Dana called as she skipped over to the pickup. "Hi, Miss Marta's friend. Shanice, right?"

Shanice nodded, looking shy.

"Aww," Dana said. "You are so cute. Oh, my God. Everyone is going to love you."

Bless Dana for putting Shanice at ease right away.

"Good music," Shanice said to Dana. "I love The Benjies."

"I love love love them, too," Dana gushed.

Much to Marta's absolute amazement, Shanice took the initiative and told Dana an abridged version of her accident and that she had been on her way to a Benjies' concert when it happened.

Much to Dana's credit, she listened and didn't put on a pity face. She said, "Life sucks sometimes, doesn't it?"

Shanice nodded. "Yeah. And it's okay if you tell everyone what happened to me."

“So they won’t stare at you the whole time wondering, right?”

“And making up their own theories,” Shanice added.

“Good point. Consider it done. Will the music bother you?” Dana asked as Marta settled Shanice into the wheelchair.

“Not at all.” Shanice smiled that endearing smile that killed Marta every time. “Mutual love for The Benjies, right?”

The two young women bumped fists and laughed when they both made fireworks with their fingers.

Marta sang Dana’s praises silently. “Oh, before I forget,” Marta said. “We brought a housewarming gift. Let’s get them out of the truck bed so I don’t end up bringing them back home.”

“You didn’t have to bring us anything, Ma’am,” Dana said.

“You want to put in a butterfly garden out back, right?” Marta lowered the tailgate, and Dana just about swooned. “Employee discount.”

“Ma’am! Oh, my God. Purple Coneflowers, Black-eyed Susans, Butterfly Weed, Blue Aster, Joe-Pye Weed.” She hugged Marta and then leaned down to hug Shanice. “I’m going to get started tomorrow right after work.”

“Which means we’ll go over the care and feeding of each one of these tomorrow, won’t we?” Marta asked. Marta was sure that Roger, her increasingly irritating boss, had assigned Dana to Marta because he thought she would hate having someone trail after her at work. Unfortunately, that had backfired because she found she liked having the company. Happy accidents seemed to be in her favor lately.

“Yes, Ma’am,” Dana said and started pulling out the potted plants. Marta helped her, and in no time, they had all ten plants neatly lined up on the side of the garage.

The song on the backyard speakers changed, and Shanice gushed, “Alicia Keys? Oh, yes, please.” Dana held her fist out for Shanice to bump, and this time Marta was the one who laughed at the ensuing finger fireworks.

As they headed into the noisy backyard, Marta let Dana and Shanice’s chatter fall into the background. She was on alert, as always. Her gaze swept from left to right. Thankfully, no one stared at Shanice. A barbecue grill and people fussing over food were on one side. There was a smattering of people in chairs holding plates of food in their laps. Others were sitting at a table. In the middle were kids—no, twenty-somethings—playing with a soccer ball on the backyard grass. On the other side, more people stood and talked while holding beverages. There was a lot to take in, but Marta was excited to see a wide variety of colors, ages, and backgrounds represented at the party. She had hoped Dana and Shanice wouldn't be the only people of color there.

Funny how she had been worried about that. She'd never thought about things like that before meeting Shanice. Deciding that all was secure, Marta let herself focus on Dana.

"So, Miss Jaleesa wants to meet you guys immediately," Dana said. "There she is." The tone in her voice was one of pure love. It became even more obvious when the woman, who must be Jaleesa, spotted them and smiled. "Isn't she a stud?" Dana whispered behind her upheld hand.

The woman was positively gorgeous. And tall. And strong. Shanice wanted biceps like Marta? Pfft. Marta wanted biceps like Jaleesa's. Jaleesa made her way over to them.

Jaleesa was a lighter-skinned Black woman with a mega-watt smile. "You must be Marta," Jaleesa said, holding out her hand.

Marta shook hands, nodded, and said, "Thank you for inviting us. This is Shanice."

Jaleesa's grin crept up her face as she stuck her hand out toward Shanice. And then the funniest thing happened. Grasping Shanice's hand, Jaleesa vigorously shook Shanice's entire arm. "Nice to meet you."

Shanice couldn't even answer; she was giggling so hard.

The four of them laughed, and Marta conveyed her thanks for breaking the ice with a smile and a nod toward Dana's Domme.

"Nice to meet you, too," Shanice said finally but couldn't help the tiny giggle that followed.

Jaleesa winked at her. "C'mon, let's meet the family."

They met Tina, Jaleesa's pale white girlfriend, who was clearly submissive but was also somehow in charge. A switch, Marta decided. Harriet was an older white woman with slightly graying hair who was submissive but stood tall with a clear sense of purpose.

And Marta hadn't realized that when Jaleesa said they were meeting the "family," that pretty much meant everyone at the party, except for the young people now playing tag in the yard. Marta and Shanice met Dana's bestie Kadesha and Dana's adorable parents. They also met Jaleesa's parents and siblings, as well as Tina's parents, who were going to Hawaii any minute now, apparently.

Marta recognized a small group of people from the coffee shop. Rikki, the owner of the shop, was there, standing tall and stoic. The worker named Brittany gushed at seeing Marta and then gushed at Shanice's cuteness. Marta wondered if Shanice hated being called 'cute' and 'adorable.' Maybe she wanted to be seen as the twenty-five-year-old grown-up woman that she was. Shanice wasn't a child. But then again, there was Bernard and the thumb sucking and the bouncing up and down in her chair. Yes, Shanice was kind of childlike. If they were going to be housemates, Marta needed to have some kind of conversation with her about all of that.

There had been so many people to meet that Marta's head was swimming. Besides Jaleesa, Tina, and Harriet, Marta retained no new names in her brain. Oh, well. She'd probably never see these people again, anyway.

After Jaleesa excused herself, saying the grill needed her, Dana led them to a long table where Rikki and some other women were now sitting.

"Hello, Miss Marta," Brittany said. "I know you just got here, but I have to head back to the coffee shop."

Rikki leaned over and teased, "And call her Domme on the way there."

"I miss her so much," Brittany wailed half-seriously.

"Life of a news reporter," Rikki said to the young woman.

Brittany said her goodbyes to everyone at the table, and Marta tried to remember the names. Brittany was obviously a submissive because she called the Dommes at the table "Miss." There was Miss Rowena, Miss Shasti, and Miss Rikki. And then there was the handsome androgynous woman with the impeccably styled hair that probably wouldn't move even if a tornado hit it. She was referred to as Daddy Vic. Maybe *she* wasn't the correct pronoun. Marta wasn't sure and wasn't about to ask.

Miss Shasti, the deep brown woman of South Asian descent, asked Marta, "How long have you two been together?"

"Oh, we're not together," Marta said quickly. Shanice simply giggled and exchanged a glance with Marta.

Shasti narrowed her eyes in clear disbelief and confusion. It was almost as if Marta had just declared that the earth was flat.

Marta didn't know what to make of the woman's lifted eyebrow and doubtful expression except to lash out silently and tell the woman to mind her own business. She took a breath and gave the table the briefest of explanations about how she and Shanice had met. She did not, however, mention the chokehold she'd put on Tyler, the nurses' aide, that fateful day.

Marta could see a thousand questions burning in Shasti's eyes and was ever thankful when Tina, Jaleesa's submissive—okay, *one* of Jaleesa's submissives—popped up at their sides and asked, "Are you two hungry? We have plenty."

"Yes, Ma'am," Shanice said politely.

Marta felt strangely proud that Shanice had such amazing manners. Not that she was Shanice's keeper or anything.

"Sure," Marta said. "Thank you." She turned to the women at the table. "Excuse us for a moment."

Tina led the way back to the grill and the food tables. She leaned down toward Shanice and half-whispered behind her hand, "Doesn't Jaleesa look so good in that apron? Grilling steaks?"

Shanice nodded vigorously. Uh, oh. Maybe Shanice was developing a crush on Tina's Domme. She could see how easy that would be.

Tina grabbed a plate and filled it at Shanice's direction. Wow, the kid was not afraid of food. Marta had pictured Shanice as a hotdog and potato chips kind of gal, but she told Tina she'd like to try a little of everything if that was okay. And apparently, it was. Back at the table, Shanice had a small sliver of steak with mushrooms and grilled onions, coleslaw, and collard greens—her favorite. The last thing was some kind of bean concoction that Tina had called three-bean salad. Shanice even made Marta put some on her own plate. "You have to try," Shanice said, sounding like a mom.

Tina carried Shanice's plate and plasticware back to the table and then excused herself. Her parents were leaving to go home and pack for their big trip.

Shanice ate a spoonful of each food and moaned at the wonderful flavors. "So good."

"Everything's homemade," Rikki said.

"It's very good," Marta added, not knowing what else to say. Small talk wasn't her forte.

Shanice attacked her steak next, except the attack wasn't going well. She had tried cutting the steak, but it proved too difficult with her one weak arm. Marta didn't say a word and pulled Shanice's plate toward her to cut the steak into small pieces.

"Thanks, Marta," Shanice said and shot her a grateful look that was so adorable that Marta's mouth fell open.

"You're welcome, kid. Now you owe me one."

"Ha ha," Shanice said and stabbed a piece of steak. "If we're really counting, I owe you, like, a million billion."

"Wow," Rikki said. "That's a lot."

Shanice simply nodded, and Marta simply welled up with emotion. She hated that her tears came so readily. Happy or sad, the tears just came. Her mother had always called Marta her "sensitive" daughter. Everyone had been surprised when Marta announced her decision to join the Army right after high school. And no one there at the table where she currently sat would ever think she'd been a tough badass Corporal at one point in her life. But that was a long time ago.

Marta blinked back her tears and turned to smile at Rikki and the others at the table. The one named Shasti looked at her with an expression that said something along the lines of, "We all see it. No sense hiding the truth there, Marta." Marta looked away quickly. She hated when people thought they knew your business. Whatever. She would probably never see any of these people again. Except for Dana on Monday. And Rikki and the rest of the coffee crew at the shop.

Apparently, Dana's Domme had instructed Dana to circulate at the party to make sure everyone felt welcomed, but she finally made it to their table and sat down. Dana nodded to each of the Dommes, including Marta, before sitting down. Marta and Shanice finished eating, and Marta agreed when Shanice said the food was excellent.

Dana said, "All made with love."

"Tasted like it," Shanice said.

Marta found her hand reaching toward Shanice's but slammed it back in her lap. What the hell? "So, butterflies like milkweed," Marta said awkwardly to Dana.

"Ooh, yes," Dana gushed. "Good idea. They'll attract Monarchs."

"The ones we had at work were on their way out," Marta said. "Wouldn't have made a good gift."

Shanice giggled. "Here's a dying plant to warm your house with."

Everyone at the table chuckled, and it made Marta's heart warm. While Dana chattered on about butterfly shelters and puddling stations, Marta noticed that even the stoic stout brunette at the end of the table smiled. The quiet woman next to the brunette was clearly her submissive. Her expression didn't change at all, however. Was her name Minjung? Marta couldn't remember, but she got the feeling that Minjung wasn't a mere submissive. No, the East Asian woman with jet-black hair pulled into a tight bun on top of her head was the stout white woman's slave. Had to be. She didn't judge them for having a Mistress/slave relationship. To each her own. As long as it was consensual slavery with agreement from both sides.

A pained cry cut Marta's thoughts short. A blond, white young man who had been playing tag was down on the ground holding his knee. "You pushed me," he cried. An older man who seemed to have a couple of male subs at the party raced toward the young man. Seamus? Yes, his name was Seamus. Marta gave herself a point for remembering that.

"I did not," a young woman of East Asian descent, her hair pulled back into two cute pigtails, said without passion. "You tripped over your own big feet."

"Did not, jerk," he said to her.

The most exasperated sigh emanated from someone at their table, and Shasti stood up. "Please excuse me while I see to this latest disaster." She headed toward the mayhem on the grass. "Madison Kim, you come here right now."

"Whoa," Shanice said, feeling the stern energy. She exchanged a glance with Marta, who felt the same way. That woman was not one to mess with.

It took several moments to calm both young people, and then it suddenly dawned on Marta. She leaned toward Rikki and said, "*Littles*?"

Rikki nodded. "Oh, yes." She gestured toward Shasti and Madison, who was now crying, and said, "They just celebrated their one-year, one-month anniversary."

"That's sweet," Marta said. And it was. Shasti enlisted the help of one of Seamus's many subs, a tall Black guy in his early thirties, maybe. He had the coolest facial hair she'd ever seen and carried himself well. He pulled out some books and put them on an empty table. What the hell? Were those coloring books? Yes, they were. So much for being vanilla.

Dana stood up and excused herself to check on her parents. Marta thought maybe it was to divert their attention from the D/s activities going on right in front of them.

Shasti plunked a bag on the table and spoke so softly to the two *littles* that Marta couldn't hear her. She said something to Seamus's sub, the one with the cool facial hair, and he looked over at their table and nodded.

He walked over and nodded submissively to all the Dommes in much the same way Dana had done. "Miss Marta," he said out loud. "Would your *little* like to join the others for coloring?"

Marta was floored by the request. One – Marta wasn't Shanice's Mommy Domme. Two – ask her yourself. Three – what the hell?

"Can I, Marta?" Shanice was sitting tall in her chair, bouncing with excitement.

Marta was tongue-tied momentarily. "Uhh, if you want to, go ahead." Duh, obviously Shanice wanted to. "Yes, yes," Marta said with more authority and stood up.

"Ma'am," Seamus's sub said, "I can take her."

"Copy that." Marta sat down feeling a little lost. "Have fun," she called after Shanice.

"I will," Shanice called back, looking over her shoulder.

Shanice looked so happy going over to color. Marta watched as Seamus petted his young *little* on the head, and Shasti spoke softly but firmly to hers. Marta turned and noticed Dana's father resting his elbow on short Dana's shoulder in a teasing gesture, and then saw Tina getting pulled into a hug by

Jaleesa after coming back outside. Even Harriet, Jaleesa's other sub, looked at them with a soulful expression that soared right into Marta's heart.

An ache set up camp in her chest. Something was happening. She looked at the women sharing her table. Rikki was beaming at the *littles*. The person called Daddy Vic was smirking good-naturedly. Even the silent slave at the end of the table was giving her stoic Domme an affectionate look.

Marta made a slight choking noise as the love surrounding her permeated her soul. She turned to see Shanice take the box of crayons from Shasti's *little,* who had apparently recovered and was now happy. Shanice's grin was incredible. She glanced back at Marta as if sensing Marta's intense gaze. Shanice's gorgeous smile lit her face broadcasting her affection for Marta. An affection that Marta, right there on a warm July evening, realized she also had for Shanice.

Oh, God, Marta was going to lose it right there in front of everyone. She put a hand over her mouth to keep it all in. Pressure built in her chest. What was it? It was a yearning. For what? For something different. A different life. A different meaning to her days.

A gentle hand came to rest on her forearm—Rikki's. Marta looked up at the coffee shop owner, blinking away tears. It was difficult, but she fought her emotions and finally caught her breath enough to move her hand away from her mouth and say, "I'm okay."

"I don't know you at all," Rikki said quietly so the others wouldn't overhear. "But it has been my absolute pleasure watching you realize how much in love you are with that young woman over there." She pulled her hand off Marta's arm.

Marta searched Rikki's face with a thousand questions, none of which Rikki could answer. Was Rikki right? Is that what she was feeling? Love?

"She'll be okay," Rikki said. "She has you. And if I'm reading things right, she has all of us, too. You both do."

That undid Marta. Rikki quickly handed her a napkin to cry into and rubbed her back. "You're okay, Marta. You've got us now. All of us."

Shanice must have sensed something and turned around. Her face fell when she noticed Marta crying.

"I'm okay," Marta squeaked. She cleared her throat and said again, much stronger this time, "I'm okay. Really. I'm fine."

"You sure?" Shanice asked, a concerned expression etched into her features.

Marta managed to get herself together and look strong. She had to in front of the kid. "Yes. Draw me a picture."

A smile lit Shanice's face, and she bopped back to her coloring.

Marta turned back to Rikki and said, "Thank you."

"Like I said. You'll both be okay."

Marta's world had just been thrown sideways. She was in love with Shanice. Huh, imagine that.

Chapter 18

Shanice

Madison held out a red crayon. “This one’s better for the cape.” She pointed to the flying Marta that Shanice had drawn on the paper. “Is she your superhero? Your Domme?”

“Marta’s not dumb.” How dare this person say things like that about Marta. Marta was amazing.

Billy, sitting on the other side of the table, burst out laughing.

Shut up, Shanice thought in her head. *These two are stupid doody heads.* She figured she’d finish her drawing, give it to Marta, who would probably hang it on the fridge later when they got back to the house, and then sit by Marta, her safe space.

“Shut up, Billy,” Madison said, and by some miracle, he did. “No, Shanice, it’s D-o-m-m-e.” She spelled the word out. “It means your Dominant, like the person who takes care of you.”

“Oh,” Shanice said, instantly regretting her mean thoughts about them. “Marta, you mean? She’s totally my superhero if you haven’t figured that out.” She tapped her paper.

“Superhero,” Billy repeated. “Seamus is my superhero. He takes care of me. The other guys do too, but I’m Papa’s special boy.”

“Miss Shasti takes care of me, too,” Madison said with a contented sigh. “She sort of rescued me, so I guess she’s my superhero, too.” Madison pushed away her unfinished picture of a bluebird and pulled over a fresh sheet of blank paper. “I’m going to draw a superhero Shasti.”

“Me, too,” Billy said, getting himself a fresh sheet of paper. “Superhero Seamus. No, no, superhero Sir.” He giggled mainly to himself and began drawing. “Super Sir.”

"Mistress signed me up for more swimming lessons," Madison said. "She made me take them at the Y for a few months before we went to visit her parents. They live in Washington, DC. We flew in a plane and went to the beach, too. Have you ever flown in a plane, Shanice? Or seen the ocean?" Before Shanice could shake her head, Madison continued. "Both were so scary, but Mistress was calm, so I was okay."

"I've been in a plane," Billy said.

"I haven't," Shanice offered.

"Maybe your Mommy Domme will take you somewhere," Madison said to Shanice. "Mistress has more trips planned for us. August is Los Angeles for more beaches, Disneyland, and maybe a trip to the San Diego Zoo if I behave. In the fall, we might go to a Vermont hotel in the woods to see the leaves change. I keep lobbying for a trip to the Bronx Zoo, but she hasn't put that on the schedule so far. And then in the spring, we might go to England. I applied for my passport already."

"That's a lot of traveling," Shanice said.

"Mistress has travel fever or something," Madison said.

"She has you now," Billy said without looking up. "She has a traveling buddy."

"Yeah, I guess," Madison acquiesced. "And then I might go to college. Next summer, maybe. She wants me to try. I have to study for the SATs first, though. I took them a long time ago, but she says they have to be more current or something. She ordered some vocabulary flashcards for me."

"Sounds boring," Billy said.

"Totally," Madison said. "So, are you in school, Shanice? Do you work? How long have you and your Domme been together? She seems really nice. She looks really strong, like she could pick you and your wheelchair up all at once. How long have you been in that wheelchair? What happened to your legs?"

It was too much. The last two questions were still ringing in Shanice's ears like a gong hit near her head. Without answering, Shanice turned to look back at Marta, who smiled and waved. She threw her a questioning thumbs-up and raised her eyebrows. Shanice threw her a tentative thumbs-up back and then returned to her drawing.

"You're so stupid," Billy hissed at Madison. "Maybe she doesn't want to talk about that."

"Sorry, Shanice," Madison said. "Mistress says I don't engage brain before engaging mouth."

"It's okay," Shanice said, taking a breath. She gave them an even shorter version of her accident than the one she'd given Dana. She did, however, sing Marta's praises for helping her out as much as she did.

"Miss Marta went and got everything out of your car?" Billy asked wide-eyed. "Do you have pictures of the car?"

"No," Shanice said. "Marta does, but I don't want to see them."

"I don't blame you," said a voice behind them. It was that handsome Deshawn who seemed to also take care of Billy. "How about we change the subject," Deshawn said. "Tell me what you're drawing. Superheroes, hmm?"

Madison took up the talking, which was okay-fine with Shanice because she felt shy around Deshawn for some reason. He was a brother and was cute; maybe that was it. No, that wasn't it, she decided after a while. He was gentle and attentive to each of them. Maybe she felt like a little sister around him. Not that she really knew how that felt. And anyway, Deshawn was a gay man, and he and Billy and that South Asian guy over there went with Seamus in some way. They were all gay for each other. Shanice hid her smile behind her hand. It was kind of like the way Dana, Tina, and the lady named Harriet were with Jaleesa. Were they all gay for each other, too? Maybe she'd ask Marta about it later. Maybe not. How would she phrase it?

Madison's incessant chatter morphed into talking about the Cincinnati Zoo and the various animals and attractions. Madison's monologue didn't need much attention from Shanice, so she kind of zoned out, trying to get Marta's eyes right. Frustrated, she sighed and looked up. Deshawn had been drawing, too, but was currently gazing off into space. She followed his gaze and realized it wasn't space. It was Jaleesa. Ho, ho! Deshawn had a crush on Jaleesa. But he was a gay man, and she…Maybe they were bi or pan or whatever. Shanice looked down and scolded herself for meddling in other people's business.

She couldn't help being nosy, though. These people were interesting. They were kind and thoughtful. Even Madison's girlfriend, Miss Shasti, was nice. Okay, she was fiercely strict, too, but only because she wanted Madison to behave well. She was protective. That was it. Was Marta that way, too? Yes, sometimes. But then, other times, she seemed nervous. She was definitely an emotional person. Like what had made Marta cry before? Shanice's heart hurt a little at that. She hoped Marta wasn't sad about something.

Madison and Billy seemed to be BFFs. He was teasing her about how lame the bird shows were at the zoo, and she was defending them. And then he said something that got everyone's attention. "Madison, you're really pretty."

"What?" Madison asked, clearly confused.

"Pretty annoying." Billy burst out laughing, earning him a smack on the arm from Madison.

Shanice exchanged an amused glance with Deshawn, who just shook his head and rolled his eyes for her benefit.

Yes, Deshawn was cute, but in a big brother kind of way. Shanice wasn't bisexual. Maybe she was asexual or something. No, that meant 'without sex' or without sexual attraction. She recalled the dream she'd had at the Chrysalis Center about Marta. That one had been way sexual. No, she wasn't asexual. Not at all. The fact that she'd never had a girlfriend was because she was kind of shy around girls. Well, before the accident, anyway. And now? Now she was damaged goods, and no one would ever ask her out. She'd kind of resolved herself to a solitary life, anyway. It was easier. And now she sort of lived with Marta. For how long, though? What if Marta found a new girlfriend? Marta would be really nice about it and help her find a place to live and not a place like Mrs. Dupont's. Shanice warmed a little recalling how firm Marta was about never letting Shanice live in a shitty place like that. She giggled inside at her chosen curse word that no one at the table knew she'd said to herself. Hee hee hee.

Shanice finished her drawing and excused herself from the coloring table. She put the picture facedown in her lap and wheeled herself across the concrete pad toward Marta.

"Whatcha got there, kid?" Marta asked.

"For you." Shanice handed Marta the drawing.

What was funny was how the pretty Miss Rikki handed Marta a napkin as if she knew Marta's waterworks would start. And they did. "Thank you so much, honey." Marta ran her fingers over the vibrant red of the billowing cape. "Look how I'm holding Bernard."

"Mm hmm," Shanice said. She had to include Bernard. Duh.

"The artist didn't sign the work," Miss Rikki said, sounding shocked. "That will never do." She reached into a small bag on the table and pulled out a pen. She handed it to Shanice.

"Really?" Shanice looked at Marta.

"Absolutely," Marta said. "And I have just the spot on the fridge to hang it."

Shanice wiggled in her wheelchair before she knew she was doing it. She clicked the pen open and signed her name in her best penmanship. As she was handing the pen back to Miss Rikki, she had regrets. She should have made it more personal. Like, "To Marta, who makes me feel safe." Or "To Marta, who makes me feel loved."

Shanice looked up into Marta's face. They locked gazes like they'd done a few times before. Shanice swallowed hard. She understood now. It had evaded her for some reason. She had a crush, a major crush, on Marta. Duh, the sex dream should have been a big clue. Shanice looked away, embarrassed. Marta must never know. That would make it so awkward at the house. They were housemates. That was it. That. Was. It.

"Guess what, Shanice?" Marta said.

"What?"

"Jaleesa invited us to go on a hike with them next Saturday."

"Uh, Marta?" Shanice said. "Have you forgotten an important detail?"

Marta chuckled. "Tina says it's a paved path, and they've seen quite a few strollers and wheelchairs on it. I mean, unless you'd rather *not* see the waterfall at the end."

"I do, I do." Shanice bounced again. "Maybe I should use your work gloves or something. Save my delicate hands."

Miss Rikki and the cute boyish-looking person next to Miss Rikki laughed at her silliness. Shanice was pretty sure the boyish person was a woman, but it was kind of hard to tell.

"You do a lot of hiking?" the boyish person asked Marta.

Marta opened her mouth to answer and then scoffed. "Back in the day."

"Military?"

Marta nodded. "Army. You?"

"Reserves. Deployed?"

"Iraq," Marta said succinctly. "You?"

"No, but thank you for serving."

"Yes," Miss Rikki agreed. "Thank you both for serving." She smiled at the boyish person, who nodded in acknowledgment.

The big woman at the other end of the table also expressed her thanks. The quiet lady next to her didn't speak but nodded and then did something weird. She turned her palms up. It didn't make any sense to Shanice.

"I served here at home for four very long years," the boyish person said. "I got out as soon as I could. I wasn't cut out for all that discipline coming at me. I'd rather give it."

"Victoria," Miss Rikki scolded under her breath.

"What? She's one of the gang, isn't she, Rik?"

Marta nodded to corroborate the statement.

"What gang?" Shanice asked innocently.

The silence at the table grew long and awkward until Marta finally said, "I'll explain it later, okay? When we get home."

"Okay." Shanice knew she'd just been blown off. That kind of thing happened all the time in the foster homes. Shanice learned it was kind of futile to even ask about stuff. She had forgotten that lesson when she opened her stupid mouth just now. She was irritated about being ignored, but it was tempered by the fact that Marta had said, 'home.' 'When we get home,' Marta had said. Warm feels settled in Shanice's chest.

A big bellowing voice sounded from the other side of the patio, "The vanillas have left the building. I repeat. The vanillas have vacated." It was Jaleesa. Shanice had no clue what Jaleesa meant by that, but apparently, the others did because Madison flew out of her coloring chair to Miss Shasti near the barbecue grill, and Billy flew to Seamus at a table along the side fence. And then both grownups did strange things. They put something around the necks of the younger ones. Collars? Shanice looked at Marta, but

Marta didn't catch her gaze.

Shanice's eyes got big as she watched the big lady put a leather collar around the quiet East Asian lady and then snap a leash onto it, of all things. Now on a leash, the woman stood up, moved the chair back, and knelt on the concrete pad next to the big lady's chair. "Good girl," the big lady said, patting the other one's head like a dog.

Shanice got uncomfortable. Was this some kind of cult or something? Was Marta going to put a dog collar on her? Shanice looked at Marta, who was blushing fiery red. Maybe this stuff embarrassed her, too. There didn't seem to be a collar in Marta's proximity, which relieved Shanice greatly.

Madison came over to Marta. "Miss Marta, I'm sorry that I never greeted you properly." She handed a ribbon to Marta and then leaned down. Marta seemed to know what to do and attached the ribbon to the collar. The ribbon read, *I disrespected a Dom/me.*

"You're a good girl, Madison," was all Marta said.

Things were very weird. It was like that book *Stranger in a Strange Land*, an old science fiction book she'd read once. She was the stranger, and this backyard had suddenly become a very strange land.

Dana came over, and Shanice was surprised to see that she, too, wore a collar. It was a pretty pink one, though. She handed Marta a ribbon and said, "Miss Marta, I'm sorry for forgetting my place at work the other day. Miss Jaleesa thought it best that you place the ribbon and then suggest any other punishment for me."

Marta attached the ribbon and said, "No other punishment necessary. You're a good submissive, Dana."

"Thank you, Ma'am." Dana headed back to Miss Jaleesa.

Shanice watched as Marta and Jaleesa exchanged some kind of knowing nod. Shanice was utterly baffled at all this weirdness but was somehow not surprised when Billy handed Miss Marta a ribbon as well. "You're a good boy," Marta told him, sending him back to Mr. Seamus.

Shanice glared at Marta. Marta must have felt the laser beam eyes boring into her and turned, red-faced, toward Shanice. Shanice leaned closer, "Do you know these people?"

"Only Dana."

"Then why are they…" Shanice's brain could not figure this one out. "Are you, like, a celebrity or something?"

Miss Rikki burst out laughing and then turned away while muttering, "Sorry."

"No, Shanice. They're showing their respect to me."

"Like some kind of *Domme* thing or something? Madison asked if you were my Domme."

"She did?" Marta looked as confused as Shanice felt.

"I'm not your Domme, sweetie. But I have been a Dominant to other women."

"What does that mean?"

Marta glanced at Miss Rikki, who seemed to be purposefully in deep conversation with Miss Shasti and Victoria. Or should it be Miss Victoria? No, no. She remembered now. It was Daddy Vic. Ahh, gender-bending. Or maybe non-binary.

Marta leaned closer and said in a low tone, "It means that some people like it when another person takes control of things. Guides them, if you will."

"Like you do for me?" Shanice asked.

"Sort of," Marta said and inhaled shakily. This must be hard for her to explain. Or maybe it was hard for her to admit. "Some people like to serve others."

"Like Harriet over there. And Deshawn."

"Very observant," Marta said, seeming proud of Shanice's observations. "Others need help managing their lives and learning how to manage themselves in the world." Shanice looked over at Madison, who was now hanging off one of Jaleesa's biceps. Literally. Her feet were dangling off the ground. It was kind of funny, actually. "Yes, like Madison," Marta said.

Like me, Shanice thought. Is that why they were at this party? So Marta could put a collar on her and boss her around? No, thank you.

"Other people only like that sort of thing in the bedroom," Marta continued. "One dominates, you know, takes charge. And the other is submissive. Some people are dominant in all aspects of their lives, and others are submissive. And then there are others—"

"Like Miss Tina," Shanice whispered after leaning in closer.

"Yes. I'm impressed that you noticed all of that. Some people are a bit of both. I mean, just think about people. Some lead, some follow, some do both."

"We all do both at different times."

"Touché, but sometimes there is an agreed-upon way to conduct a relationship between people. See Miss Shasti over there talking with Miss Jaleesa? She's called a Mommy Domme. I didn't figure that out until she resolved the scuffle earlier."

Shanice had no words. She was getting hung up on the word "Mommy." Someone who acted like a Mommy toward someone else who wanted her to act like their Mommy? She turned to look at Billy. Mr. Seamus must be a Daddy figure to Billy, then. Wow. Just wow.

"Can we talk about this more later?" Shanice asked. It was a lot to take in.

"Sure," Marta said, putting her arm on Shanice's forearm and rubbing twice before removing it. The touch was reassuring. Shanice liked it. But she didn't like the idea of a collar. That was…weird. And so was the lady on the leash. That was weird, too.

"Cookies?" Madison said, right next to Shanice's ear, making her jump. "I baked them, with Mistress's help, of course. It's part of my therapy. Dr. Sumner thinks it'll help me overcome my bad association with cookies."

"Thank you," was all Shanice could say, and took one cookie. She had no idea what the heck Madison was talking about, but if cookies were part of therapy, sign her up.

Shanice lasted another half hour. Her legs, pointing down for so long, were starting to swell. She didn't say anything, though, because this was Marta's friend Dana's party, and she didn't want to be the cause of any bad feelings.

"Yeah, you're right," Marta said to Shanice. "We should get you home."

Shanice's jaw dropped open. She hadn't said a word.

Marta smiled and said, "You're fidgeting, and I know you're uncomfortable. Maybe a bath when we get home? A hot soaking one?"

"Okay," Shanice said. She was still embarrassed that Marta kind of had to see her naked when she put her in and got her out of the tub.

"We can add bubbles if you want."

Now that perked Shanice right up. "Okay," she said much more enthusiastically.

"We're going to have to head out," Marta said to the women at the table. "We have a big day tomorrow. First day of occupational therapy, and my sister and her family are coming over for dinner."

"They are?" Shanice hadn't known that. Maybe that's what Marta had been doing on her phone. She was texting Nora.

"I let it slip that we had kittens in the house, and she lost her mind needing to see them." Marta made a silly face and added to Shanice, "Oh, and she said something about seeing you, too. Not me, mind you. Just you."

Shanice scrunched up her face as she giggled. Yeah, she and Nora had shared some good stories about Marta while in the Chrysalis Center together.

They said their goodbyes, and Miss Jaleesa and Dana walked them out to the pickup truck. It was weird. Even though Miss Tina was Miss Jaleesa's girlfriend, Jaleesa had her arm around Dana's shoulders, kind of protectively like a girlfriend. Whoa, Shanice realized something. Miss Jaleesa had two girlfriends. Maybe more. Her question was answered. They *were* all gay for each other. That was almost too much for Shanice's brain to understand.

Once on the road home, Shanice blurted, "I have to clean my room. It's Nora's room, and she's coming over."

Marta burst out laughing. "We have to clean the whole damn house."

"I can do that while you're at work tomorrow. I mean, I'll do what I can."

"I've already asked Mrs. Pulaski to do the cleaning when she comes over. I used to pay her to do that when she took care of my mom."

"Oh," Shanice said, not sure why this bit of news hurt her feelings. Did Marta think Shanice couldn't do it on her own? Ugh. She was tired. Too tired to delve further into it. Once home, she barely woke up when Marta carried her into the house, put her on the toilet, and then got her into bed, tucking Bernard into her arms. "Love you," Shanice heard Marta say as she left the room.

Shanice's eyes popped open, but Marta was gone already. Didn't matter. She wouldn't have had the nerve to ask her what she meant by it. "What is love, anyway?" Shanice murmured to Bernard as she fell back to sleep.

Chapter 19

Marta

Amazingly, the week went by quickly. Even Marta's supervisor, Roger, hadn't been much of an ass until she asked for Saturday off to go hiking. There was no contest when it came down to working or giving Shanice the opportunity to make new friends. And a small part of Marta knew that her own soul craved friendship, too. Both Shanice and Dana had been put in her path for a reason. Marta just wasn't sure what those reasons were, though, but she wasn't going to pass up the outreach of friendship. Yes, it was only a hike, but honestly? It was so much more.

The occupational therapist had come on Monday afternoon and assessed Shanice's ability to care for herself. The two main issues were getting on the toilet and into the bathtub on her own. The therapist didn't want to work on either of these until they had installed adjustable handrails on the toilet and gotten a different kind of wheelchair for Shanice to move in and out of more easily. She also recommended a tub bench that would make it easier for Shanice to get in and out on her own as well as a handheld showerhead mounted lower and within Shanice's reach on the new bench. She showed them options for all the items on her laptop, and Shanice and Marta exchanged glances. These things were pricey. But Shanice needed them. After the therapist left that day, Shanice got busy making a list of medical supply stores for them to hit all over Denton Heights and the greater Cincinnati area. Hopefully, they could find some gently used, less expensive items. The therapist reminded them that Shanice's insurance might cover some of the cost, and Shanice added that to her list of calls to make the next day. One of the things the occupational therapist tried to hit home was that Shanice was adapting to a new body and a literal new sense of balance. Those things would take time, she'd counseled. Made sense.

Nora and her family came by Monday evening for an incredible visit. Nora was still using a walker, though, because of her obesity, she said. Nora brought a salad and beef stew for them to have for dinner. Yes, it was their mother's recipe. Nothing like comfort food. Even Nora's husband, Brian, wasn't a total ass that evening and was gentle with Shanice, asking her questions about the accident but not staying on the subject too long. One of the coolest things was when Shanice showed Marta's nephew Elliot Marta's gaming system. And even though the two of them made fun of the "archaic" system and the "lame" games, they played for over an hour until it was time for the big surgery right there on the kitchen table.

Shanice looked optimistically hopeful and nervous all at the same time as Nora undid the childish stitches in Bernard's leg. Nora was able to carefully add more stuffing after Shanice approved the machine-washable polyester Fiberfil material. Once they were both satisfied with Bernard's new 'boyish figure' as Nora called it, Nora stitched the leg back on expertly using a curved needle that Marta had seen her use before. The last part of the surgery was the most nerve-wracking for Shanice, but Nora was calm and cool and told Shanice everything she would do to replace his button eye with a real one. Shanice picked out the new eye from a selection that Nora brought. Crazily, it was almost an exact match to Bernard's existing eye. Marta and Brian exchanged a knowing glance at that point because Nora's craft room was stuffed to the gills with all manner of craft items which apparently included musk ox eyes.

The eye surgery was completed in less than two minutes, and Shanice gushed over Bernard when Nora handed him back to her. Marta teared up because, of course, she did. What amazed Marta was how easily her family took to Shanice. She was childlike in many ways, but they didn't seem put off by it. Even Elliot said Shanice was "cool" on his way out.

When her family headed out to go home, Brian and Elliot went to the car while Nora hung back with Marta on the front landing. Shanice was in the back bedroom checking on the kittens at Marta's request.

"I want two," Nora said.

"Of?"

"Those kittens, of course. Brian doesn't know it yet."

"You might have to arm wrestle Shanice for them. I don't know."

"Just let me know what you decide," Nora said. "But I'm serious about taking two, okay?"

"I'll tell Shanice and let you know what she says. Hey, did you ever take that quiz thing I sent you?" Marta asked as gently as she could.

"Yes," Nora answered succinctly but then added. "I never knew there was a thing called Overeaters Anonymous."

"And?" Marta swathed herself with all the patience she could muster. Nora was *not* the kind of person you told what to do. She'd dig in her heels and do the exact opposite. That's why Marta had only suggested the Overeaters Anonymous quiz after researching the twelve-step program.

"I have a sponsor."

"You what?" Marta gushed. "Does that mean you joined?"

Nora smiled and let Marta hug her. "I took the quiz and got, like, twelve yes answers out of fifteen. So, I found a Zoom meeting. I mean, Elliot had to help me get Zoom going and all that, but I've been to a lot of online meetings already."

"And you have a sponsor. Nora, that's fantastic."

"I hired a registered dietician or whatever they're called. She sent me a food plan where I have to weigh and measure my food. At first, I thought it would be a deal breaker, but it's fine. And Marta, it's good. I don't feel hungry. I don't feel anxious. And my sponsor says if I get anxious and want to go back 'into the food'— that's what they call it. She says I call her, and we examine what's going on together."

Marta was speechless. She pulled her sister into a hug over the walker. When she stepped back, Nora also had tears in her eyes. "Let me know what I can do to help you," Marta said, not knowing what that would be.

"Actually, you can do two things," Nora said quickly. "It's time."

"For?"

"To update the house. It's time for both of us to accept that Mom's gone. Mom *and* Dad. So, when you're ready, I want to come over and help you rip out all that old carpet, toss Mom's chair to the street, and move you into the primary bedroom."

"Mom's room?"

"She's gone, Pip," Nora said gently. She waited another beat and said, "It's not Mom's bedroom anymore."

Marta didn't say anything. She knew her mother was gone, but to hear the words out loud like that?

"I'm glad you didn't listen to me about taking down the ramp," Nora said, clearly shifting the conversation. "Weird."

"Yeah," Marta agreed. "Weird."

"She looks good, Marta," Nora said, obviously referring to Shanice.

"I know."

"You do, too."

Marta narrowed her eyes. "What do you mean?"

"She's good for you. That's all I'm going to say."

Marta was glad that was all Nora would say because even though Marta had strong feelings for Shanice, she would not and could not let those feelings out. They might get in the way of Shanice's recovery. Things were good. No sense in complicating it.

~~~

Saturday, the day of the hike, dawned bright and almost too warm, but they outfitted Shanice's old wheelchair with a bag that fit perfectly on the back and loaded it up with thermoses of water and healthy snacks of apples and grapes.

Shanice was excited as they pulled into the paved parking lot at Patriot's Memorial Park. And she hadn't even balked at the early seven A.M. meetup time. Apparently, Jaleesa needed to get to the hair salon she owned by ten to open up.

"Look, Marta." Shanice pointed to a metal statue near the flagpole. "That's you." There were three soldiers depicted. One of them was a white woman.

Marta smiled. Shanice was clearly intrigued by Marta's service, but Marta wasn't one to readily talk about it. "She's much prettier than me," Marta said and got out of the driver's seat.
~~~

"You're pretty, Marta," Shanice said, wiggling her way to the edge of the passenger seat.

"Humph," Marta grunted.

Once in the old chair, Shanice said, "I wish we could use my new chair."

"Right? That thing's the Maserati of wheelchairs."

"I know," Shanice gushed. "Detachable sides for easy commode transfer. Adjustable backrest. Leg lifts."

"We don't want to mess up the new one, though." Marta made sure Shanice was secure in the chair and then draped the bag on the back of the handles. "How's the pooping in privacy thing going?"

"Marta!" Shanice screeched and smacked Marta's thigh. Their new friends were just getting out of a sweet black Ford F-150. Now that was a pickup Marta could wrap herself around. She'd never be able to afford it in this lifetime, though.

"What?" Marta said innocently. "I just mean, now Mrs. Pulaski doesn't have to see your shiny butt every time you have to go boomsy."

Shanice laughed, saying, "You don't have to see my butt either now."

"Aww, but it's so cute."

"What was cute?" Dana asked. "Hi, Miss Marta," she added quickly, responding to Jaleesa's raised eyebrows.

"She's excited," Jaleesa said to Marta.

"It's okay," Marta said back. Wow. Protocols were important to this group.

"Sorry," Dana said.

"You're good," Marta said. "Shanice was just bragging about being able to get onto the toilet by herself without help."

Their new friends gushed their excitement as Shanice withered in her chair, mortified that Marta had brought up such a delicate matter.

"Shanice," Tina said, obviously seeing her discomfort. "It's okay, honey. You have new challenges now, right?"

Shanice nodded.

"We're excited to share in your successes," Jaleesa said. "However, *poop*-ular they are."

The entire group burst out laughing. Even Shanice laughed. That was a good sign. And Marta was glad to know she wasn't the only one with bad Dad jokes.

"Okay," Jaleesa said, taking the lead after the laughter died down. "Family and extended family, let's hit this trail and see a waterfall."

Shanice bounced in her chair and grabbed her wheels when Marta said, "Wait, I forgot one thing." She reached into the bag behind the wheelchair and pulled out a paper-wrapped present for Shanice. "Open it."

Shanice pulled out a pair of small leather gloves that didn't have fingertips. "Wheelchair gloves? Really?"

"Like 'em?"

Shanice didn't answer with words. She looked up at Marta with an expression that could only be described as puppy-dog eyes.

"Oh, you guys are so sweet," Dana gushed.

"I'm getting a cavity over here," Jaleesa quipped, earning her a smack on the arm from Tina.

"Upward and onward?" Marta said.

"Onward and upward," Shanice answered, leading the way onto the paved pathway.

Marta was pleased to see Shanice and Dana move ahead of them, obviously enjoying each other's company. Marta surmised they were about the same age, so that just made sense.

"So, how long have you been at Carter's?" Jaleesa asked. She held Tina's hand as they walked, and it made Marta wonder if Dana ever got jealous.

"Too long," Marta said with a scoff.

"Then find something else to do," Jaleesa said matter-of-factly.

Marta wanted to say that she wasn't Jaleesa's sub and didn't need her advice but took a breath instead. She briefly described her work at the nursery and followed it by saying, "I like the physical work. And until Dana came along, I thought I liked the solitude."

"Not so much anymore?"

Marta shook her head. "It's nice to have someone to banter with or to just listen to."

"Dana does like to talk," Tina said and then chuckled, gesturing to the animated conversation ahead of them.

"And then there's the boss," Marta shared, not sure why she was sharing at all. She must feel comfortable with Jaleesa and Tina. "He's not being very flexible with my schedule. I need time off. For her." Marta pointed toward Shanice, who was doing an amazing job wheeling herself alongside Dana. "For things like this. She needs this." *And maybe I do, too,* Marta thought privately.

"Might be time for a change then," Tina suggested softly.

"I'd hire you in a micro-second," Jaleesa said, "but I don't think you're a hairstylist. Or have I read you wrong?"

Marta chuckled. "That I am not. And a desk job is not for me. Computers? No thanks. And I can't go backward, you know? I have to make at least what I'm making now."

"We'll keep our ears and eyes open," Jaleesa offered.

"Thanks," Marta said. Tina might be right. It might be time for a change to something more flexible and maybe less cow-manurey.

A slight hill was coming up, and Dana moved behind the chair to relieve Shanice.

"Let her do it," Marta called from behind. She knew Dana meant well, but she didn't want Shanice to rely on others when things got a bit hard. "When the wheels start heading the wrong way, jump in," Marta said, garnering a chuckle from everyone, including a couple walking behind them.

Shanice almost made it to the top of the hill when Dana had to jump in.

"That was epic, Shanice," Dana said.

"Cardiac Hill," Shanice said breathlessly. "Oh, my God. Thank you."

"No, problem." Dana pushed the wheelchair until Shanice had caught her breath. About a half hour into the hike, they stopped at a bench for some well-deserved water and grapes, which Shanice generously offered to their new friends.

"Red-winged blackbird," Jaleesa said and pointed to a tree.

"I hear a blue jay," Tina said, "but I don't see her."

"Whoa, woodpecker," Dana said, pointing.

"What kind?" Jaleesa asked.

"Oh, shoot. I forgot what you said it was last time. Something about sap."

"The funny thing about the *yellow*-bellied sapsucker," Jaleesa said with a laugh, "is that its most prominent feature is the *red* head and chin. Now, what we're really after is a *Pileated* woodpecker. You know that cartoon Woody Woodpecker laugh?"

When Shanice shook her head, Dana demonstrated making everyone laugh.

"Supposedly, that's what the Pileated woodpecker sounds like," Tina said. "It's on Jaleesa's bird bucket list." She pulled up a picture of the bird on her phone. "Jaleesa says you usually hear them but rarely see them. That's why she loves hiking new trails."

"And it's a great way to get fresh air, move your muscles, and be with your family," Jaleesa said, pulling Dana and Tina into side hugs, one on either side.

Marta felt the love among them. She exchanged a happy glance with Shanice, and only then did she realize her hand had been resting on Shanice's shoulder. She pulled it away quickly.

Unbeknownst to Marta and Shanice, the waterfall was just around the next bend. It wasn't a huge waterfall, but it was steady and had an impressive splash in the stream down below. Marta wondered how the people had gotten down to the creek. Probably by climbing the hillside beyond the barriers. Something that Shanice would never do. And that made Marta a little sad. That thought and many others like it since meeting Shanice steeled her resolve to ensure that Shanice had good experiences and lived a fulfilling life.

They took pictures at the waterfall, and Jaleesa even got a stranger to take a picture of the five of them with Jaleesa's phone. Jaleesa sent it to Marta and Shanice's phones immediately afterward. Tina insisted on one with only Shanice and Marta, and when Marta saw it, she almost teared up but didn't. Shanice's smile was so big and genuine that Marta's heart was crushed under the weight of it. Taking her on this outing had put a little sunbeam in the kid. Yeah, this outing was infinitely more important than the risk of pissing off her boss.

"Thank you," Marta said to their new friends as they were about to part ways in the parking lot.

"Of course," Jaleesa said. "Oh, Harriet sent her regards. I let her stay home to paint."

"She's an artist," Tina clarified. "She likes the quiet when we all leave."

Jaleesa chuckled. "She sure does."

Marta figured they wouldn't see Jaleesa and her family again for a while after this hike, but there they were, making plans to meet up at Rikki's Coffee Shop the very next day.

When they got home from the hike, spirits were high, stomachs were growling, and Shanices were curious. Well, just the one Shanice.

They sat down for a meal of leftover Nora stew, and Shanice said, "Soooo, what *gang* are you in with Miss Rikki and Daddy Vic?" It had been an entire week since that conversation had been mentioned. It must have taken Shanice that long to muster up the courage to ask.

Marta took a swig of flavored seltzer water they'd picked up at the grocery store the other night and said, "The BDSM gang. The Dominance-and-submission gang. The we're-all-Dommes gang." She let that sit there and took a forkful of stew.

Silence grew between them, and Marta noticed that Shanice was neither eating nor talking.

"Shanice?"

"Do you have me here so you can put a dog collar on me?"

It was a punch to the chest. "Absolutely not." Marta exhaled the hurt from her heart. More softly, she said, "Let me explain about the collar stuff. Not everyone likes to wear one. Miss Tina didn't have one on, right? And Dana didn't have hers on today, right?"

Shanice nodded a couple of times.

"The collar is a symbol, mainly. It's usually given to the submissive by the Dominant. It's not meant to humiliate the submissive." *Unless that's what they want, but she's not ready to understand that part yet.* "By giving the collar to a sub, the Dominant is making a very sincere promise to take care of the sub's needs, whatever those are. Dana needs guidance and direction, I think. And love."

"Sex?"

"I think so," Marta said, although she didn't know their arrangement. "Others only want the sex part, and they take the collar off after a play session. A sex session. Jess…my recent ex was like that. She wasn't a twenty-four-seven submissive. Only when she came over here."

"Are you a twenty-four/seven Dominant?" Shanice asked, finally taking a bite of food. That was a good sign. She wasn't as upset now that Marta had started explaining.

"I've never been a twenty-four/seven Domme, but that doesn't mean I couldn't be. I've never really had a relationship long enough to find out."

"I could tell that they liked wearing those collar things. Even the quiet Asian lady on her knees."

Marta simply nodded. She hoped Shanice wasn't about to ask about Minjung because Marta was pretty sure Minjung was a slave, and she had no idea how she would explain that to Shanice. And, besides, Marta didn't quite understand it herself. To each her own, she always said.

"Madison…" Shanice started to say and then stopped.

"She's a *little*," Marta said. "From the way I see it, Madison can do lots of adulting but likes having Shasti to guide her and help her with life stuff."

Shanice looked Marta right in the eyes, and it seemed like a thousand thoughts were swirling through her mind until she finally said, "Like you do for me."

"We can't really know that because we don't know what Shasti does for Madison."

"Okay." Shanice got pensive again. "So, with this whole collar stuff, what does the *sub-person* promise to the other one? Like, why in the world would someone agree to wear a collar? It's like ownership or something. Slavery."

"Not at all," Marta said and hoped again that Shanice wouldn't ask about Minjung. She wished she could remember the Domme's name, but it wouldn't come to her. "There are rules of engagement, if you will. There are deliberate spoken and sometimes written agreements between people entering a D/s relationship."

"Dominant/submissive relationship, you mean?"

"Mm hmm." Marta nodded and offered Shanice more stew which she took with the politest thank you. "When Jessica and I entered into our D/s relationship, we told each other what our needs were, and then we promised to fulfill each other's needs to the best of our abilities with some exceptions. We agreed that everything we did had to be consensual."

"She had to okay anything you did. And same for you?"

"Mm hmm," Marta said. "Sometimes someone agrees to something, but it turns out to be something they realize they don't want, so they use their safewords. Red means stop. Yellow means pause—"

"And green means go," Shanice finished. "Like at the coffee shop."

"Right. Now, there were things that Jessica wanted me to do with and to her that I didn't want to do. Those were my hard limits, and I told her about them. We discussed our hard limits before we even did anything."

"That's a good thing," Shanice said. "And I won't ask you what those were because I know that's private between you guys."

"Thank you," Marta said with a laugh. "That's very understanding of you. And listen, I imagine that all those Dominants and submissives at the party, including the ones wearing collars, had conversations like the one I had with Jessica."

"Why did she leave you?"

Marta sighed. "Remember how I said that I had hard limits? Things I wouldn't do?"

Shanice nodded.

"She met someone else who would."

"Oh."

"That's okay," Marta said. Although she hadn't been quite ready to give up her weekly liaisons with Jessica, she'd had no choice. Oddly, she was finding that she really hadn't missed them. Not much, anyway.

"Billy's one of those *littles*, too. Isn't he?"

"Yes."

"Am I one?"

Marta blinked twice. "Only you can say if you are or aren't."

"I don't know. Maybe I like the way you tuck me in at night. And I have Bernard when most grown-ups don't sleep with a stuffie. And then there's that other thing I do."

Marta put her thumb to her lips without saying a word.

"Yes," Shanice said. "That thing."

"Which is okay, kid."

"And maybe I like your guidance, how you outline my day, and how you hired Mrs. Pulaski to help me. And how you're my superhero and all."

"I'm not a Mommy Domme, though," Marta protested. She wasn't sure a D/s relationship was on the table with the kid. Her Dominance had been discovered in the military for quick hookups and honed over the years for physical sex only. She'd never had a relationship like Jaleesa had with Tina, Dana, or even Harriet. What was the kid implying? Marta was *not* a Mommy Domme.

Uncomfortable with the conversation's direction, Marta stood up abruptly, picked up her dinner plate and silverware, and put them in the sink to soak. She kept her back to Shanice and said, "I have some bills to pay in the living room. Do you want to check on the itty bitty complaint committee in the back room?"

Shanice burst out laughing. "You mean the kittens?"

"Noisiest, most complainiest little things I've ever known."

"They just need a lot of help surviving right now."

Speaking of needing help, Marta thought. She softened her gaze and said, "After that, how about you do your PT in the living room while I do the bills? You have to be stronger and more fit than you've ever been in your life. And we also need to oil up those scars like Elizabeth suggested."

"Okay," Shanice said. She put her dinner dishes in the sink and wheeled out of the kitchen toward the kittens' room. Marta knew she was avoiding the whole Mommy Domme little girl discussion because she was not a Mommy Domme. No fucking way. A quasi-sadistic Dominant in the bedroom, yes. All day. But a Mommy Domme? No. Highly doubtful. Less than a ten-percent chance.

As Marta sat at her mother's antique rolltop desk sorting the bills, concerning thoughts came to the forefront. Marta knew she had the urge to nurture and guide the kid. No. She needed to stop thinking of her as a kid. She wasn't. Shanice was a grown woman who'd had a rough go of it in life.

Marta, nestled in her parents' and older sister's love and security, had become strong and independent. Although she still owned Seymour, the awesomest green frog stuffie ever, she didn't need to hold him to feel better. Once upon a time, absolutely. Maybe Shanice never had that security as a child. Growing up, moving from foster home to foster home had to be difficult. Living in an institution in her teen years? And now this accident? Jeez-us, Shanice couldn't catch a break.

Marta tapped her pen on the electric bill opened on the desk. She had become fiercely protective since the moment she heard Shanice scream in that hospital room. Maybe Marta could help Shanice catch that break. Absolutely. Marta took a deep breath, determined to give the kid every advantage to have a happy, fulfilled, successful life. And…fuck. She had thought of Shanice as 'the kid' again.

"Oh, my God," Marta said out loud. *Was* she a Mommy Domme? No way. She dropped the pen and looked down the long hallway where Shanice had gone. At the party, they had all assumed Shanice was Marta's *little.* That means they all assumed she was…"A Mommy Domme," Marta whispered out loud. "No fucking way." Instant dizziness hit her. She rubbed her forehead and then her temples. Unfortunately, Shanice picked that moment to come back into the room.

"What's wrong?" Shanice said and came over. She put a hand on Marta's forearm.

Marta soaked in the concern in those baby brown eyes staring right back at her and softened her expression. "I'm okay, sweetie. Just paying bills."

"Oh," Shanice said. "About that. I want to pay my half. I have an appointment to go to Johnson Tech Monday to see about working from home."

"You didn't tell me."

"I just now got a reply text from Mrs. Washington." Shanice waved her phone back and forth. "She thinks there's a really good chance that management will approve a stay-at-home work situation given my condition."

Marta snorted. "Your 'condition.'"

"Right? What else should we call it, though? Anyway, if you can't drive me over there tomorrow at four o'clock, then maybe I can ask Mrs. Pulaski."

"I can drive you," Marta said quickly. There was no way she was going to subject Shanice to Mrs. Pulaski's driving if she could help it.

"Thank you. And I want to start paying my share around here."

Marta sighed. A whole bunch of thoughts raced through her gray matter. She wanted to tell Shanice emphatically, 'No!' but then she also wanted Shanice to feel like an independent contributing adult who could manage in the world. What her brain finally settled on was this. "How about we set up a joint bank account? And we each contribute the same amount each month. We'll figure out what that is later because, you know, the kittens are getting hungrier by the day and will soon eat us out of house and home."

Shanice giggled and said, "We *could* set up a joint account, or we could join modern times, and I could pay you using Venmo or Paypal or CashMeOut."

Marta blinked comically, letting Shanice know she had no idea what those things meant.

"No clue what I just said?" There was a lilting tease in Shanice's voice.

"None whatsoever," Marta said. "My mom and I did the joint household bank account thing, and that's what I'm used to, so if you don't mind this senior citizen being set in her ways, can we try it that way?"

Shanice chuckled and nodded. "What bank?"

"JW Bank."

"Me, too," Shanice said excitedly. "It'll be easy then. I'll need to bring some mail with me to show proof of address."

Marta put up one finger, rooted around the pile of bills on the desk, and handed her a bill from the surgeon's office. "The tide is rolling in," Marta announced. At Shanice's confused expression, Marta clarified, "Your hospital bills are starting to come in now."

"Oh," Shanice said, her voice tinged with dread.

"You'll be okay," Marta said gently. "We'll figure this out."

"Okay," Shanice said. She sighed and added, "Nora was hinting about taking two kittens, you know."

"She told me," Marta said, knowing that Shanice was totally changing the subject. Marta didn't blame her one iota. "I said I'd ask you."

"They should go to a good home, and Nora will take care of them." Shanice narrowed her eyes. "But does that mean we can keep Mama Cat and one of the kittens?"

"Fuck yes," Marta blurted.

"Potty mouth, Mama." Shanice gasped. "I mean Marta. It was because I just said, '*Mama* Cat.' I promise."

"It's okay," Marta said, thinking Shanice was overreacting to her slip. It was, however, the second time she'd called Marta 'Mama.' Maybe the kid needed a Mommy Domme, and maybe, just maybe, Marta was that person. She cleared her throat and said, "So anyway. If we set up a joint account, I can pay the bills from our mutual household expenses account."

"Sounds fine," Shanice said. "Maybe we can do that someday this week. My follow-up appointment with the surgeon is Wednesday in Cincinnati, though. And Nora said Mama Cat and the kittens need to go to the Vet for checkups. She said the kittens were old enough now. And I need to get new glasses. I found my prescription in my stuff."

Marta sank back comically in her seat. "Whoa, whoa, whoa. We're going to be busier than the bees."

Shanice giggled.

Marta added, "Will you make those appointments for us this week? In the late afternoon or evening?"

"Sure."

"What time is your surgeon's appointment?"

"They were able to change it to five o'clock," Shanice said. "To give us time to get down there."

"Built-in office assistant," Marta said, punching a fist in the air. "I love this."

"You're silly," Shanice said. "But if you'll excuse me, I have a date with three-pound weights."

"Proper form," Marta said.

"Yes, Ma'am."

Ma'am. She called me Ma'am. A quick swap of the last two letters, and

you get...*Mama*.

Chapter 20

Shanice

Shanice lay in bed, tired from the full day of hiking and PT and everything, but she was also kind of wired. The hike to the waterfall that morning had been so much fun. Shanice really liked getting to know Dana and Tina and Jaleesa. They were so nice. That whole Dominant/submissive thing seemed weird when explained, but after watching her new friends interact at the party and then again today, it seemed like love, mutual respect, and fun. The D/s labels were a way to distinctly define the role each one was in, making it uber clear to all involved. And then, during the hike, when Marta told Dana *not* to help her up Cardiac Hill, this crazy rush of determination ran through Shanice. Marta acted like she had the power and authority to influence Shanice's life. But it was more than that. Marta had challenged her, just like Marta constantly challenged her to do more PT with correct form. Marta wanted Shanice to succeed, and Shanice found herself wanting to please the woman who had taken her in.

Shanice clutched Bernard tight. It was amazing to have someone in her corner like that, rooting for her. Someone like Marta. And Marta did say that she liked to be a Dominant. And maybe Shanice felt able to be a submissive like Dana. It was obvious that Dana looked up to both Jaleesa and Tina for guidance. Shanice could get on board with something like that with Marta. Marta had already proven to be her superhero, after all. Oh, wait. Marta said she was only a Domme in the bedroom for sex or something. The only thing…there was that dream Shanice had a while back. That was definitely a sex dream. But maybe Marta didn't think of her that way. Maybe Marta—

A soft knock sounded on her closed bedroom door. "You still awake?" Marta called softly.

"Come in." Shanice made her voice strong so Marta wouldn't think she was disturbing her.

Marta came into the room, followed quickly by Snowball. Snowball jumped on the bed and chirped right in Shanice's face.

Marta sighed dramatically. "I think I've lost my cat to you."

Shanice smiled and petted the cat in all the right places. In the two weeks she'd been living with Marta and Snowball, she'd learned all the cat's favorite spots for petting. "She's such a lush," Shanice said with a chuckle.

"She is," Marta said. "I came to see if you needed anything. Water?"

"I'm fine."

"How are your arms and hands? That was quite a workout you had today, and then we threw a few PT sessions on top of it."

"The gloves helped. Thank you for getting those for me. But you don't have to buy me—"

"I know," Marta interrupted. "I just wanted to."

Shanice scooted over so Marta could sit on the side of the small bed. Snowball, possibly insulted, jumped off the bed and left the room, making them both laugh. Wordlessly, Marta sat and brushed Shanice's out-of-control hair off her forehead. It might be time for a trim. A smaller, more manageable 'fro would be nice. Ooh, or maybe braids. But that could wait. Marta would have to drive her, after all, and Marta had done too much already.

Shanice soaked in Marta's intense gaze. Her heart was responding, but she didn't quite know what to do with it, so she picked up Bernard and handed him to Marta.

"Well, hi, Bernard." Marta pulled him into a hug. She held him up and kissed his head. "You are doing a fabulous job taking care of our Shanice. Aren't you?"

"He is," Shanice said, feeling giddy because Marta had said '*our* Shanice,' like she belonged to both Bernard *and* Marta.

Marta kissed him one last time, right on the nose, and handed him back to Shanice. "Okay," Marta said, "if you don't need anything. I need to get to bed."

"Wake me up before you go," Shanice blurted. But then felt stupid.

"You can sleep in, silly."

"No," came the quick answer. Shanice didn't want to miss a minute with Marta. Having coffee together in the morning had quickly become one of her favorite things.

They locked gazes again, and Marta smiled that melting smile that always hit Shanice right in the…everywhere.

Marta stroked Shanice's shoulder and said, "You're a beautiful soul, Shanice."

Shanice shivered. She couldn't help it. Marta's words did that to her.

"Are you cold?" Marta pulled her hand away.

What to say? What to say? "I'm okay. Just tired."

"You'll be okay, Shanice," Marta said gently.

"I will with…" *Ack!* No, she couldn't say it.

"Finish your thought," Marta prodded quietly.

"I'll be okay with you helping me," Shanice stammered. "Guiding me and stuff. Driving me places."

"It's my pleasure. We're making it work, right?"

"Mm hmm," Shanice nodded, knowing full well what she wanted to say but didn't dare. Marta could *not* know that Shanice wanted to be like Bernard—held in Marta's arms and kissed on the nose. Nah, not just the nose. The lips. And other places.

"You okay?" Marta asked with an amused expression.

"Mm hmm," was all Shanice seemed to be able to get out.

"All right then," Marta said. "Holler if you need me."

"Mm hmm."

~~~

Sunday without Marta or Mrs. Pulaski was kind of lonely. Since Shanice could transfer more easily with the new wheelchair, Marta told Mrs. Pulaski to come over less often with the understanding that Shanice would call the neighbor if she needed help. And then there was Mama Cat. She had
~~~

been jonesing to get out of that bedroom for a few days now. She probably needed a well-deserved break from those adorable but demanding kittens. Thankfully Shanice had been able to score an evening vet appointment for tomorrow through the vet's online scheduling page. The sooner Mama Cat got a clean bill of health, the sooner she could roam the house. Yes, that was a priority.

Before the vet appointment, Shanice had to go to Johnson Tech late tomorrow afternoon to meet with Mrs. Washington. For the life of her, Shanice couldn't remember if the building was wheelchair accessible. They would find out soon enough, wouldn't they?

Shanice picked up the deck of cards she'd been practicing with and got ready to try her hands at the riffle shuffle again. The first part she could do now, although she hadn't shown Marta yet. It was the cascade finish where everything went to heck. Her hands and thumbs were strong enough to get the cards to overlap, but bending the two decks back the other way? Yep, fifty-two pickup. Every time.

"Dang it," Shanice said when the cards went flying. Thank goodness Marta wasn't there to witness her ineptness. She picked up the cards using the plastic grabber thingy that Marta had given her to use, and wondered how in the world she was ever going to repay Marta for all this help she was giving her. Marta went to her job in the mornings and then came home to a second job of taking care of Shanice. It kind of wasn't fair to Marta. *'Kind of wasn't?'* It wasn't. At all.

Shanice knew she was helping Marta by being her home secretary and by contributing to household expenses, but that wasn't enough by a long shot. And then there would be Wednesday's appointment with the surgeon. Marta had to drive her all the way into Cincinnati. Shanice was about to make herself more upset by conjecturing all the bad news the doctors were going to tell her, but she heard a sound outside. Was that Marta's pickup pulling into the driveway? Shanice checked her phone for the time. It was only ten o'clock. Maybe Marta had forgotten her lunch or something.

Shanice pulled her chair away from the kitchen table and faced the front door. Marta came in, didn't take her shoes off like always, and barely looked at Shanice. She lay her keys, phone, and wallet on the table and said,

"I have to…I need to…" Marta looked lost and then said, "I'll be in my room."

"Okay," was all Shanice could say. "Are you okay?" Marta didn't turn but simply waved her hand overhead as she headed down the hallway. Snowball followed her but wasn't allowed entrance as the bedroom door clicked shut firmly.

Alarm bells raced through Shanice. Even her stumps flared as the nerves fired in confusion. What did that hand wave mean? Why was Marta home at such a weird time? Shanice knew better than to disturb Marta but didn't know what to do with herself.

Water. Marta always brought her water, so maybe she needed some. It was an irrational thought, but Shanice set about washing out her own sippy cup and filling it up with ice and water for Marta. It would be ready for her when she came back out.

Shanice set the cup on the kitchen table, intending to check over that week's schedule of appointments, when Marta's phone vibrated. Shanice didn't mean to pry, but it was a text from someone named Jeff. To her credit, Shanice didn't read it. After a few minutes, Marta's phone vibrated again. Another text from Jeff. And then one from someone named Jessica.

Shanice inhaled sharply. Wasn't that Marta's recent ex? Oh, no. Did something happen? Did Marta try to get back together with Jessica only to be shot down? And how was the guy named Jeff involved?

After two more incoming texts from Jessica, Shanice had had enough. Without putting much brain power into the decision, she grabbed the phone and the sippy cup of cold water and headed to Marta's room. She knocked once and let herself in.

"Marta," Shanice said quietly, just in case Marta was sleeping. "Your phone is blowing up from people named Jeff and Jessica."

Marta was lying on her bed in the darkened room facing the wall. She merely grunted.

"Something happened," Shanice said, stating an obvious fact. Duh.

"I fucked up."

There was no way Shanice was going to tease Marta about her potty mouth, and she wasn't sure *what* she was going to say until she asked, "What happened?" When the only answer she got was silence, Shanice said, "I have your phone. And I brought some water for you."

"Water?" Marta rolled over onto her back. "You, you brought me water?"

"Yeah. You always bring me water, so I thought..." Honestly, Shanice didn't know *what* she thought. She only wanted to help.

Marta patted the bed in invitation.

Shanice's eyebrows shot to the sky. Okay. This was going to take a minute. She'd kind of never been in Marta's room before and had definitely never tried to transfer from her new chair to this bed. Oh, it was the same height as Nora's. It took her a minute, but she did it fairly quickly, albeit awkwardly. Marta enfolded her in her arms, and they lay together with Shanice's head in the well of Marta's shoulder. Shanice didn't know what to do with her arms, so she folded them tight against her body. Marta stroked her back as if Shanice was the one needing comfort.

Shanice didn't break the silence. Marta did.

"I fucked up, Shanice," Marta said again.

"How?"

Marta sighed and then kissed the top of Shanice's head, sending Shanice into an almost swoon. "I quit my job. Just now. Wow. I did that, didn't I?" She was quiet for a moment and then said, "I just told them I was quitting and then walked out." She paused again. "I have no income."

The hand stroking Shanice's back stopped.

The dread Shanice had somehow managed to bury came back in full force. She knew she shouldn't have trusted her new situation. She stiffened in Marta's arms; she couldn't help it.

Silence filled the room, and it was heavy. It was too heavy for Shanice to break all on her own, so she simply deflated as she waited for the Mama Deborah words, '*You do see that circumstances have changed, don't you? You understand, right?*' Shanice remained quiet and wondered how long she'd have to find another place to live.

Shanice sat up. "Marta?"

"Yeah?"

"I'll get started."

"Doing?"

"Packing."

"For?" Marta asked, clearly confused.

"Moving out, obviously."

"What the hell, kid?" Marta said and bolted upright. "Oh, no no no no no. I'll find a new job. No worries about that. You're here with me for as long as you want to be. If you move out, it will be your idea, not mine. I'm ready, willing, and able to work. I'm strong and reasonably intelligent. There's a new job out there for me, and I'll start looking first thing tomorrow."

"You *are* strong," Shanice agreed. "And someone will hire you immediately because you're awesome and not a jerk."

Marta burst out laughing. "Well, thanks for that."

"No, I mean that someone will hire you because you like working and you're honest and dedicated." Shanice sighed. "I'm saying this all wrong."

"No, no, you're fine." Marta lay back down and pulled Shanice to her. It was as if holding Shanice comforted Marta, and that was fine with Shanice. "I understand what you're trying to say." Marta then went into a recounting of events from that morning. Shanice had no idea that Marta's boss, Roger, had been harassing her by making her work in the rain and shoveling cow doo-doo. *Those* were jerk moves, for sure. *He* was a jerk, and Shanice told her so.

Marta chuckled and then let out a long sigh as if releasing tension. "He *is* a jerk. I mean, I'm just sorry it took me so long to finally realize that I didn't have to take his shit anymore. And that I didn't have to shovel shit anymore, either. The office workers were shocked when I walked back into the office, propped the manure-covered shovel against his door, and said right to him, 'Don't forget to punch out.' And then I punched out."

"And then you told him you quit?"

"Yep."

"Brave," Shanice said, totally admiring the guts Marta showed.

"Or incredibly stupid."

"You'll find another—"

"I know." Marta nudged Shanice up into a sitting position. "Okay, how about this? Tomorrow, first thing, we'll set up that joint bank account. We'll make it one of those accounts where we both have to sign the checks or whatever. That way, you won't think I'm going to swindle you or something."

"And vice versa," Shanice added.

"Touché," Marta said. She squeezed Shanice's shoulder briefly as a gesture of comfort, at least, that's how Shanice took it. "I know life hasn't been kind to you, and people have made all kinds of promises and broken them. Words have little weight, so I want to *show* you that I mean to stay present for you and in your life."

Shanice appreciated what Marta was saying, but time would tell. The cardboard boxes in Nora's room would remain filled, though, and her kernel of dread would still be there, but she tucked it away as best she could.

"And," Marta continued since she was on some kind of roll, "this will totally make no sense at all, but let's hit up the hardware store while I still have money. I have to shore up the ramp and build you another one out back. And the kitchen counter sticks out too far for your chair. I have to modify that. I'll make a list. Oh, and then…" Marta bopped Shanice playfully on the nose before saying, "…I want to stop at that bookshop on Market Street where they sell those cute stuffies. It's about time Bernard had a buddy, don't you think?"

Joy hit Shanice's heart so quickly that it almost made her dizzy. "Yes," she said. "Yes, to all of that."

"Good, let me shower, and then we'll hit the road. Lunch out after shopping, and then it'll be time to meet our new friends at the coffee shop."

"Marta?"

"Yes, honey?"

"If I'm staying, can I meet Seymour?"

Marta gasped comically. "What? You haven't met his highness yet?" She bounced her way off the end of the bed and turned on the light. She reached up on a high shelf pulling the cutest, yet faded, fuzzy green frog down. "He's kind of old and fragile," Marta said, handing him to Shanice. "So please be careful."

"Of course." Shanice took Seymour and petted his smooth back. "You are so cute." She kissed him right on his worn and faded nose and then gently hugged him. "Thank you for taking care of Marta all these years." *I'd like to take it from here*, she added, but only in her head.

~~~

Shanice clutched her new fox stuffie as Marta wheeled her into Rikki's Coffee Shop. And even though Shanice felt like Bernard might get jealous, her new stuffie was perfect with her big green eyes, soft fur, and awesome fluffy tail. Marta suggested that maybe Bernard could be her stay-at-home friend, and the new still-nameless fox could be the one she took out and about.

Marta backed into the coffee shop, and when they turned around, they saw a big group of people surrounding a small family. Marta moved them off to the side so they wouldn't be in the way.

"Thanks again, everyone," a short Hispanic-looking man said. "Carla and I are so grateful for everything you all have done for us. A woman holding the hand of a child, maybe four years old or so, stood next to him. She beamed her agreement and nodded. Was she the dude's wife or girlfriend? Shanice didn't know. All she knew was that they'd happened upon what looked like a monumental moment in this family's life.

Miss Rikki put her hand on the man's shoulder. "Let us know how things are going once you get settled in Pittsburgh, Diego. We wish you all the best."

"I will," he said. "Thank you." Shanice saw that the man had tears in his eyes. Aww.

The woman beside him leaned down and said something to the young child.

"Tank you, Miss Riri," the child blurted, making everyone laugh. Shanice even heard Marta chuckle behind her.

"You're welcome, Isabella," Miss Rikki said. "We'll miss you." She leaned down and accepted the hug the young Isabella was offering.

They said a few more goodbyes, got hugs from many people, and then made their way toward the front door. Shanice watched as the man named
~~~

Diego nodded at Marta, who returned the nod.

"Did you know them?" Shanice asked as soon as the family was gone.

"No, but I think the guy worked here or something."

"Oh," Shanice said.

"I see Jaleesa and the gang." Marta maneuvered Shanice's new wheelchair around tables and chairs to the comfy couch section near the back wall.

"Hey, hey," Miss Jaleesa said, giving hugs all around.

Tina and then Dana were next in line for hugs, followed quickly by Miss Shasti and Madison. It was quite comical to see Madison busting at the gills to see Shanice's new fox stuffie. After Madison mashed it in a fur-crushing hug, Shanice quietly gave the fox CPR while Madison spouted random facts about foxes and the different kinds at the Cincinnati Zoo. Shanice had never heard of a bat-eared fox before and now kind of wanted to go to the zoo to see it. She'd been to the zoo once as a foster when some charity group brought them there for a visit.

"So glad you could join us," Miss Rikki said to Marta and Shanice as she walked up. She looked like an Irish Goddess, and Shanice found herself getting nervous for some reason. Was it a crush? Like the one she had on Marta? Miss Rikki greeted Marta, and they chatted for a few moments. Aha, Shanice knew what it was. With the possible exception of the brief time she'd spent with Mama Deborah, Shanice felt like she belonged somewhere. Maybe she had peeps now. Ooey gooey joy squeed inside her.

With all this going on inside, Miss Rikki leaned toward Shanice and said, "Oh. My. Goodness. Your fox is so cute."

Shanice blurted, "Hi, Miss Riri." *Ack! What was that? That's not her name.*

Miss Rikki didn't seem to care. "What's your cutie's name?"

Shanice shrugged. She hadn't thought of a name yet.

The Irish goddess-princess smiled. "I love the new transport."

Miss Jaleesa and everyone else gushed, oohed, and ahhed over her new wheelchair. Thankfully Marta took up the conversation and pointed out all the new features. Shanice just held onto her fox and soaked it all in.

"Did you say thank you to Miss Riri?" Marta asked Shanice.

"Thank you," Shanice said. Wait. Did Marta just go with the flow and call her Miss Riri, too?

Miss Riri didn't seem to mind and took drink orders before heading back behind the front counter. After she left, the conversation took on a more serious note. Apparently, Miss Riri—hee hee, Shanice giggled at the new nickname. Anyway, apparently, Miss Riri was moving into an apartment right over their heads, and they were discussing particulars about helping her move.

"I have a pickup truck," Marta offered. "And I suddenly have all kinds of free time now."

All conversation stopped. Miss Jaleesa said, "You okay?"

It was uber-obvious to Shanice that Marta was holding back her emotions, yet somehow, she managed to tell the tale about quitting her job that morning. Many concerned expressions were shot toward Shanice, but Shanice didn't know what to say, so she said nothing.

"Do you need something quickly?" Miss Shasti asked.

Shanice fully expected Marta to say she had it all under control but surprised Shanice by saying, "Yes." It was clear to everyone that admitting this was troublesome to her.

"I may have a solution," Miss Shasti said. "Bear with me for a moment." She stood up and excused herself.

Shanice wasn't sure what was happening, but in no time, Miss Riri, the girl named Brittany, and the woman named Lydia came over with all their coffees.

Miss Riri said directly to Marta, "I want to show you something. It's in the back."

Marta looked startled but got up and followed Miss Riri behind the counter and beyond.

Miss Shasti patted Shanice on the knee and said, "She'll be right back. Okay?" The look of compassion calmed Shanice's sudden nerves somewhat.

"Yes, Ma'am," Shanice said.

Madison had a sad expression on her face, and it was then that Shanice remembered. She pulled the bag from the back of the wheelchair onto her lap and pulled out a fresh box of crayons and two brand-new coloring books.

"Madison," Shanice said. "Look, Marta bought us these. I know you love birds, so this one is for you."

"Me?" Madison looked startled and read, "'Drawing Wild Birds Coloring Book.'"

"What do you say, Madison?" Miss Shasti said gently.

"Mistress," Madison whined. "You promised."

Miss Shasti rolled her eyes, shot a teasing laser beam glare at Miss Jaleesa, and said, "What do you say, *Bucko*?"

Miss Jaleesa, Tina, and Dana broke out laughing. Shanice didn't quite understand, so Dana explained that Miss Jaleesa always called Madison *Bucko*, so now Madison wanted everyone to call her that.

Shanice was in on the joke now and started chuckling.

"Thank you, Shanice," Madison said. "That was very nice of you and Miss Marta to buy me a coloring book." And, contrary to her usual ways, Madison remained quiet as she began coloring the first bird in the book.

Dana leaped up and found a clipboard for Shanice to lean her own coloring book on in her lap. She'd chosen a *Frozen* coloring book and opened it to the first page.

She was content listening to the others chat, but inside, she was worried about Marta. After a long fifteen minutes, Marta finally came back looking a lot more relaxed.

"Good news?" Miss Shasti asked.

Marta nodded.

"What?" Shanice said, not able to hold it in anymore.

"I just got a new job, kid," Marta said and broke into a big smile. Before Shanice could ask, Marta explained to the group that she would be the new Diego. She was going to be the back kitchen manager in charge of food, inventory, dishwashing, and miscellaneous. Marta laughed and said she wasn't sure what the "miscellaneous" part entailed, but she didn't care.

"So, kid?" Marta said to Shanice. "We're okay. I'm starting Friday, so we have all week to get our zillion and one appointments in."

Shanice did a happy dance in her chair, and Marta followed up with her seated white girl dance. Instantaneously, their new friends joined in with their own versions. Shanice caught Marta's gaze, and they shared a relieved look between them.

"We'll be okay," Marta said again low so only Shanice could hear. The hand that snaked into hers and held it completed Shanice's best day ever.

Chapter 21

Marta

Marta wasn't exactly nervous on her first day working for Rikki, but she did want to make a good impression. Having Shanice help out was going to guarantee that because Shanice had already designed a new organization system for the back storage room off the kitchen.

"Rikki was floored by your ideas in here," Marta said to Shanice as she moved a box of Fair Trade Certified French Roast Coffee beans to Shanice's new Fair Trade shelf.

"It was kind of crazy in here," Shanice said from inside the storage room. She was carefully labeling the last few sections of shelving with her new scheme. "That's a lot of stuff." She pointed to the mountain of boxes that had come down from the upstairs area waiting to be stored. "They keep bringing more. I hope it'll all fit."

"With your brilliant organization scheme, it will." Marta beamed at Shanice.

Shanice looked back at Marta with a shy smile. They locked gazes again like they had been doing for the past few weeks, but Marta didn't look away this time. Shanice seemed to be more settled and more grounded in recent days. Maybe because their visit to Johnson Tech on Monday had been a success, and Shanice was officially getting back to work next week but from home.

Marta walked over and squatted down in front of Shanice's wheelchair. Taking one of Shanice's hands in hers, she said, "Thank you for helping today. I'm glad you don't start your job until Monday." *This way, we have more time together*, Marta wanted to add but didn't.

Shanice swallowed hard as if she was nervous or something. "I'm excited to get to work, actually. Parvati's teaming up with me to work on a new account. Maybe they think I need help or something."

"You don't. I have no doubt you can stand toe to toe with this Parvati woman."

"Toe to toe," Shanice echoed with a chuckle but then looked down, her smile fading.

Marta used the side of her index finger to lift Shanice's chin up. "You'll show them that you've still got it, right? I mean, c'mon." She gestured around her. "Look at how smart you are. Sharp as a tack."

Shanice looked up, her expression hopeful. Her deep brown eyes held depths Marta had only begun to explore. She was powerless to stop what she did next. Without breaking eye contact, Marta stroked Shanice's cheek with the back of two fingers. Part of her understood that she was doing what she'd been telling Shanice to do all along. She was feeling her feels. And she did more than simply feel them; she actually spoke them out loud when she said, "You're a very pretty young woman, Shanice." Marta's voice broke on Shanice's name. Her emotions were right there; they were always right there, dang it.

Shanice looked incredibly uncomfortable and fluffed her hair with one hand. "I'm not. I need to go to Jaleesa's salon soon."

"You're perfect any way you are," Marta said but made a mental note to get Shanice to the salon if that's what she wanted. She hated when Shanice downplayed herself like that. Every woman did it, though, didn't they? Marta broke the moment and went out to get another box to put on the shelves.

"The kittens are growing fast, aren't they?" Shanice called after her, clearly changing the subject.

"Did you see those people at the vet's office? They were so excited to have kittens in their midst."

"I know," Shanice squeed. "I think every single person came in for a cuddle. I'm glad they were all healthy. Even Mama Cat."

"Who is now roaming freely in the house," Marta said, holding up the box she had just fetched. Shanice marked it on the inventory clipboard Rikki had given them.

"Snowball has been an excellent host, accepting Mama Cat into her house. Did you see how she tried to play with Mama Cat yesterday?"

Marta laughed. "Yeah, and Mama Cat was having none of it. She's probably worn out from her babies. Nora's impatient about having to wait three more weeks before her two are weaned and ready to go. I'm glad you picked the gray one for us to keep."

"She's the grayest," Shanice said, waiting a second before breaking out in laughter.

It took Marta a moment to get the joke. "The 'grayest' like *greatest.*" Marta laughed again. "Good one, Shanice."

Shanice did a happy dance in her chair, and Marta answered with a happy standing dance. Marta's phone chimed an incoming text.

"Jeff again?" Shanice asked.

"Mm hmm," Marta said. "I wish I'd gotten to know him better when I worked at Carter's. He's a good guy. Might become a good friend."

"Seems like he had your back the whole time, and you didn't know it," Shanice said. "Maybe he had a little crush on you?"

"Maybe, but they all knew the score down there," Marta said. "In one of his texts, he told me his sister is a lesbian, and he's very protective of her. So, I think maybe he was protective of me, too."

"Could be," Shanice said with a nod. "I hate that your stupid boss didn't think a woman should be doing manual labor like you did. That's what Jeff told you he heard your ex-boss say, right?"

"Yep. Roger's stuck in old-fashioned thinking. He's a bit of a misogynist."

"Your new boss isn't," Shanice said with a smile. "And you're making more money here, too."

"I know," she mouthed and nodded exaggeratedly. "And I'll have more flexible hours if we have appointments and stuff to take care of. She is incredibly understanding."

Marta inhaled sharply as she noticed Shanice fighting to hold back tears. "Oh, honey, what happened? Are you okay?"

It took a moment, but Shanice bit back her emotions. "I'm just grateful for you and for everyone that's helped me. I never know who to trust, but…"

"But you think maybe you can start to begin to perhaps maybe trust…me?"

Shanice nodded, and then the tears came out in full force. Marta wrapped her arms around Shanice and rocked her gently. She kissed the crown of Shanice's head and hummed to her like she'd done that one night when emotions had overtaken Shanice. Marta vowed silently that keeping Shanice safe, happy, and thriving were her new goals in life. "I've got you, honey. I've got you."

Once Shanice seemed settled enough and had wiped the tears from her face, Marta let go. "Music?" she asked, thinking maybe they needed a bit of a distraction from all the feels.

"Sure," Shanice said and then jumped when Marta's music app came on loud and strong.

"Oops, sorry." Marta turned it down.

Shanice bopped her head from side to side. "What is this?"

"*Rush*," Marta said. "The song's called *Tom Sawyer*. Like it?"

"Old school," Shanice said. "I like it."

Marta patted her chest two times and bopped along with the song's rhythm. They worked in silence for a while listening to Marta's more tame music, when Shanice asked out of the blue, "Why is Miss Riri moving into the apartment upstairs?"

Marta wasn't sure how much she could share but figured it was common knowledge, so she said, "Rikki's aunt passed away, and apparently, the house has to be sold to pay bills. Miss Riri said something like, 'There are a lot of bills to be paid.' Something like that. As soon as she gets moved in upstairs, there will be an estate sale at the house, and then it will be sold."

"Oh," Shanice said. "I'm sorry her aunt died."

"Yeah, kind of sucks. But like us, Miss Riri's starting a new chapter in her life."

"New chapter," Shanice said, sitting up taller. "Yes, a new chapter that includes superheroes and kittens. Who could ask for anything more?"

Marta beamed with pride. Shanice was looking to the positive things in her life. The results of the visit to the surgeon's office on Wednesday had been mixed. Although they were impressed with how strong she was, they also said her stumps weren't ready, and it would be at least six more months before they could re-evaluate her for prosthetics. But if Shanice were now looking toward the good things, then Marta would, too. New friends, new job, and.... She wasn't sure how to classify Shanice at the moment; Shanice was just Shanice. Marta shrugged inwardly as she stowed another box of coffee. She'd think about it later.

"*Hole*," Marta screeched when the song changed. "*Celebrity Skin*." She reached with both hands for Shanice's and pulled her out of the storage room and into the spacious kitchen. She spun Shanice's chair around as they danced. Marta turned in circles as she circumnavigated the wheelchair. She took one handle of the chair and said, "Ready?" Before Shanice could answer, Marta spun her around twice, much to Shanice's delight.

Shanice was giggling up a storm when Rikki walked in and laughed. "This is fantastic."

Marta slowed her moves but didn't stop bopping. Neither did Shanice, who did something amazing. She put her hands out toward Rikki, who laughed but gave in and joined them in the dance.

When the song ended, they broke out laughing. Marta turned her music off now that she and Shanice weren't alone.

"I knew I did the right thing hiring you," Rikki said.

That was incredible to hear, but Marta hoped she'd live up to Rikki's expectations. "Thank you, Ma'am."

"No, no, no," Rikki said. "That'll just confuse me if you call me that. Just *Rikki* is fine."

Marta knew she couldn't. "You got it, Boss," she said with a questioning eyebrow lift.

Rikki chuckled. "All right. Good compromise." She glanced at the storage room. "That looks amazing, you guys. Oh, Marta, I heard you say you needed to repair the ramp at your house. Deshawn is a licensed carpenter. I can give you his number if you want."

"That would be great," Marta said, surprising herself. She usually liked to do things on her own without help, but maybe having a professional help her out would be good. She didn't want to compromise anything that had to do with Shanice. "Know anybody that puts in vinyl flooring? The carpet in the house needs to go. It's hard for her to get around on it sometimes."

"Deshawn might do flooring. I'm not sure, but tell you what, you can ask tomorrow while we move me from the house. I'm counting on that pickup of yours. And I need this one's organization skills," Rikki said, turning toward Shanice.

"We'll be there," Marta said. "Right, kid?"

Shanice nodded once, but the smile on her face was priceless.

"C'mon," Rikki said. "Lunch is on me out front. Shanice, bring the fox. Did you give her a name yet?"

Shanice looked stricken and choked out, "Riri." Yes, the kid had named the fox after a certain redheaded barista she was apparently smitten with.

Rikki's mouth dropped open. "I'm honored. Thank you."

Marta handed Shanice the stuffie from the shelf where she had been supervising all morning, and they followed Rikki out front for a well-deserved break.

~~~

"Long day," Marta said as she tucked Shanice into bed. They had both decided to turn in early, and Marta stood next to the bed in her usual athletic shorts and a loose T-shirt, her standard sleep uniform. "Wait, what's wrong with this scene?" She tapped her chin and then put a finger in the air as if suddenly remembering. She leaned over Shanice, squishing her underneath her body, and grabbed Bernard. "Oh, I'm sorry," she teased. "Didn't see you there."

Shanice just giggled and made grabby hands for Bernard. Once in her clutches, Shanice said a meek "Thank you."

Marta sat on the edge of the bed and brushed Shanice's flyaway hair off her face. Yeah, a trip to Jaleesa's shop was in order. "Thanks for your help today," Marta said softly. "You made my first day there memorable."

Shanice nodded, clutched Bernard tighter, and then shivered.

"Are you cold?" Marta asked in alarm. She hoped Shanice wasn't getting sick. Maybe the central air-conditioner was on too low. "I'll go turn the air con—"
~~~

"No. Stay," Shanice blurted, grabbing Marta's hand as she stood up.

"Stay?"

"Yes. I'm okay."

Marta searched Shanice's face and then nodded. "Okay. For a little while." She sat back down on the bed. "Until you've warmed up."

"You could—" Shanice didn't finish her sentence. "Like that one time." There was another pause. "When I was crying that night."

Realization dawned on Marta. She understood what Shanice was asking, and her expression softened. Marta searched Shanice's face and saw something she hadn't seen before. Desire. Shanice was good at hiding her emotions, but this one was plain to see.

Marta nodded, and Shanice moved over to give her room. Marta lay on her back and patted the well of her shoulder in invitation. Shanice wasted no time and laid her head where requested. Marta's arm went around and pulled her closer.

"Mmm," Shanice murmured and then said something that floored Marta. "You're a pretty woman, too, Marta."

"Pfft," Marta scoffed, hating that she couldn't take the compliment.

"You are." Shanice tapped Marta on her stomach and then let the hand stay there. Marta's heart skipped a beat when she put her hand on top of Shanice's. A soft moan of contentment sounded near her ear, and Marta smiled. Yes. This felt right.

They lay quietly for a while. Shanice's hand on her stomach was doing all kinds of things to Marta's libido. Aroused, Marta turned on her side so she could look Shanice in the eye. With her face inches from Shanice's, Marta's questioning smile was returned. Shanice's gentle nature seeped into Marta's mind and body. Marta silently reached up and stroked Shanice's forehead, down her nose, and then traced her lips. She felt Shanice's exhales become more labored, kind of like her own.

"Is this okay?" Marta asked.

"Yes," came the breathy answer.

Marta leaned up on one elbow. She searched Shanice's eyes for permission and seemed to get it. She moved her lips to within an inch of Shanice's. Both were breathing hard. Shanice whimpered as if struggling to make a decision and then, in one swift move, closed the gap.

Marta melded into the touch. Shanice's lips were soft yet exploring. Marta moaned into Shanice's mouth. She hadn't meant to. It had just happened. The kiss lasted a few more moments, but no words were spoken afterward. Marta nudged Shanice onto her back and then moved her lips to Shanice's forehead and kissed her there. She kissed Shanice's cheeks and then nibbled on an earlobe. That got a shiver from Shanice, and then two arms went around Marta's neck, pulling her closer. That was the greenest of green lights, so Marta moved over Shanice but stayed balanced on her knees and elbows as she traced a path of soft kisses down Shanice's face to her chin and beyond. Shanice shivered when Marta placed a heavy kiss on her neck, not enough to bruise, but enough to get a reaction.

Marta sensed that the light was still green and undid the top button on Shanice's sleep shirt. She kissed the lovely collarbones there. Another button came undone. Kisses peppered Shanice's chest and the top swell of her breasts.

"Marta," Shanice said breathlessly.

"Mmm," Marta said, coming to a halt. "You okay?" she whispered.

"Yes," Shanice said.

"Color?"

Shanice giggled. "Yellow."

"Copy that," Marta said, speed-kissing her way back to Shanice's lips. She moved off of Shanice and lay on her side. A possessive hand landed on Shanice's stomach, not too low. Shanice had called 'yellow' after all.

"I like you," Shanice said. "A lot."

"I like you a lot, too," Marta said with a chuckle. "I hoped you could tell."

"Mmm," Shanice said with a moan. She reached down for Marta's hand and pulled it up to the third button that was still fastened.

"You want me to keep going?" Marta asked as another surge of arousal hit her.

"Yes."

Marta didn't need to be told twice. She undid the next button and, instead of kissing Shanice, undid the next few until the sleep shirt was entirely undone. Shanice shivered again, and Marta took that as a sign to keep moving.

Marta splayed her hand on the bare skin of Shanice's stomach just below her breasts but let her hand rest there. She wanted to give Shanice every opportunity to stop her forward motion. Sensing all was well, Marta propped herself up on her elbow and moved her face to within inches of Shanice's. The smile she gave Shanice was returned, and Marta began another round of kissing. This time, though, her hand stroked Shanice's stomach and then moved up to cup first one breast and then the other. Oh, how she wanted to get her lips around those nipples. Dang, it was too dark to see Shanice's body.

The squirming woman beneath her was aroused. She seemed ready. Marta moved her swirling hand lower until she brushed the lovely curls covering Shanice's mons.

Marta was just about to inspect lower when Shanice blurted, "Marta!"

Marta stopped her movement. "You okay?"

"Yellow," Shanice said. "Red."

Marta pulled her hand away and sat up. "What's wrong, honey?"

"I just...It's...The thing is...." Shanice sighed. "I've never done this before. I'm a virgin." She sighed.

"Oh," Marta said, not expecting that at all. "Oh," she said again. "I..I can...Do you—"

"I want to keep going," Shanice interrupted, then moaned in arousal. "I just don't know what to do."

"I'll show you," Marta said gently. "Just remember to feel your feels."

"Oh, I'm feeling them," Shanice quipped. "I'm feeling them."

"Permission to continue?" Marta asked, feeling incredibly awkward. She hadn't planned on this happening tonight. Or, like, ever, but here they were. And it felt right. And amazing. When Shanice didn't answer, Marta asked, "Color?"

"Green. Green means go."

"I'm going," Marta said with an eyebrow waggle. She leaned down for another series of passionate kisses as her hand snaked lower. "You are an incredible kisser," Marta said as her hand found the wetness she had expected. "Ahh, beautiful, Shanice." Marta stroked the aroused woman underneath her. She nudged the legs open wider with her hand and then slowly and deliberately circled Shanice's center. How she wished she could see Shanice's body right now, but maybe it was better this way. Marta needed to earn Shanice's trust.

Marta made broad strokes at first and then tighter. There would be no penetration since they hadn't talked about that. Marta's well-coated fingertips brushed over the swollen clit emitting a gasp from its owner.

Shanice's hand reached down and grabbed Marta's wrist. "Don't stop," Shanice gasped. And Marta didn't. Shanice held on, not guiding Marta's hand or changing the speed. Her grip on Marta's wrist was positively endearing.

Shanice's hips arched up and bucked slightly. Marta sped up the pace.

"Yes, yes, yes," Shanice said in encouragement.

Marta stayed right where she was, knowing that Shanice would release any moment. The hand around her wrist tightened. The hips beneath Marta's working hand arched high, froze momentarily, and then bucked as the orgasm hit.

"Uhh, uhh, uhh," Shanice moaned nonsensically.

"Good girl," Marta encouraged, not slowing her strokes until the hand squeezing her wrist loosened.

Shanice fell flat on her back and sighed a long moaning sigh. "Oh. My. God."

Marta chuckled and pulled her hand away from Shanice's sensitive area. "You did so well, sweetie. I'm so proud of you."

"Mmm," Shanice moaned in answer, still out of breath. "I didn't know…Mmm."

"Didn't know what?"

"I didn't know it could be like that."

"You ain't seen nothing yet, kid," Marta said with another chuckle.

"Hold me?"

"Yes, it would be my pleasure." Marta pulled the spent woman into her arms and kissed her gently. "That was epic, Shanice. Thank you for letting me be your first."

"Mm hmm," Shanice said. "All my other girls were busy tonight."

Marta burst out laughing, not expecting that response.

Once Shanice caught her breath, she rolled over and said, "I want to, uh…but I don't know what to do for you."

"Tomorrow is another day," Marta said. "For now, let's get some sleep."

They both broke out laughing when Snowball jumped on the bed and got right in between them.

"Three's a crowd, Snowball," Marta quipped but made room for the cat anyway.

"Marta?" Shanice said. "I mean it. I want to learn how to make you feel good, too."

"That can be arranged," Marta said. She was incredibly aroused but wanted to wait. This was all new to Shanice, and the moment they'd just shared was enough for tonight. "How do you feel about morning sex?"

"I have no idea," Shanice said with a laugh. "But does this mean we're…"

"Going out? A couple? Together? Girlfriend and girlfriend?"

"Yes," Shanice said. "Does it mean those things?"

"It does," Marta said succinctly.

"I don't want a dog collar."

Marta burst out laughing for the umpteenth time that day. "No dog collar. Check."

"But," Shanice said shyly, "maybe we can talk about the kind of relationship Madison and Miss Shasti have."

"I was wondering if you'd want that," Marta said quietly.

"You were wondering? Does that mean you have been thinking about, you know, us?"

"Humph," Marta said. "Yes. For a while now."

"Me, too," Shanice said. "But I wasn't sure. I mean…"

"It's okay. Trust comes hard for you. Me, too, if I'm being honest." Marta pulled Shanice as close as she could around the white fluffball between them. "I have one request. For tomorrow morning."

"What's that?" Shanice asked.

"No second guessing what happened here tonight. I want to be with you, Shanice. I want you in my life."

"Me, too," Shanice said, squishing the cat as she leaned over for several passionate kisses. The squirming cat ruined the moment, but that was okay. There were many more moments on the horizon for them.

"Okay," Marta said. "Hurry up and sleep so we can wake up and have that morning sex."

"Mmm," Shanice moaned contentedly, burrowing into Marta's embrace as much as she could.

Only after Shanice's breathing got slow and steady did Marta let herself relax enough to feel content. It was a feeling she hadn't had in a long, long time. Maybe that's what happened when you let your guard down long enough to let someone amazing in.

Chapter 22

Shanice

Shanice woke feeling more content than she ever had. As soon as Marta's arms squeezed tightly, she remembered why. It wasn't sexual arousal that flashed through her, but something else. It was a flash of belonging. Maybe not that exactly, but something like it.

"No regrets," came the gentle reminder from the amazing superhero holding her.

"None whatsoever." Shanice rolled onto her side, blinking the sleep out of her eyes, only to see Marta doing the same. It was still dark outside. They'd both woken up before Marta's alarm.

Shanice brushed one of Marta's wavy blonde locks off her forehead. Marta searched Shanice's eyes. For what? Shanice wasn't sure but leaned in for a kiss, hoping that was it.

Marta's soft moan as their lips met made Shanice smile, and the kiss was lost. "Mmm," Marta said. "I could do this all day."

"Me, too," Shanice said. "But I have to, you know, go to the…."

"Me, too," Marta said with a giggle. "It's never like in the movies. How can people just wake up and have mind-blowing sex without peeing first? That's just fiction."

Shanice laughed as she sat up. "And before brushing their teeth." She spun around before backing into the chair that was locked against the side of the bed.

"It wouldn't be fair to race you," Marta said.

"Yeah, because you'd lose." Shanice unlocked her wheels and bolted for the door.

Marta bounced her way off the end of the bed and almost made it past

Shanice, but the wheelchair now filled the bedroom doorway. "Aww," Marta groaned good-naturedly. "If only I could fly over you."

"Not all superheroes fly," Shanice reminded Marta, heading out of the bedroom.

"I'll go set up the coffee," Marta said.

"You could use the bathroom in your mother's room," Shanice suggested just as she was about to close the bathroom door behind her.

The silence following the suggestion grew so long that Shanice called, "Marta?"

"I'm okay," Marta said from the kitchen. "I'll just use your bathroom when you're done. And then I'll meet you back in that super small bed."

"Okay." Shanice sighed and then set about doing her morning routine. She even took a quick sponge bath as best she could. Hair? Nah. She'd do something about her mop later. Her first official workday was on Monday, so there would be no screen time with Parvati or anything like that today. But there was Marta. Shanice suddenly had the urge to make herself look good for Marta. Now that they were girlfriends, Shanice wanted to please her. She squeed as she thought about being someone's official girlfriend. That had happened, right?

"Hey," came the superhero's voice from outside the bathroom door. "Any day now?" The teasing lilt in Marta's voice was unmistakable.

"I'm done," Shanice said. She couldn't help the grin on her face. Yes, she was someone's girlfriend.

Shanice got back in the twin bed and didn't have to wait long before Marta dove onto it, making the bed bounce.

Shanice couldn't help her giggles. She loved when Marta was playful, but she was also giggling from nerves. She knew Marta would take the lead, but still.

The gentle caress across Shanice's face, the intense expression, and the murmured, "You're beautiful, Shanice," rocketed Shanice into high arousal. Her soft moan seemed to be all the permission Marta needed as soft searching lips found hers. Shanice wrapped her arms around Marta's neck and practically pulled Marta on top of her in her fervor. Marta took the hint and adjusted her position.

Marta let one thigh land between Shanice's legs. Shanice moaned, letting Marta know that the light was very green. Keeping her thigh pressed against Shanice's center, Marta began a trail of kisses all over Shanice's face, even making a comment about kissing the small cut on Shanice's face to make it all better. When Marta's lips hit her neck, shivers ran through Shanice's body.

She understood something in that moment. Sex was more than just an activity to achieve orgasm. Anyone could do that with their own hands. But this? What Marta was doing? This was lovemaking.

She moaned as Marta kissed each button on her sleep shirt before opening it. She opened the shirt wide and bared Shanice's body.

Marta inhaled sharply. "You're more beautiful than I imagined." She ran her fingertips over Shanice's breasts making the nipples harden. Soft lips replaced the gentle fingers. The soft lips hardened, and the tip of Marta's tongue lashed back and forth, causing arousal to seep up from the core of the earth to fill Shanice's body. It was too much.

"Yellow," Shanice said, and Marta stopped her movements.

"You okay, sweetie?"

"Equal time." She tugged at Marta's tight t-shirt.

Marta chuckled, reached behind her neck, and pulled off the T-shirt in one swift motion. Shanice didn't have time to comment because Marta reached for one of Shanice's hands and placed it on her own breast. Marta was so pretty. Her breasts were nice. Soft. Not small. Not big, though. They were perfect. And, wow, Marta's nipples were getting hard. Shanice was doing that. She had power, too. Who knew?

A surge of strength coursed through Shanice's core to her arms, and she pushed Marta up and over onto her back. Shanice kept eye contact as she climbed over Marta's body, her knees on either side of Marta's thighs. She leaned down and kissed Marta in much the same way Marta had done. She followed the same path, and when Marta moaned, Shanice wanted to shout to the world that she was the one causing that. Her. The loner nerd who wrote computer code for a living.

Shanice wasn't sure what to do after that, so she let Marta take over and flop Shanice onto her back again. Shanice's breathing got even heavier when she saw unmistakable lust in Marta's eyes. Wow. Intense.

Marta kissed her way down Shanice's body quickly. One hand massaged one of Shanice's breasts while the other rested on Shanice's thigh. Upper thigh. Close to—

"Yes," Shanice said as the hand moved to cup her center. Kisses traveled down Shanice's torso to her mound. Kisses were placed there, and then the thing Shanice never thought would happen in her lifetime happened.

The hand covering her mound became two fingers that split her open, and a tongue landed gently on her clit. Shanice jumped at the contact. She reached down and put her hand on Marta's head in encouragement.

Marta purred at the unspoken feedback. *Purred* was the only word Shanice had to describe Marta's low growling moans that were almost predatory. The hand fondling Shanice's breast moved lower to the real action. The fingers on this hand began a slow traversing of Shanice's wetness. Shanice was almost embarrassed at the way Marta was touching her. Almost. The amazing feels threatening to overwhelm her won out.

"So pretty," Marta said, talking directly to Shanice's center.

There were no more words until Marta's lips engulfed Shanice's clit, and Shanice moaned out the only word she knew. "Yes, yes, yes." Shanice kept her hand wound tightly in Marta's locks as the orgasm built. Words became unintelligible as she screeched her release and bucked her hips, throwing Marta off. Marta, the superhero she was, latched back on and pulled out another smaller release.

Shanice released her grasp on Marta's hair and threw her hands overhead in surrender. She was breathing hard, moaning in time with the aftershocks as they hit.

"Yellow, yellow," Shanice said, pulling at Marta to let up. She'd become too sensitive for any more touching.

Wordlessly, Marta moved over to Shanice's side and pulled her close. She kissed Shanice's forehead and rocked her until Shanice's breathing evened out. "That was epic, sweetie," Marta said with another kiss to Shanice's forehead.

With one big inhale and a controlled exhale, Shanice moaned her content. “Yes, it was.” One more sighed exhale, and Shanice was on top of Marta, causing her to yelp in surprise. Marta quickly changed her tune, though, and moaned her approval.

“Tomorrow has arrived,” Shanice said cryptically and returned to kissing Marta passionately. Tasting herself on Marta’s lips was so intimate that she almost smiled at the surprise.

“Hmm?” Marta said, sounding confused.

“Last night, you said, ‘Tomorrow is another day.’ Well, guess what? Tomorrow is here.”

Marta laughed in a way that told Shanice they both knew the jig was up.

“Tell me what to do,” Shanice said.

Marta moaned low in her throat. “Kiss me like I kissed you.”

Shanice complied and was amazed at how much Marta’s moans turned her on. Yes, this was definitely more than sex. They were making love. Shanice kissed Marta’s ample breasts and did the same sucking and tongue flicking. Marta approved this activity with her insistent moans. Without preamble, Marta grabbed one of Shanice’s hands and thrust the fingers toward her center. She guided the inexperienced fingers around her clit, and it wasn’t long before Marta arched her pelvis. She bucked her hips until a low groan signaled her release. Shanice’s fingers continued to work on their own until Marta stopped their movement.

Marta moaned as a few aftershocks hit her, then commanded breathlessly, “Come here.” She patted her chest. Shanice moved up and put her head on her favorite spot. Marta’s arms wrapped around her as a satisfied sigh came from Marta’s core.

Marta kissed Shanice’s head and said, “I think I knew the moment I laid eyes on you in that hospital bed. You were all alone and so helpless. But I didn’t realize what it was at the time. I mean, I didn’t know you. How could I be in love with a stranger? It was your grateful smile. The way you looked at me. The relief in your eyes.”

Shanice snuggled tightly against her superhero but didn’t interrupt.

“I was devastated beyond belief the day I went to the hospital, and you weren’t there. You’d already been moved to the Chrysalis Center, but I didn’t know that. I thought I had lost you.” The arms around Shanice tightened for a moment. "But then I found you again. And then that other time, do you remember it, the morning I ingloriously quit my job?"

Shanice nodded.

"You brought me a cup of water. And it was in *your* cup. You could have in no way understood what that meant to me. Most people are takers. You're not. Although maybe you need to ask for help more often, but I'll fuss at you about that another time. But when you brought me that water, you were showing that you wanted to help me. That you didn't want to see me hurting."

"I didn't know what to do," Shanice admitted.

"It was at Dana's housewarming, though, that I finally realized I was in love with you, Shanice. Everyone saw it." Marta nudged Shanice off her shoulder and sat up enough to caress Shanice's face. "All the love displayed among those people just sent me over the edge. When you turned and saw me so upset? That was moments after I realized I was deeply in love with you and wanted to take care of you. Make a life with you, you know?"

"Yes. I know," Shanice said. "I think it was that same night I officially allowed myself to admit I had a major crush on you, but I was never going to tell you. And honestly, I'm pretty certain my crush on you started the moment you superheroed your way into my life and manhandled Tyler."

Marta laughed. "So, I guess we have Tyler to thank for our meeting."

"Oh, God. I guess." Shanice sighed and let Marta kiss her gently. When they broke apart, Shanice said. "But there were so many other things that conspired for us to meet. Nora was in the hospital at the same time, on the same floor."

"Do you know her surgery date had changed a couple of times? I guess the universe was rearranging things for us."

"And Tyler forgot he needed to have a female in the room with him when undressing a female patient," Shanice said with a scowl.

Marta scoffed at that one. "Who knows? I'm just glad you have a good healthy set of lungs on you that got right into my brain and moved my feet."

"My hero." Another round of kissing ensued. "Marta?" Shanice said once she broke away for much needed oxygen.

"Yes, sweetie?"

"I love you."

Tears welled up in Marta's eyes.

"Oh, I didn't mean to make you—"

A finger went over her lips. "Hush," Marta said. "That's just me. I love you, too, sweetie, and I'm glad you came into my life. Now, if all this talking is done, can we get back to the kissing?"

Shanice nodded emphatically and leaned up to let Marta's soul-searching kiss send them into another round of lovemaking that almost caused Marta to be late for her second day of work.

~~~

Shanice sat at the kitchen table with her laptop open but could barely focus on the coding project on the screen. Parvati sent her the project the day before so Shanice could look it over and be ready to work on it on Monday, her first official day back at work. Marta had suggested she get a jumpstart on the work project, and Shanice had agreed. She'd already been out too long from work and felt she needed to be up to speed the moment the proverbial bell rang to start her first day back. That way, everyone would see she was strong and capable.

The only problem? Shanice had morning sex on the brain. She firmly decided that morning sex was an amazing way to start one's day, giving it five stars and a 'highly recommend,' but the memory of it was distracting as all heck. She'd given Marta two orgasms. *Me,* Shanice thought, biting her lower lip. *I did that.* They even showered together afterward. Shanice sat on her bench seat in the tub while Marta washed every inch of her. The care and gentleness Marta took was otherworldly. She even had to rush her own shower so she wouldn't be late for the coffee shop.

Shanice picked up her phone and reread their text exchange from earlier that morning.

MARTA: Got here with ten minutes to spare!

SHANICE: Yay!
~~~

MARTA: Meeting more of the workers and getting to experience what a busy Saturday is like here at the coffee shop. I may not be able to text until lunchtime.

SHANICE: I understand. I'm working on that coding project like you suggested.

MARTA: Good girl.

MARTA: Guess what?

SHANICE: What?

MARTA: I love you.

SHANICE: I love you, too.

MARTA: Oops, the boss is here. Gotta go. (kiss emoji)

SHANICE: (kiss emoji)

Shanice reread the line where Marta said she loved her. She took a screenshot of it and filed it in a newly created photo album, 'Favorite Things.' Her heart swelled with so much feeling that she almost started crying. Ahh, this must be how Marta always feels, with emotions bubbling up on their own.

Enough. Shanice put the phone face down on the table. The volume was up, though, because she didn't want to miss Marta's lunchtime text. And, yeah, she needed to get into the coding project so she could tell Marta how productive she'd been.

Shanice sighed and resigned herself to look at the notes on the legal pad she'd taken during her brief phone call with Parvati Friday afternoon. Parvati said the feedback from the beta testing group from Reynolds

Trucking specifically mentioned the app's reefer truck subroutines. The app kept giving error codes or just locked up.

"Okay," Shanice said out loud, "I'm not a trucker, but what do we know about refrigerated trucks?" She wrote down the criteria from Parvati's follow-up email. Maximum freight weight, maximum dimensions and capacity of the trailer, temperature fluctuations, time schedules, and quite a few more. Yes, this was going to take a while because Shanice would have to check each variable against the code to see what might be causing the lockups and error messages.

She read over the feedback from the drivers, and a couple of things emerged. Obviously, none of the coders realized that reefer trucks were sometimes used to haul dry goods, too, so the temperature variable needed to be overridden for those trips. She checked on the code. Nope, there was no allowance for that. Should she dig into the code now or wait for Parvati? She wasn't supposed to be officially working, but she was chomping at the bit to get back into it. She loved coding. It was problem-solving with a million moving parts.

The first time one of her subroutines had been used in a larger project, she was over the moon. She'd helped out. She'd made something real that wasn't just a game for the Coding Club. Real people would use it for their real-world lives. It had been so rewarding that she knew she'd found her calling. Coding for the trucking and transportation industry probably wasn't one of those careers she ever thought she'd have, but it was really satisfying.

She made notes on a fresh page of her legal pad, opened a new screen on her work laptop, and typed in the code that would hopefully take care of the dry loads' issue. She decided not to incorporate the new code into the existing project until Parvati had a chance to look it over and approve it. Yeah, good idea. The company probably wanted to see if she could think straight after her accident.

Shanice laughed. It wasn't the accident that had her not thinking straight. It was Marta. Her kisses and caresses and the way she locked onto Shanice's gaze. Those were the things causing Shanice's brain to overload that morning.

"Exactly," Shanice said out loud. "Who knows how I might ruin the code in my distracted state." Notes and temporary coding were enough for now.

She looked over the project again and saw another mistake. The program only allowed for Fahrenheit temperatures. A quick toggle subroutine and the user could set the default to whichever temperature scale applied. And, yes, she mused, the scale should be displayed either way.

"Make it not only user friendly but user *proof*," Mr. Johnson always said.

She spent the better part of the morning combing over the project's original code, looking for more bugs, until her phone dinged an incoming text message.

MARTA: Guess what?

SHANICE: You love me?

MARTA: (gasp emoji) Are you psychic or something?

SHANICE: I love you, too.

MARTA: (kiss emoji)

MARTA: Can you put this on our family calendar? MOVE Rikki on the fifteenth. She said she'd understand if you have to work, being such an important computer scientist and all.

SHANICE: (shocked emoji) I'm not that important.

MARTA: You are to me.

Shanice melted at the texted words on her screen. They texted for a while longer, but too soon, Marta had to go. She took Marta up on her suggestion by wrapping her arms around herself as if Marta were hugging her. Being loved was amazing, but why did it scare her so much?

Chapter 23

Marta

It was the first Saturday in September, the Saturday of Labor Day weekend to be exact, and Marta and Shanice were sitting in Rocco's diner with nine of their new friends.

"Did you get enough to eat, sweetie?" Marta asked and used a napkin to wipe Shanice's chin. Shanice nodded.

"How long?" Shasti demanded with a knowing expression.

Marta looked at Shanice, asking permission with her expression. There really was no hiding it anymore because they couldn't help making googly eyes at each other. When Shanice nodded, Marta said to the group, "One month on Monday."

A cheer went up at the overlarge table. "Knew it," Dana said, pointing to Shanice.

"Who had one month?" Jaleesa asked with a laugh earning her a good-natured smack from her girlfriend, Tina.

"Shut up, you guys," Marta said but didn't really mean it.

"Miss Marta," Madison said, her hand raised.

"Yes, Madison?" Marta exchanged an amused glance with Madison's Domme, Shasti.

"For your anniversary on Monday, can we go to the zoo to celebrate?"

"Madison Kim," Shasti said sternly. "Do not interject yourself into others' plans. We've talked about this."

"Sorry," Madison said to her Domme. "Sorry, Miss Marta."

"We'd love to go to the zoo with you sometime, but I'll have to take a raincheck on that date because I need to ask my boss about taking next Saturday off for some house reno."

All eyes were on Rikki, who didn't seem flustered by the sudden flow of attention toward her. She was always so cool and calm and put together. It made Marta wonder why Rikki didn't have a partner. Oh, right. The last breakup had been a bad one. Once bitten, as they say.

"Of course," Rikki said. "What are you having done?"

"I'm not *having* it done. I'm doing it." Marta sighed. "The carpets have to go. Her chair has trouble on them, and they're ancient anyway. I've asked Deshawn to help rebuild the ramp out front and help build one out back. And eventually, new vinyl flooring will go in."

"I can help with all of it," Victoria offered. "My father was a contractor and had me do a little bit of everything, so sign me up."

"Oh, no," Marta protested. "I didn't mean to rope you into—"

"No one can rope Daddy Vic," Madison said with a giggle.

The entire table broke out in laughter except for Marta and Shanice, who exchanged glances. They had no idea what was so funny.

Rikki leaned over and said low, "Shasti is quite the rigger. And Madison is quite the rope bunny."

"Ahh," Marta said with understanding. To Shanice's confused expression, Marta said, "I'll demonstrate on you when we get home."

Shanice's wide-eyed expression had them all cooing and reassuring Shanice that all would be well and that she would love Shibari rope play. Shanice still looked doubtful.

At the end of the table, Rowena said, "Minjung can demonstrate if you wish to borrow her." She pointed to her submissive sitting quietly at her side, hands folded in her lap, gaze downward.

"Uh, thanks," Marta said. "That's very generous. Perhaps when the ties get a bit more complex." Marta smiled at the Domme at the end of the table. She hadn't quite gotten a bead on Rowena and didn't want to rankle her in any shape or form. She was new to having a friends' group like this and hadn't quite worked out all the dynamics.

"Minjung could be part of a demonstration at the Christmas Masquerade Ball," Rikki said to Rowena, who beamed.

Ahh, yes. Rowena did like to be seen as important. That much Marta had figured out.

"Perfect idea. Will Shasti do the rigger honors?" Rowena suggested.

If the question threw Shasti, she didn't show it. She simply said, "Perhaps a suspension. I've been itching to try one of those."

"We'll set up some sessions at your place, then," Rowena said firmly as if the matter was decided. Shasti simply nodded.

Jaleesa changed the direction of the conversation. She said to Marta and Shanice, "Tina, Dana, and I will be at your house bright and early next Saturday morning to help out."

"Harriet might like to come, too," Tina offered. "She loves helping."

"True, true," Jaleesa agreed and turned back to Marta. "What time?"

"Seriously," Marta protested, "I didn't mention it to recruit workers."

Shanice tugged at her sleeve, and Marta lowered her head so Shanice could whisper in her ear.

"Okay," Marta said with a sigh. "I've been told it's okay to accept help, especially when it has been so generously offered."

A cheer went up around the table.

"Did I mention we're painting, too?" Marta added sheepishly.

Jaleesa's laugh was the biggest of all, but what struck Marta's heart the most was the tiny grin on the slave Minjung's face. Good. She wasn't just a mindless object. Marta had learned from her former sub Jessica that temporarily playing a bimbo or inanimate object could be intensely freeing, but it wasn't a twenty-four-seven thing. Marta looked away so she didn't bring attention to Rowena's slave and get her in trouble.

"Hey, we help each other in our community," Rikki said. "Look how fast you all moved me into the apartment over the shop. I'd still be packing if I hadn't asked for help." She patted Marta's forearm, essentially conveying that she understood how hard it was to ask.

They hammered out the details for the renovations and then got another round of coffees from their clearly seasoned, middle-aged waitress.

"Thank you, Marlene," Rikki said.

"You're welcome, honey," Marlene answered. "Can I get anybody anything? I'm not kicking you out. I love to see ladies out and about living their best lives."

Her comment made the table of women chuckle. No one needed

anything except for another glass of water that Rowena ordered for Minjung.

After Marlene brought the water, Rikki said, “Can we make this brunch a monthly thing? Casual. Not mandatory. First Saturday of every month. Ten o’clock here at Rocco’s if you can make it.”

“Let’s do it,” Victoria seconded the unofficial motion. A round of “Sounds good” and “I’m in” moved the motion forward.

Marta loved the idea, especially for Shanice’s sake, but she knew Rikki would have to approve the time off on Saturdays. Something could be worked out, maybe not every month, but a few, hopefully.

Rikki said, “We’ve been batting around the idea of forming a council of sorts. My Aunt Tilda was an amazing leader in our community, but I am not her. I can lead for now, but I see this as a community effort.”

Shasti said, “Tilda always talked about a formal Denton Heights BDSM group, but I’d like to make sure the women are represented. Maybe we can form one group with two councils. One for the guys and one for the women. Or women-identified.” Clearly, she was rethinking her suggestion. “With so many people defining their genders or non-gender, I suppose we’ll have to leave that open, won’t we?”

There was general head nodding around the table, and Rowena offered, “I like the idea of calling it a women’s board, but one that is open. And I’m positive that Seamus would be interested in forming some kind of men’s board.”

“I’ve heard him say he’d like more formal checks and balances,” Rikki said. “Aunt Tilda always told me the vanillas didn’t understand our lifestyles. She said we needed to police ourselves before bringing anyone else in.”

“I like it,” Victoria said, her hair perfectly coiffed and unmoving. “A council or committee would ensure that one person wasn’t taking on the sole role of judge and executioner if we’re going to police ourselves.” She nodded at Rikki in solidarity. Victoria and Rikki were long-time friends. The two of them and Shasti had been disciples of Rikki’s aunt. Okay, *disciples* was probably too strong a word, but Marta couldn’t think of a better one at the moment.

"It will make planning these masquerade balls so much easier, too," Rikki said with a relieved sigh. Marta hadn't realized until then how much responsibility Rikki had taken on in their community. It had been obvious that Rikki was their de facto leader, and sitting here with the group, Marta witnessed it firsthand.

"I'm in," Jaleesa said, looking toward Tina for approval. Tina lay her head on Jaleesa's shoulder as if she were proud of her Domme for volunteering.

Marta's voice joined the others in agreement. Shanice's beaming approval made Marta feel good. Honestly, Marta had no clue what she had just signed up for, but she had experience working within group dynamics. Of course, she'd worn greens, khaki, and camo while doing it, but the concept was similar.

"So, we're in agreement then?" Rikki looked at each Domme in turn. After each one nodded, Rikki said, "Okay then. The Denton Heights BDSM Women's Collective is officially born."

"We can offer up our home for the first meeting," Jaleesa offered.

"Sound good?" Rikki asked, looking around the table. "Good. I'll send out a group text so we can hammer out a date for the first official meeting. I'll also contact Seamus and let him know what we gals are up to."

"Good idea," Rowena agreed. "Those boys can get their stingers out of whack so easily."

Enemy artillery exploded out of nowhere.

"Get down," Marta boomed and tried to move Shanice out of the way. Damn. Locked. Marta dove under the table. With her heart pounding, she searched for the source of the ambush. It wasn't until Dana slowly crawled under the table that Marta realized what had happened.

"You're okay," Dana said softly. "It was just the busboy. He dropped an entire tray of something. Everyone jumped. I even screamed."

Marta struggled to catch her breath. It didn't matter that she'd just embarrassed herself in front of her new friends and boss. She was worried about Shanice. She looked toward the wheelchair and then back at Dana for the strength she hoped she'd find there.

"You're okay, Miss Marta. Shanice is okay. We're all fine."

Marta nodded, took a moment to collect herself, and then patted Dana's forearm. "Thank you," she whispered.

Rikki pulled her chair out and squatted down. "Do you need help getting up?"

Marta shook her head. "No."

Once back in her seat, no one except Shanice looked at her. "Are you okay, Mama?"

Marta nodded. "But I think I need to call Dr. Fieldston's office ASAP." In the back of her mind, she realized Shanice had called her Mama. She was still so shaken, though, that it barely registered.

"PTSD?" Victoria asked gently.

"Affirmative."

More faces turned in her direction. She wasn't sure why she shared what she did next, but she felt safe in this group of new friends. She couldn't look at them yet, so she looked at her hands in her lap instead. They were shaking as she spoke.

"I realized early on, as far back as boot camp, that they were outfitting us with so much ammo that each of us could take out a small village on our own. But I wanted to serve my country. My entire company got shipped out for Operation Iraqi Freedom. I was stationed in Baghdad as a vehicle mechanic, but sometimes I did checkpoint security or drove transport. War always seemed like such a noble thing, but…"

"You don't have to go on," Shanice said softly when Marta hesitated.

Marta looked up at Shanice. "Is it okay if I do?"

Shanice nodded.

"Only if you want to," Shasti said, speaking for the group. "We're here to support you, Marta. Both of you."

"We've got you," Rikki said gently.

Marta nodded, emotion building in her chest. Shanice's hand snaked into hers; maybe that's where she found the courage to continue. "I thought I was over this."

"Your protective instincts are on high alert now," Jaleesa offered. "You have more at stake." She gestured toward Shanice.

Marta smiled at Shanice, who then did something so endearing that

Marta almost lost it. Shanice handed the fox stuffie to Marta for comfort. Marta squeezed the soft treasure and wiped at her eyes. "Thank you," she mouthed to Shanice, who nodded encouragement.

"War is brutal," Marta continued to the group. "The things I've seen. Bombed-out villages. Bodies. Soldiers. Civilians." She closed her eyes to the vivid memories. "Suicide bombers could come out of nowhere. A transport vehicle ahead of mine ran over an IED. The truck blew up. There were no survivors. Our vehicle took shrapnel, but we had no casualties. I knew those soldiers in the lead truck. The bonds you make within your squad differ from any I've ever known. These were life and death bonds. That's what they always told us, anyway."

Marta looked up at the sympathetic faces. "I hate crowds, as you can probably understand. I need my back to the wall to keep tabs on the space." She gestured to the wall behind her. "Loud, unexpected noises? Well, you witnessed what could happen. Some veterans I know have anger or substance abuse issues. For me, I go inward. I've tried to keep the whole world out, but not anymore. I discovered that wasn't any way to live."

Marta looked at Dana. "When I got assigned an apprentice at the nursery, I realized I liked having someone to talk to." She turned toward Shanice. "And then, when this damsel in distress needed me, I fully understood it was time to rejoin the human race. And I think she's beginning to understand how much I also need her."

A series of awws filled the space, and Marta let the love bask over her. She kissed the back of Shanice's hand. "Please be patient with me," Marta said to Shanice. Shanice nodded and kissed Marta's hand in return.

"I hope you'll all be patient with me," Marta said to the group, her eyes welling with tears.

A chorus of quiet yet reassuring encouragement filled the table, and Marta let herself be consoled by her new friends.

Once the brunch bills were paid, the entire group walked Marta and Shanice to Marta's pickup truck. They exchanged phone numbers and shored up plans for the renovation project the following Saturday. Marta was floored that everyone was going to come and that they had divvied up snacks and beverages to bring, so Marta and Shanice "wouldn't have to worry about that sort of thing." Of course, now that this was really happening, she needed to get the house ready. Jeff would come to help. And Nora, Brian, and Elliot. They were coming over tomorrow to get Nora's new kittens, so she'd put them to work. A lot of the furniture needed to be tossed or donated. And the rooms needed to be emptied. Marta tried not to be overwhelmed. She'd had enough for one day.

After their final goodbyes, Marta was just about to back the truck out of the space when she heard someone call her name.

"Miss Marta! Miss Marta!" Madison was running toward the driver's side window.

"What's up, little one?"

"I understand about your crowds' thing now," Madison said, looking sheepish. "So, we don't have to go to the zoo, like, ever. Okay? I retract my request."

"I think we can still go," Marta said, knowing that Shanice had expressed interest in going at some point.

"We can?" Madison's face lit up.

"I'll ask my research department," Marta gestured toward Shanice, "to find out what days at the zoo are typically the least crowded."

"I can do that," Shanice said with authority.

"Yay," Madison said, clearly gleeful. "Thank you so much. Best stay away from Halloween and other holiday events. It's always crowded then."

"Noted," Marta said.

Madison said her goodbyes again and literally skipped back to Shasti's old BMW. Would Shanice be more comfortable in a car like that? Would a different vehicle make things easier? Maybe something with a backseat or trunk to store the chair. She hated that Shanice's chair always got dumped in the pickup bed, exposed to the weather. And winter would be there soon enough.

"Mama?" Shanice asked gently, a worried lilt to her voice.

"I'm okay, baby girl," Marta said, smiling at her charge. "I was just thinking about vehicles. I want to make sure you're taken care of."

"Are you going somewhere?"

"No, no, no," Marta said, turning to reassure Shanice. "No, I just mean that maybe we need a new vehicle. Like one with a place for your chair *inside.*"

"And maybe a car with hand controls that I can drive."

"A van," Marta said as lightbulbs turned on over her head. "Holy crap, yes. An accessible van with one of those electric ramps that you can operate yourself to get in and out on your own." Marta nodded her head a few times. "A savings account. I'll set one up for us on Monday. No, it's Labor Day. Tuesday then."

"You love opening bank accounts," Shanice teased.

Marta simply waggled her eyebrows. "Helps keep the goal in sight. We should do some research. Find out the good vans and how much we need to save."

"My bills, though," Shanice said dejectedly. Her shoulders slumped down.

Marta took off her seatbelt and leaned over to hold Shanice. "Those will get paid. But we'll also save for the future. We have a van to get you first. Then an electric wheelchair. Or maybe that first. I don't know. And hopefully, your silly stumps will be ready for prosthetics soon."

"It's a lot, Mama," Shanice said.

Marta kissed Shanice's forehead. "I know it is, but you know what?"

"What?"

"Two things. First, it's okay if you want to call me Mama. You seem to want to, and I'm okay with that."

"I can't help it."

"It's fine," Marta said. "I kind of like it. Second thing. I love you, and as far as I can tell, we're in this together. You and me."

"Me and you."

"We'll figure all this out," Marta said. "Okay?"

Shanice's genuine smile was all the answer Marta needed.

"Let me get you home. I believe someone needs to learn what Shibari rope is all about."

"That sounds scary, Mama."

"Nah. I'll be gentle. And then I think the Reds are on TV later this afternoon."

"Can we have popcorn?" Shanice bopped in her seat.

"Of course," Marta said. "Anything for you."

Marta pulled the pickup out of the parking spot and noticed Rikki's old Subaru idling at the far end of the lot. Wow. She'd been waiting to make sure Marta and Shanice were okay. That was friendship.

At the red light heading onto the main road, Marta reached over and held Shanice's hand. "Love you, baby girl."

"Love you, too, Mama."

Marta kissed the hand in hers.

Chapter 24

Shanice

It was the second Saturday in September, and it had been one whole month and five days since Marta became Shanice's real-life girlfriend. Nora had screeched her excitement at their relationship the day she came over to take the two mewling black kittens home. Shanice thought Nora's names for the cats were brilliant. The girl cat was Cinder, and the boy cat was Coal. Marta just looked at Nora funny. Nora just waved her off like she always did.

That same day, Nora and Marta packed up their mother's clothes. Marta was kind of crying the whole time, which made Shanice's heart hurt, too. But Nora said all the right words, and Marta seemed to get herself together after a while. A donation truck came to pick up the clothes and a lot of the old still-usable furniture. Marta's old co-worker Jeff came by to help. He was so nice. Even though they had just met, he and Nora's husband Brian got along like old-time friends. Marta told Shanice later that getting rid of the clothes and furniture was hard, but she knew it was time.

Now it was one week later, and Shanice took a sip of water from her spot on the driveway. It was hot for September, but she couldn't complain since she wasn't doing much of the grunt work. Not yet, anyway. Once the carpeting was pulled out and everything cleaned up, Shanice would join the painting party. They were really taking on a lot today. So many people had come over to help, including Nora and Brian. Mrs. Pulaski came over too, and even though she was an older lady in her sixties or something, she had definitely come ready to work. She wore leather work gloves and safety goggles and everything. Marta had done a triple-take when she saw their neighbor, but Shanice thought she looked awesome. Nora also looked awesome. She'd lost some weight on her interesting diet program that not only had a food plan, but a psychology-type plan, too. It was working for her.

Miss Shasti assigned Nora, Brian, and Mrs. Pulaski to rip out the old carpet in the primary bedroom, but Miss Jaleesa sent Dana in to work with them because Nora wasn't supposed to put much strain on her knee. Jaleesa, Tina, and Harriet worked on the living room carpets. Shanice didn't really know Harriet at all, but when she'd smiled at Shanice that morning, a sugary warm feeling erupted in Shanice's heart. All their new friends were so nice.

Miss Rowena, Daddy Vic, and Minjung were in Nora's old room ripping out the carpeting in there. Madison was a 'floater' helping wherever needed.

The only untouched room was Marta's, where the cats were held up for the day. They were absolutely positively *not* happy about that, but Marta made a fort for them to hide in. Kia, the gray kitty they kept who was named after Shanice's beloved car, thought it was a fun game. Snowball and Mama Cat? Not so much. Shanice vowed to give them extra treats later once things settled down.

A lot of the old furniture had either been donated or was sitting by the side of the road for bulk pickup. The stack of rolled-up old carpeting was getting bigger and bigger next to the discarded furniture. Yeesh, there was a lot of it. "A new start," Marta kept saying.

You would think they would have been too wired for morning sex that morning, but they had both been ready and willing. Marta introduced her to something called 'Go Around the World' and then proceeded to kiss Shanice on every part of her body—even her stumps. Shanice definitely liked the new game, especially because Marta lingered in certain lovely places.

Of course, now that Shanice's libido had been stirred, she was always ready. Marta had been a fantastic teacher and put up with Shanice's "yellow" and "red" calls with grace and patience. Shanice told Marta about the bathtub sex dream she'd had in the rehab center, and Marta put it on their "list" of things to do. Rope play was definitely on their list of things to do again. Who knew being tied up by someone you trust was a turn-on? Shanice, that's who.

Shanice knew that Marta wasn't getting to do all the harder sex things she wanted to, not yet anyway, and that made Shanice a little insecure, especially when Marta's ex Jessica kept texting. When Shanice asked Marta about it, Marta didn't shrug her off. She told the truth. Jessica apparently found the grass wasn't greener with her new love partner and wanted to come back to Marta. Marta informed her that she'd moved on and was quite happy. That had gone a long way in settling Shanice's anxious fears. Marta was real. Marta was staying. Marta was "coming into the present," she'd told Shanice. Shanice wasn't exactly sure what that meant, but apparently, it included whole house renovations.

With all the people working inside, Shanice hadn't known how to help, so she wheeled herself out the back door on the newly installed ramp to the driveway, where she now sat watching Deshawn and Marta replace rotted plywood on the wheelchair ramp. Deshawn had graciously offered his time and expertise free of charge. After Deshawn's initial inspection the other day, they even went to the DIY home store for more materials. As Shanice sat on the driveway, she admired Marta's muscles, gleaming with sweat as she swung the hammer. And that toolbelt, yes, please. Maybe she'd ask Marta to wear that in the house sometimes. Before they—

"Caught," Madison said with a playfully accusing tone.

"Yep," Shanice said. There was no sense denying it.

"Mistress is coming out with lemonade and cookies for everyone," Madison said as she set up folding chairs. While she did that, she talked Shanice's ear off about her August trip to California and the San Diego Zoo with Miss Shasti. The stories were interesting but kind of tiring, too, because Madison rarely seemed to take a breath. Shanice was polite, though. She nodded in all the right places and said, "Oh, wow," at the appropriate times.

True to Madison's words, Miss Shasti came out with a tray laden with a pitcher of lemonade, plastic cups, napkins, and cookies. Dana followed right behind and set up a card table for the snacks.

"Break time," Miss Shasti called to everyone and poured a cup of lemonade for Shanice.

"Thank you, Ma'am," Shanice said, remembering her manners. Marta was trying to teach her etiquette in their community, and sometimes

Shanice forgot. Madison? Yeesh. She forgot all the time. It was crazy.

Miss Shasti touched Shanice's forearm and said, "Miss Rikki, Miss Lydia, and Brittany will be here in time to help with the painting." She followed her statement with a wink and a knowing smile. Yes, everyone knew about Shanice's crush on Miss Riri. "Oh, honey." Miss Shasti grabbed one of Shanice's hands. "How did you get that scar on your palm?"

Everyone in the house had come out for their break by this time. Marta and Deshawn had walked over as well. Shanice looked up at Marta for guidance.

"It's up to you, sweetie," Marta said. "It's your story to tell or not."

"Okay." Shanice looked down, rubbed the scar on the palm of her hand, and then relayed the story about running away from the last foster house she ever stepped foot in and how she had impaled her hand on the spikes on their back fence. She even got brave and told them why she'd fled that day. As she told the tale, she was well aware that the conversations around her had stopped, and they were all listening. That was okay. They were friends. She hoped.

"I'm so sorry that happened to you," Miss Shasti said. She was a doctor, so it was natural she would ask about a scar like that. Miss Shasti exchanged a glance with Marta, but Shanice couldn't interpret it.

Shanice got a lot of attention after her story. Many extended their sorrow that she'd had to put up with 'predators,' as Miss Jaleesa called the bad foster parents. Shanice wanted to tell about the good times with Miss Deborah and Miss Lauren, just so everyone didn't think she'd been tortured her entire childhood, but the conversation had changed to the Cincinnati Reds' run for a playoff bid.

Miss Shasti told Marta about a therapist she highly recommended that might help Shanice process events like that from her childhood. When asked, Miss Shasti said she would gladly share the therapist's contact information. Miss Shasti then had to excuse herself to discourage Madison from picking through the discarded furniture by the road.

"We'll discuss the idea of therapy later," Marta said to Shanice privately. "Once the dust settles, okay?"

Shanice shrugged. "Okay."

"And, as always," Marta said, "you have the ultimate choice whether you want to go or not."

"Okay." Shanice had no idea what to think about therapy. But, like Marta said, they'd talk about it later.

"Hey, since we're on a break," Marta said, "can we show them your new skill?"

"It's nothing," Shanice said. "You need to show them *your* new skill."

"Deal."

Madison sulked as she made her way back up the driveway, head down, probably disappointed about not being able to explore. She perked up, though, when Marta whispered something into her ear. Madison took off running into the house and returned in no time to hand Marta the requested items.

Marta got the silence of their gathered friends and said, "We'd like to show you our new party tricks." Everyone gathered around. "When I first met Shanice, I couldn't do this." She handed the colorful Rubik's cube to Shanice, who began twisting the sides at lightning speed. "And she couldn't do this." Marta took the deck of cards and expertly showed them the riffle shuffle with the cascade finish. Marta shuffled the cards one more time, and in that time, Shanice was done with the cube. Their friends clapped and got very excited, congratulating Shanice mostly. Marta gestured for Shanice to mix up the cube, much to Madison's very vocal dismay.

"But now," Marta handed the cards to Shanice, who gave her the cube, "we can both do both." Marta nodded toward Shanice.

"Go ahead, Mama," Shanice said. "It's going to take you a lot longer." Everyone laughed at Shanice's teasing, which was good because Shanice had called Marta 'Mama.' Marta had said it was okay, but she'd never done it in front of Nora or Brian or Mrs. Pulaski.

"No way," Nora said and maneuvered to stand next to her sister. "Is that Dad's cube?"

Marta nodded and twisted the sides of the cube quickly but not as quickly as Shanice. Oh, yes. It was uber obvious to Shanice that Marta had been practicing. She had noticed the spare Rubik's cube in the kitchen at Rikki's Coffee Shop.

Shanice did several flawless riffle shuffles with the flourishy cascade finish and got lots of applause. She bowed in her chair, but her eyes were on Marta. Yes, she was doing every step correctly and, in no time, held up the finished cube to thunderous applause and a hug from Nora.

Marta just laughed and tossed the cube back to Shanice.

"Gotta get back to it, baby girl." Marta leaned down for a kiss. Everyone oohed and ahhed and then headed back to their assigned jobs.

Shanice watched Marta head back toward the ramp but veer off as a pickup truck pulled up. It was Jeff. Yay, he made it. Marta hugged him when he got out of the pickup and pointed toward Shanice. He came over to Shanice, hugged her neck, and even said he liked the new braids that Jaleesa had done for her. Everyone else had seen them by now, but not him, and it was nice that he noticed. After a few more pleasantries, he excused himself to work with Deshawn and Marta. Shanice liked Jeff. He was strong but gentle and had taken over as Dana's mentor at the landscaping place. Dana said she liked him, too, which put Marta's mind at ease. She'd said leaving Dana without a mentor was her only guilty regret about quitting her job. But when Jeff volunteered to mentor Dana, her guilt vanished. He was going to come back to the house another day, too. He, Marta, Deshawn, and Daddy Vic were going to install the new luxury vinyl flooring throughout the house.

Now, Daddy Vic? She was nice, but kind of closed off. She always had a serious expression on her face, so much so that Shanice never knew what to say to her. So, she didn't.

Nora patted Shanice on the shoulder, knocking her out of her thoughts. "I'm amazed that you were able to teach her that." She pointed to the Rubik's cube in Shanice's lap.

"She worked hard at it," Shanice said.

"She does work hard," Mrs. Pulaski agreed. "I think the new job agrees with her. Don't you think?" The question was directed at Nora, and Shanice could sense a gossip session about to start. Yeah, she wanted no part in that.

"I'll just go inside and put these away," Shanice said, holding up the cube and cards.

"Okay, honey," Nora said distractedly.

Shanice had just turned the corner toward the back entrance when she heard Mrs. Pulaski say, "She looks happy."

"She does," Nora answered. "She's making a home now with someone who loves her."

"She is," Mrs. Pulaski agreed. "It's so nice to see."

Shanice grinned. They were talking about her.

"Yes," Nora said, "Happiness was always within her grasp, but she just hadn't reached for it until now. She's taking care of Shanice, making a home with her. I've never seen Marta this happy, this content."

Shanice gasped. They weren't talking about her. They were talking about Marta. Her heart gushed warm feels for the two gossiping women. They truly loved Marta and had each been looking out for her in their own ways. "I'm joining the 'take care of Marta' club, too," Shanice said to the universe and headed inside.

~~~

Shanice nestled her wheelchair into the well of the desk she and Marta had picked out for the new office, which used to be Nora's room. Not only did the new luxury vinyl flooring look fresh and amazing, but it was so much easier to get around the house now. She opened one of the drawers and pulled out a pad of paper. She had a coding project to work on, but Marta thought maybe this other project was more important. She was probably right since the coding project could wait until Monday. This other thing, though? She'd been putting it off because it was going to be hard. She had been avoiding it ever since her new psychologist Dr. Sumner suggested it.

Shanice smiled, thinking about her therapist. She was a sister. And she was so nice. It was November now, and she'd been seeing Dr. Sumner once a week for almost two months at this point. It was her and Marta's three-month anniversary, and it was a day before Shanice's twenty-sixth birthday. They were going out for a lobster dinner in a little while to celebrate, but Marta wanted Shanice to at least get a start on writing the letter to her birth mother. The only problem? What to say? There had been so many feelings
~~~

about her birth mother throughout her life—abandonment, fear, anger, betrayal, confusion. So many feelings. She didn't know where to start.

'Feel your feels,' Marta always said.

All right. Here goes. Shanice took a cleansing breath and clicked open the gel pen. Marta had teasingly told her to plant her feet, back her ears, and get started. *So here we go.* The pen hit the paper.

> To the mother who birthed me,
>
> Hi, my name is Shanice Ward, but you know that. You named me. Dr. Sumner suggested I write you a letter. When I asked her what to say, she told me to write whatever was in my heart.
>
> So, I finally found out your name when I turned eighteen, and they gave me my birth certificate. It was proof that I was born and not hatched, Marta joked to me. More about who Marta is in a minute. I searched online but couldn't find you. I made calls, and then Marta and I finally found out that you had died when I was, like, two years old. So, you've been gone most of my life. All those daydreams and hopes of finding you were for naught. All those wishes that you would show up one day, take me in your arms, bring me home, and tell me it was all a mistake, were just that. Wishes. And I'm sorry you passed away before I had a chance to meet you.
>
> The nice woman from the Institute for the Blind I talked to on the phone found your records. She told me you were homebound your entire life in a home for the disabled in Cincinnati. You were blind from birth, she said. Your family had given you up, too. The woman at the Institute searched for more information but couldn't find any. She said she would contact me if she

found something, but I haven't heard from her in a month, so I guess there was nothing more to find. She couldn't find the name of my father, either, but since I have your last name, I guess you never married him or whatever. I shouldn't dwell on that, Dr. Sumner said. And Marta said, "It is what it is." She says that a lot.

So, who's Marta? My hero. She found me when I was recovering from a stupid car crash, which wasn't my fault. Oh, I got $1500 for my car. That went right back into medical bills. Oh, well. Marta says it will take longer for the lawsuit to settle between the truck company and all of us affected by the accident. Marta says not to count on getting anything because corporations have ways of getting out of almost anything. A small part of me hopes I can get something. I mean, I'm kind of disabled now. But I don't want to think of it that way. Marta says it's my new normal. She says I should think of myself as *differently*-abled. Not handicapped or disabled because DIS-abled means NOT abled. And I am quite capable, she tells me. I love her.

She takes me running, you know. She pushes my chair around the neighborhoods like those moms who run with their babies in strollers. Marta says it gives her a better workout and that I'm getting a workout in my core because I have to keep my balance as we go. I like that she includes me that way. She's special. Yes, really special.

Tomorrow is my birthday. We're having a birthday party for me here (at the house). I'll be twenty-six. Marta called me an old lady. Ha ha. She's thirty-six. Marta and I have now been together for exactly three months today. She got me an early birthday present—tickets to a Benjies concert in March. She doesn't like crowded places, so this is an exceptional gift. But tonight, she's taking me to this restaurant that has steak and lobster. She knows I like lobster. No, I LOVE lobster. Maybe I'll ask her to take me to Maine sometime, where we can have it every single day.

Oh, and you know what? Marta understands about my food issues. "Food insecurities," she and Dr. Sumner call it. She bought me a lockable food locker. I didn't know there was such a thing, but it's totally portable. It's so that I have food that's mine, and no one can take it from me. The foster parents sometimes punished us by sending us to bed without dinner. And sometimes dinner was just oatmeal or something. Yeah, like gruel. What a cliché, right?

Anyway, Marta lets me pick food to keep in there, non-perishable stuff, and we make sure we 'rotate out the stock' as she calls it. I keep it in our office. And, truth be told, it's really just my office. Marta has, like, five books on the bookshelf and some envelopes. That's about it. I think she wants me to have my own private space or something. I work from home and have my computers and printers set up in here. So far, it's working out great. I can do video calls and share screens with Parvati if necessary. Parvati is my coworker. She's very nice, and we got a commendation recently for some code we wrote for a new client. Mr. Johnson, my boss, was really impressed with our work, so now Parvati and I are kind of permanent partners.

So, Marta and I live together. We live in the primary

bedroom. They don't call it a master bedroom anymore because, you know, that's kind of racist. Anyway, Marta and I sleep there. As a couple. You understand, right? We have three cats, and all of them sleep with us. Sometimes we kick them out, but that's private between me and Marta. I know you get what I'm saying. I'm a Scorpio, and she's a Cancer which means we're totally compatible in love as long as we communicate with each other.

It's funny how I'm picturing you receiving this letter up in heaven. I hope you have your sight back up there. Just like I hope I get my feet back. I picture them dancing around heaven without me but waiting to reunite with the rest of me. It's silly and kind of weird, but Marta thinks it's a 'perfect' way to think about it.

And listen, just so you know, I'm not hoping to get up there to heaven any time soon. Not anymore. I used to. Often. I haven't told Marta about those times, but I will. It's just hard to think about my low times now. I told her and all our friends about when I ran away from that last foster house. Marta says it was fine. She said it's okay for our friends to know some stuff that happened to me because they are incredibly supportive. They totally are.

Speaking of friends. Here's a list. Miss Riri is like the alpha Domme. She's the one everyone looks up to, including me. She gives me coloring books and activity books all the time. And I've never had so many crayons, colored pencils, and markers in my life. Yes, I have a crush on her, but not the kind of crush I have on Marta. Totally different.

Miss Jaleesa has this whole family. She's goofy, but everyone knows she's in charge. Miss Tina is her girlfriend and is soooo nice. She's a good cook. She and Marta talk about recipes and cooking techniques all the time. Marta has to cook at the coffee shop where she works—just snacks and baked goods, but she's trying out different recipes. I totally get to sample them. Dana is their friend, too, and is like a big sister to me.

Madison is like me because her girlfriend takes care of her the same way Marta takes care of me. But Madison is all over the place, meaning her brain thinks so fast that she can't even finish one thought before the next one comes out. I like her, though. She and I hang out sometimes when the grownups talk or have their meetings. Miss Shasti is Madison's girlfriend. She's a doctor and is fierce, but she is definitely someone I want on my team in a zombie apocalypse. Actually, I want all those people I mentioned on my team. I should tell Marta that, just so she knows.

So, bottom line, I have a family now. I have people who look out for me and who take care of me. Marta is my partner in life now. She loves me, and I love her. When we decided to be girlfriends, she asked me this question: "Do you trust me to be in your corner? To keep you safe and help you with whatever you need?" I said yes, of course, but then she was speechless when I turned around and asked her the same question. Finally, after a hundred years, she answered me by saying, "Yes," and then had to wipe away her tears. She is an emotional person, and it's so cute and endearing. I call her "Mama" now, even though she insists she's not a

Mommy Domme. She said she might accept a “caregiver” label. All in all, she takes amazing care of me.

Oh, and guess what? Next month, around Christmas, we’re going to put in for a Domestic Partnership. It’s like getting married, but a little different (I’m not really sure how it’s different, though). You just have to show at least six months of shared bills and stuff. Way back in June, she put my cell phone under her plan, so that means we can be like a married couple in December. Yay!

Did you know that Marta holds my hand when we’re waiting at a stoplight? She says she can’t think of a better use of her time while we’re waiting. She’s kind of romantic like that. She drives me to my appointments and just everywhere. Her big sister Nora is like a big sister to me, too. My heart gets full when she comes over. I’m glad Marta had her as a big sister her whole life.

Oh, I forgot about our awesome neighbor, Mrs. Pulaski. She paid Deshawn to build a ramp at her house so I could visit ‘any time.’ And I have, but Marta says I need to text first to make sure she’ll be home and ready for company. I taught Mrs. Pulaski how to play the game called BS. It’s called something else, but I don’t want to write it down. It’s kind of a curse word.

Anyway, I wanted you to know that I am well taken care of and that I’m finally happy.

I look forward to meeting you sometime in the WAY

future up there in heaven. I hope you are happy, too.

Take care,
Shanice Ward

P.S. – Dr. Sumner says this doesn't have to be the only letter I write to you. I can write more at a later time. Marta says I can write to you 'whenever the spirit moves me.' She's funny with her sayings. Bye for now.

"Mama?" Shanice called from the office. She placed the letter in a folder and tucked it safely in the back of the file cabinet built into her new desk.

Marta knocked once on the closed door and then let herself in. "Ready to head out for our lobster dinner?"

"Yep," Shanice said. "I did it. I wrote it."

"Yeah?" Marta walked over and smashed Shanice's head lovingly against her torso. This was Marta's new way of hugging Shanice. It was nice. "How did it go? How do you feel?"

"I feel…" Shanice sighed. "I don't really know, actually. No, you know what? I feel like it's a good beginning. I mean, I can write to her anytime I want to. Hopefully, she'll get my letter. Like through God-mail or something."

Marta chuckled, kissed the top of Shanice's head, and said, "That's a great way to think of it." She stepped back. "Okay, you only have a few more hours left to be twenty-five, so let's go have that fancy dinner. And don't forget foxy Riri."

"Which one?" Shanice said with a gleaming side-eye.

"You're just trying to make me jealous," Marta teased. "Your travel stuffie, not my boss."

"Oh, no," Shanice cried out. "I forgot to tell my birth mom about Bernard and Riri. I didn't tell her the names of our cats or the names I gave the dumpster cats. And I didn't tell her about Mama Deborah."

"Looks like you have enough topics for your next letter, don't you?"

Shanice nodded. "Yep," was all she said. What she didn't say was that Marta had been a significant topic in the first letter to her birth mother and would most likely, like one hundred percent, be a major topic in the next one, too.

"You're grinning like you're keeping a secret, little girl," Marta said, her eyes narrowed.

"The only secret I have is how much I love you."

"That is no secret," Marta said. "But it's okay. I have ways of getting things out of you." She raised her tickle fingers, making Shanice squirm at the sight.

"Red," Shanice called.

"No fair." Marta chuckled and dropped her hands. "And listen, it's A-ok to have secrets, my love. But as we discussed with Dr. Sumner, if those secrets can harm you, you shouldn't keep them."

"It's not like that," Shanice said, knowing Marta would worry. "I just said some private thoughts to my birth mother. That's all."

"It's time," Marta said.

"I'm ready."

"You misunderstand me, little one," Marta said with a mischievous grin. She waggled an eyebrow. "I'm overdue for a kiss. It's not every day I get to kiss a quarter-century-old person."

"Mama!" Shanice screeched, but her protests were muffled by Marta's insistent kisses. Shanice gave in and wrapped her arms around Marta's neck. She was breathless when they broke apart. "Mama?"

"Mm hmm?"

"Later, as an anniversary gift, do you think we can, I mean, um…"

"Green means go, my love," Marta said. "And I've been thinking. It's about time you learned what the words *edging* and *denial* mean. Because tomorrow, when you'll be a mature twenty-six, you're going to finally learn what a blended orgasm is."

"What's—"

"Nope," Marta interrupted. "You're not quite old enough to know yet. And don't text Madison."

"How do you always know what I'm thinking?"

"I don't," Marta said. "It was a lucky guess. And no internet searching. That will just spoil the fun."

"Soooo, will this blended thing be something I can do to you at some point?"

Marta faked a swoon and said, "I'm counting on it, love."

Shanice started a happy dance in her chair, and Marta joined in before wheeling her out of the office and toward the front door.

Yes, the things she'd written to her birth mother were true. She loved and trusted Marta. She felt taken care of, but it was more than that. With Marta, she'd finally found…home.

~~~ The End ~~~
~~~

Newsletter Signup

Sign up for Danielle Grainger's newsletter to keep up with new releases. She also likes to recommend books to read (other than her own, of course)

Find the sign-up on Danielle's website:
www.daniellegrainger.com

Reviews

Reviews help get books like this one to readers who enjoy books like them. It's often difficult for readers of certain, err, tastes to find books they enjoy. Would you consider writing a review? Get the word out?

Thank you for the help.

About the Author

Danielle Grainger

Danielle Grainger is an instructor who currently resides in the southeastern USA with several pampered fur babies. She has always been an avid reader and ventured into writing after reading several novels she felt didn't accurately represent the BDSM lifestyle. With so many rampant misconceptions, she took a chance and crafted admittedly idealized versions of possible experiences. Dani hopes not only to entertain her readers but to enlighten and educate them as well.

Dani's Website:
www.daniellegrainger.com

Dani's Facebook:
facebook.com/danielle.grainger.7777

Dani's Instagram:
DaniGrainger84

Dani's Pinterest:
danigrainger84

Dani's Goodreads Page:

www.goodreads.com/author/show/19699760.Danielle_Grainger

Additional Resources

REIKI ENERGY HEALING:

https://www.reiki.org/faqs

"Reiki is a Japanese technique for stress reduction and relaxation that also promotes healing. It is administered by 'laying on hands' and is based on the idea that an unseen 'life force energy' flows through us and is what causes us to be alive. If one's 'life force energy' is low, then we are more likely to get sick or feel stress, and if it is high, we are more capable of being happy and healthy."

https://www.reiki.org/articles/reiki-hospitals

"At hospitals and clinics across America, Reiki is beginning to gain acceptance as a meaningful and cost-effective way to improve patient care."

INTERACTING WITH PEOPLE WHO HAVE DISABILITIES:

https://www.wikihow.com/Interact-With-People-Who-Have-Disabilities

"Someone who is disabled should be afforded the same amount of respect as anyone else. View others as people, not impairments. Focus on the person at hand and their individual personality."

https://www.dhs.state.il.us

"The most important thing to remember when you interact with people with disabilities is that they are people. Their disability is just one of the many characteristics they have. People with disabilities have the same needs we all do: first and foremost among them is to be treated with dignity and respect. When you interact with people with disabilities, focus on their abilities, not their disabilities. People with disabilities are unique individuals who have a wealth of knowledge, skills, talents, interests, and experiences that add tremendous diversity, resourcefulness, and creative energy to our society. Remember, people with disabilities may do things in different ways than people without them however, they can achieve the same outcomes."

HELPING SOMEONE WITH PTSD:

https://www.therecoveryvillage.com/mental-health/ptsd/how-to-help-a-friend-with-ptsd/

"It's often extremely hard for people with PTSD to open up because they fear judgment. They might fear what people will think of them as far as their experiences leading to the development of PTSD. They may fear that they will be treated differently or stigmatized. Provide a safe space for your friend that they know will be judgment-free. Prepare yourself to potentially listen to difficult or upsetting stories that your friend needs to get off their chest. Listening is critical for social support. While you shouldn't push someone into talking, when they're ready to talk, let them know you're there to listen. Practice active listening to show you're engaged, but don't try to compare your feelings or experiences to those of your friend. Even if you've experienced PTSD, you don't have to say you understand, because maybe you don't know their exact experience. Listening is enough."

OVEREATERS ANONYMOUS:

oa.org

"Overeaters Anonymous (OA) is a community of people who support each other in order to recover from compulsive eating and food behaviors. We welcome everyone who feels they have a problem with food."

oa.org/quiz

"Do you have a problem with food? Take our quiz to compare your answers with the experiences of our members."

Get your own "Bernard" at the Aurora Gifts website.

https://auroragift.com
(Search for Muskox)

Books by Danielle Grainger

THE DENTON HEIGHTS SERIES

The Denton Heights Series comes BEFORE the Bernadette Series. This group of books tells the stories of the beloved characters who populate the Bernadette Series world and live the BDSM lifestyle. We find out more of the origin stories of Madison and Shasti; Jaleesa, Tina, Harriet, Dana, Deshawn, and Kari; Marta and Shanice; Rowena and Minjung; Lisa and Rachel. The Denton Heights series is basically the "Prequel" to the Bernadette Series.

Under Her Wing (Denton Heights Book 1)

(The Shasti and Madison Story)

A lesbian age-gap erotic romance with light BDSM aspects.

2023 GOLDIE FINALIST

Madison Kim finds herself on a bus headed to Denton Heights, Ohio, a suburb of Cincinnati. Her mother sent her there without notice to care for an elderly Korean woman Madison had never met. Madison is twenty-two-and-three-quarters years old, has a high school diploma, but isn't smart enough to go to college...so they tell her. Now she spends her time caring for Mrs. Park, going to the beloved Cincinnati Zoo, and watching movies on her outdated phone. She's not really sure why she's there, but she's taking it day by day. And then she meets strong nurturing Miss Shasti at a tea dance.

Shasti Balakrishnan has been looking for someone to call hers for more years than she cares to count. She wants a woman to love and care for in a nurturing Mommy Domme/little girl scenario. She's thirty-two and already a partner in a thriving medical clinic in Denton Heights, but truth be told – she's lonely. She thought she'd found a companion in Amber back in D.C., but that fizzled out once they realized they weren't what each other wanted—or needed. And then she meets adorably precocious Madison at a tea dance.

ISBN: 978-1-953734-10-5 (e-Book)
ISBN: 978-1-953734-13-6 (Paperback)

In Her Cage (Denton Heights Book 2)

(The Jaleesa and Tina Story)

A lesbian/asexual interracial polyamorous erotic romance with BDSM aspects including Dominance and submission.

Jaleesa Whitmore is a lesbian Domme in and out of fast relationships fueled by sex. She didn't understand addiction. Not yet, anyway. Although she had almost one full year sober, she was done with it. She was moments from heading down the familiar road of drinking that always made her feel good and filled that void. She was about to get her life back on its old track when a fateful encounter with a stranger, who would become a trusted friend, halted her downslide. She didn't know it then, but this encounter would not only lead her to a series of events and people that would change how she looked at life but how she approached it.

Tina Jenkins likes women but is asexual and afraid to try for another relationship. She does understand addiction. Just shy of eleven years clean of her opioid addiction following a dental procedure right out of high school, her parents carefully constructed and monitored everything in her world. It didn't matter that she was thirty-one years old and still living in the pink bedroom in her childhood home. It didn't matter that her mother now had to work from home, and her parents had to track her location and do routine searches of her bag, car, computer, phone, and room. None of it mattered because she was clean.

And then asexual Tina meets promiscuous Jaleesa. And everything changed. For both of them.

ISBN: 978-1-953734-28-0 (e-Book)
ISBN: 978-1-953734-29-7 (Paperback)

Within Her Grasp (Denton Heights Book 3)

(The Marta and Shanice Story)

A lesbian age gap interracial erotic romance with light BDSM aspects.

"Within Her Grasp" is an age-gap interracial lesbian romance that tells the tale of two women who had settled for unhappy lives. And then they meet.

White, thirty-something Marta Ingersoll was done with people. She just wanted to be left alone at work and at home, thank you. Her inside cat and the outside stray were all she needed. And her sister, Nora, too, of course. But that was it. And then, one fateful afternoon, her instincts to save a woman in obvious distress kicked in, and her life was shoved onto a strange new course.

Black, twenty-something Shanice Ward never got a break. Life had thrown challenge after challenge at the young woman, and this latest thing was too much, but it wouldn't stop. Woken up from a sound sleep by someone trying to remove her clothing, she shrieked for him to leave her alone. He didn't, but then, the most amazing thing happened. She discovered that superheroes were real, and one had just flown into her room to save her, and her life was shoved onto a strange new course.

ISBN: 978-1-953734-30-3 (e-Book)
ISBN: 978-1-953734-31-0 (Paperback)

THE BERNADETTE SERIES

Dr. Bernadette Garneau holds a Ph.D. in Mathematics and has just gotten out of a four-year relationship. Shortly after the breakup, she began an exploration of her repressed sexual desires. One message from a beautiful and powerful online Mistress and Bernadette leaps into the world of BDSM. The Mistress takes charge, and Bernadette reels in the heady power this stranger has over her. She has gotten a taste of the life, and she wants more. She needs more. Several online and in-person experiences with BDSM and Power Exchange have led to cravings she doesn't quite understand. A brief sexual exchange with an online Goddess unleashes an incredible pain-to-pleasure connection that she hadn't understood before. As she sifts through the posers and one-night stands, she homes in on what her submissive nature needs from a Domme.

The Bernadette Series follows Bernadette's journey into the world of BDSM and her search for love and sexual satisfaction. As she said, "I want a monogamous partner who wants to not only love and nurture me but who also wants to drape me over her lovely couch and have her way with me."

Wrecking Bernadette
(Book One in the Bernadette Series)

A lesbian erotic novel with heavy BDSM aspects featuring Dominance and submission.

Dr. Bernadette Garneau holds a Ph.D. in Mathematics and is four months out of a four-year relationship. One good thing about breaking up is that Bernadette is free to explore her repressed sexual desires. One message from a beautiful and powerful online Mistress, and Bernadette leaps into the world of BDSM. Mistress Ciara takes charge, and Bernadette reels in the heady power this stranger has over her. She has gotten a taste of the *life*, and she wants more. She *needs* more.

ISBN: 978-1-953734-00-6 (e-Book)
ISBN: 978-1-953734-14-3 (Paperback)

(S)mothering Bernadette
(Book Two in the Bernadette Series)

A lesbian erotic novel with heavy BDSM aspects featuring Mommy Domme, little girl.

Dr. Bernadette Garneau's universe is pushing her toward change. Her initial experiences with BDSM and Power Exchange have led to cravings she doesn't quite understand. A brief sexual exchange with an online Goddess unleashes an incredible pain-to-pleasure connection she hadn't understood until that encounter. But after sleeping on it, she clearly understands that this Goddess would never be the long-term relationship she seems to be seeking.

Disappointed, she wonders if she should just give up and move back to California to be closer to her family. That is until she meets Mama_Luvs, an online Mommy Domme. The woman is nurturing yet stern from the start and is just ... perfect. And then Mama_Luvs wants to meet. Starry-eyed Bernadette packs for a New Year's Eve weekend, hoping that this time she's found *the one* – the one who wants to love and nurture her but who also wants to drape her over a couch and have her way with her.

ISBN: 978-1-953734-01-3 (e-Book)
ISBN: 978-1-953734-15-0 (Paperback)

Becoming Bernadette
(Book Three in the Bernadette Series)

A lesbian erotic novel with heavy BDSM aspects featuring Dominance and submission.

University professor Dr. Bernadette Garneau has fallen in love with the world of BDSM. She has a nascent interest in the pain-to-pleasure connection, but she has yet to find partners interested in nurturing the soul within her body that they play with. Admittedly, she's had incredible sexual encounters with experienced Dommes, but all of them left her feeling cold for whatever reason. Most of them simply wanted a sadistic roll in the hay. Bernadette wants a strong Domme who will love and nurture her *before* flogging her on a St. Andrew's cross and *afterward* when her body is spent.

One afternoon, she finally musters up the courage to venture out and meet some new friends in the local BDSM community. In walks a tall, handsome butch woman with fantastic hair and a confident stride. When this woman asks Bernadette, "Are you collared," Bernadette truthfully answers, "No," and accepts a dinner invitation for that very evening. She is walking on stars when she gets home at 2 a.m. after an ethereal sexual liaison. On the one hand, she wonders who she is becoming – she's never been this promiscuous. And on the other hand, she wonders if this strong butch woman could finally be the Domme of her dreams.

ISBN: 978-1-953734-02-0 (e-Book)
ISBN: 978-1-953734-12-9 (Paperback)

<u>Desiring Bernadette</u>
<u>(Book Four in the Bernadette Series)</u>

A lesbian erotic romance novel with heavy BDSM aspects featuring Dominance and submission.

Rikki Carmichael finally feels that deep Dominant/submissive relationship she has been craving ever since her Aunt Tilda introduced her to *the life*. She embraced her dominant side early on, but finding a suitable submissive woman who wanted more than a quick roll in the dungeon proved elusive. That is until Professor Bernadette Garneau arrived on the scene. Now collared and committed to Rikki, will Bernadette prove to be different, or will she turn out like all the others — fickle and full of lies and deception?

And will this perfect sub stay with her when she realizes Rikki's ship is sinking? She'd almost lost the coffee shop she owns when creditors came knocking down her door en masse seeking payment for debts that weren't hers. Rikki managed to keep most of her staff and friends in the dark about it, but she has not been able to get out from under it. With high stakes all around, Rikki looks for the peace she is seeking within her relationship with Bernadette. If this one fails, it may be time to leave the life entirely and go live in a cabin somewhere isolated in the woods. But buying a cabin takes money – money she just doesn't have.

ISBN: 978-1-953734-03-7 (e-Book)
ISBN: 978-1-953734-09-9 (Paperback)

Loving Bernadette
(Book Five in the Bernadette Series)

A lesbian erotic romance novel with heavy BDSM aspects featuring Dominance and submission.

Bernadette Garneau, a beloved professor of mathematics, is a natural submissive. She likes structure and rules and finally found a way of life and a woman who would provide those things for her. The BDSM community she stumbled upon in Denton Heights, Ohio is where she found Rikki Carmichael, now her dominant partner and fiancée. Rikki is everything she's dreamed of. Yes, Bernadette found the captain of her ship. With Rikki's support and guidance, maybe other parts of her life can finally come together, too – like the respect she deserves but hasn't gotten at the university. Why won't anyone see that she deserves to teach those upper-level courses? And to move out of that closet of an office? What do they know that she does not?

Rikki Carmichael, the respected owner of Rikki's Coffee Shop in town, has finally found the woman of her dreams in super-smart and super-real Bernadette Garneau. Bernadette is a submissive who instinctively knows how to take care of Rikki and accepts Rikki's need to be in charge. Bernadette is the first submissive Rikki's ever had that wasn't solely out for her own gain. Once Rikki can climb out of the deep financial debt she's found herself in, she will finally make their engagement to be married public.

Miscommunication, faulty assumptions, and unmet expectations threaten this union seemingly made in heaven. When life comes at them hard and fast, they must rely on their bond and their loving self-made family of friends.

ISBN: 978-1-953734-08-2 (e-Book)
ISBN: 978-1-953734-11-2 (Paperback)

www.ingramcontent.com/pod-product-compliance
Lightning Source LLC
Chambersburg PA
CBHW051243260626
47162CB00002B/580